WARRIOR
PRIME

OTHER NOVELS BY VICTOR GISCHLER

Suicide Squeeze

Gun Monkeys

The Pistol Poets

Shotgun Opera

Go-Go Girls of the Apocalypse

Vampire a Go-Go

The Deputy

Three on a Light

Stay

Gestapo Mars

A FIRE BENEATH THE SKIN TRILOGY

Ink Mage

The Tattooed Duchess

A Painted Goddess

WARRIOR
PRIME

Ink Mage Legacy

VICTOR GISCHLER

Text copyright © 2019 by Victor Gischler
All rights reserved.

Published by 47North, Seattle

www.apub.com

Amazon, the Amazon logo, and 47North are trademarks of Amazon.com, Inc., or its affiliates.

ISBN-13: 9781542091466
ISBN-10: 1542091462

Cover Design by Faceout Studio, Spencer Fuller

Cover illustrated by Deborah Wolfe Ltd.

Printed in the United States of America

WARRIOR
PRIME

PROLOGUE

Ambassador Korick sat with Prince Kha'narahn in one of the box seats and waited for the demonstration to begin. Below them, Fyrians of lesser nobility and rich merchants filled the tiers of bench seating. The small domed arena had filled up fast. Korick had been led to believe witnessing this event was a high privilege, so the men here were likely some of the most important people in the city. Korick tried to remember as many names and faces as he could as the prince pointed them out.

Servants came with wine, and Korick took all he could get. His understanding was that the display was somewhat gruesome. His background was in diplomacy. He had no military experience, knew nothing of weapons except that they could do horrid things to the human body. Korick had fallen off his horse once while hunting and had sprained his ankle. That was the extent of his experience with pain. The idea of being in a battle with all those thrusting swords and hacking axes . . . well, no thank you.

He gulped his wine, motioned to the servant for more.

Korick almost spilled his drink when the horns blew. The sudden fanfare had caught him by surprise.

The prince leaned toward him and said, "It begins." He had a light accent, but his Helvan was nearly flawless. "Look. They bring her out now."

In spite of his anxiety, Korick leaned forward to see. He was curious, and attending this exact event had been part of his mission after all. When he eventually dispatched the envoy back to the king, he'd be obliged to send along as much information as possible.

"Here she comes now," the prince said. "A good specimen, don't you think?"

She was escorted onto the floor of the arena by a dozen brutish men, their armor consisting of small, overlapping bronze rectangles. The metal was even sewn into knee-length kilts. Greaves of the same metal and also bracers. Scimitars hung from wide belts, and they held long spears formally in front of them. The men were dusky and dour, the hair on their heads braided in tight rows in the style of most of the Fyrian working class and military men.

But when the prince had spoken of a good specimen, he hadn't meant any of the soldiers.

He'd been talking about the girl.

She probably wasn't as tiny as she appeared walking among the hulking warriors, but she was slight and lithe. She was nude, and Korick wondered if that was to show off the tattoo, although he couldn't see it from this angle. More likely the men just enjoyed seeing her form.

Korick supposed some men would find her attractive, although she was too lean for his tastes. Too many ribs showing. Hair cut short like a boy's, perhaps to be out of the way during combat. Nose and cheekbones sharp, eyes dark and mysterious.

It didn't matter. Her appearance wasn't important.

The prince leaned in again and said, "I'm adding this one to my personal stable. Meddigar said she tested very well."

Korick's ears perked up. Meddigar was another person on his list. The ambassador was obliged to dig up as much information about the man as possible. As the prince's pet magician, Meddigar had been chiefly responsible for the prince's recent rise in social and political status. According to Korick's spies, Meddigar had ventured into the deep desert of Fyria, urged on by rumors and an old map. No one could find out where the man had gone, but when he'd returned, he brought with him the secret of the Prime.

And the Prime was everything. It was how one made an average person into an ink mage.

Wizards in Helva had lost the secret decades ago. And the distant sound of saber rattling could be heard in the high chambers of the grand sultan's palace. It seemed absurd. The world had known peace and prosperity these last twenty years after the failed Perranese invasion of Helva. Nobody wanted more blood and death.

But the grand sultan heard the call of his ancient ancestors, voices from centuries ago when Fyria was the seat of a vast empire that included Helva to the north and other nations to the south. And he was a strong-willed man, strong enough to bind the half dozen lesser sultans to him. Fyria was united in a way it had not been for nearly four hundred years. Each day, the empire added men to its army.

And now it could produce ink mages at will? No wonder the king had been concerned. It was a dicey time to be an ambassador.

The soldiers unlocked the chains on the girl's wrists and ankles and then withdrew. The only remainder of her bondage was a thin metal collar around her neck. More brilliant than brass but not quite gold.

A portcullis across the arena rose slowly with the metallic clank of gears and chains. Four men emerged. They seemed of the same type as the earlier soldiers, large and formidable, but they didn't have the same magnificent armor or weapons. Simple boiled leather, wooden shields, no spears, but each held a curved scimitar. The expressions on their faces ranged from anger to fear. The largest of them, a man with muscles on top of muscles, gripped his sword with a white-knuckled fury as if impatient to get on with it.

"New ink mages must be publicly blooded of course," the prince said. "Generally, this is to assure the man purchasing the ink mage that he is not being cheated. In this case, obviously, I would not cheat

3

myself, but it is tradition." The prince shrugged. "And if you can provide the gentry with a good show, well, it's not a terrible thing to court their appreciation."

The servants brought more wine, and Korick accepted eagerly. There was also a plate of greasy spiced meats that the Fyrians seemed to like so much. Not quite pork, definitely not lamb, some animal Korick had never heard off. The prince grabbed a handful and stuffed it into his fat mouth, licking his fingers and smacking his lips. The juices dripped into his forked beard.

Korick hid his distaste and drank the wine.

The girl searched the crowd until she found the prince. She took a half dozen steps toward him and bowed. The prince raised a hand acknowledging her.

"The girl was given to me to forgive a debt," the prince said. "The parents, alas, were not blessed with sons. It is a good arrangement that benefits everyone."

Korick rather doubted everyone felt they benefited equally.

"It is more difficult to find the soldiers actually." The prince gestured to the men in the cheap leather armor, holding the wooden shields. "We use deserters or other offenders, but our army is so well disciplined these days, instances of misbehavior are few. These particular men were part of a garrison in Norrica."

Korick mentally pictured a map of the region. Norrica was a small island nation off the coast of Fyria. The grand sultan had claimed it without opposition a decade ago.

"They raped some local girls," the prince continued. "Usually company punishment would suffice, but the garrison captain is a stickler. He sent the men along to us. Otherwise we would have had to scrape the dungeons for common criminals. They're good enough to get the job done but do not put on the best show."

Korick had kept his eye on the girl as the prince prattled. After bowing to the prince, she'd turned to bow to the rest of the onlookers. And that's when Korick had seen it.

The Prime.

The tattoo down the girl's back must still have been fresh because it was a bright red. Korick had been informed it would eventually fade to a steely blue. The lines of the tattoo spread across her shoulders and up her neck to the base of her skull. The lines followed the length of her back to curl down below the tailbone. Along the lines, on either side of her spine, runes had been inked small and precise. Some ancient language perhaps.

Korick couldn't claim an intimate knowledge of ink magic, but one thing most everyone knew was that the Prime tattoo was the key. It was the tattoo that allowed the ink mage to go on and get other tattoos, each one granting some marvelous power.

Or so he'd heard. The stories often stretched credibility. This display would be Korick's first opportunity to see an ink mage in action.

Another fanfare of trumpets startled him again. Fyrians loved trumpets.

The girl snapped into a defensive crouch, hands up, eyes alert. Her expression remained stoic even as the four warriors spread out to come at her in a semicircle. They knew enough to take her seriously, and none seemed eager to be the first to attack.

The two on the ends charged her full speed. If she'd turned to face one, it would have left her back exposed to the other. So she fought neither. Instead she ran flat out toward the other two.

The nearest screamed fury and swung his scimitar hard at neck level. She wilted to the ground, the blade passing two inches over her. She rolled into a ball and barreled into the legs of the next warrior, upending him.

He went down hard, holding on to his sword, but fumbling the shield.

The girl came out of the roll and snatched up the fallen shield, twisted her body around, and hurled it. She did all this in one fluid motion, like steps to a well-rehearsed dance.

The round shield flew through the air at one of the charging men so fast, he didn't have time to react. It hit him square in the mouth with a crack so loud, all the spectators flinched and gasped. The soldier's head spun around, blood and teeth flying. He went down, crawled along the ground, groaning and pawing at his ruined face.

The girl stamped a bare foot down hard on the fallen soldier's wrist, and when his fist popped open, she bent, grabbed his sword, and sprang up again just in time to deflect the blade of the other charging warrior.

The girl's hand became a blur, and suddenly the man was stumbling back, blood gushing from his throat. He dropped his sword and shield, hands coming up to staunch the flow. Red seeped between his fingers.

Korick was afraid to blink lest he miss something. The girl moved with utter confidence, no hesitation. Her face remained blank, only her eyes showing intense concentration.

She swung the sword down at the one near her feet. Another slit throat, and the man died in an instant.

The remaining warrior was the biggest, muscles rippling as he gripped the scimitar tightly. He glanced around, clearly afraid, but didn't see an exit. He squared off with the girl, in no hurry to make the first move. She closed in on him slowly, and he backed up a step at a time.

"The Prime allows her perfect perception," the prince said. "Perfect control over her own body. She is a living weapon. It usually does not go this fast. This girl is something special, I think."

The soldier realized he would eventually be backed against the wall and lose all initiative. His face hardened, and he rushed forward, screaming and bringing his blade down fast, aiming for the center of her face.

She sidestepped, grabbing his sword wrist as the blade came down. She twisted his body, yanking the wrist, pulling the big man all the way through the swing, using his momentum to her advantage. She dropped to one knee, and the soldier flipped over her, landing hard on his back.

He tried to get up, but she slammed both of his ears with her open palms. He screamed again, this time in pain.

She kicked him over onto his belly, stood on top of him, one of her bare feet on his neck. He struggled to get up, but she wrapped up one of his massive arms in a tight grip, her own arms looking thin and feeble by comparison. She twisted, drawing the arm back at a painful angle. He babbled frantically in Fyrian.

Korick understood only a smattering of the language, but the man's tone was clear. He was pleading for her not to break his arm. Begging for his life.

"Observe," the prince said. "She is no stronger than any other waif of a girl. There are tattoos that can give an ink mage strength, of course, as strong as an ogre is what I've heard. But that is not the case here. All of her power comes from the Prime. She can determine the perfect angle, the amount of leverage needed. The Prime gives her a sublime self-awareness of what her body is capable of."

She braced one foot against the soldier's back, the other still on his neck, and pulled, using all her weight to bend the arm. The two froze for a second, and momentarily, it seemed to Korick as if the girl might not have the strength after all. The crowd held its collective breath.

The wet, sickening snap of the man's arm was so sudden and loud, Korick winced, even all the way up in the prince's box. The soldier screamed, much louder and longer than any of his other screams.

The crowd erupted in wild applause.

The girl let go of his arm, and it flopped limply down next to him. He sobbed quietly.

She stepped away from him, circled around, keeping one eye on him in case he had any fight left. She picked up the man's scimitar and, with seeming indifference, brought it down on the soldier's neck.

More applause from the appreciative spectators.

"Oh, yes," the prince said. "I think it likely she will be my new favorite."

Korick smiled weakly.

No wonder the king of Helva had made investigating the ink mages a priority. With seeming ease, a young girl, naked and without weapons, had killed four seasoned warriors. How many of these ink mages did Fyria have? How many could they make? An army of such creatures would be devastating.

He wondered if the prince had agreed to show him the blooding of the new ink mages for just this purpose. A show of Fyrian strength.

"Might I excuse myself a moment, Highness?" Korick asked. "I want to refresh myself before the next display."

"Of course," the prince said. "Hurry back. You don't want to miss this next one."

Korick rose, bowed, and hurriedly found his deputy waiting in one of the anterooms with the other underlings.

"Mullen," Korick said, "I don't want you to wait for me. Go and find the king's envoy and have him waiting for me at the embassy when I return tonight. I must brief him immediately and book passage for him on the next possible ship."

Mullen's thin moustache twitched. The deputy ambassador was a fussy little man with delusions of grandeur, always overdressing and overly formal. Korick got the impression the deputy was waiting for him to make a mistake so he could take over Korick's job.

"I'm afraid I don't know where the envoy is, sir," Mullen said.

"What do you mean you don't know?"

"He left the embassy last night and hasn't been seen since."

Korick blustered. "Well, where did he go? Did he say anything?"

Mullen cleared his throat. "He said he was off to find a drink."

CHAPTER
ONE

The splitting headache was offset somewhat by the woman's soft back-side pushing up against him. She snored lightly.

When Peyne Erlich tried to sit up, little gnomes inside his head hammered away at the backs of his eyeballs. He groaned and fell back onto his pillow. The woman stirred but didn't wake.

Peyne paused to consider how he'd come to be here.

He'd gotten off the ship, and a carriage had been waiting for him. The seaside capital of Fyria was a bustling city, and Peyne had been thankful not to have to find the embassy on his own. Upon arriving, he'd been told the ambassador was away.

No matter. He was finally off that cramped ship with a new city to explore, and there was no bad time for a goblet of wine. He'd found himself in the expatriate quarter where merchants and dignitaries from other lands congregated. Peyne had found a tavern full of men and women from Helva, and while he did want to explore this strange and exotic city, there'd been some relief to being able to order a drink with-out having to wrestle with a different language.

He'd struck up a conversation with a merchant woman who was bringing Klaarian lumber from the evergreen forests in the north to trade for Fyrian spices and silks. Odd that he could remember that but not her name. Peyne had reached the halfway point in his twenties, and the woman was at least a decade older, but her raw sexual aggression had enticed him, and she curved in all the right places, and her room was conveniently just upstairs.

And she hadn't been some tittering, blushing virgin. She'd known what she'd wanted and had made her expectations clear. Peyne had been hard-pressed to keep up with her.

Whatever her name was.

Peyne decided he was in no condition to attempt moving again. He rolled over, shut his eyes.

Then the pounding.

Peyne put his hands over his eyes and groaned. At first he thought the pounding came from inside his head but then realized somebody was banging on the door.

The woman stirred next to him. "Stop that bloody racket and fuck off." She pulled the blanket over her head.

Peyne raised an eyebrow. *Well then.*

The pounding on the door grew more insistent, and a voice on the other side said, "Lord Erlich, your presence at the embassy is required immediately."

Peyne thought he recognized the voice of the persnickety little deputy. "Mullen?"

"Yes. The ambassador has men combing the city for you."

Peyne groaned. "I *just* got here. What could be so urgent so soon?"

"Nevertheless. If you could come with me."

"For the love of Dumo," the woman shouted from beneath the covers. "If you know this man, then just go. I'm trying to sleep."

"One moment." Peyne heroically rose from the bed, brain throbbing with redoubled savagery. He circled the room, collecting his clothes. Tunic, doublet, breeches. He had to crawl under the bed for one of his boots.

He dressed hastily, turned to the lump under the bedcovers. "Madam, unfortunately, as you've heard, I've been called away, but I wanted to assure you it's been a profound pleasure—"

"Just go!"

Ah.

"But I just got here." Peyne held both sides of his head, trying not to groan.

He sat at a table with Ambassador Korick on the embassy's upper veranda. The ambassador sipped tea, a local brew, strong with an aroma of citrus.

"These things happen." Korick sipped again.

"I'd hoped to see something of the city after coming all this way," Peyne said.

"I think you saw quite enough last night," Korick said.

"The expatriate quarter," Peyne corrected. "I didn't even meet any Fyrians."

"Nevertheless," insisted the ambassador.

Mullen arrived and handed Peyne a cup filled with some sour-smelling liquid. "One of the old women who works in the kitchens says this will help. Some home brew concoction."

Peyne sniffed the drink, grimaced. "Is it safe?"

Mullen shrugged. "I doubt it could make you feel any worse."

A fair point.

"Don't sip," Mullen told him. "You're supposed to guzzle it all in one go."

Peyne saluted the two men with the cup. "Bury me someplace with a nice view."

He tilted the cup back and drank it all down as instructed. The brew tasted like rotten fruit.

He belched. "Oh, sorry. Excuse me a moment, will you?"

Peyne pushed back from the table, turned away, and leaned against the railing overlooking the embassy courtyard. He belched several more times. The taste was like death, but he had to admit he did feel somewhat better.

He looked down into the courtyard. Two Fyrian servants carried a trunk across the cobblestones and loaded it onto the back of a carriage.

Peyne pointed. "That's my trunk."

"Yes," Korick said. "We had it brought down from your room."

"It was just taken *up* to my room," Peyne said. "I haven't even *seen* my room. For Dumo's sake, *I just got here.*"

"So you keep saying," Korick said. "But there is no time to lose. I've already booked passage for you on a trader ship. It won't be quite as luxurious as the royal envoy ship that brought you, I'm afraid."

"Delightful."

"The ship needs to sail with the tide in the next hour, which means you need to go in the next few minutes," Korick said. "Therefore, I'm going to need you to *pay attention*. I can't commit anything to writing, but this message must be carried to his majesty."

Peyne pouted. "I still don't see why it can't wait a few days."

"Lord Erlich!" The ambassador drew himself up, back stiff. "I appreciate you are the king's friend. Indeed, it's why you were chosen as envoy. It needed to be somebody the king trusted. But *I* am his majesty's ambassador to Fyria. I decide what can wait and what is urgent. You will follow my instructions to the letter. Is that clear?"

Peyne held up a placating hand. "Okay. I know. I'm sorry. I want to help." He wasn't on vacation after all. His mission was serious. Fyria had been growing as a concern back in Helva the last few years, and the king was counting on Peyne. He couldn't foul this up.

Korick cleared his throat. "Very well." He glanced around, then lowered his voice and said, "What do you know about ink mages?"

One of the officers screamed at them to get their asses up the gangplank.

"That tone doesn't bode well for a pleasant voyage," Peyne shot back.

The officer on deck made an exasperated gesture, then turned away. Peyne told the servants to take his trunk aboard and find his cabin.

He paused to look at the ship. It wasn't new and sleek like the one that had brought him here. It was a fat tub meant to haul cargo a long distance in no particular hurry. Two tall masts and the old-fashioned square sails. Peyne was no nautical expert, but he'd been given to believe shipbuilders had favored the triangular sails in recent years. Well, she seemed seaworthy enough at least. Peyne sighed and headed up the gangplank.

The deck was a tumult of activity. Sailors securing lines and hatches. Last-minute cargo being brought about by crews of men with block and tackle. Peyne had to step lively to keep out of the way.

He stopped a skinny, weathered sailor with a crude mermaid tattoo on his chest. "Where do I find the person in charge?"

The sailor pointed. "Boss lady's there on the quarterdeck."

"Obliged."

Peyne climbed the steps to the quarterdeck and saw her standing between the ship's wheel and the mizzenmast. A handsome woman, brown hair leaning toward red in a long braid down to the middle of her back. He suspected a good shape, but it was difficult to tell. She wore the blousy clothing favored by the locals, smart probably given the heat. Loose pants of a deep green fabric, bound at the ankles. Strappy leather sandals. A blouse of matching green fabric, bound at the wrists. The jeweled hilt of a short dagger stuck up from a wide sash around her waist.

Peyne watched her closely as she berated a group of men clumsily loading some barrels. One had gotten away and almost flattened several sailors as it rolled across the deck. There was a fierce self-assurance in her voice that made her all the more attractive. Perhaps this wouldn't be such a dismal voyage after all.

She turned toward Peyne, approached him with a wry smile. "Lord Erlich, welcome aboard the *Pride of Klaar*. Another few minutes and I'd have left without you. I can't afford to miss the tide."

"Yes, uh . . . yes." He knew he was staring but couldn't stop himself. He felt sure he knew this woman from somewhere.

She frowned. "It's *me*, you idiot. You spent last night in my bed."

Peyne blinked. "Oh? Oh!" Yes, he recognized the face now. He'd seen her before only in candlelight. In the full light of day, she looked slightly older than he'd estimated the previous evening, but striking with a spray of freckles across her nose. "You look different with your hair in a braid like that."

"Helps keep it out of the way while working. And you'd had quite a bit of wine, so I forgive your fuzzy memory."

He squinted at her. "You're . . . the captain?"

"I'm Emma Terrigan, and I'm the owner," she said. "The captain works for me."

Peyne absorbed all that as quickly as possible, then smiled and said, "Well, I'm certainly glad to have the pleasure of your company. I was afraid it was going to be a lonely voyage."

Emma snorted. "Thanks. I'm good for a while. I appreciate your helping me scratch an itch last night, but you're going to need to stay out of my way. This is work time. As soon as my crew finishes loading the olives and dates, we're shoving off. I have merchants waiting in Sherrik, and I want my money."

"Ah."

"There's more good news."

Peyne smiled tightly. "Do tell."

"I need to kick you out of your cabin," she said.

"What? Why?"

"We need the cabin for someone else."

"That's outrageous." He tried to sound indignant but feared it came across as whiny. "His majesty's ambassador Lord Korick made the arrangements himself."

Emma shrugged. "Too bad. In Fyria, princes outrank ambassadors, and this request comes from Prince Kha'narahn."

Peyne's eyes widened. "Is *he* on board?"

"Of course not. Important men don't run errands. They send flunkies," she said. "Like you."

"I think I liked you better last night."

"That's them over there." She lifted her chin toward the starboard railing on the main deck. "Those two. They're the prince's people."

"They don't look like anything special."

"They're traveling incognito," Emma said.

"If they're traveling incognito, then why are you telling me?"

"You're still his majesty's envoy. I thought you should know. But I do a lot of business in Fyria, so you didn't hear it from me."

"If we could return to the issue of my accommodations . . ."

"I've had a storage compartment cleared for you."

"Is *storage compartment* nautical slang for luxury cabin?"

"It's a place we stored rope and casks of anchor chain oil," Emma said. "It's all the way forward. I've already had a crewman take your trunk."

"Well, thanks for that anyway."

Emma chuckled. "I'm sure you'll settle right in. Remember, stay out of the way." She winked, turned, and left to harangue the men loading the cargo.

Peyne went belowdecks and made his way forward until he found his room, which was small. *Very* small. He was only a tad more than average height, but he had to hunch over slightly to keep from hitting his head. His trunk took up far too much space, and his bed was a pile of straw on a pallet with blankets thrown over it.

No, he would definitely not spend any more time than necessary in here. The place smelled stale and oily. He opened the single, small porthole for fresh air. He checked his belongings inside the trunk. Everything seemed in order. In fact, since he was still wearing yesterday's clothes, nothing had been touched at all.

Peyne eyed a bucket in the corner and was pleasantly surprised to see some thoughtful soul had left him fresh water. He stripped, splashed water around the best he could for a makeshift bath, and used a towel from his trunk to dry himself.

He looked over the garments in the trunk. He would never admit to anyone else he was a bit of a clotheshorse, but he did admit it to himself. He liked to look good. The black outfit was his most dashing, but in this Fyrian heat perhaps not the best choice.

So the brown breeches with the scarlet piping up the sides and the off-white tunic would have to do. He rolled the sleeves up to his elbows. He thought about the vest but decided to keep it casual. He left his rapier and dagger in the trunk.

A vague sense of movement beneath his feet.

Peyne looked out the porthole, saw the ship moving away from the dock.

He slicked his hair back and went topside.

Most of the crew had sprung into action across the deck or scrambled up the rigging. Sails were unfurled and caught the wind as the *Pride of Klaar* left the bay for open sea.

Peyne spotted the two Fyrians looking back at the dwindling city. He joined them at the rail.

"A beautiful city. I wish I'd had time to explore it further."

A tight smile and a curt nod of greeting from the tall one. He had broad shoulders and lighter skin than most of the other Fyrians Peyne had seen. His beard was too short to be forked, and his eyes looked dark and humorless. His midnight-black hair shaved close. A thin scimitar hung from his belt, and he seemed the sort of man able and eager to use it. He wore a simple blue tunic and breeches, but Peyne could easily imagine him in heavy armor.

There was something else stuck in the man's belt. At first, Peyne thought it was a dagger, but the object was more like a scepter except shorter, ornate, and brassy, with a carved metal globe the size of a peach pit at the top.

The other Fyrian didn't acknowledge Peyne at all, immobile, hood drawn forward to cover the face. The day seemed a bit warm to be so completely covered, but it was hardly Peyne's business.

"I'm Peyne Erlich." He held out his hand.

The man looked down at the hand and then shook it reluctantly. "Kayman."

He offered no last name, and Peyne didn't ask.

"Not exactly the most luxurious ship, is it?" Peyne said with a chuckle. "But at least we have good weather. A flat sea suits me just fine."

"I'm sure. If you'll excuse me."

He took the other Fyrian by the arm and turned aft, walking away from Peyne in no particular hurry, but definitely *away*.

The shorter one glanced back at him.

The face took Peyne's breath away. Mostly it was surprise. He hadn't expected a woman's face. But there was more. The face looked somehow strong and vulnerable at the same time, the eyes so haunted. Peyne was instantly captivated, but in the same moment, she turned away again, Kayman leading her belowdecks.

Perhaps the woman was Kayman's consort. He could only speculate. Kayman didn't seem the sort to answer personal questions. Anyway, he should have guessed the man might not be talkative. Emma had told him the couple was traveling incognito.

He looked around. Well, never mind. The sun was bright, the sky blue, and Peyne quite enjoyed the smell of the salt air. He spotted Emma and a group of officers on the quarterdeck, all facing away from him.

Peyne climbed the steps to the quarterdeck, stood next to her. They ignored him, all looking silently back at their own wake as they stood along the rail.

"So," Peyne said, "what are we doing?"

"Captain Arnol, this is Lord Erlich." Emma gestured to a grizzled man next to her.

The old sailor grunted and nodded, his gaze not wavering from the ocean behind them. He wore a floppy hat with a brim pulled low to shade his eyes. He was small but hard as if put together with sticks and wire. Bushy white sideburns curved down each side of his face, not quite connecting on his chin to make a beard. He smoked a stubby brown chuma stick, the smoke lost in the wind.

"Good to meet you, Captain," Peyne said. "Are we looking at anything in particular?"

Arnol pointed.

Peyne didn't see anything at first, squinting. Then he spied it in the long distance behind them. A glint of white. A sail.

"This is a common shipping lane, yes?" Peyne said. "Are we worried?"

"No." Emma shook her head slowly. "Not worried at all."

Peyne looked at everyone. *These are some grim expressions for people who claim not to be worried.*

"Who's got the best eyes?" Emma asked.

"Teena," Arnol said.

"Get her up in the crow's nest."

Arnol snapped a finger, and one of the junior officers scurried away to carry out the command.

A minute later, Peyne saw the girl scrambling up the rigging, skinny and barefoot, ragged breeches cut just above the knee, her dark hair in a braid like Emma's. She climbed effortlessly and was in the crow's nest a second later.

A few minutes passed, and finally Emma asked, "Well?"

The captain barked something in another language that Peyne thought might have been Fyrian. An officer passed along the command to a sailor who in turn passed it up the mainmast.

In a few seconds the answer was passed back in the same language. Arnol grunted. "Narrow beam and low in the water."

"Not a cargo ship," Emma said.

"No."

Word came down the mast again, and the captain nodded as he listened, face hardening. "She's got a couple knots on us," he told Emma. "Maybe three."

Emma squinted up at the sun. "When?"

"About an hour after dark," Arnol said. "Give or take."

"Pass the word."

Arnol nodded at the junior officer, and a low muttering among the crew traveled the length of the ship.

"I can't help but think that when you told me earlier there was nothing to worry about, you weren't being completely honest," Peyne said.

"Precautions," Emma told him. "When a ship appears out of nowhere, it always raises questions, but as you say, it's a common shipping lane."

"What are we going to do?"

"Watch and wait," Emma said.

"Anything I can do to help?"

She shook her head slowly. "Not that I can think of."

"Then I'll go get something to eat," Peyne said.

Since it was between mealtimes, all the cook would allow Peyne to scrounge was a strip of overspiced beef jerky and an apple that had seen better days. He ate with little pleasure, then made his way back to his cramped cabin, where he kicked off his boots and flopped on his makeshift bed.

Peyne let his mind wander, but it didn't get far, and soon he dozed.

CHAPTER
TWO

"Something's happening on deck," Kayman said. "I'm going to have a look."

"Do you want me to come with you?" she asked.

"Stay here and out of sight," he ordered. "Talk to no one."

She nodded. *Yes, you've told me that a hundred times.*

He left and shut the cabin door behind him.

She let out a long sigh, relieved to be free of his company. Even if only for a little while. She was glad Kayman had his own cabin. At least she could escape from him in sleep.

Her name was Zayda Yond, or at least it used to be. Her betters still called her Zayda, but her new masters told her that her family name now meant nothing, and it would do her well to forget it. Indeed, mentioning it at all would bring harsh punishment. That was her *old* life. It had been erased in favor of a new one. A life as a slave.

She tried—and mostly failed—to comfort herself with the fact it could be worse.

Much worse.

Zayda was keenly aware she was not unattractive. She'd been told so by the men who'd traded her and debated how best to sell her. When her parents had fallen into crushing debt, it would not have been unheard of for her father to sell her to the brothels. She wanted to think he was a better man than that, but thankfully he hadn't been put to the test. It had hurt her father enough to see her taken away by the prince's men. He'd wept openly. She wanted to think her being dragged off to a life of prostitution would have been too much for him.

Zayda had only the vaguest notion of what her father's business entailed. He owned warehouses on the riverfront, and various trade goods would come and go, her father speculating when the price was right to buy or an opportune time to sell. They had lived the comfortable upper-middle class life of a prominent merchant. Zayda had been wonderfully spoiled, had, in fact, only recently become aware how spoiled she'd been.

A series of bad business decisions followed by a fire in her father's warehouses at the exact wrong time had ruined him, and the money-lenders had gouged him beyond recovery. To risk losing everything and become beggars in the street had been too much for him. Selling Zayda had allowed him to save the family home and start fresh.

She reached inside her clothing and tugged at the metal collar. It was not, she had to admit, especially uncomfortable. Simply the fact of its existence galled.

The collar would never come off. Not as long as she lived. It assured complete obedience to her masters.

She touched the back of her neck. The tattoo still seemed strange, and she thought she could feel it, the ink humming just below the surface of her skin. It was an illusion, a trick of the mind. The wizard had told her in time, she wouldn't even think about the tattoo, but for now it was *all* she could think about.

Zayda had been made to understand that although she was being enslaved, she was also being given a high honor. Few were suitable, but she'd been tested—a process of spell casting she didn't understand at all—and Zayda had been selected to receive the Prime.

The memory of the old wizard remained vivid and unpleasant. Zayda had been bathed by servants, old women resigned to their lot in life. Then she'd been toweled dry and taken to the wizard. She'd stood before him naked and humiliated, but if he'd had any lewd interest in her, he'd kept it hidden. She'd been ordered to turn around, flinched at the feel of his dry, coarse hands on her back. She'd been chastised sharply and told to keep still. If Zayda moved in a way that ruined the inking of the tattoo, then it would all be for nothing, and they would have to find another use for her.

The stings of the inking needle were like fiery fly bites, and by the end, her legs and back were sore, muscles burning. But she hadn't dared move.

And then it was done. The Prime had been inked down her back and the collar fastened around her neck.

She'd known in that moment there was no going back. Her life had been changed forever, although to what extent she could only guess.

Then the wizard had instructed her on *tapping into the spirit*.

Zayda hadn't understood. The term was not familiar to her. The wizard had been surprisingly patient. He'd said to close her eyes, to reach out with her mind.

It was only difficult the first time, groping within herself, trying to connect to something that seemed just out of reach. Finally, she found it, the deep well of power stored within herself.

Zayda tapped into the spirit.

And immediately the way she perceived herself and the rest of the world changed in a way she could not possibly have imagined.

She seemed to live within the world at a higher level. When the soldiers had attacked her at the blooding, they had looked ridiculously slow, as if she were being besieged by drunken toddlers. By contrast she had a perfect awareness of her own body, could sense the blood in every vein. And with awareness came control. She understood the limits of the shell of flesh that contained her, knew how to push those limits.

And she could banish any unwanted emotion that might hinder her. The men at the blooding were simply problems to be eliminated. When she'd released the spirit, the knowledge she was now a killer flooded in, sickened her. Zayda tried to take heart in the fact the men had deserved it. Murderers and rapists. She took confidence in knowing she could defend herself. She was a living weapon.

Zayda told her body what to do, and it obeyed.

Even now, aboard the *Pride of Klaar*, she felt a tinge of seasickness and knew she could make it go away. She could tap into the spirit and command her stomach to calm itself, keep the queasiness at bay.

But the old wizard had warned her not to rely on the spirit for mundane things. The behavior could become addictive. She could latch on to the spirit and refuse to let go and burn herself out. It had happened to ink mages before, or at least that's what she'd been told.

At the same time, the wizard had told her that tapping into the spirit was like a muscle. It could be exercised and grow stronger.

Zayda would have to find that balance for herself.

For now, she was glad for the silence. Solitude was in short supply these days. She lay on the narrow bunk, a long sigh leaking out of her, and closed her eyes. She was more tired mentally than physically. She tried to clear her mind, to forget who she was.

She tried to forget her entire existence.

At last she dozed, walking the tightrope between sleep and wakefulness.

Peace. Quiet.

Then a slam so hard, it bounced her out of the bunk, the earsplitting crack of timber. She hit the deck hard. In trying to right herself, she discovered the floor pitched at an angle. Muffled shouts and screams coming from above.

Zayda reached for her scimitar.

The splintering crack of wood brought Peyne out of a sound sleep. He stood abruptly, bumping his head on the low ceiling.

"Fuck!"

He bent over, rubbing his head, blinking the stars from his eyes. He stood, took a step, and went down.

Was the floor at some strange angle? He was drunk again. That must be it. Where was he?

He remembered. Aboard ship. He was sober.

Peyne pulled on his boots as he listened to sailors shouting above. The all too familiar clang on clang of sword blades sent a stab of panic through him. He strapped on his rapier, dagger hanging from the belt on the other side, and rushed up the steps two at a time to the main deck.

Lanterns and torches cast flickering light over the chaos on deck. Another ship had smashed broadside at an intercept angle up against the *Pride of Klaar*. Black-clad men with scimitars boiled over the gunwale, leaping down to the *Pride of Klaar*'s deck to clash with Arnol and his crew. The attackers' faces were wrapped in black cloth, with only a narrow slit for the eyes. The two groups collided with the ring of steel, shouts of rage and pain as men went down on both sides.

Peyne drew his rapier but made no move to join the fray. He found himself torn between wanting to be helpful and the desire to save his own skin. He watched Arnol lead a line of pikemen into the mass of attackers, attempting to drive them back. Pikes pierced throats and chests and limbs, the blood spraying so thick over the deck, the men were slipping in it.

No, Peyne definitely didn't want any part of that.

He backed toward the quarterdeck, intending to climb the steps and put himself above the fighting. He never had the chance. The tide of battle shifted, and a wave of bodies slammed into him. He was knocked to the deck and lost himself among the legs. He tried to rise, but bodies crowded from every direction, sending him back down again.

Somebody tripped over him, fell on top. This caused a chain reaction, and more bodies piled up on top of the others. The din of battle still raged all around, but all Peyne could see were legs and feet.

He pushed his way out of the pile and crawled fast across the deck. When he reached an opening in the melee, he lurched to his feet just in time to see one of the black-clad attackers rushing at him, sword raised, screaming a savage war cry.

Peyne brought up the rapier for a parry. Metal rang. He readied a thrust, but again the throng of combatants washed over him. Arnol's pikemen pressed in, looking to stem the tide, and Peyne was caught up in it. A pike slid right past him and sank into the belly of an attacker. A different attacker swung his scimitar.

Peyne ducked, and the blade raked the face of a sailor behind him. The man screamed agony and dropped his pike, hands going up to staunch the blood spraying from his face.

Peyne backed away, bumped into somebody behind him, turned, and saw it was another of the attackers. He was too close for a proper blade thrust, so he punched hard with his sword hand, the knuckle guard smashing into the man's face. Peyne heard and felt teeth and bone crack. The attacker staggered back, eyes crossing.

The battle swirled around him, knocking him back and forth until by dumb luck it spit him out near the steps up to the quarterdeck. He ran toward them, looked up when he heard a woman's voice shouting in fury.

Emma stood with her back to the ship's wheel, a long dagger in each hand, fighting gypsy fashion. Rips in her clothing, braid pulled loose. The helmsman hung limp over the wheel, blood dripping down his arms. Two of the attackers moved cautiously toward Emma. A third lay dead at her feet. She obviously had no intention of making it easy for them.

Peyne flew up the steps to the quarterdeck.

One of the men in black leapt at Emma, scimitar slashing. The other turned on Peyne.

Emma caught the blade of the scimitar with crossed daggers, blocking it past her as she sidestepped, spinning with surprising grace and speed, slashing across the man's throat just under the ear. Blood splattered as the man screamed and stumbled back.

The attacker approached cautiously, scimitar up and ready. Peyne took up the stance his fencing instructor had taught him years ago for receiving an attack. Peyne had little experience in battle. Men pressing in on him from every direction was one of the most disorienting experiences of his life. He felt slightly more confident one on one.

Slightly.

The clash of blades rang across the quarterdeck as Peyne and the marauder exchanged thrusts and parries. Peyne was playing his game now, and it was one of patience, watching and waiting for an opening. A quick thrust caught the man on the wrist. Another parry and thrust, and he jabbed the man a shallow gash on the shoulder. Within ten seconds, the man bled from four different wounds, all infuriating insect stings.

The man in black lost any semblance of poise, screamed, and charged wildly, swinging the scimitar at Peyne's head. The exact lapse in discipline Peyne had been waiting for. He ducked underneath the scimitar and thrust, extending fully, his thin blade sinking deep into his opponent's belly.

The man grunted, slid off the blade, and crumbled to the deck.

Peyne glanced at Emma. In the time it had taken him to dispatch his opponent, Emma had killed another three, the bodies in a semicircle around her as she brought up her twin daggers, eyes darting for the next attacker. Peyne considered. Perhaps sport-fencing tactics were not the most appropriate for actual combat.

An earsplitting scrape and splintering crack drew their attention, the deck lurching under their feet. Was the ship breaking apart? A row of men on the enemy vessel used long wooden poles to push off from the *Pride of Klaar.*

Three short blasts on a horn, and the men in black began a fighting withdrawal toward their ship.

Emma scanned the scene, eyes intense. "We've got to take their ship."

"Take their ship?" Peyne said incredulously. "Let the bastards go, I say, and good riddance."

She grabbed him by the arm and pulled him nose to nose. "Idiot. Their battering ram is below the waterline. The sea is filling the holds right now. The other ship is the only thing holding us up. They withdraw, and we go *down.*"

"Then we should probably take their ship," Peyne said.

"An astute observation. Pass the word to Arnol. I have to make sure everyone is out of the upper cabins." She left at a run, not waiting for his reaction.

Peyne looked at the mayhem on the main deck below. He wasn't eager to reenter the fray, but that's where Arnol was, and Peyne didn't want to go down with the ship. He sped down the stairs and skirted the edge of battle until he found Arnol, egging on his pikemen.

"Emma says we have to take their ship," Peyne shouted over the din of clashing arms.

"I've already given the order." The captain gestured to a group of sailors aft.

They were casting lines onto the other ship, grappling hooks catching against the gunwale. Sailors lined up to haul on the lines, drawing the enemy ship closer. Men in black rushed to cast off the grappling hooks almost as fast as they flew across from the *Pride of Klaar.* Crossbow bolts flew back and forth. An agonized scream whenever one of the bolts found its mark, bodies tumbling over the side, splashing into the gap between vessels.

Some of Arnol's men swung on ropes out of the rigging to land among the men on the other ship, blades flashing. Slowly, the sailors manning the grappling hooks pulled the opposing ship within a few feet.

Out of nowhere, the sailors produced a half-dozen wide planks, laying them across the gunwales of both vessels as makeshift bridges. The other ship was lower in the water, and the planks angled downward.

"Now, now, now!" screamed Arnol. "Everyone goes! Get the lead out of your backsides! Nobody stays!"

The sailors swarmed across, screaming desperate war cries. Three seconds later, Peyne stood alone on the main deck. No. Not quite alone. The mortally wounded quivered and moaned around him. He wondered briefly if anything could be done for them. The deck was thick and slippery with blood.

A scream of pain caught his attention. He turned and saw one of the attackers being stabbed by a shorter figure. The man clutched at his guts, staggered back, and fell.

He recognized the shorter figure as the Fyrian woman. A dozen dead men in black lay in a circle around her. Blood splattered across her face and hands. None of it appeared to be hers. She stood calm, uninjured amid the carnage.

Peyne noticed the other Fyrian's body lying among the dead. He'd been a rude asshole, and Peyne couldn't summon any remorse at seeing his corpse. But if the girl had been his consort, then his death might be disorienting for her.

"Come on," he called to her. "We've got to get off this ship." Not that he was eager to board the other vessel. He could only hope Arnol and his men were winning.

The woman ignored him, went to the body of the other Fyrian, and frantically searched through his clothing.

Peyne took her by the arm. "We've got to go *now*!"

She jerked away, jabbering at him harshly in Fyrian. He didn't understand a word but recognized the tone.

He backed away, forced himself to speak calmly. "We can't stay. The ship is going to sink." He gestured at the vessel around him, then mimed with his hand the ship going down.

She looked at him for a long moment, face blank, then turned and jogged away.

Peyne blinked. "Hey!"

She took the stairs down, disappearing below the deck. A voice in Peyne's head said, *Leave her. If she wants to drown, that's her business.*

But he found himself running after her, calling for her to come back.

He followed her footfalls two decks down, came off the stairs into knee-deep water. He found her slamming a shoulder against a cabin door.

"Forget it," Peyne told her. "It's locked, and there's nothing in there worth drowning for anyway. Can we please go?"

With sudden rage and frustration, she slammed her sword blade into the door. A scream that was half-growl tore from her throat.

Peyne stepped back, startled. She turned to him, eyes so fierce Peyne thought she might take a swipe at him next. She held the hilt of the scimitar with a death grip.

Her gaze fell to the dagger at his belt, her hand darting out and snatching it before Peyne could even blink.

He grabbed at the empty sheath. "Hey!"

She's fast!

She turned back to the door again, bent to work the iron lock with the dagger tip. Peyne opened his mouth to object again, but the ship groaned and creaked, the deck tilting under his feet.

A small utterance of triumph from the girl as the lock clicked open. She pushed the door inward.

A rush of water tore through the corridor and slammed into them. Peyne lost his footing and went under, the water sweeping him into the girl. They tumbled together into the cabin. There was a brief moment of disorientation, Peyne trying to figure which way was up. He surfaced at last, sputtering and coughing, salt water stinging his eyes.

The water was chest deep. It there hadn't been a whale-oil lamp hanging from the ceiling in the corner, they would have been in total darkness. The thought of being belowdecks and blind on a sinking ship terrified him.

Enough. I'm leaving and to blazes with her.

She surfaced near him, gasping for air. She grinned, relief in her eyes as she held up what she'd been looking for, the small scepter thing Peyne had seen before in the other Fyrian's possession. *She risked her life for that? A trinket?*

Now that she had what she wanted, she seemed just as eager to depart as Peyne. She struggled against the current, the water still coming into the cabin, up to her chin now. Peyne followed. They climbed the stairs to the deck, the water foaming up after them. It rose faster now. The *Pride of Klaar* wouldn't last much longer.

He looked around, taking in the scene. Bodies littered the deck. All lay still now. A fire aft cast an eerie flickering light over everything.

The other ship was gone.

"Fuckers!"

They'd left him. All because that stupid woman needed . . . whatever the hell that thing was. They'd sailed away and left him on a sinking ship in the middle of the ocean.

He went to the railing, careful of his footing. The ship listed badly, and if he stumbled, he could keep on tumbling right over the side. He squinted out to sea. He could just make out the fuzzy orange light of the other ship's lanterns in the darkness.

"Hey!" he shouted. "We're still here!"

It occurred to him that Emma's crew might have failed to take the enemy ship. In which case he was shouting for the marauders to come back and get him. Not that it mattered. They were too far to hear.

A tug at his sleeve, and his head snapped around to see the girl gesturing emphatically across the deck.

The ship's longboat.

"Good thinking!"

The longboat was on the wrong side of the ship, lifting higher above the water as the other side sank. Lowering the vessel would be awkward but still doable if they hurried.

They crossed the deck, leaning against the tilt, then threw their legs over the railing to climb into the longboat. Peyne motioned the girl to the aft pulley, and he took the one forward. He mimed pulling the ropes. She nodded.

The process went smoothly at first, but then something gave way in the ship, and she started to roll. Slowly, but not slowly enough.

"Hurry! Get her down fast!"

The girl didn't need to know his language to understand the urgency. They both worked the ropes like mad. A few seconds later, Peyne's end touched water, but the stern was still three feet in the air.

"Come on!" he shouted. "Get it down!"

She yanked on the ropes, spitting violent words at the pulley. There must have been some kind of snag.

The ship rolled faster. This was it. She was going over. The aft end of the longboat smacked hard against the ship's hull. When the *Pride of Klaar* flipped, it would drag the longboat over with it.

Peyne lurched aft. He had to unsnag the pulley. They had only seconds until—

The girl barked something angry in Fyrian and swept her sword across the ropes.

And then suddenly Peyne was flying, the longboat falling away beneath him. The sensation lasted only a split second. The longboat rose up to meet him again quickly, and he landed hard in the bottom. There would be bruises. He looked up to see the girl had hit hard too. She was pushing herself up, trying to get her bearings.

The prow of the longboat began to lift out of the water.

Peyne hadn't cast off the forward line.

"Shit!"

He leapt at the line, cast it off, and the longboat plopped back into the water.

The *Pride of Klaar* rolled over.

"Get the oars," he said. "We've got to get away from her. I don't want to get tangled in the rigging or some damn thing."

He scanned the interior of the longboat. No oars.

"Are you fucking kidding me? Damn the eyes of every god and titan and fuck this fucking boat!"

Peyne leaned out, began paddling with one hand. The girl saw what he was doing, leaned out the other side, and began paddling. With agonizing slowness, they moved away from the sinking ship.

They needn't have worried.

Once rolled over, the *Pride of Klaar* took its own sweet time to sink. Sixty yards away, Peyne and the girl lay panting in the longboat and watched her go. Down . . . down . . . down. At last, the sea swallowed the ship whole. Not a scrap of debris remained, as if the vessel had never existed.

The longboat bobbed on the quiet water. Peyne turned his head back and forth, the empty sea stretched vast and eternal in every direction.

"Well," he said, "this is much better."

CHAPTER THREE

Peyne pointed to his hand. "Hand."

"Hand," the girl repeated.

He lay in the prow. At the other end of the longboat, the girl sat in the stern, legs pulled up under her. It was hot, and she must have been uncomfortable in her cloak, the hood pulled forward to shade her face. The sun beat down mercilessly. Peyne pulled his own shirt up to cover his head after enduring the sun for an hour.

He didn't see how they could last. The longboat had no food or water. The days were endless and hot. There was no land in sight, and Peyne had given up scanning the ocean for signs of other ships. He'd hoped to glimpse a sail on the horizon, but no such luck. They were fortunate to have a boat beneath them, but in every other way, the situation was dire.

So why not learn a new language?

Peyne tugged on an earlobe. "Ear."

"Ear," she repeated.

She'd mimed the request that she wanted to learn Peyne's language. She knew almost no Helvan, and Peyne certainly didn't know Fyrian.

And anyway, there wasn't much else to do.

Her focus impressed him. She didn't tire. Her attention never wavered, and when he'd go back and quiz her on the words she'd learned, she never missed one and her accent was perfect.

At last he indicated he'd had enough of language lessons for the time being. When she understood, something immediately changed in her expression and posture, shoulders slumping, fatigue taking over her face. Almost as if she'd let go of something inside her, whatever was helping her concentrate on words. She curled in the stern and went to sleep.

Peyne dozed.

A heavy *thunk* woke him.

He sat up, looked around. The girl still slept. At her feet, the odd little scepter had fallen out of her clothing and landed in the bottom of the longboat. He leaned forward and picked it up, reclined again and examined the object.

The thing was heavier than it looked, well crafted. He thought it might be some tool, but its use wasn't self-evident. A weapon? It didn't seem especially lethal or practical as a weapon.

He felt the girl's eyes on him.

Peyne looked up slowly.

She held out her hand and said something in a low, even voice. She was clearly pretending to be calm but wasn't. Their language lessons hadn't gotten as far as *please return my property to me*, but her meaning was clear.

"You almost got us killed for this," Peyne said. The resentment in his voice surprised him, but he didn't stop. "We're here in this damn boat in the middle of the godforsaken ocean for *this*."

He leaned out, held the scepter over the water. "How about I just drop it? It'll sink fast, I bet."

The girl gasped.

Peyne immediately regretted his cruelty. The girl's eyes filled with tears, and she began talking so fast that Peyne might not have understood her even if they'd shared a language.

"I'm sorry. I was joking, okay?" He scooted forward, handed her the scepter. "Just take it. I didn't mean anything."

She snatched the scepter back from him, hugged it to her chest. For a moment, she seemed okay. Then she started sobbing, her whole body shaking, fat tears rolling down her cheek.

Peyne made what he hoped were soothing *shooshing* sounds. "Hey, it's okay. Calm down. I made a bad joke."

She wiped her eyes, sucked in a ragged breath. After a moment, she turned away, wrapping herself in her cloak.

Peyne sighed and leaned back into his spot. His entire world had shrunk to the length and width of a longboat, and he'd just alienated the only other person in it.

They slept, the longboat bobbing in the sweltering heat. Night brought relief. A full moon glittered on the waves, and Peyne might have appreciated the beauty under other circumstances. By morning, he could think of nothing but food and water. He'd heard stories of sailors lost at sea for days. How they could stand it? Day two adrift was only just beginning, and Peyne didn't see how he could go on without a drink of clean water.

He realized he might be a bit spoiled. Life at court had done little to prepare him for such hardships. He hoped to get out of this alive so he could go on being spoiled. He closed his eyes and tried to imagine servants—young, pretty, female servants—bringing him roast goose or pork and goblets of wine. But always it came back to water and his increasing thirst. He'd never touch a drop of wine again if he could just have a single cup of cool water right now.

He and the girl passed time with more language lessons. He was less enthusiastic for it today, but at least practicing was a distraction.

Night fell again, and he slept restlessly. The sun rose, and Peyne was nearly mad with thirst. He considered the seawater. It certainly looked very wet, but he knew better. Drinking salt water would only make his situation worse. *Much* worse.

The girl spent all her time hidden within the folds of her cloak. Late afternoon, she poked her head out and tried to initiate another language lesson.

Peyne waved her away. He didn't have the energy. Despair was a heavy weight on his chest. Night fell again, and he closed his eyes thinking they might not ever open again.

He dreamed.

Peyne was back aboard the *Pride of Klaar*. Everything was fine. In this strange world of slumber, it seemed normal to be back aboard ship, and the ordeal in the longboat was the dream. He searched the ship for Emma. He wanted to find comfort in her arms, this strong impressive woman.

But he couldn't find her. He called out, and she answered, but her voice seemed distant and muffled. The interior of the ship became a labyrinth. He turned a corner only to find another corridor that led to still another winding passage.

The earsplitting crack of wood startled him. Somehow the sound seemed more real and immediate than everything else around him. Water flooded the corridor, rising impossibly fast. It splashed wet and salty on his face and cold enough to startle—

His eyes flickered open. A head hovered over him in silhouette against the dull, flat gray sky.

"Emma." Peyne's throat was so dry it hurt to talk.

The head babbled Fyrian at him.

Not Emma.

A wave crashed over the gunwale, filling his eyes and mouth with seawater. Peyne coughed and sputtered, his eyes stinging. He felt hands on him.

The girl was trying to yank him up by his shirt. Her babbling had an urgent edge to it. The ocean poured into the longboat. Peyne sat up, blinking to clear his vision, and tried to orient himself.

The longboat was sinking.

"Got to be . . . fucking . . . kidding me," he croaked.

The longboat bobbed against a huge gray rock. Peyne's brain labored to put the puzzle pieces together. He looked down, saw the crack in the hull near the prow, water pouring through. A swell must have lifted them and brought them down hard against the boulder.

Nobody would accuse Peyne of being a nautical expert or wise in the ways of the sea, but it was his general understanding that giant rocks just didn't rise up randomly from the ocean floor. Or did they? Peyne tried to remember if he'd ever heard such a thing. It occurred to him he had no idea what he was talking about. For all he knew, boulders sprouted from the water every five miles like markers on the King's Highway.

The girl frantically tugged at his sleeve. Whatever she was saying, she seemed pretty emphatic about it. He looked where she was pointing. There were more scattered rocks in the water ahead, the foaming waves crashing into them. Beyond the maze of rocks, Peyne saw it in the dim light of dawn.

"Land!" Peyne wiped his eyes and looked again. It had to be an island. Didn't matter. Anything was better than the sinking longboat. Reaching the island was maybe a half-mile swim. Maybe even a bit more. He wasn't at his best, weak from hunger and thirst, but there was no other choice than to try to make it. The longboat would sink out from under them in a few short minutes.

The girl must already have been thinking the same thing. She dove headfirst into the water. If she hadn't been so rash, Peyne would have suggested she take off the cloak first. She surfaced a few yards away, turned, and motioned for him to follow.

He hesitated. There was no other choice, yet still he balked. He wasn't a bad swimmer but hadn't gone out of his way to practice either. He looked at the island again, growing clearer in the brightening light of dawn. He could make it. He had to.

Peyne dove into the water.

He surfaced, saw the girl ten yards ahead of him, and stroked after her.

It was difficult to tell if he were making progress or not. The ocean between the rocks sloshed around, shoving him in one direction, then another.

A wave crashed down and sent him under. He tumbled and kicked and surfaced, and another wave slammed him into one of the rocks. Pain shot through his shoulder. He opened his mouth to scream hurt and frustration when the next wave slapped him in the face, filling his mouth with water and pushing him down again.

Something yanked him by the collar, and a second later, he was up again. The girl had him, dragged him along as she swam forward, one-armed, kicking furiously. Peyne's dead weight held her back, and they both tossed in the roiling ocean between jagged rocks.

Peyne spit water, coughed. "It's okay. I'm all right."

She released him, and they swam together toward the island. Once past the field of rocks, the ocean calmed. Instead of a foamy tumult, the sea now swelled gently, the tide seeming to be with them as they were carried toward land.

Peyne swam, legs kicking, arms stroking. His eyes burned with salt. Every muscle in his body screamed. He looked up. The island still seemed a million miles away.

No. Don't look. Keep your head down. Breathe. Swim. Breathe.

He swam. Time melted away, became meaningless. Peyne thought of nothing but kicking his legs, stroking with his arms. Over and over.

The pain started in the center of his back between his shoulder blades. A hot ache spread to his shoulders and neck.

Keep going. Swim. Breathe. Swim.

His legs were heavier than lead. His strokes had diminished to a feeble doggy paddle. Every muscle burned.

I'm not going to make it. I'm not going to make it. I'm not—

His foot touched bottom.

Peyne stood chest deep in the water, the surf crashing around him. He trudged, doggedly putting one foot in front of the other until he was out of the water. He took five more steps to reach dry ground, then allowed himself to collapse. He lay face first in the hot sand, a groan of pain and relief leaking out of him.

Five feet away, the girl sprawled in the sand, panting.

Peyne closed his eyes. His relief in making it to land lasted all of thirty seconds. Hunger and thirst returned to haunt him.

He opened his eyes again and saw the girl on her knees, sitting back on her feet, hands palm down, flat on her thighs. Her head was up, eyes closed. She breathed in sharply through her nose, turned her head side to side, breathed in again, kept repeating the process. The exhaustion from the hard swim had seemingly vanished.

Peyne had heard the monks of some religious orders liked to . . . what was the word. Meditate. Not that Peyne saw the use of it.

The girl's face was utterly calm, and she seemed not to feel the effects of the arduous swim at all.

Her eyes popped open, and she stood. She pointed to the tree line, gestured for Peyne to get to his feet.

To blazes with that. "A bit tired actually."

"Water." She pointed again. "Water."

For obvious reasons, *water* had been one of the first words in her language lessons.

The girl mimed drinking. "Water."

Peyne heaved himself to his feet. His arms and legs protested. His parched mouth and throat overruled his limbs. He didn't even care how she knew, didn't even care if it was a lie.

The chance for water was impossible to resist.

She led him into the palm trees. Within twenty yards, sand gave way to coarse grass. The undergrowth grew up around them. In another fifty yards, Peyne found himself climbing a rocky slope. When it grew steep, he stopped, leaning on a boulder.

"Climbing . . . some enormous . . . mountain . . . after swimming . . . a hundred miles . . . isn't exactly . . . what I had in mind," he panted.

"Water," she insisted.

Peyne rolled his eyes. "Fine. Lead on."

They continued up a narrow ravine, the greenery becoming more lush as they climbed, the trees leaning in to form a canopy above them. Peyne noticed with appreciation it was cooler up here. Vines and moss covered the rocks.

He paused, cocked his head, listening. "I can hear it."

The rush of falling water was close.

Peyne followed the girl with renewed hope.

They rounded a large outcropping of rock, and there it was. A small waterfall fell about a dozen feet into a small pool below. On the far side of the pool, water overflowed the edges, forming streams that disappeared down the hill.

Peyne and the girl rushed forward, both going to their bellies at the edge of the pool. Peyne stuck his face directly into the water, sucking in great mouthfuls. His dry mouth and throat flared in pain at the sudden influx of cold water. But then, almost immediately, the liquid soothed him. He drank and drank until his belly was tight.

He dunked his head completely under the water, surfaced, and looked at the girl.

She brought water to her mouth with both hands but paused to look back at him.

In a blur, everything came back to him, what they'd been through. They'd survived the marauder attack, the *Pride of Klaar* sinking beneath them, the near catastrophe with the longboat, adrift on the open sea without oars, and a marathon swim through rough waters to reach land.

"Well," Peyne said in a light tone, "that was fun. How about we never do it again?"

She couldn't possibly have understood completely what he'd said, but something in his demeanor must have registered. She threw her head back and laughed wildly.

Her face changed completely. Something bright lit in her eyes.

And then she plunged her head completely under the fresh, cool water.

CHAPTER
FOUR

"You *smelled* the water?"

She handed him a piece of fruit. "Yes."

"There was an entire ocean behind you."

She shrugged. "Salt water smells different."

These were *not* satisfactory answers, but Peyne decided not to pursue the line of questioning. For now.

He took a bite of the fruit, a sweet explosion of juice in his mouth. "What's this called again?"

"Mango," the girl said.

He'd had bananas before. The traders brought them as far as Merridan occasionally, although by the time they made it so far north, they were dotted with brown specks. But mangoes were new to him. Delicious.

However, after three days of nothing but bananas and mangoes, a big dish of greasy pork would have suited Peyne just fine. And a skin of wine.

But he wasn't dead, and he wasn't starving or wasting away from thirst. He lounged in the shade of the overhanging palms near the pool. His sunburn had partly faded. All things considered, Peyne had been incredibly fortunate.

He cast a sideways look at the girl. Her name was Zayda. They'd gotten around to introducing themselves when the language lessons had continued. With death imminent, her name hadn't mattered. Now it did. She sat cross-legged in the patch of shade, eating her own mango, the hood thrown back on her cloak.

"Are you wearing anything under that?" he asked.

She froze in midchew, raised an eyebrow at him.

He laughed. "I'm not trying to disrobe you. It just occurred to me you must be dreadfully hot. Wearing the cloak made sense when we were adrift. Probably saved you a lot of sunburn. Seems unnecessary now."

She looked away, shrugged. "I'm not hot."

He didn't believe it but said, "Suit yourself."

She pointed upward. "I'm climbing the hill. Above where the water comes down."

"Waterfall."

"Yes. It does."

"It's called a waterfall," Peyne told her.

She nodded. "I'm going to climb the rocks above the waterfall. To the top."

"Why?"

"To see." She pointed in every direction. "All around."

"Do you want me to come with you?" *Please say no.*

"Faster with just self," she said.

"By myself," he corrected.

"Faster by myself."

"You're picking up my language surprisingly well," Peyne said suspiciously. It wasn't the first time her uncanny aptitude had caught his attention.

A moment of concern on her face was immediately hidden by a bright smile. "Because you're a good teacher."

Peyne knew a dodge when he heard one but let it go. "Well, see if you can spot a comfortable inn from up there."

He leaned back and closed his eyes. Peyne had rapidly mastered the art of island life. Eat a mango. Take a nap. Drink from the pool. Repeat. He glanced up a few minutes later and spotted her among the rocks high above the waterfall.

She's surefooted and a quick climber. I hope she doesn't break her neck. Peyne dozed.

A gentle breeze brought the exotic scent of some flower. The sound of falling water soothed him. Oh, yes. Peyne's situation could be better, but it could also be far worse. He had food. He had water. He had shade. It could be *far* worse. Now was the time for recuperation after his ordeal. Then, once rested, he could put his mind to getting off this stupid island.

"It's not an island."

Peyne's eyes popped open. Zayda stood over him. He hadn't even heard her approach. "Did I say that out loud?"

Her eyes narrowed. "Say what out loud?"

"Never mind." He sat up and stretched. "How do you know we're not on an island?"

She pointed to the hill she'd just climbed. "I looked all around. Water only on this side." She gestured behind her toward the beach.

"Did you see roads or a town or . . . or *anything?*"

"No, but I think I know where we are. This coast is called *Alaaykraba*. It means . . ." She gestured with her hand, groping for the right translation. "The Dragon Teeth Shore. All the rocks like teeth."

"Yeah, I get it."

"All the rocks not good for ships, so very few towns for ships," she explained. "How do you say towns for ships?"

"Ports."

Her face went strangely calm, drained itself of expression. "Ports," she repeated, and in the next second, she seemed to return to normal.

"Okay, then I guess if we can figure out where we are, then we can make some kind of plan for getting back to civilization," Peyne said. "Whatever direction we choose, it looks like we're in for a good bit of walking, and Dumo knows when we'll actually stumble across a village."

They discussed likely plans for about an hour, neither in any real hurry to make a decision. Zayda felt confident they were much closer to the Fyrian border than to the Helvan lands northward. The tropical jungle was an uninhabited buffer zone between the two kingdoms. Peyne tried to remember any maps he might have seen at some point. The captain of the ship always seemed to know where he was going, so Peyne had little motivation to consult maps. If one went north through the jungle, it would eventually give way to the grasslands and then the baronies and duchies of Helva beyond. A long, *long* walk by anyone's reckoning. Not that he recalled ever hearing about any roads through the jungle. A smarter strategy would be to head back south to Fyria. They'd come to a port sooner or later and then maybe catch a ship. He and Zayda agreed on the plan until a better one presented itself.

Both of them disliked the thought of leaving their water source behind.

"At least we can take as many of these bananas and mangoes as we can carry," Peyne said. "I fancy we'll see more along the way, but I'd rather not chance it."

"We can only carry a little," Zayda said.

"I had an idea about that. If we tied up the hood part of your cloak, we could use it as a sack and take turns carrying food." Peyne waited for her reaction, knowing already she wouldn't be keen on the idea.

She frowned, tried to hide her reaction, and knew she'd failed. She simply looked at him, not talking.

"What are you hiding, Zayda?" He tried to sound like an adult attempting patience with a stubborn child, but really he was worried she might be hiding some weapon. He remembered the little scepter, her unfriendly traveling companion on the *Pride of Klaar*. What did he really know about this girl?

She met his gaze, face firm but not malevolent. Maybe she was deciding, trying to think of some excuse.

They glared at each other for a long, awkward moment.

Peyne was about to say something more when Zayda's shoulders slumped. She sighed, bent, and grabbed the hem of her cloak. A pause, her eyes coming up again briefly to meet his. He saw resignation there.

Zayda pulled the cloak up over her head and let it drop.

She wore a halter top underneath, something much more appropriate for the climate as Peyne had suspected. Ivory-colored material, trimmed in a deep red. The fabric was so light and flimsy that little imagination was needed to guess what was underneath. A single thin strap, tied at the back of the neck, held the garment up. Attractive, in a hard, slender, athletic sort of way.

But his attention was drawn to the thin collar around her neck. It seemed well wrought yet too simple to be jewelry. His eyes fell to the sash around her waist. The little scepter was tucked in there. It appeared to be made of the same type of metal.

Slowly, she turned. The halter top left her back completely exposed.

The blue lines of the tattoo stretched down her spine and across her shoulders, runes meticulously inked along the lines. Peyne had seen tattoos before, crude dragons or mermaids etched on the leathery skin of seasoned sailors. Never anything this elaborate.

He tried to remember everything Ambassador Korick had told him about ink mages.

"I should have guessed sooner," Peyne said. "You were picking up my language with remarkable ease."

"That's about twenty-five yards." Peyne held up the scepter. "How's that?"

Zayda shook her head. "I've been this far from Kayman many times. Anyway, ink mages would be of little use if they were always kept this close."

The duo stood facing each other on the beach. The sun beat down on them, but a breeze coming off the sea made the weather tolerable, bordering on pleasant. She motioned him back another twenty yards.

"Still the same," she shouted over the crash of the surf.

"I'll go slowly," Peyne shouted back. "Tell me when to stop."

He backed up one deliberate step at a time. For some reason, he held the scepter up over his head. Probably didn't make any difference. At the two-hundred-yard mark, Zayda waved her arms. He couldn't hear what she was shouting, but guessed she wanted him to stop.

"I'll try a bit more!" Probably she couldn't hear him at this distance, but she'd get the idea soon enough. He slowly took ten more steps back.

Zayda waved her arms more frantically, her shouts shrill but unintelligible. She ran toward him at full speed, feet kicking up sand.

Peyne stopped, watched her come, and then walked back toward her.

In seconds, she was in front of him, panting, one hand reaching out, demanding the scepter. Peyne gave it to her immediately.

She clutched it to her chest, anxiety draining away from her face.

"What happened?" he asked.

"I started to feel afraid," she told him. "When you kept going"—she put one hand over her chest—"like panic in here."

"You wanted to test the limits," Peyne reminded her. "Should we try again? A little farther?"

"No!" she said quickly, fear flashing in her eyes.

"What happens if you get too far from the scepter?"

"This." She tugged at the metal collar. "It makes an explosion. The head goes off."

"What?"

She made a tumbling gesture with her hand to indicate her head flying through the air.

"That's barbaric."

"It is how they keep the ink mages under control," she said. "Otherwise ink mages would overpower their masters."

Peyne hadn't thought of that. The tattoos made an ordinary person into something much more powerful. Why would anyone as powerful as an ink mage let herself be a slave? So of course the masters had to invent a way to keep them in line.

He remembered taunting Zayda by holding the scepter over the side of the longboat and immediately felt a stab of guilt. If he'd dropped the thing into the water out of spite, or simply fumbled it into the sea, the scepter would have gone down and down and down until it was far enough away to pop the poor girl's head off.

No wonder she'd been frantic. He couldn't blame her.

"At least we have an idea of the limit now," he said.

"Maybe."

"What do you mean? We just tested it."

"But I've been farther away from the scepter with Kayman," she said. "He must do something that lets me, but I don't know how."

"Does it do anything else?" Peyne nodded at the scepter.

"There is a command to cause pain," she said. "For discipline if I am disobedient. Other things too maybe, but I'm not sure. I hadn't been bonded with Kayman for long."

"Bonded?"

"A link to the scepter and to me," Zayda explained. "So if I try to kill him, the scepter knows and . . . boom."

Boom indeed.

"How do you get it off?"

"It doesn't come off," she said. "Ink mages are slaves forever."

◆　◆　◆

Peyne watched the dying embers of the small campfire, unable to sleep. Even at night it was hot, and he considered a dip in the pool only a few yards away. But the heat wasn't what was keeping him awake. Okay, maybe a little. This entire adventure had been damned uncomfortable, but that wasn't what occupied him.

He still had questions.

"Why don't they just put the tattoos on themselves?"

The girl stirred a few feet from him, made a small grunt. He'd probably disturbed her on the edge of sleep.

"What?"

"The princes and the sultans," Peyne said. "Why not just have the tattoos inked on themselves? Then they could be powerful."

"Women take the tattoos better," she said. "They test us. Very few men are able to take the ink, maybe one in a hundred, maybe one in five hundred. With women it is more like one in ten. But even then, they don't take all. Only those with the deepest wells of . . . I don't know the word yet. The strength inside of us."

"Then you should be flattered, I suppose," Peyne said. "That they found you strong enough."

"I don't feel flattered," she said. "I feel like a slave."

"How'd they pick you?" Peyne asked. "Do they just roam the streets, randomly testing young women?"

She told Peyne the story of her family's bankruptcy and being sold into slavery.

That sort of thing hadn't been done in Helva for two centuries, but Peyne had heard rumors. Zayda might not feel fortunate, but perhaps she was after all. Much worse could happen to pretty young girls.

You should thank your lucky stars. You could have been sold to the brothels. But he didn't say it out loud. He had his tactless moments, but this wasn't one of them. A slave was a slave. Asking a slave to see the bright side was idiotic. And Zayda was already acutely aware of the alternatives.

"Why are women more suited to the ink than men?" he asked.

"I don't know. They didn't tell me. But . . ."

After a few seconds, Peyne said, "It's okay. Just say whatever you're thinking."

"I think women are stronger than men," she said. "I don't mean muscles. I mean inside. A kind of willpower. Men could never go through childbirth. And when my father is sick, he lies in bed all day. Mother always keeps working."

A slow smile spread across his face. Sure. It was as good an explanation as any. And then he drifted off slowly and easily into a deep, peaceful sleep.

CHAPTER FIVE

The walk south had been easy the first day, a relaxed march along the sand, camping under palm trees and drifting off to the sound of surf and wind. They awoke with the dawn and began the hike anew.

Halfway through the day, the white sand beach narrowed and narrowed until the sea encroached, forming a saltwater marsh to block the way in front of them. Mangroves crowded out the palms. It stank like rot, and the closer they approached, the more often clouds of fat mosquitoes swarmed around them. They briefly discussed options. There were few. Heading south to Fyria instead of north toward Helva still seemed the best bet. They'd have to go around the marsh.

The two backtracked a mile until they found a likely spot to head inland.

The jungle canopy closed over them. Wide palm fronds blocked most of the sun, but the trees also closed them off from the ocean breeze. In an hour, they both poured sweat, the humidity heavy and cloying.

Peyne followed what he thought was a narrow game trail, which soon became overgrown and then vanished altogether. He drew his rapier. The weapon was a quality bit of steel, and he hated blunting the edge to use it as a machete, but there'd be no forward progress unless he chopped his way through.

In a few short hours, Peyne's clothes were sticking to him. His eyes stung with sweat. His arm and shoulder ached from swinging the sword. He called a halt, leaning against a tree, panting. The waterfall and the pool of clear water seemed like some long-lost paradise.

"Five minutes," Peyne said. "Then we'll get started again."

Zayda closed her eyes, face calm as she took in long breaths through her nose.

When her eyes opened a second later, she pointed back east. "Water."

Peyne didn't need to be told twice. He hacked his way east, eager for a drink.

They found the stream in a shallow gully, a thin trickle bubbling over rocks. It wasn't as cool and clear as the pool constantly stirred by the waterfall, but they drank deeply, relief flooding them.

Zayda stood, wiping her mouth with the back of her hand. She hooked her thumbs into the vines she'd fashioned into straps for the backpack made out of her cloak. It was full of bananas and mangoes. "Are you hungry?"

Peyne flopped on his back next to the stream. He wasn't sure he could move. Not for a while. "Later."

Zayda stood, something going tense in her posture, her head turning slowly, eyes squinting into the jungle. "Somebody's out there."

Peyne propped himself up on one elbow. "We're in the middle of nowhere. How could there possibly—"

He stopped himself, listened. He heard nothing. And that was the problem. He heard way *too much* nothing. As they'd moved inland, away from the constant racket of wind and surf, the constant caw and tweet of jungle birds had risen in volume and variety.

Now the utter quiet was absolute and unnerving. Not a breath of wind. Not the rustle of a single leaf.

"I don't have a very good feeling all of a sudden," he said.

"Get on your feet," Zayda told him. "Draw your sword."

Peyne suddenly looked frightened.

She hadn't meant to sound so commanding. Her tone surprised even her. But she needed him to be ready, and he obeyed, lurching to his feet and lifting his sword with reluctance. Zayda wished belatedly she'd taken a turn hacking through the jungle so Peyne could have rested his sword arm.

No matter. When trouble came, it didn't pause for you to make ready.

She tapped back into the spirit, connecting to that well of strength and power within herself.

Zayda opened her senses up to the world around her.

Being tapped into the spirit gave her perfect control of those senses. She isolated her hearing, divided each sound into a category to form an auditory picture. There was Peyne's breathing, the rustling of his clothes, his steps on the wet ground as he turned to survey his surroundings. She set aside those sounds as a known quantity.

She let the sounds of the area filter in, her brain sorting. Breathing and footfalls behind her, more on her left, and at least one on her right. The crunch of a leaf under a foot that only she could hear. They were closing in, positioning themselves.

"There are five or six behind us," she said. "Two on the right, and three or four on the left. Maybe more in reserve beyond. Their footfalls are light, so probably not armored. They are about to charge us, so brace yourself."

Peyne licked his lips nervously, eyes darting side to side, trying to take in all his surroundings at once. "That's all? You can't tell me the color of their eyes?"

Bravado. But she could hear the strain underneath. He was trying to cover the fear. Was that for her benefit? He needn't have bothered. When Zayda was connected to the spirit, she didn't feel any emotion she didn't wish to. She squeezed her fear down into a tight ball, rolled it into a dark cellar within herself, and slammed the door.

She caught sight of the first attacker at the very edge of her peripheral vision.

He exploded from the foliage, thrusting a spear ahead of him. For anyone else, this would have been a startling, deadly occurrence. Not for Zayda.

Time.

Slowed.

Or at least it seemed to. In fact, there was nothing at all different about the flow of time. Rather her perception had slowed the world around her. She instantly took in every detail of the scene. Her every sense had been raised to the absolute height of human possibility.

Zayda had heard of the primitive jungle tribes but hadn't known what they looked like. Short, bare arms and legs, thin but wiry with muscle. Crude symbols in muddy orange paint on his chest and face. A thin loincloth of some rough fabric. Animal hide sandals. The man's hair was shaved off on the back and side of his head, a black mop sprouting up from the top like a mushroom. If Zayda had wanted, she could have studied each pore on the man's face. Her eyes missed nothing, mind processing every image.

Understandably, she focused on the spearhead being jabbed at her. Five-foot wooden shaft, expertly hewn from the branch of a jungle tree. A stone spearhead, edges jagged and unpleasant. The angle of the thrust suggested he was going for her throat.

More movement on all sides. At least a dozen springing from their hiding places.

She stepped aside at the last second, spear thrust passing her face, missing by three inches. She plucked the spear from the man's hands, spun it around, and slammed the butt end into her attacker's face. A sharp crack of his jaw breaking. He stumbled back, spitting blood.

Zayda turned and hurled the spear.

Another of the primitives slid off Peyne's blade, thick blood running down the steel like syrup.

The spear landed in the back of another tribesman coming up behind him. Peyne heard the scream, turned just in time to see the man fall at his feet.

Zayda had already drawn the scimitar and danced among the other tribesmen, dodging spear thrusts, slashing and hacking as she went. They might as well have been stabbing at a ghost. She passed, and they'd look down at their own bellies, innards spilling out as they screamed and died.

In scant seconds, it was over, a ring of bleeding, quivering bodies in a circle around her.

A scream, pain and fear. Not quite over yet after all.

Peyne had run one of them through the belly and out the other side. The tribesman coughed, blood spilling down his chin. Peyne tried to yank his sword free, shoving the dying man away with his other hand.

"Get off, you bastard!"

The final surviving tribesman leapt on Peyne's back. A skinny arm went around his throat, and suddenly Peyne froze. A stone dagger prodded the flesh just below his ear. The tribesman babbled angrily.

"What's he bloody saying?" Peyne demanded.

"He wants you to drop your sword." Zayda could just make out what the tribesman was saying. The language was definitely Fyrian but some primitive version, the accent harsh and, frankly, offensive to her ear.

"By all means," Peyne said. "Happy to oblige."

He let go of the rapier, still stuck through the other tribesman. The dead man fell to the ground, taking the sword with him.

"Tell him if he just goes away we won't follow him," Peyne suggested.

The tribesman barked something rude.

"He says . . . I'm not sure how to translate," Zayda said. "Go and have sexual relations with yourself."

"Oh, come on," Peyne said. "I realize he and his friends just tried to kill us, but that's no reason to be disrespectful."

"Maybe better if I talk to him," Zayda suggested.

"I'd venture to guess that out of the three of us here, I am, in fact, the only professional diplomat," Peyne said. "But by all means, work your charms."

"You need to be smart about this," she told the tribesman in Fyrian, speaking slowly and trying to match his accent.

"Shut your whore mouth," he said. "Drop your sword, or I jab this hog sticker into your soft man's pretty white flesh."

"Look around you," she said. "Your friends are dead. I did that. It wasn't even very difficult. You kill him, what do you think happens next?"

His eyes flicked to the bodies, then back to her stoic face. She could tell he was thinking. She gauged the distance between herself and the tribesman. She knew how quickly and decisively she could move and was *certain* she could get there and kill the man before he harmed Peyne.

Well, *almost* certain.

But she could see he was relenting, muscles relaxing. He wanted a way out of this. Zayne predicted that next would come some kind of offer, maybe even what Peyne had already suggested. *Just let me walk away, and we can forget this ever happened.*

The tribesman opened his mouth to say something.

He went stiff, an arrow coming through his gaping maw, blood and shards of teeth flying out. Zayda took note of the gleaming steel arrowhead, specked with blood.

The tribesman shuddered once, eyes rolling back. He let go of Peyne and slid to the ground with a dull thud, landing in a sitting position, hunched over. The arrow had entered through the back of his skull.

Zayda had sensed something out there in the jungle but had focused only on the tribesman with the dagger at Peyne's throat. She wouldn't make that mistake again.

They emerged from the jungle slowly, tentative, a half dozen of them, arrows nocked and ready to loose. They looked similar to the first group, but Zayda figured they must be a different tribe. The markings on their faces and chests were made with a gray-blue paint, hair completely shaved except for one thin line down the middle. Short swords with wide blades hung from braided belts. Each wore a necklace of teeth.

Human teeth.

One of them stepped forward and spoke directly to Zayda but glanced curiously at Peyne. Again, a primitive version of Fyrian, but the accent was smoother.

"What's he saying?" Peyne asked.

"He asks if you're a man of Helva," she said. "Do I tell him?"

"I suppose it depends," Peyne said. "Is he friendly with Helvans? Or does he consider us a delicious change from mangoes and bananas?"

Another quick exchange between Zayda and the newcomer.

"He says there are other men of Helva close by, and he'll take us to them," Zayda told Peyne. "But he wants us to hand over our weapons."

Peyne gestured to the rapier still stuck through the tribesman he'd slain. "Help yourself."

One of the primitives yanked the sword from the dead savage with a hard tug.

They looked at Zayda expectantly.

Six of them. It likely wouldn't matter if she had her scimitar or not. If she wanted them dead, they'd be dead. She thought this without an iota of arrogance. Simply a fact. And anyway, Peyne obviously wanted to proceed without bloodshed, so these warriors could take him to his countrymen.

She turned the scimitar around in her hand, offered the hilt to the nearest tribesman, who took it, then eyed the scepter stuck into her sash.

"It's not a weapon," she said. "I'm keeping it."

He looked at the corpses all around her. "Okay."

Primitive, she thought. *Not stupid.*

A gagging sound drew her attention. Peyne was bent double, giving back the banana he'd had for breakfast.

Next to him, one of the newcomers knelt next to the tribesman with the arrow through his head. With a short, curved knife, he carved teeth from the corpse's mouth.

If Zayda hadn't been tapped into the spirit, she might have gagged too.

CHAPTER
SIX

When it had become clear Peyne and Zayda would cooperate, the tribesmen had lowered their bows and formed a single-file line into the jungle, Peyne and Zayda in the middle of the pack. They hiked silently and at a steady pace for nearly three hours, veering west and a little north.

Then the jungle opened into a clearing before them, a village of maybe a hundred squat huts made of dried grass and sticks, like giant birds' nests turned upside down. Across the village, Peyne spotted the pavilion, about a dozen large tents. Two flags flew from the post of the biggest tent. The first was the flag of Helva. The smaller flag displayed a coat of arms he didn't recognize.

Someone of low rank, or I'd know them.

Peyne might have been an indolent layabout, but hanging around court, drinking his fill of wine, and propositioning the daughters of lesser nobility had given him the opportunity to see many coats of arms. The owner of the tent wasn't someone who frequented the court.

The tribesmen led him and Zayda through the village toward the Helvan pavilion. Women worked at various tasks, repairing huts, tending fire, or nursing babies. Toddlers of either gender ran around bare-ass naked. The village wasn't as squalid as Peyne would have imagined, and on the whole, the villagers seemed reasonably happy and healthy.

They halted at a large cook fire around which the tents were arranged. A native woman labored over a big iron pot.

The spokesman for the tribesmen babbled his nonsense talk at Zayda.

She turned to Peyne and said, "He says to wait here. He's fetching the head Helva man."

Peyne shrugged. "I guess fetching the head Helva man is better than fetching the Helva man's head." He grinned at his own witticism.

Zayda very slowly and deliberately rolled her eyes.

Peyne smiled, more warmly this time. *This girl has something. There's spice in her.*

The tribesman returned with a man Peyne didn't immediately recognize as Helvan. He had the dark-brown skin of the southern islanders, but when he spoke, it was in perfect Helvan with no accent.

"I'm Lord Mardis Kain," he said in a smooth baritone.

Kain was a big man, a foot taller than Peyne and half again as wide. He wore a loose red shirt of light material, likely in deference to the heat, but Peyne could easily imagine him in full plate armor. A wide handsome face with a broad nose. No moustache, but beard trimmed to a neat point. An abundance of black hair pulled into a topknot. A formidable-looking long sword hung from a wide belt.

"A pleasure," Peyne said. "Peyne Erlich at your service. I suppose you're wondering how we came to be—"

"You don't mean Peyne Erlich the king's envoy, do you?"

"Oh . . . uh . . . yes, actually."

"We thought you'd been lost at sea."

"We were lost," Peyne said. "We found ourselves."

"A fascinating story, I'm sure. We have much to talk about." His eyes slid to Zayda. "The woman is Fyrian?"

"Uh, my translator actually," Peyne said. "Difficult to do the king's business in Fyria if one doesn't speak the language." He gestured to her with a flourish. "Zayda."

"A pleasure to meet you, Lord Kain," she said in perfect Helvan. She lowered her head, more than a nod, not quite a bow.

"The pleasure is all mine, madam." Kain's eyes flicked back to Peyne. "Still, if we could talk alone, Lord Erlich. My people can see to your translator, make sure she's provided with refreshment."

Peyne hesitated.

"I could use water and a meal, thank you, Lord Kain," Zayda said.

"Very well. I'll see you later then, Zayda," Peyne said loftily, as if to a servant.

"Come. Let's talk in my tent where we can be comfortable and away from prying eyes." Kain took him to his tent and threw back the flap, ushering Peyne inside. "I have a skin of good wine in my bags somewhere."

"In that case, Lord Kain, I believe we're going to be great friends," Peyne said.

They sat in the tent across from each other in folding camp chairs. Kain leaned in close to refill Peyne's wine goblet from the large skin. When he and Zayda had been beached on the dragon-toothed shore, and Zayda had smelled out the water, Peyne's life had been saved. But it was only now, sipping a middling red wine, that he felt truly happy again to be alive.

"I fear I now owe you a debt I can never repay, Lord Kain." Peyne sipped, relishing the slightly too-sweet flavor.

"Please call me Mardis."

Peyne lifted his goblet in salute. "And I'm Peyne."

They drank enthusiastically to being on a first-name basis.

"I came into the jungle with a hundred men," Mardis said.

Peyne leaned forward to demonstrate he was paying attention. Mardis had listened dutifully as Peyne had related his recent adventures. It was only polite Peyne return the favor. He'd exaggerated only slightly in explaining how he'd rescued Zayda from the sinking (and burning!) *Pride of Klaar* and dragged her limp form ashore, barely saving her life. Peyne didn't consider this self-aggrandizing. Mardis was sharing his wine after all. He deserved a thrilling tale.

"Our mission is to open the old trading road from the grasslands down to Fyria," Mardis said.

"I didn't know there *was* a trade road," Peyne admitted.

"Something they tried a few decades ago," Mardis said. "In the end, it wasn't profitable."

"I would imagine not," Peyne said. "Ships can bring a lot more cargo and faster."

"But not necessarily cheaper. Anything coming through Helvan ports is subject to tariff. And bigger ports like Sherrik add a local tax on top of that. The jungle road was a free route. Anything that could easily be packed onto a mule caravan was a good bet, spices, the better-quality silks."

"Until somebody caught on," Peyne guessed.

"The Fyrians," Mardis said. "They began charging an exit tax on their end. As soon as the profits dried up, the road became meaningless. It's barely an overgrown path now. At one point during our expedition, it vanished completely, and my men and I spent half a day finding it again. Of my hundred men, I have only twenty with me here. The rest are divided into squads, clearing the overgrown parts. About twenty miles back, there's a camp with men guarding the horses. The rest of us pushed through unmounted. Stealthier that way. Plus, the Mashi don't ride, and we need them for guides."

Peyne raised an eyebrow. "Mashi?"

"This is their village," Mardis said. "It was fairly easy to win them over. They love anything metal, which is scarce in the jungle, swords and arrowheads and the like. Gives them an advantage in their ongoing feud with the Katoki."

"Let me guess," Peyne said. "Those unpleasant people with the orange body paint."

"Yes, and if you've seen their stone weapons, then you understand why good steel gives the Mashi an advantage."

"What's the feud about?"

Mardis shook his head. "Don't know and don't care. I have my orders."

Peyne sipped wine. "So you're reopening the road. Starting up the trade route again? Is that the purpose?"

"Purpose?" Mardis looked at him as if not understanding the question. "The purpose is so we can start the war of course."

Zayda sat cross-legged near the cooking fire. She'd been given stew—something with meat, a nice change from the fruit—and had been generally left alone. The Helvan men spared her sideways glances as they went about their business. Of the Mashi men—she'd been told that's what they were called—she saw nothing. Back skulking through the jungle on some errand, she suspected.

The women of the tribe specifically avoided meeting her gaze as they tended the fire and stirred the stewpot. She wondered if this were some custom or if she'd offended them in some way.

The sun went down, and darkness consumed the jungle. Her world shrank to a flickering circle of firelight. Peyne remained in the tent talking to his countryman. She should have guessed he would forget about her when he was back with his own kind.

Not that she cared.

Just because Peyne was handsome with a square jaw and thick, rich chestnut hair, and eyes the most haunting shade of blue she'd ever seen, didn't mean she missed his company.

63

She blinked, the thought she'd so keenly noticed such things startling her. *Ugh . . . this is not the time or the place or . . . or anything. I need to focus on getting out of this jungle.*

And he was tall.

Stop it.

Her hands drifted back to the scepter tucked into her sash. The cool metal on her fingertips was a small comfort. She kept worrying she'd lose it. Which was foolish.

If she lost it, she'd be dead already.

"Sister."

Zayda flinched, startled, her head spinning around.

At the edge of the firelight knelt one of the Mashi women. She bent forward, prostrate, forehead against the ground, arms straight out.

"Are you talking to me?" *Stupid question. Who else is around?*

"Forgive me for disturbing you, sister," the native woman said. "I was sent to bring you."

"Get off your face," Zayda snapped. "We're none of us slaves here."

The woman rose, sitting back on her feet.

Zayda flushed with embarrassment. She hadn't meant to speak so harshly. "I didn't mean to be rude. What's your name?"

"Dureen."

"I'm Zayda. Bring me where?"

"To the old woman."

"That's a bit cryptic," Zayda said. "Does she have a name?"

"She has always been known as the old woman all my life," Dureen said. "For all the years of my mother also."

"What does the old woman want?"

"It is not for me to say, sister."

Zayda didn't understand all this *sister* talk. Perhaps it was simply a local custom among the Mashi women. And maybe this invitation from the old woman was some belated attempt at hospitality. An invitation from one of the village elders. After all, Zayda had been sitting alone by the fire for some time while Peyne consulted with the other Helvan.

You'd think he'd at least check on me.

Never mind. It didn't matter.

Zayda stood, dusted herself off. "I'll come with you, Dureen. Why not?"

Dureen lit a torch from the flames of the cook fire, then headed into the jungle, glancing back over her shoulder periodically to make sure Zayda was still there.

The jungle was eerie in the dark, Dureen's torch making strange shadows of the gnarled trees. Thick liana vines rose up the trunks to crisscross in the darkness overhead. They had a tentacle-like quality in the flickering torchlight, and Zayda found herself irrationally uneasy.

If she'd wanted, she could tap into the spirit, push all trepidation aside.

No. It can become addictive.

Abruptly, Dureen stopped, held the torch out in front of her. "The old woman awaits you."

Zayda peered ahead. In front of her, the liana vines tangled together, forming a tunnel in the jungle as if some arboreal god had reached down to knit them together.

"It's dark."

Dureen handed her the torch. "I'll wait. I know the jungle. The dark doesn't bother me."

Zayda held the torch aloft and entered the tunnel. The vines arched above her like nature's own temple, woven together so intricately that she could hardly believe such a configuration happened by chance. She'd heard of druids who sang to the trees, encouraging them to grow in one direction or another. Maybe this was some similar craft at work.

The tunnel zigged and zagged and opened into a large chamber, the walls a tight latticework of liana, the ceiling curving into a dome above.

Another cook fire, smaller than in the camp of the Helvans, with an iron kettle warming. The old woman sat on a short, three-legged stool, poking at the fire with a crooked stick.

She was the oldest person Zayda had ever seen, at least by how she looked. Gray hair, thin, kinked, and wiry, stuck out in every direction. Skin brown and lined and splotched, papery thin and clinging to frail bones. Deep lines in her face. Zayda thought one sturdy mule kick would scatter her like a stack of dried kindling. She wore clothes similar to the other Mashi women, the one exception being a fine, silken shawl of deep red wrapped around her shoulders.

She looked up, caught Zayda's gaze. One eye was moist and milky white. The other a bright, alert blue.

Most Fyrians didn't have blue eyes. She hadn't seen any other Mashi with blue eyes either.

"Sit if you like, Zayda,"

The old woman nodded toward a large flat rock on the other side of the fire. Zayda sat, knees coming up high enough for her to rest her elbows.

"The tea will be ready soon."

Zayda didn't want tea. "You sent for me?"

"An invitation, sister."

"How are we sisters?" Zayda asked. "Is that how Mashi women refer to each other?"

"I am not Mashi," she said. "When the old tribe faded to dust, the Mashi came. When they are gone, I will still be here."

"How sisters then?"

The old woman studied her for a long moment with her one good eye. Slowly she turned and let the shawl drop. On her wrinkled, spotted skin, yet still clear and unmistakable, the lines of the Prime tattoo were inked down her back.

"Did you say *start* the war?" Peyne asked.

"If we wait for the Fyrians to attack, then they'll do so at the time and place of their own choosing. Gant doesn't want to give them that advantage." Mardis sipped wine, then cleared his throat. "My pardon. His Royal Highness *King* Gant. No offense meant."

"I call him Ferris and none taken," Peyne said. "Starting a war just . . . well, look, I know the man, okay? We're friends. I'm friends with the king, and I know how that sounds, and I promise I'm not trying to impress you, but *let's start a war* just doesn't sound like Ferris." Peyne drained his goblet, looking at the wineskin pointedly.

"I've never met the king, so I'll have to take your word for it," Mardis said. "If it makes a difference, most of the officers feel the war has begun already. I mean, nobody's stabbing anyone with spears yet, but for all intents and purposes, Helva is at odds with Fyria. We are philosophically opposed."

"What exactly is the Helvan philosophy?" Peyne held his goblet in a way that must certainly indicate he needed a refill.

"Damned if I know," Mardis said. "I think it amounts to the basic fact they'd like to invade and take all our stuff, and we'd prefer preventing that. The sultan has his heart set on the entire world. He feels he shouldn't settle for less."

Peyne reached over, grabbed the wineskin, and filled his own goblet. Manners be damned. He took a big gulp, felt it wash warm down his throat into his belly. He took his comfort where he could get it. "A war. Seriously. A war?"

"As I said, many around court feel the war's already begun," Mardis said. "The swords simply haven't left their scabbards yet. If Gant can find a way to snatch the initiative, then why not?"

"And he thinks the Fyrians have forgotten the road, is that it? Gant wants to use it for a sneak attack." Peyne drained the goblet, filled it again.

"Or if the Fyrians haven't forgotten it, we hold the road to prevent them coming up through the grasslands. In either case, controlling the road is better than not controlling it. Obviously." Mardis took back the wineskin and refilled his goblet. "These are all theories and educated guesses naturally. I was sent to secure the road. That's the only thing I *know* with certainty. Marshal Pascale might be sharing the details of his battle plan with his generals, but he hasn't taken the time to enlighten *me*."

"Pascale? What happened to Jon Gorten? He's been marshal of the armies for a decade."

Mardis shook his head sadly. "Times are changing, my friend."

"I haven't been gone *that* long," Peyne protested.

"Maybe not, but the changes were a long time coming," Mardis said. "Gorten was a complacent, peace-time general, slow to see what was happening right under his nose and slow to act."

Peyne had always thought Gorten thoughtful and level-headed. "Pascale is brash and ill-tempered and has possibly the worst moustache I've ever seen."

"Some translate brash and ill-tempered as ambitious and confident," Mardis said. "I would not presume to judge the man's moustache."

Peyne had more to say but bit his tongue. Like it or not, Pascale was now a powerful man in Helva. He was just the sort of thin-skinned twat who'd hold a grudge if he caught wind somebody was bad-mouthing him, and really Peyne had only just met Mardis Kain. Who knew where the man placed his loyalties?

Peyne let the news sink in. What other political upheavals had taken place in his absence? Weeks had passed since he had left home. He knew little of Helva's military. How big were the armies? How many ships were in the navy? He didn't even know where in Helva there were forts or strongholds, or what they guarded. He damned himself for his poor attention span. As a man high in the king's favor, he'd had multiple opportunities to listen in on military discussions. Instead he'd guzzled wine and chased chambermaids.

And what of the Fyrians? How many troops could they muster on short notice? Or have they been planning for years? Yes, obviously. It was why Peyne had been dispatched to Fyria in the first place. The war was coming and any information that might help—

Ink mages.

Idiot. Of course. The ambassador even told me how important it was to report on the ink mages. A single ink mage is worth ten regular soldiers. He remembered the image of Zayda's flashing blade dealing death to the tribesmen. *More like fifty.*

Ink mages could make all the difference in the war. And Peyne had one. She'd even explained, albeit basically, how the tattoo worked. He had to get her back to Helva. The scholars would know what to ask her. It might make all the difference.

"Mardis, I'm sorry for this, but I'm going to have to presume upon your hospitality."

"Don't fret, my friend," Mardis said. "I have more wine in our supply tent. I'll send the porter."

"No, that's not it. I mean, well, yes, actually, do send the porter, but it's more than that," Peyne said. "I'm going to need two of your horses and enough supplies to get me and my translator back to the capital."

"You're an ink mage." Not a question. The Prime was obvious down the old woman's back. Zayda would never have guessed she'd meet another ink mage here in this remote place. The only others she'd seen were created by the sultan's pet wizard.

"A very select sisterhood, don't you think?" the old woman said.

"What about the woman who came for me," Zayda asked. "Dureen."

The old woman shook her head. "Not an ink mage. She just used the term in case you recognized it."

"I'm not in a sisterhood." Zayda tugged at the metal collar. "I'm a slave."

The old woman frowned. Something hardened in her good eye. "I thought such things were over centuries ago. So long, I thought they might just have been stories. Tell me."

As Zayda told her story, they sipped tea from earthen mugs.

When she'd finished, the woman looked fatigued, as if Zayda's tale was a heavy weight she'd placed on her new companion's back.

"I'm sorry. I would help you if I could, but this is an ancient evil and beyond my skills."

"It's okay," Zayda said. "I'm told they don't come off. I doubt there's anyone anywhere who can help me."

"You're too young to be without hope."

"I don't want to hope and then be disappointed."

"Perhaps . . . I can give you some hope," the old woman said. "Not much. A glimmer."

Hope seemed a dangerous thing. The collar made hope a lie.

"For twelve generations, the women in my family have been ink mages," the old woman began. "The knowledge passed from mother to daughter. I know things, legends maybe or truths. Who can say which is which?"

"Stories." Zayda sighed. "Stories can't help me."

"Don't underestimate stories. You're writing your own even now," the old woman said. "You decide what the end will be. What story do you want your children to know?"

"Then tell your story. I'll listen." Zayda sipped tea.

"Once there were two great wizards, each wanting to be greater than the other. Their war almost broke the world," the woman told her. "But these men didn't invent the magic they wielded so powerfully.

The magic was born ages before these two wizards. The wise call Fyria the cradle of all magic. Certainly the ink magic was first made there."

She took a stick from the fire, began to draw something in the dirt. Zayda leaned forward, recognized the Fyrian coast and realized the old woman was drawing a map.

"In the deepest part of the desert where there is no living thing," said the old woman. "Begin at the Last Village." She poked a point on the map with her stick, then dragged a line south. "Find the Valley of the Seven Guardians. From there . . ." A noncommittal shrug.

Zayda took a long look at the map. Not that she needed to memorize it. She could tap into the spirit any time she wanted and recall every word of this conversation exactly, every detail of the simple map the old woman had scraped into the dirt.

"Is this why you brought me here?" Zayda asked. "To show me this?"

"I didn't know why. Only that you were a sister. It has been many years, more than your lifetime three times over. I have no daughters. I cast aside three husbands until I realized finally it was me. I cannot bear children, and yet I have a legacy to pass along."

The old woman sighed, all her long years seeming to catch up with her at once. "I have a gift for you . . . if you will accept it."

♦ ♦ ♦

"That probably seems like a reasonable request," Mardis said. "But if I give you two horses, that means two of my men will go without. It might seem a small difference, but if I go into battle, I'll want every man. And if I have to retreat, I don't want to leave anyone behind."

"Please," Peyne said. "It's . . . important."

Mardis sat back, chewing his lower lip. Peyne guessed what the man must be thinking. Technically, Peyne wasn't Mardis's superior. He held no place in the chain of command, either military or political. On the other hand, Peyne was close with the king and had been dispatched

20

to Fyria, presumably for an important reason. Casually dismissing a request from one of the king's closest friends was probably not smart.

"Perhaps if I knew the nature of your dilemma I might figure some way to lend assistance," Mardis suggested.

Shrewd. *He's not saying no. But he's not offering me his horses either.*

Now it was Peyne's turn to tread carefully. He sized up the man in front of him, decided Mardis could be trusted. Anyway, what choice did he have?

"Have you heard of ink mages?" Peyne asked.

"A gift for me?" Zayda raised an eyebrow. "Why?"

"Because there's no one else to give it to," the old woman said. "Eventually, my time will come. Not soon, but it is inevitable. I must pass on the gift lest it be lost to history."

"I don't want your gift." Zayda sat back suddenly, crossing her arms, not looking the old woman in the eye. "I don't want any of this."

The old woman sighed, a long, sad sound. "You are a slave, then."

Zayda lifted her head abruptly, now meeting the old woman's crooked gaze with fire in her eyes.

"Good," the old woman said. "You might think yourself a slave, but at least you don't like the idea. At least there is some fight in you."

"I told you. The collar doesn't come off."

"The collar doesn't make you a slave," the old woman said. "Only accepting it does."

The held each other's gaze for a moment.

"Tell me about this gift," Zayda said.

"First you must take off your top," the old woman said. "You must be bathed. Your skin must be clean and blemish-free to receive the tattoo."

"I'd always thought ink mages were something of legend," Mardis said. "I remember the light in the sky twenty years ago. I was just a child. But they said that had something to do with ink mages. Stories and legends."

"They're true," Peyne said. "I mean, I can't verify *every* story you might have heard about ink mages, but enough are true. I've seen what she can do with my own eyes."

"She?" Understanding slowly bloomed in Mardis's expression. "The girl isn't your translator, is she?"

Peyne shook his head. "And she's just one little girl. Now I want you to imagine an entire army of them coming through the jungle on your newly cleared road."

◆ ◆ ◆

When the wizard Meddigar had inked the Prime down her back, Zayda's world had expanded by leaps and bounds. The new tattoo given her by the old woman had much the same effect. Even in the gloom of night, the world was perfectly clear around her, one of the side benefits of the moon tattoo.

Zayda untied the strap of her halter top, looked down at the new ink. The crescent moon glowed a faint silver between her breasts. The feeling of the old woman's rough, dry hands on her as she applied the tattoo had faded, and now only the hum of power beneath her skin remained.

Two tattoos. Only two, and yet she felt as if she could take on the world.

Zayda had heard the stories, tales of ink mages with dozens or even hundreds of tattoos covering every square inch of skin. How could such beings be anything but gods?

She paused beneath an opening in the jungle canopy, squinted at the crescent moon in the night sky. It perfectly matched the tattoo on her chest. The old woman had explained the tattoo moon would always match the moon in the sky. As it grew to a quarter moon and then a full moon, so too would her power grow.

She found her way easily back to the Helvan camp and circled behind the large tent where Peyne met with his countryman. How much longer would they be in there? Zayda had been hoping they'd show her a place to sleep. Or did they expect her to curl up next to the campfire like some stray cur?

Zayda cocked her head and listened. She tapped into the spirit, separating out all extraneous sounds and focusing only on the voices of the two men.

"In light of this new development, I think I can let you have two of my horses," Mardis said. "An army of ink mages sounds horrifying. The king will want to know. They'll want to see the girl firsthand. A demonstration will mean more than stories."

"I appreciate your understanding," Peyne said. "The sooner we can leave, the better. I'll deliver the girl to court. The king's wise men will know what to do with her from there."

Zayda backed away from the tent, not wanting to hear more. They'd discussed packing her off as if she were cargo, as if she had nothing to say about her destiny. Her hand went automatically to the collar around her neck. Then it drifted to the scepter in her sash. As long as she held on to it, she was still master of her own fate.

At least to a certain extent.

She felt a sudden stab of disappointment and anger toward Peyne. She'd come to trust him, but what did she really know about the man? Had that been his plan all along, to deliver her like some prize, an enemy weapon to be examined and duplicated?

No. She wasn't being fair. It had always been Peyne's plan to return to Helva, and she'd assumed she was going with him. With the collar around her neck, what kind of life would she have in Fyria? The laws of her own land made her a slave. And really, she did trust Peyne. She had a feeling about him, and she always trusted her own judgment in such matters. Peyne meant her no harm.

But her fate would likely be out of Peyne's hands. She was an ink mage, and she'd probably be poked and prodded by Helvan wizards trying to learn what made her tick. Zayda didn't want that to happen.

She refused to *let* it happen.

Again, she found herself absently tugging at the collar. The old woman had given her an extraordinary gift with the moon tattoo, but she'd also given her another gift, one potentially even greater.

The knowledge that there might be a way to get the collar off, and that the secret perhaps lay somewhere deep in the Fyrian desert.

Stories and legends.

But the old woman said stories could be powerful. I'm writing mine now, aren't I?

She turned and headed back into the jungle. Silvery moonlight filtered down through the trees, the tattoo transforming the light into raw power. It surged through her veins, pulsed beneath her skin.

She could walk all night.

CHAPTER
SEVEN

Demanding physical labor had always been high on Peyne's list of things to avoid. He'd always felt slightly guilty standing idle and watching while other men sweat and toiled.

Which was why he excused himself on such occasions.

This time, as there were only endless miles of jungle in every direction, he was forced to observe as the locals felled the necessary lumber, shaped the ends into points with small hatchets, and then grunted and heaved and muscled the palisade into place.

Peyne felt really bad about it.

Mardis and his men were also standing around and watching while the Mashi did all the heavy lifting. Mardis called it *supervising*.

"Across this narrow stretch of road is the perfect place for the palisade." Mardis stood next to Peyne, looking proud of himself. He gestured extravagantly as he listed the merits of the location. "The river crosses the road about knee-deep. We built the footbridge first, just wide enough for a single small wagon to pass. Those rock formations rise up on the right, and the river drains into a nasty bog on the left. An enemy force could go around, of course, but it would be difficult and slow. Troops trudging out of the bog would be easy pickings for crossbowmen. I feel confident a couple dozen men could easily hold the position against a couple hundred."

Peyne nodded along as the man spoke even though the particulars of the fortification were of little interest to him. Mardis had been ordered to hold the road and was clearly taking his mission seriously.

"We brought the large iron hinges all the way from the capitol in anticipation of this construction," Mardis said. "As soon as the gate is attached, we'll be ready to fend off whatever might come. Then we start on barracks and other support buildings. I'm expecting a company of infantry to garrison the place in a few weeks. If everything goes as planned, this will all be happening, *I hope*, right under the sultan's nose."

"Impressive. I'm sure Pascale will be pleased." Peyne cleared his throat. "No sign of Zayda, then?"

Mardis frowned, shaking his head. "I picked my fastest two riders and sent them up and down the road. No sign of her. If she struck off through the jungle, then finding her again is impossible."

"I see."

Peyne's first thought upon discovering Zayda missing was that something had happened to her. A quick search of the area failed to turn up any sign of a struggle.

Did I say something wrong, give her a reason to be wary of me?

He couldn't think of anything. Perhaps she'd meant to part ways with him all along and had simply been waiting for the right opportunity. And he'd seen she could defend herself. Her leaving was almost certainly her own choice.

Peyne felt, he admitted to himself, slightly offended.

But Peyne's personal feelings weren't the crucial consideration. He'd had an ink mage in the palm of his hand and had lost her. With war looming, knowing as much as possible about the tattooed sorcerers might make the difference between victory and defeat. Peyne never should have let the girl out of his sight.

Mardis had withdrawn his offer to lend Peyne a couple of his horses, pointing out there was no longer quite the urgency for the envoy to get home. When the garrison troops arrived, Mardis would send Peyne back with the message courier.

In the meantime, Peyne felt obligated to lend his support to Mardis's mission.

His support mostly amounted to staying out of the way.

"I feel things here are well in hand," Mardis said. "But feel free to offer suggestions if I've missed anything."

"Fire."

Mardis raised an eyebrow. "Eh?"

"The trees you're using for the palisade are still green, but eventually they'll dry out," Peyne said. "If I were trying to break through, I'd torch the whole thing."

"Reasonable," Mardis said. "I've already sent some of the Mashi into the bog with buckets. There's a tree there with a certain kind of sap. Very flame retardant. We'll coat the entire fortification."

"Don't put any on the bridge."

"No?"

"A fire arrow from the wall could send the whole thing up," Peyne said. "Whatever keeps them on the other side of the river."

"A good idea," Mardis admitted. "But there's plenty of time. Our scouts indicate the Fyrian's are clueless as to our presence. I honestly don't feel we'll need to defend this position at all. Our primary function will be to support an eventual invasion . . . or, at least, that's one contingency."

By which time I'll happily be long gone, Peyne thought.

"The women will set up the tents before all the Mashi withdraw," Mardis said. "We'll have a good meal soon and naturally some wine to toast the completion of the wall. I was thinking of dubbing the place

Gant's Crossing in honor of his majesty. If all goes well, it might be the new southernmost point of Helva."

"Did you say the Mashi were withdrawing?" Peyne asked.

"A few will stay with us to continue as guides," Mardis said. "But the tribe as a whole will fulfill their obligation upon completion of the palisade. We needed the raw muscle for the construction."

Peyne took a good long look at the palisade. Once they'd hung the gate, it would be an effective deterrent to anyone attempting to use the narrow road to travel north. Compared to the towering ramparts of Sherrik or Merridan, the simple wall of rough-hewn tree trunks driven into the ground and lashed tightly with leather was almost laughable.

But here in this remote place, the palisade represented . . . well. . . . *some* sort of accomplishment. Would the wall withstand the entire might of the Fyrian army? No. Obviously not. But some smaller scouting force attempting to come north would be in for a nasty surprise.

"A job well done," Peyne pronounced.

Mardis beamed.

Peyne shook the man's hand. "I look forward to drinking to your great success." *Or to anything really.*

Zayda didn't get far.

When she'd left Peyne and the Helvan camp the previous night, she'd set a quick pace, determination driving her on. It hadn't lasted. The weight of her decision had begun to drag on her. She was alone in a strange place. Peyne might not have been perfect company, but there was a jovial air about him that helped Zayda forget she was stranded in the jungle with a slave collar around her neck.

Did she actually miss Peyne? In her current predicament, almost any company was better than none.

Right?

No. She'd constantly been in Kayman's company from the day the vile man had taken control of her, had reinforced with his every command the reality that she was a slave. She'd cherished every second she could contrive to be away from him, preferring to be alone the rest of her life than ever lay eyes on that man again.

And since he was dead, well, no risk of that.

But there could always be another Kayman or even somebody worse if she were identified as a runaway slave and taken by the Fyrian authorities. The idea she would venture into the deep desert based on the old woman's story now seemed like sheer lunacy. Who was she to rediscover the magic of the ancients lost for centuries?

And she was exhausted.

She abandoned her plan to hike all night by moonlight and found a dry patch of grass under a tree. She curled on the hard ground, laying her head on her arm. It didn't matter how uncomfortable it was. She was so tired, she'd be asleep in minutes.

Except minutes later, she wasn't.

Her mind spun with anxiety, refused to let her body surrender to fatigue. All of her decisions were wrong. She'd never make it on her own. How would she even get out of this endless jungle?

Softly, she began to cry.

It was a silly, little girl's indulgence, and she was ashamed of her own weakness. On the other hand, who was she trying to impress? There was no one to see her tears.

So she let herself cry until she was finished, then let out a long cathartic sigh and finally drifted off.

She awoke with a start, surprised to see the sun high enough in the sky to indicate late afternoon. Zayda had been even more exhausted than she'd thought.

Who wouldn't be? Is all this even happening to me or am I stuck inside somebody else's nightmare?

She stood, yawned, and stretched. The narrow road was still only a dozen yards away. Her intent was to use it as a guide until she was out of the jungle. She dusted herself off.

Zayda felt . . . better.

So much had happened. So much lay ahead of her. A good cry and a night's sleep was hardly the cure for every dilemma, but it hadn't hurt. She managed to scrape up a modicum of determination. Her slender hands balled into fists.

I'm going to walk out of this jungle. I'm going to find my way south. I'm going to get whatever I need to survive the deep desert. And I'm going to get this collar off.

Ugh. Such daunting thoughts made her want to lie down again and go back to sleep. Handling things one at a time might be the only way to stay sane. First order of business? She was hungry. Okay, simple enough. Find some food, then . . .

Her head came up at the sound of hoofbeats.

She backed into the thick foliage, squatted, and watched, holding her breath.

The rider appeared a moment later atop a huge jet-black stallion at a slow gallop. The soldier wore the same type of armor as Mardis Kain's men. He disappeared around the bend, and Zayda waited until the sound of the hooves had completely faded before emerging from her hiding place.

She'd wondered if they would send somebody to look for her. Her instincts had been right to stay off the road.

Zayda spent the next two hours searching for food and water. She was sitting cross-legged between two plants with enormous green leaves when she heard the rider returning. She stopped chewing a piece of fruit, going completely still. She needn't have worried. The rider didn't even slow as he passed her.

He's going back to report he didn't find me. Maybe that's the end of it.

But she couldn't take the chance. She decided to wait until nightfall and travel by moonlight as she'd originally intended. She lounged in the shade until sundown. The moon wouldn't appear for another hour. She considered setting out anyway, but how stupid would it be to come this far only to trip over a gnarly root and break her neck?

Her patience had been nearly exhausted by the time the sliver of a moon rose in the sky. Her moon tattoo hummed with a distant warmth. She could feel her well of spirit slowly being filled by the moonlight.

And this is just a crescent moon. What will a full moon feel like?

She set off through the jungle, keeping the road in sight for guidance, a steady pace but nothing too brisk.

An hour later, she stopped abruptly. Had she heard something? She tapped into the spirit, drinking deeply. She wasn't worried about using too much. The moonlight would replenish her.

Zayda opened her senses to the night.

She set aside the sounds of cooing night birds, the wind in the canopy above, the rustling of rodents in the underbrush. She isolated the sounds she was searching for.

Footsteps.

Not just from one person but from many. The dry crack of feet on dead leaves and twigs. The dull thud on the dirt-packed road. The sucking squish of soft mud. A line—more than one line—across the road and on both sides. They all came at a slow walk. If she focused with all her concentration, she could make out individuals. She stopped counting at forty when she finally saw them coming.

Katoki tribe. They probably thought they were being stealthy under cover of darkness, but Zayda saw them clearly, the muddy orange war paint plain. They crept forward in a ragged line, spears at the ready, another line of tribesmen behind them, and yet another line . . .

An army. There are hundreds of them.

At least a score of warriors approached on her side of the road, slow and quiet through the foliage. They'd be right on top of her in a minute.

She backed against the trunk of a tree, slid down into the bushes, trying to make herself small.

Options. She could hunker down, wait for them to pass her in the darkness. If she kept silent, there was a reasonable chance they'd go right by without seeing her. But if they did spot her, she'd be smack in the middle of the army. She could head into the jungle, let them pass. If they heard her leaving, they'd likely give chase. She could see far better than they could, but this was their jungle.

A sudden high-pitched cry went up, echoing in the still night. It was meant to sound like the call of some jungle bird, but Zayda wasn't fooled.

At the sound of the call, the Katoki halted. Zayda gently pushed aside the shrubbery in front of her face so she could watch them from her hiding spot. The tribesmen on either side of the road stood at ease. The others parted, allowing another group of tribesmen to advance up the road between them, four stout men carrying a bamboo pallet on their shoulders, each at a corner. Atop the pallet, an old man sat cross-legged in a nest of palm fronds.

Zayda had thought there could not possibly be anyone more ancient than the old woman who'd given her the moon tattoo, but the shriveled creature on the pallet might be the winner of that contest. Toothless, eyes closed, his face seemed to be trying to sink into itself. Dull brown hanging from frail bones. Zayda could count every rib. Gnarled, bony hands folded in his lap. Hairless like some strange tree frog. The orange symbols on his body were more elaborate than those of his fellow tribesmen.

The warriors carrying the pallet came forward a dozen yards and gently set it in the middle of the road. They backed away from the old man with respectful bows.

He sat motionless for long seconds, and Zayda wondered if the man was even alive. Then he lifted one hand into air above his head, thin fingers spread. He began to mumble unintelligible syllables, too quiet to hear at first, but in scant moments his voice filled the sky with a strength belying his feeble appearance. She sometimes had trouble understanding the dialect of the tribesmen, but this was something altogether different. The words touched her mind only briefly before flittering away and leaving no trace.

Like Meddigar! Zayda's thoughts returned to the wizard who'd inked the Prime down her back. *I could never remember the words to the spells he cast. Like the words didn't want to be remembered.*

The old man took a small earthen jug from between his legs, set it in front of him, and removed the lid. He passed a hand over the open mouth of the jug, the words to his spell flying from his lips faster now.

The wind picked up, shaking the canopy above Zayda. She'd thought it just a gust, but it blew harder, a forceful wind coming from the direction of the ocean, like the prelude to one of the great tropical gales that plagued the coastal towns during storm season.

In the next ten seconds, the temperature dropped abruptly, and her teeth began chattering, breath visible from her mouth. She wrapped her arms around herself, suddenly lamenting the loss of her cloak.

But there was no need. She remembered she was tapped into the spirit. She ordered her body to ignore the cold, and it did.

The old man chanted at a fevered pitch as his hand trembled over the jug. Zayda watched, wide-eyed and mesmerized.

Something white oozed up from the earthen jug, spilling over the sides. At first, Zayda thought it some strange liquid, but then she realized it was mist. It spread out from the old man, creeping along the ground at first only ankle deep. The fog expanded, knee-deep, then over a man's head. Then it seemed to fill the whole world, engulfing all the Katoki and rolling toward her.

Yeah, time to go, young lady.

She rose from her hiding place, turned, and left in a crouch, moving slowly and picking her way so as not to be noticed, deftly placing each footstep to avoid snapping a twig or cracking a dry leaf. When she felt safely out of range of the Katoki, she'd pick up the pace.

But the fog caught up with her much faster than anticipated. Within a minute, the soup was all around her, limiting her vision in every direction to three feet. Great lumpy monsters rose up in front of her, only to resolve themselves into a mass of vines or clump of bushes.

Zayda shoved down a sudden surge of anxiety at the thought it would be all too easy to get hopelessly turned around. She was positive the road was to her right. If she found that and stuck to it, then she couldn't get lost. All she had to do was stay ahead of the Katoki.

The moonlight, which had been refilling her spirit, had dwindled to a trickle. Not much filtered through the fog. Good to know. The tattoo was still very new to her. Trial and error were needed to fully understand how and what it did. The old woman had given her only the basics.

She stopped suddenly.

Where was the road? The fog had warped her sense of direction. If she kept walking in the wrong direction . . .

Zayda sensed movement to the right. She held her breath. Was that a noise to the left?

Without moonlight to replenish her, she hesitated to tap into her own well, but she had to know. She tapped into the spirit, opened her senses, straining with her ears. Yes, the footfalls were clear now, too close for comfort. The warriors advanced from behind and on both sides, and if they were following the road, then she could use their positions to get ahead of them.

She kept moving at a diagonal to the right, still trying to find the road but also hoping to stay ahead of the Katoki.

If they weren't following the road, if they were coming after her instead, then everything she was doing was taking her farther away from where she intended to go. Self-doubt began to eat at her. She was afraid to move but couldn't remain still either. The tribesmen would have her surrounded. Maybe if she just changed direction slightly, she could—

Her foot hit the road, the hard-packed dirt unmistakable.

Zayda broke into a steady jog, back the way she'd come, back toward Peyne.

She let her imagination get the better of her, thinking the Katoki must be right on her heels, surging toward her through the fog, an army of hundreds, maybe thousands.

She broke into a run.

CHAPTER
EIGHT

When they brought in the hog, Peyne's mouth literally began to water. The Mashi guides had gone into the jungle and come back with the animal, a huge saber-toothed thing big enough to easily feed those remaining at the palisade. It had been spit-roasting all day over the campfire while construction of the gates was completed.

Peyne and Mardis had been toasting the finished palisade for a good hour and now dove greedily into the wild pork, served with some kind of native stewed greens, also prepared by the Mashi.

"Absolutely fantastic," Peyne said around a mouthful of food. "You set a good table, Mardis. I'm impressed at your ability to remain civilized here in the wild."

Mardis lifted his goblet of wine in salute. "Kind words, sir." He drained his wine, smacked his lips. "I'll have my porter fetch another bottle of the good stuff, then we can—"

One of Mardis's men abruptly opened the tent flap and entered. He wore a dark-green tunic over chain mail, a long sword dangling from a wide belt. "Sorry to disturb you, Lord Kain, but you might want to see this."

Mardis frowned. "Always during dinner. Very well. Let's have a look."

Peyne wiped his mouth with a napkin and followed Mardis out of the tent.

And into the thickest fog he'd ever seen. He spun completely around, his vision limited to a few feet in every direction. The campfire was a hazy orange blur twenty yards away, the shadows of men moving around it.

Peyne shivered. "It's suddenly very cold. Does that happen often in this climate?"

"No." To the soldier, he said, "Pass the word among the men. Armor and weapons. Tell them to make ready just in case, but keep it quiet."

The soldier saluted, then vanished into the fog.

"It's just weather," Peyne said. "I mean, *unusual* weather, but still."

"I'm just getting to know this jungle, and I don't like anything unusual," Mardis said. "Come. I want to check the palisade."

The short walk to the wall became strange and otherworldly in the thick fog, men seeming to coalesce out of nothing as they passed, only to dissolve again into nothing. Although Mardis had ordered the men to keep quiet, Peyne heard the muffled clank of armor and weapons as the men prepared for . . .

Does Mardis think we're being attacked by the weather? Or does he suspect something else?

"How many men are here?" Peyne asked.

"Forty. And a half dozen of the Mashi guides," Mardis said. "The rest are scattered back along the road, securing checkpoints and establishing resupply depots."

"That's not much of an army."

"They're good men," Mardis said sharply.

"Of course."

"Come on. Up here for a look." Mardis gestured at the ladder leading up to the platform.

Mardis had told Peyne that eventually proper watchtowers would be constructed, but for now, a crude platform had been erected on either side of the gate. A few soldiers could stand guard and keep watch on the road beyond the palisade.

Peyne followed Mardis up the ladder.

The guard at the top pointed into the fog. "It rolled in fast. Can't see a bloody thing."

Peyne peered into the mist. The footbridge and river were completely obscured. He looked down. He couldn't even see the ground directly at the foot of the palisade.

"I don't like it," the guard said, a young man with peach fuzz for a beard. "All eerie how it come in sudden like that."

"Easy, lad," Mardis said. "Eyes front."

"No point. Can't see nothin'."

"Then use your ears," Mardis told him.

The three of them stood stock still, heads turned, leaning slightly out over the rough-hewn wooden wall. They stayed that way for a minute. Two.

Peyne could just barely hear it, a constant low rustling not completely swallowed by the fog. Movement.

"There's somebody out there," Peyne whispered.

Mardis cast him a sideways glance, nodded.

Peyne looked straight down at a spot before the gate. For just a split second, the fog thinned, and Peyne thought he saw . . .

"Get me a torch."

Mardis's eyes narrowed. "They'll see."

"You don't think they know we're here?"

Mardis sighed, turned, and bent, calling down the ladder in a hoarse whisper. "Pass up a torch."

A few moments later, a soldier brought up a torch and handed it to Peyne. He took the torch, leaned out over the palisade, squinting into the murk.

Then he threw the torch.

It tumbled end over end toward the spot in front of the gate, flaring orange briefly before sputtering out.

But in the quick flash of light, Peyne saw them.

Hunched up figures, at least a dozen of them. They had hold of something long and brought it fast toward the . . .

Peyne shouted down to the men on his side of the wall, "Brace the gate!"

The words were barely out of his mouth when the battering ram slammed into the gate, the crack of splintering wood breaking the eerie silence.

"Katoki!" screamed Mardis.

The tribesmen had felled a huge tree for a battering ram. They brought it against the gate again.

The Helvan camp abandoned silence and rushed the gates, officers screaming orders at the troops.

The twang of crossbows drew Peyne's attention. The two guards on the other platform fired into the fog below. No way to tell if they hit anything.

And that's the point, right? No way is this fog a coincidence.

"Pikes! I want two rows!" Mardis was already on his way back down the ladder.

Peyne hurried after him.

Getting his men lined up in the fog proved difficult. It was impossible at a glance to see if they were all in position, and Mardis found himself running up and down the line, shouting to his other officers, all the time the sound of the battering ram slamming against the gate sending a cold chill up Peyne's spine.

When Mardis finally had two rows of ten pikemen each, he shouted, "First row, down!"

The men in the front row went to one knee.

The battering ram hit again, and Peyne heard the metallic clang of a hinge popping off. The gate was barred on the inside with a green piece of wood about as thick as Peyne's calf. A temporary measure. Mardis's builders hadn't yet fashioned a proper bar reinforced with iron. Peyne was surprised the gate had held this long.

"Pikes at the ready!" Mardis shouted.

Both rows lowered their pikes toward the gate, braced for whatever might come.

The rest of the soldiers spread out in a semicircle behind the pikemen, drew swords. Peyne did likewise, palm sweaty on the rapier's hilt, heart thumping away in his chest.

He tried to summon a mental image of the situation. Mardis had insisted that anyone trying to go around the palisade would either have to climb over enormous rock formations on one side or wade through a deep bog on the other. But how long had the Katoki been lying in wait, preparing, needing only for the fog to roll in before launching their assault? Maybe they were planning to attack from all directions.

Peyne's eyes darted side to side. Pointless. In this preternatural fog, there was nothing to see.

"Steady, men, steady," Mardis shouted to his men. "Remember, they're savages. We have the discipline and the weapons and—"

The final slam of the battering ram, the sharp crack of wood, the ring of another hinge popping. An enormous crash that could only have been the gates themselves falling inward. Peyne felt his heart leap into his throat.

The whoop of war cries rose from what must have been hundreds of voices filling the night. The racket of running feet, a lethal stampede coming right at them.

The pikemen took a halting step back. They couldn't see a thing.

"Hold your ground!" Mardis commanded.

Dark shapes formed in the fog ahead, and suddenly the Katoki were on them.

They slammed into the first line of pikes, war cries turning into shrieks of pain, a din of rage and death. The tribesmen who made it through hit the second line a split second later, some impaling themselves on the pikes, but many more streamed through, swinging cudgels and thrusting spears. A number of Mardis's men went down, swept under by the tide of Katoki.

In an instant, Peyne was surrounded, both by Helvan swordsmen and the tribesmen. A Katoki came roaring from the fog, cudgel held high. Peyne swiped at him with the rapier, making contact but unable to tell if he'd done much damage before the man faded back into the murk. Another attacked him from behind, and Peyne turned only just in time to thrust his blade through the Katoki's belly. He fell to the ground, pawing feebly at the blood oozing from his wound.

Bodies jostled Peyne from all sides, some armored, others not. He could see no one plainly unless he was within three feet. He stabbed another tribesman, who was then swept away into the fog by the tide of battle.

Something struck him at the base of the skull, and Peyne staggered, pain flashing white hot. He took three steps, the world titling out of control, and when he blinked his eyes open next, he was on the ground. He tried to push himself up, failed. Peyne's head swam, darkness narrowing his vision. He strained to stay conscious.

The battle shifted, bodies coming through the fog, feet stepping on his hands and legs. Somebody tripped over his head and landed hard on his back, knocking the air out of him.

He sucked in a long, cold lungful of air, let it out slowly.

Peyne's head didn't quite clear, but he was awake. He lifted his gaze, looking right, then left. He saw the orange blur of the campfire in the fog. He crawled toward it, worried that getting to his feet would draw unwanted attention. Not that he felt confident he could *get* to his feet.

An eternity later, he crawled within the circle of firelight and collapsed, the racket of battle an uproar some ambiguous distance behind him. He rolled onto his back, eyes crossing, fighting off the urge to surrender to darkness. The warmth of the fire was some small comfort. It would be so easy just to close his eyes, to drift . . . peacefully . . .

An enormous figure rose up out of the fog, stepping over him. He lifted a stone axe, face full of battle lust, wicked grin missing a number of teeth.

Peyne swallowed hard. *I'm going to die.*

A flash of metal so fast, Peyne wasn't sure he'd seen it.

The Katoki standing over him froze, grin wilting into stunned disbelief. A red ring formed around his throat, began to drip down into his matted chest hair. And very slowly, the tribesman's head slipped . . .

. . . off.

It landed with a thud next to Peyne.

The tribesmen stood headless a moment before collapsing into a pile of meat at Peyne's feet.

And then the world blurred again. He felt hands on him. He was being lifted, but at the same time, it felt like falling.

"I've got you." A woman's voice.

He was tossed over something, hung awkwardly. The smell of horse.

Peyne was jostled up and down as the horse galloped. He tried to pick his head up to see where they were going. Useless.

Fuck it.

He went to sleep.

CHAPTER NINE

The sensation felt very similar to some of his hangovers.

Except nearly all the pain throbbed in a single knot at the base of his skull. He thought about opening his eyes, but no. He wasn't ready yet. He stretched, felt along his limbs, rolled his ankles. He'd been wrong about the pain. It was all over. Not so severely as the head injury, but a sort of dull ache that seemed to say, *You should just lie there, old boy. No point rushing it.*

Peyne's ribs felt bruised too. Probably from being thrown across . . .

The horse.

He remembered now, bouncing along through the fog, tossed over the horse like a sack of seed potatoes.

Peyne opened his eyes.

The desert stretched out before him, the blur of heat rising from the cracked ground. The sight had been . . . unexpected.

He sat up and fought off a bit of dizziness, blinked and took deep breaths until it cleared. He gently touched the base of his skull. An enormous knot and something vaguely sticky. He looked at his fingers. Blood, mostly dried. He remembered being struck during the battle.

It all seemed like something far away and a long time ago.

He took stock of his surroundings. The jungle rose up lush and green behind him. Peyne appeared to be in some middle ground where the green world succumbed to the encroaching desert. Peyne had been sleeping in the sand but under the shade of a short palm tree. A saddle for a pillow. He looked around, saw the horse twenty yards away, tied to another palm and munching on a patch of coarse grass.

Peyne's boots were right next to him, neatly placed side by side.

He wanted water. Didn't see any.

He pulled on his boots, tried to stand, and was surprised to succeed. A stiff breeze mussed his hair. It was not altogether unpleasant, easing the heat somewhat. Peyne inhaled deeply, hoping to smell the ocean. He didn't and wondered how far a ride it might be to a seaport.

A distant voice cut through the wind and startled him. He turned and saw Zayda emerge from the jungle, something slung over one shoulder.

"Where the blazes have *you* been?" he shouted, but she was too far to hear.

He waited until she was closer and tried again. "We didn't know what had happed. I was worried about you, you know?"

Zayda flashed a bright smile. "I was worried about *you*. You've been delirious for two days. I thought you might never come around."

"Wait . . . what . . . ?" sputtered Peyne. *"Two days?"*

"I thought you might die."

"Sorry to disappoint you."

The smile fell from Zayda's face. "I came to get you, didn't I?"

"But where did you *go?*"

"I ran away."

Peyne screamed, clenching his fists. "Dumo damn you, I know *that*! Why? Where did you go?"

"You're not being very nice right now," Zayda said.

"Not nice? Damn your eyes, girl, answer my . . . wait. What is that? Is that water?" He now recognized the thing slung across her shoulder as a waterskin. "Give me that."

She handed it over.

Peyne snatched it frantically, thumbed out the cork, and tilted it back. He drank greedily, paused, panting for breath, then drank more.

"I hope you didn't have to walk far for that," Peyne said.

"There's a stream about two-minutes' walk past the tree line," Zayda said. "Never mind. Drink what you need."

Peyne took another large gulp, then handed the water back to her. He'd emptied at least a third of the skin. "Thanks."

"I'll get more."

"Don't bother," Peyne said. "We'll get more on the way back."

"Back?" Both her eyebrows rose in a *don't be ridiculous* expression. "We're not going back that way."

"Good thinking," Peyne said. "If the Katoki have overrun Mardis's palisade, then it's probably not safe."

Zayda rolled her eyes and headed back into the jungle with the waterskin.

Peyne gently lowered himself into a sitting position beneath the shade of the palm, leaning back against the trunk. The water had helped considerably. His skull still throbbed, but it was down to a low roar.

In his desperation to quench his thirst, Peyne realized he still didn't know why Zayda had run away. When the girl returned, he'd have to set her straight. With the world nearly at war, this was no time for juvenile indulgences. He needed to get her back to Helva as soon as possible, so the king's wise men might learn the secrets of ink magic.

And then Ferris Gant could put a fat coin purse in his hand by way of a thank-you.

The thought further eased the pain in his head.

Peyne had just about dozed off when Zayda returned with a full waterskin.

"We're ready to go," she said.

"Agreed." Peyne stood and stretched. "If we angle east, we'll eventually hit the coast and then we can get a ship."

"No."

"I know. We don't have any money, but if we can find somebody of sufficient authority, I can establish a line of credit."

"No." She picked up the saddle, walked toward the horse.

Peyne followed her. "I'm not saying there won't be difficulties. Be optimistic. A port town will eventually see a Helvan ship pass through, then there's our chance."

"No." She slung the saddle onto the horse, cinched the straps tight.

"Come now," Peyne said. "I realize our situation isn't optimal, but you're being a bit too pessimistic, don't you think?"

"When I say no, I mean, no, I'm not going back to Helva." Zayda put her foot into the stirrup, heaved herself up into the saddle.

"Of course we are."

"I'm not."

"Yes, that was the plan. Don't be silly."

"No!" barked Zayda. "I heard you and Mardis Kain talking. I'm not going. Not now. Not ever."

"You know, I'm really being very patient. I'm not sure what the problem is here."

"I'm not a slave!" Zayda said heatedly.

"We don't want to make you a slave," Peyne shot back.

She tugged violently at her collar. "*This* does. And it will never come off if I go with you. The old woman said there were answers in the deep desert, that I might be free again."

"Well, then the old woman can just take a flying . . . old woman? Who are you talking about?"

"Back in the Mashi village," Zayda said. "She told me of the ancient magicians before giving me the tattoo."

"You got another tattoo?"

She averted her eyes, nibbling her lower lip. Peyne guessed the conversation had gone in a direction Zayda hadn't intended.

"Maybe you should tell me all about it," Peyne suggested.

She sighed and let the story spill out, the villager Dureen who'd come to take her to the old woman—the sister—and then the old woman telling her about the origins of ink magic in the deep desert, and finally getting the new tattoo.

She finished her story, and Peyne took note she'd neglected to say what the new tattoo actually did. "Let me see it."

One of Zayda's slim hands automatically came up to cover the spot between her breasts.

Peyne rolled his eyes. "Never mind. There'll be time for that later. The important thing is we get to a safe place, and marching back into Fyria doesn't qualify for either of us. They're about to go to war with my home country, and as soon as somebody recognizes what that collar means, they'll pack you off to the prince. So. To reiterate. We angle east. We'll hit the coast sooner or later, and then we arrange a ship."

Her face hardened. "No."

Peyne sighed, pinched the bridge of his nose between thumb and forefinger. This shouldn't be so difficult. "It's really pointless to keep arguing like this."

"I agree." Zayda put a foot into the stirrup and heaved herself into the saddle. She clicked her tongue, and the horse headed south at a trot.

"Are you serious?" Peyne jogged to catch up, grabbed the horse's reins, and yanked the animal to a halt.

Zayda glared down at him. "Let go of the reins."

"This nonsense has gone on quite far enough," Peyne said. "Now, you're going to listen to me, and the first thing we're going to do is—"

Zayda's hand fell to the hilt of her scimitar. "Let. Go."

Peyne froze. Then he slowly removed his hand and took a step back. They held each other's gaze for a long, tense moment.

"If I ever lose this stupid thing"—Zayda gestured to the scepter in her sash—"then my head comes off. Imagine living your whole life like that, knowing that if you were careless, or somebody robbed you, then your head might explode. What would you do to get the collar off?"

Anything, thought Peyne. *Anything to be free of it.*

Zayda didn't need him to respond. She saw the answer in his face. "Then you know that I'm doing what I must."

They looked at each other another long moment.

She held out her hand.

He hesitated, just a moment, then took it. She swung him up behind her in the saddle.

"Hold on to my waist," she said. "It's okay."

He did as instructed.

"And I know what you're thinking," she said. "So stop thinking it right now. It won't do you any good."

"Please. You can't possibly know what I'm thinking. I happen to be a complex person. Practically a riddle."

"You're thinking you'll humor me for now," Zayda said. "And then talk me into your way of thinking eventually or trick me onto a ship or some clever thing. Won't happen. I'm going south."

Peyne cleared his throat. "That new tattoo doesn't give you mind-reading powers, does it?"

Zayda didn't answer but grinned, knowing he couldn't see. She gave the horse a kick with her heels, and the steed lifted its head, snorting loudly as if to say *about time* and trotted across the baked land.

CHAPTER
TEN

His official title was the Prince's All Knowing and Infallible Court Magician, an appellation that had been made up just for him.

Meddigar shook his head, chuckling. *Fyrians do love their titles. I doubt I'll ever get used to it.*

Infallible. That would be nice.

But, he admitted to himself, he wasn't doing so badly. He was in high favor among Fyria's greats. He had a palace of his own. Not so big compared to some, not as big as the prince's palace certainly nor most of the nobility or even as large as some of the more prominent merchants. A palace nonetheless.

And women. Dumo forgive him for all the things he'd done with so many women. When the prince was happy, he could be extremely generous.

And so far, Meddigar had done nothing less than make the prince one of the most powerful men in Fyria second only, many would say, to the grand sultan himself.

Not bad for a boy from the grasslands. The Fyrians embrace very few foreigners to the royal bosom.

All because Meddigar had had the good fortune not to die in the deep desert.

He crossed the workshop to the cabinet where he kept the strange liquid metal for the collars, opened it, and took out an iron pot with a secure lid. The object was heavy. He carried it to his workbench with a grunt.

Not that the desert hadn't done its very best to kill him. No food. No water. By sheer dumb luck had he stumbled upon the lost city.

And dumb luck was something akin to lightning. It very seldom struck the same place twice.

The wizard removed the lid and looked into the pot, lined inside with smooth ceramic. The brassy, liquid metal within shimmered in the lantern light. He should have been used to the sight by now but still wasn't.

Meddigar had come out of the deep desert with a supply of the metal along with other untold magical treasures, two enormous pack dromadan loaded down with ancient artifacts. Chief among his finds were the secrets of ink magic and how to apply the Prime to an appropriately receptive subject. Various inks and needles and stencils and other arcane items.

The collars had been a surprise.

At first, Meddigar hadn't understood what they were for. Plundering the ancient workshops of long-dead wizards wasn't an exact science. He'd had to piece together scraps of information from dusty tomes and tattered scrolls. The process had pushed his ancient Fyrian to the limits. The classes at the university in Tul-Agnon had been good—wizards serious about magic were obliged to study the old tongue—but classroom instruction even with the best of mentors seldom prepared one for conditions in the field.

But Meddigar had persevered. He'd learned the function of the collars and how they were made. Enslaving the ink mages had been distasteful to him at first, but the more he thought about the process, the more he understood.

Wizards guarded their secrets closely. Since they couldn't ink the Prime on their own backs, that meant they either had to trust somebody else to put it on them or that whomever the wizard selected to receive the tattoo had to be trustworthy. A risk either way. Either the wizard had to share the secret of how the tattoo was inked, or he had to chance that he was creating a mage who might eventually grow more powerful than him.

The collars took the trust, and therefore the risk, out of the equation. The collars and the control scepters assured obedience. An ink mage could obey or die.

A knock at the door.

"Come."

Nila entered the workshop. A pretty young thing but with a permanent expression like she'd just smelled bad cheese. Brown, flawless skin, eyes a light sandy brown, full red lips. She'd be fat in coming years, Meddigar suspected, but was pleasantly curvy now. She wore a flowing turquoise gown and matching head wrap, thin material to accommodate the heat. How such an attractive woman could be so constantly sour was one of the little mysteries Meddigar had given up on in the year she'd been his apprentice.

She nodded slightly, a minimal show of respect for her master, then said, "Prince Kha'narahn wants to know about this morning's batch."

"None were suitable," Meddigar lied.

Nila narrowed her eyes. "Not a single one?"

Meddigar frowned. If he were back among his own people, an apprentice would not be so forward as to question her master. But he was here in Fyria and hadn't picked Nila to be his apprentice. The prince had provided her ostensibly as a gift. And she was apt enough, intelligent, and properly educated. Technically her abilities were superior.

But to Meddigar, the prince's motivations were fairly transparent. Nila served two purposes: to act as the prince's spy and to learn the secrets of ink magic through her normal duties as an apprentice. After all, it was tradition that the master pass on his secrets to the pupil.

Eventually.

He stroked his dark beard, gray just starting to creep in at the corners of his mouth. He'd reached the far end of middle age. *But I have many good years left in me. Don't be too eager for my secrets, little Nila. Not yet. Your prince will have to wait.*

Nila stood next to him, looked into the pot. "That's the last of it?"

"Yes. I thought I'd make good use of my time in case we find a suitable girl in the next batch, but these materials are rare and valuable," Meddigar said. "Of the nine women I tested this morning, two might do in a pinch. I don't think the prince would want us wasting resources on mediocrity. Do you?"

Nila opened her mouth for a quick retort but caught herself. She understood the difference between stepping right up to the line and crossing it. "Your wisdom in this is, of course, undisputed."

And don't forget it.

He dipped a ceramic ladle into the liquid metal. Ceramic worked best. Other metals reacted badly, and the shimmering liquid seemed to cling to anything wooden. He dipped the ladle into the pot, filling the bowl two-thirds of the way. He pivoted to the mold on the workbench, filled the first slot, a thin line twenty inches long.

"You'll be heading back to the deep desert soon?" she asked suddenly.

Meddigar stiffened but tried to keep the annoyance off his face. *Clever girl. She suspects.* "Why do you ask that?"

"The liquid metal." She nodded at the pot. "I'm eager to see the lost city, and if we're running out . . ."

Damn her.

And therein lay the predicament. In getting lost both to and from the city, Meddigar, out of his head from hunger and dehydration, had gotten hopelessly turned around.

He had no idea, not one, where the lost city might be located.

Probably how it got lost in the first place.

Oh, he knew the *general* direction. South into the deep desert. Obviously. Perhaps if he retraced his steps, something would seem familiar.

He kept filling the mold, to buy himself a few seconds to think. He dipped the ladle into the pot three more times, filling as many lines. The metal poured out like a thick, brassy gravy.

"I hadn't thought to bring you, actually," Meddigar said lightly as he shuffled scrolls from one side of his worktable to another, not looking at her. "It is an unpleasant journey. I'd thought to spare you."

"My place is at your side," Nila said. "Both to learn and assist."

And if he refused to take her, the prince would hear and grow suspicious.

"Hold that thought," the wizard told her. "And stand away."

She took three steps back.

Meddigar's hand dipped into a pouch on his belt. He pinched a small portion of the powder there, a mix he'd concocted himself to go with the spell, also a thing of his own invention. He sprinkled the powder over the liquid metal in the mold as the word of the incantation began to tumble from his lips. From the corner of his eyes, he saw Nila, her eyes narrowed in concentration as she tried to follow the words of the spell. All useless effort of course. Spells had to be studied, their words elusive, resisting being remembered.

He passed his hand over the mold as the arcane syllables trailed off. There was a blur in the air around the liquid metal, a vibration, and then it was over.

Nila leaned in to examine the lines of metal. "May I?"

"By all means."

She picked up one of the brassy lines. Instead of spilling through her fingers like liquid, it hung limp in her grip.

"It feels . . . odd," Nila said. "Not like liquid, but not solid either."

"Not its final form, obviously," Meddigar explained. "But like this we can manipulate the alloy, fasten it around the neck of our new ink mage. Then the last command word makes it solid. A bit of a cheat actually. I had to invent a spell that would duplicate the process."

She shifted the limp length of metal from one hand to the other. "You'll teach me?"

"In time. But as you've pointed out, we're short of the metal. Perhaps in a few months an expedition can be properly arranged." *That should put her off for a while.*

"I began preparations last week," Nila said. "The prince happened to hear about it and is expediting matters."

"What?"

"No need to wait with the authority of the prince behind us. I assumed you'd be pleased."

"Indeed," Meddigar said. "Pleased."

Meddigar's plan had been simple. Return to the deep desert and do everything possible to locate the lost city again. If he found it, then he would replenish the rare supplies needed to ink the Prime and fashion the collars.

And if the city proved impossible to locate again, he would simply disappear. The prince had lavished fabulous wealth upon the wizard, and if Meddigar spirited himself away with only a fraction of such riches, he could set himself up nicely. He knew a number of wards that would foil any magical search for him.

Nila coming along was an unexpected complication.

Never mind. Misfortunes could be arranged. Nila need not alter his plan one whit.

◆ ◆ ◆

His Royal Majesty Ferris Gant sat on his throne trying not to look bored. It seemed somehow a sin that the palace's great hall in the capital of Merridan should ring with the tedious whine of various government ministers. The soaring vaulted ceiling echoed with the dullest details of trade agreements, the minutiae of the bureaucracies that kept the city running, the pleas of a menagerie of minor nobility all hoping for some boon.

How long since he'd been hunting? Too long. But of course a king couldn't simply slip off with a few comrades and go hunting. No, it had to be a production, bodyguards and chefs to prepare a luncheon and minstrels and ladies-in-waiting to ooh and aah over whatever he happened to kill.

Being king is a damned awful headache.

The minister of agriculture droned on about crop rotations. With heroic effort, Gant stifled a yawn.

Nothing of real importance ever happened at court. Urgent and weighty matters always happened in a back room with a pitcher of wine and away from prying eyes. A handful of men conducted the great affairs of Helva. A thousand expendable peons handled the myriad details.

No. Gant chastised himself. He must never think of those people as small or expendable. That was his uncle talking. Gant's Uncle Pemrod had been an effective king but not a good man. There had to be a way to do both.

And work in some hunting too, for Dumo's sake.

The minister finished, and Gant nodded and smiled, indicating he appreciated the report, then dismissed the man with a casual gesture.

The chamberlain stepped up to announce the final business of the day. Evet Murnan was a skinny, storklike man with a comical beak of a nose and an unfortunate overbite. But his intelligence was of the sharpest variety, and he had an infallible knowledge of every noble house from the most influential duke in Merridan to every backwater baron in Klaar. His political instincts were beyond reproach.

Murnan raised his voice theatrically. "Your Royal Majesty, it is with distinct honor that I present the Fyrian Imperial Ambassador Hreel'Kishna."

The ambassador was short and alarmingly fat. Breathtaking obesity had become a new trend among the Fyrian aristocracy, a conspicuous physical show of wealth and leisure. Hreel'Kishna was light skinned for a Fyrian, black moustache curled extravagantly on either side, his beard sharp and abbreviated, jutting out from the uppermost of his triple chin. He wore a turban with an enormous emerald in the center, flowing green robes, and a belt of gold links.

His girth kept him from achieving a proper bow, but everyone knew what he was trying to do, so it was fine. Gant nodded a greeting, hoping the man had something significant to say but knowing he didn't.

"His most sublime imperial and supreme grand sultan of the Fyrian Empire sends his sincere greetings," the ambassador said. "It is with utmost respect and the fervent desire for friendship between our two great nations that I have come again to offer you a daily report on the search for the lost ship the *Pride of Klaar*."

Dumo damn your eyes, you insipid lard ass. Get on with it.

"Alas, there remains no sign of the vessel."

The tone of regret in the ambassador's voice seemed so genuine, Gant was forced to consider the man might actually mean it.

"There is, however, some news," the ambassador said.

A pause.

Just tell me, you buffoon. Gant had stopped himself from rolling his eyes. He'd learned very early that as king his every gesture and facial expression was monitored. A furrowed brow might send outlying territories into rebellion. A sneeze could start a war.

So. Fine. He was expected to say something.

"Helva is ever grateful for Fyria's ongoing friendship," Gant said. "And any news you might be able to share would naturally be appreciated." It was the bare minimum etiquette required, but it would suffice.

"The Fyrian high council of sultans has been led to believe that insurgent activity has increased beyond even our expectations," the ambassador said. "Our sources report that these elements have expanded their activities to the areas in and around the Fyrian coastline. We think it possible, even likely, that an insurgent ship may have intercepted the *Pride of Klaar.*"

Gant took a deep breath and very slowly sat forward in his seat, frowning down at the Fyrian ambassador. "The ship was out of Klaar?"

"Yes, your majesty."

"Am I given to understand that Fyrian insurgents have now taken to attacking Helvan ships?" Gant asked.

"Ah." The ambassador shifted nervously. "Not as a rule, no, your majesty."

"I see," Gant said. "Then this is . . . a unique situation."

"Aptly stated, your majesty," the ambassador said. "A unique situation. Just so."

"Then the attack had nothing to do with the fact that my envoy— and personal friend—was aboard the ship at the time?"

"An understandable query," the ambassador said. "While the safety of your friend Peyne Erlich is uppermost in all our minds, we believe the attack had nothing to do with his presence aboard the vessel."

"Then why?"

Hreel'Kishna's eyes widened into a question. "Why, your majesty?"

"Then why was the ship attacked?"

"There were Fyrians aboard bound for Helva, your majesty," explained the ambassador. "A man and a woman meant to join me here at the consulate in Merridan. So you see, your majesty, we grieve along with you. We've both lost valued members of our respective nations in the incident."

Gant thought about that. A second stretched into two, then ten.

At last, Gant said, "Who were they?"

The ambassador blinked. "Majesty?"

"The two Fyrians aboard the *Pride of Klaar*," Gant said. "They must have been very important people if the insurgents found them worthy of an attack on the ship."

"Ah. Yes. Well . . ." The ambassador fidgeted. "The two people in question were meant to rotate in, letting others go home to visit family. All very routine."

"Routine?" Gant raised an eyebrow. "And these routine people merited a risky attack on a ship at sea?"

"I . . ." The ambassador tugged at his collar, forced a smile. "It is a justifiable question, your majesty. The motivations of the insurgents are not always known to us, but they seek to disrupt even our most mundane actions. Such is the way of the small-minded. They are unable to effect meaningful change, so they resort to petty harassment."

"These insurgents," Gant said, "what do they want?"

The ambassador dismissed the question with an easy gesture. "They are beneath your notice, your majesty. There are always malcontents who feel an otherwise peaceful and prosperous nation owes them something special. It is a Fyrian internal affair. Pay it no mind, your majesty."

"Your so-called internal affair attacked a Helvan ship," Gant said. "My citizens were aboard."

Hreel'Kishna frowned. He was slow to hide his impatience with this line of questioning. Gant could guess the man's thoughts. The ambassador had come to pay a courtesy call, not expecting to be questioned like this. Nonetheless, Gant was still well within the bounds of diplomatic etiquette.

"Naturally, Fyria regrets such a thing has happened," the ambassador said. "Steps have already been taken to patrol our waters more diligently."

"Please convey Helva's appreciation to the sultan," Gant said.

The ambassador attempted another of his awkward bows before taking his place again with the other dignitaries and nobility.

Gant stood, signaling that this session at court had reached its conclusion.

Chamberlain Murnan stepped forward. "Ladies and gentlemen, the queen."

The queen emerged from a side aisle, escorted by the captain of her personal guard. He wore a gleaming golden breastplate, and a silky horsetail sprouted from the top of his polished helm. The queen was a handsome woman in the early part of her middle years, hair a rich brown piled up in braids atop her head, a tiara of dazzling diamonds holding it all in place. Her gown was cut simply, but the light-blue fabric was of the highest quality.

The captain escorted her to the bottom of the dais where Gant met her and took her arm. Together, king and queen walked down the center aisle of the great hall, heads held high, occasionally greeting an important minister or nodding to a distant relation.

So much of Gant's job was just this. Being seen. Look at the handsome king in his regal uniform. Isn't the queen lovely? They're so happy together. Peace and stability stemmed from such simple things.

They left the hall behind and entered the residential wing. Away from the prying eyes at court, they could talk freely.

"How are the boys?" Gant asked.

"With the tutors," she said. "Although Tavin would rather be riding."

Ferris laughed. Of course he would. What boy wouldn't? "You're a good mother, Tonia. Thanks for looking after them so well."

She looked pleased at that. "You're still coming to see them tomorrow?"

"Unless some catastrophe crops up, yes."

"I'll tell them."

Gant and Tonia had engaged in sex exactly twice, and the result had been two wonderful healthy boys, Tavin, fourteen, and Sarlan, twelve.

Tonia had been selected specifically for her demeanor and lineage and fulfilled her role as queen admirably.

They paused where one hall crossed another.

"Ferris, if you ever need to talk, you know, I'm available for that sort of thing," Tonia said.

"That's a nice offer," Gant said. "If I don't have to rush off after I see the boys, maybe we can have tea."

"Okay." She gave him a little wave. "See you in the morning."

Gant watched her walk down the hall toward her apartments and wondered idly if she'd taken a lover. She had always seemed satisfied in her role as a mother, but was she ever lonely? He continued to muse on this as he turned the other way and headed toward his own quarters.

Gant entered, shutting the door behind him. "Denrick?"

He crossed the sumptuous drawing room and entered the study beyond. Denrick's overstuffed chair near the window was empty, but the flames in the fireplace hadn't burned low yet.

"Denrick!"

He entered from the other doorway. "Oh, stop yelling. I haven't gone deaf. Yet."

Gant laughed. "Not that you'd ever admit it, you grizzled old turnip."

Denrick drew a heavy fur robe tighter around himself. "I'm not *that* much older than you." He paused to let Gant kiss him on the cheek, then plopped down into the easy chair. He pulled out a book from between the cushions. "So how was being king today?"

"Dull. I'd rather be hunting."

"Hunting." Denrick wrinkled his nose. "I'll take a good book any day."

Gant took a good long look at his friend. They'd been together for years, and while it was true that Denrick was only a dozen years Gant's senior, the past decade had worn on the man. He seemed shrunken inside the big fluffy robe. He was always cold and spent most of his time in his chair, with a fire going and maybe a pot of tea.

I need to get him out of here. Maybe we could take a trip.

He dismissed the notion immediately. Ferris Gant was king, his every twitch scrutinized. The idea he could run off with his longtime lover was lunacy. They were already getting away with more than Gant had ever guessed possible.

Think of something else.

"The Fyrian ambassador came to court today."

Denrick closed his book, set it aside. "Peyne?"

"His ship was attacked. The ambassador says they've been having trouble with insurgents. He didn't offer many details."

"You're worried about him."

"Of course," Gant said. "I've been sort of a mentor to him ever since he was a boy. He's a friend."

"Also he saved your life a couple of times," Denrick said.

Gant smiled. "One of his most endearing qualities."

"Without rock solid information, I say you keep hoping for the best," suggested Denrick. "The Fyrians can concoct any story they like for their own purposes. I'm sure your own spies are investigating."

A look from Gant confirmed it was true.

"And anyway," continued Denrick, "Peyne is a resourceful young fellow. Don't count him out."

Korick sat in his office atop the Helvan embassy in Fyria. The shutters of the wide windows had been thrown open, and the servant songs reached him from the neighborhood below.

The Fyrian upper class preferred to eat dinner late after the heat of the day had faded. The cooking songs floated out from dozens of open windows blending in the night. It sounded quite lovely actually, very unlike any music he might hear in Helva. The aroma of exotic spices wafted in through the window.

Korick turned his desk chair toward the window and poured a glass of the good sherry he'd imported for his personal use. No more work for tonight.

A knock at the door, tentative.

Now what?

"Come in please."

The door opened and Mullen entered. "Normally I wouldn't disturb you at this hour." He fidgeted with a small envelope in his hands.

Korick saw that the seal had been broken. Mullen had read it. "Tell me."

"A report from the Red City, relayed from the Fyrian consulate there," Mullen said. "We now know that the *Pride of Klaar* was lost." Mullen saw the ambassador's distressed expression and hurried on, saying, "However there is a bit of good news also. The woman who owned the vessel and her captain organized a counterattack. They boarded and seized the enemy ship. The Red City was the nearest port of opportunity to effect repairs and resupply."

Ambassador Korick brightened. "Damn. Jolly good show. I knew those people in Klaar were made of gritty stuff. Must be those hard winters that make them mean. We should arrange a medal for the woman. Good for morale."

Mullen cleared his throat.

"There's more?"

"Peyne Erlich was not among the survivors," Mullen said.

Korick sighed. He took the glass of sherry and tossed it all down in one go.

"The king will want to know. Erlich was a personal friend." Korick turned his chair back to his desk. "I'll write the letter tonight. Let's make sure it goes out with the morning missives."

CHAPTER
ELEVEN

They sold the horse and saddle in the small oasis town of Moizan.

"Horses are rare here," Zayda had told Peyne. "If we trade shrewdly, we can get a dromadan with enough left for food and water to get us across the desert." She'd been vague about their next destination. Peyne would certainly find some reason to object. Men, her mother had taught her, are best kept on a need-to-know basis. Under duress, their simple minds could process only so much at a time.

She stood with Peyne now in the town square near the guarded well. In the most remote desert towns, water often came at a premium, costing more than wine in some cases. Those not from the small town—one might even call it an overgrown village—would have to pay to drink.

Zayda counted out silver coins into Peyne's hand. "That's ten. Get food from the market and buy extra waterskins, then fill them at the well."

"How come I only get ten?" Peyne asked.

"Because you only *need* ten," Zayda said.

"But the man paid you forty-two for the horse," Peyne said. "A ridiculous amount of silver for such a pedestrian animal, I might add."

"I wanted fifty," she said. "I told you, they fetch such prices in Fyria. We don't have so many horses here. The man drove a harder bargain than I thought he would. I think he knew we were in a bind. He'll turn around and sell it to the army for double. The Fyrian cavalry is desperate for horses."

"I should probably make a note of that," Peyne said. "Although I'm sure the Helvan military already knows. I still don't see why I can't get a few more coins to work with."

"Because I'm buying a dromadan and all the tack that goes with it, along with a few other necessities, and I might not have enough as it is," Zayda said. "I'll need to bargain better than I did when selling the horse."

Peyne scratched his chin thoughtfully. "If that's the case, then perhaps I should handle it. I've done my fair bit of haggling, and I could probably—"

Zayda barked a scornful laugh. "You'd be lucky to come away with your teeth, my soft little lordling. This is Fyria, and the animal breeders are cutthroat. The old ladies selling fruit in the market will be more than a match for you, and water prices have been fixed at a flat rate by imperial law for a century. Ten silver is plenty, and I want *change*."

Peyne held up a hand to forestall any further harangue. "I can see I'm going to have to *prove* myself. I think you might be pleasantly surprised what I can do with ten silver. We'll meet back here after we've each made our respective purchases by which time I might, in fact, own this entire village."

He turned on his heel and walked away, chin in the air, adopting his haughtiest demeanor.

Zayda hid a smile. Somehow the man had a way of being irritating that was . . . *ugh*. She didn't know how to put it. Never mind. She headed off toward the dromadan corrals.

She found them on the edge of town and leaned on one of the gates, sizing up the animals. They varied in size and the color of their shaggy fur, but all had the same musty stink. In the heat of midday, the stench was nearly unbearable, the animals together like this.

The dromadan were enormous, shaggy lumbering beasts. Not fast, but tough. They could walk for hundreds of miles with riders and cargo, and a few gulps of water would last them for days in the vast desert. At the shoulder, they could stand ten or twelve feet tall, and wide enough for two people to ride side by side in the saddle. The beast's back legs were shorter than the front legs, so riders generally climbed a short rope ladder at the ass end and then shimmied forward to the saddle. Its broad back could carry a ton of cargo. Its head was shaggy and round, a stubby snout below huge, stupid eyes.

The animals would never win a beauty contest, but they were the backbone of travel and commerce in the wide inland parts of Fyria where the distance from one oasis to another could be as much as two weeks travel.

"All strong and very healthy," came a voice from behind her.

She turned, nodding to the man without saying anything. He wore a cream-colored robe of light material with thin blue vertical stripes. A fez sat atop his head at a jaunty angle. No moustache but a full black beard outlining a broad, friendly face.

"They are good animals," he said. "If the lady has questions, I can answer them. My family has bred dromadan for nine generations. I am Aimud."

"Hello," Zayda said. "I was hoping so make a purchase." She sighed. "But I suppose not."

"No?" Aimud raised an eyebrow. "You are not looking for a dromadan?"

"I was," Zayda said. "But I'd hoped for a big one."

"But look, across the corral." Aimud gestured. "Three or four very large, none bigger. Strong animals."

She paused. "I suppose that one in the middle. He's not as big as I'd hoped, but if the price were right . . ."

"For you, thirty silver. A bargain."

"Oh no. Sorry to waste your time." She started walking away.

Aimud scurried to get in front of her. "Let's not be hasty. For such a pretty lady, I suppose I can let the animal go for twenty-five."

"Really, I'm sorry," she said. "If you'll excuse me, I'm already late to meet somebody."

"Twenty-three," Aimud said. "But you must have cast some witch's spell over me, for I am literally making nothing. I'll go bankrupt to make such deals."

Zayda paused reluctantly, or at least hoping it appeared that way. "I . . . suppose that's fair."

Aimud began to smile.

"That price includes the saddle and harness, of course," Zayda said.

Aimud blanched. "The lady is not only very pretty but has a keen sense of humor."

And thus the dance began.

In the end, nearly an hour later, dromadan, saddle, and harness had cost her thirty silver. She rode atop the gigantic beast, swaying in the saddle, marveling how everything looked so different from more than a dozen feet in the air. Zayda was from a much larger town and seldom traveled, so she hadn't ridden a dromadan in years.

But it was a docile animal and responded to her commands without fuss. The beast was fairly idiotproof actually, its only drawback a lack of speed. A dromadan could manage a sort of shuffling gallop for fifteen or twenty minutes, but its real strength was doggedly stomping across endless miles of desert without rest.

She tugged the reins to a halt near one of the many hitching posts. She climbed out of the saddle and slid down the dromadan's back to dismount.

Zayda scanned the town square and frowned. No sign of Peyne. The errands she'd assigned him would take fifteen minutes at most.

She felt a sudden tight feeling in her stomach at the thought he'd gone. He wanted to find a ship, to get back to his homeland. No. How far could the man get on ten silver?

She chastised herself. What did she care about him anyway?

But she found herself scanning the square. Something could have happened to him. Or maybe he'd simply been distracted in some shop. The area near the town's well was a premium location, and there were a number of merchants. A rug maker, a silversmith, a cooper, a tavern . . .

A tavern. Zayda's eyes narrowed. *Of course.*

Her hands formed into little fists as she stomped across the square toward the seedy establishment.

Of all the stupid . . . of all the times to . . . idiot man!

Zayda burst into the dank tavern and was met with a dense layer of smoke. She waved it away, squinted into the depths of the place. The barkeep leaned on the bar, chin resting in a palm. He turned lazily to see Zayda standing in the doorway, seemed not to care, and went back to watching the commotion at the far end of the room.

She moved toward the crowd. A very scantily clad woman moved past her quickly with a tray of drinks, eliciting a sloppy cheer when she reached the men. Zayda arrived a moment later and took in the scene.

A semicircle of men leaned in to look at something on the floor. They were dressed in the robes of upper-class merchants, men of means, obviously, to have free time in the middle of the day to haunt the local tavern.

Now that Zayda had moved closer she could see what the crowd was looking at. Two more men on the floor knelt next to a large pile of coins. Zayda understood now. She'd seen her father and male cousins play this game. One shook a pair of dice in his hands, while the other looked on expectantly. The one shaking the dice was . . .

"Peyne!"

Every head turned to look at her just as Peyne released the dice. The clatter across the wooden floor drew their attention back to the game. The dice spun to a stop, coming up three.

Wild cheering from everyone except the man on the floor across from Peyne who rolled his eyes. Some of the men patted Peyne on the back.

He saw Zayda and said, "Just a moment, gentlemen. I think the young lady would like to have a word."

He stood and came toward her swaying, a sloppy grin on his face.

Contemptible bastard! He's been drinking. I gave him money for food and water, and he's been drinking! Her face felt hot, fury raging in her veins.

"Good news," he said when he was standing next to her. "I'm on the verge of tripling the money you gave me."

"I will murder you," she said through clenched teeth.

One of the men fired off something in Fyrian, and the crowd laughed.

"Didn't quite catch that," Peyne told Zayda.

"He says you need to control your woman," she said. "As if I'd ever—"

"Sorry. Hold that thought," Peyne said. "If I roll three one more time, I win the whole pot. I don't really understand the rules, but these nice gentlemen have been kind enough to explain as we go along."

Zayda had heard about people being paralyzed with anger. All she could do was stare daggers at the man.

"Be right back," Peyne said. "Wish me luck."

He returned to the game, his opponent handing him the dice. Peyne shook them in his fist, then tossed.

Zayda edged forward, held her breath.

The dice bounced and spun.

And came up eight.

Zayda felt sick.

The men cheered, many patting the back of Peyne's opponent. Peyne himself shook the man's hand. He rose from his place on the floor and staggered to Zayda, grinning like an idiot and shrugging at his loss.

"Well, I was close," he slurred. He dug into his pocket and came out with a silver piece. "One coin left. The least I can do is buy a final drink for my new friends."

One of the men knew Helvan and translated for all his friends. A boisterous cheer erupted from the throng. He staggered back, tripping and nearly falling before his former opponent in the dice game caught him, a huge gap-toothed grin indicating his amusement. Peyne had to hang onto the guy to keep from hitting the floor.

When he was upright again, Peyne tossed the last silver coin on the bar, and the proprietor began filling mugs of spiced ale from an earthen pitcher. The men gathered around.

Peyne emerged from the crowd, a stupid sloppy grin on his idiot face. *Look at the fool. Buying a round of drinks with his last coin. Now what do we eat?*

He stood in front of her, smiling down, eyelids heavy. "Well, that was fun." He lowered his voice. "Go out to the square. Get the food and water. Don't skimp. Tell them your husband will be out to pay directly. Try to hurry."

"Pay with what, you ass?" Fury filled her face. "I should kill—"

He latched onto her forearm and squeezed slightly. He pitched his voice lower, barely above a whisper. "Please. Do. What. I. Ask."

Zayda's stared into his eyes, clear and alert, no sign of inebriation.

She considered, sizing him up for a moment, then nodded once.

On her way out, she glanced over her shoulder, saw him heading back to the men, ostensibly to partake of the merriment.

The wizened woman at the produce stand began loading a basket with various fruits and root vegetables that would keep while traveling a long distance. She told Zayda her sister across the square sold various dried meats, also good for traveling. Zayda paid a few copper for several bundles of kindling. Firewood had been relatively easy to come by in the jungle. Not so in the desert. She purchased two simple hats made from dried woven palm fronds. Cheap but effective for keeping the sun from baking heads.

After Zayda had purchased six more waterskins from a vendor near the well and paid to have them filled, she added up the grand total in her head.

I just spent nineteen silver. What am I doing? These people will riot when they find out they're not being paid.

The merchants gathered around her, shuffling impatiently as she smiled and told them her husband would be along any moment to pay them. Her face hurt from smiling, and she half didn't believe it herself, thinking Peyne had probably slipped out the tavern's back door.

She'd barely completed this thought when Peyne arrived, gesturing in grand fashion as if he were the sultan himself who'd just arrived to offer the town his blessings.

He produced a fat coin purse and looked at the merchants expectantly. "Now, I believe I owe you fine people some money."

Zayda's jaw dropped. She recovered quickly, watching Peyne place silver into the palms of those gathered. The merchants' impatience vanished in an instant. They grinned and bowed, happy for the business.

"Thank you one and all," Peyne said loudly. "These provisions will be invaluable on our trip to the coast where we hope to catch a ship."

Zayda opened her mouth to contradict him, but he shot her a look.

He's lying. He wants people to think that's the direction we're heading.

The merchants wished him well, turning to wander back to their stands and shops.

Peyne looked down at the food and water, baskets of fruit, sacks of meat, and numerous waterskins. "You should have had them load all this on the pack animal."

"Funny how people don't let you leave with their goods on a pack animal when you haven't paid them yet."

"Just help me. We have to hurry." He began gathering up the supplies. "Where's this animal you purchased?"

Zayda pointed thirty feet away where it was tethered.

"Bloody hell." Peyne gaped. "*That's* the animal you bought."

"I told you," she said. "A dromadan."

"It looks like one of the grassland bison ate a whale."

"Can we just go?" she said. "You're the one who wanted to hurry."

They rapidly loaded the provisions, lashing them to the animal's harness. Zayda showed Peyne how to ascend the ladder, then shimmy up the dromadan's back.

Once settled into the saddle atop the beast's shoulders, Peyne looked around, eyes wide. "If I fall off this thing, I'll break my neck."

"Then don't fall." She handed him one of the hats. "For the sun."

"How fashionable." He put the hat on, cinched the string under his chin.

Zayda grabbed the reins and gave them a flick.

The dromadan lurched forward, making a low rumbling sound from the throat. Peyne rocked in the saddle, latching onto Zayda's arm.

Zayda couldn't help it. She grinned. "Easy, big man. I'll keep you safe."

He frowned at her but didn't let go. Within a minute, he caught on to the rhythm of the animal's gate, holding on to Zayda without being flung from the saddle.

"Take us as if we're heading for the coast," Peyne said. "When we're out of sight, turn south for a while. That should throw them off."

"Where did that money come from?" she asked.

He waved the question away. "Later. Right now we need to get out of here. How fast can this thing go?"

"Not very and not for long."

They made it to the edge of town, Peyne growing more anxious every step of the way.

"I don't think I can stress enough that we must go faster," he said.

Zayda turned the animal due south. "Fine. But you're going to be disappointed." She snapped the reins sharply and made a sharp noise with her tongue.

The dromadan broke into a lumbering trot, bouncing its passengers in the saddle.

"My ass," Peyne said through gritted teeth. "Dumo help my ass."

CHAPTER
TWELVE

The town was now a blotch on the horizon behind them.

Peyne's neck was sore from looking back at it.

"Can you finally tell me what all that was about?" Zayda stabbed him with her eyes. "Or will I be sorry I asked?"

"That was all about my solving our financial woes," Peyne said. "Heroically and with extreme cleverness."

"And no small amount of modesty," Zayda observed dryly.

"I'm not sure teaching you my language was the best choice."

Zayda jerked the reins, and the dromadan lurched to a halt.

"Why are you stopping? Don't stop." He looked behind them again. "Stop stopping and start going."

"Peyne."

"There's no point in worrying about—"

"I want to know what happened."

"I . . . got the money we needed."

"I *saw* you lose."

"You know, it turns out they were nice fellows," Peyne said. "I explained my situation, and . . . you know, I wouldn't believe this either, but the fellow I was playing against agreed to lend me the money to—"

"Liar!" She shoved him. Hard.

Peyne flew out of the saddle, arms windmilling. He bounced off the meaty foreleg of the dromadan and a second later landed flat on his back, the air huffing out of him. He worked his mouth a moment like some pathetic fish trying to suck in air.

When he could breathe again, he said, "Okay. Okay. Listen, I faked being drunk. I pretended to fall, and when he caught me, I picked his pocket. I slipped my hand into his robes and lifted his purse."

Zayda leaned out, glaring down at him. "You're a cheat and a thief!"

"No!" Peyne insisted from flat on his back. "I could tell from the beginning that they were using loaded dice. The game was fixed. I only did what I did because they were cheating me. I swear."

"But you still went into the tavern looking to gamble," Zayda said.

"Not true."

"Then why?"

Peyne frowned. "Why what?"

"Why did you go into the tavern in the first place?"

"I didn't see the harm in a quick drink, and anyway—"

"Asshole!"

"They invited me to their dice game, and I saw an opportunity," Peyne said. "I'll admit it didn't quite work out as planned."

"I hate you."

"What was I supposed to do?" Peyne demanded. "Let them cheat me?"

"It would not have been an issue if you'd stayed out of the tavern in the first place."

"Yeah, well . . ." Peyne sat up, dusted himself off. "I . . . I guess you're right."

"You're damn right . . ." She blinked. "I am? I mean, of course I am."

"I'm sorry."

She hesitated, suspicious. "Well . . . you should be."

"I know," he said. "You have every right to be upset."

Zayda hesitated again. "This is a trick."

He shook his head. "It's not. You're right. I had no business going into the tavern in the first place. I made a mistake, and I kept trying to fix it, getting in deeper and deeper. But I did get our money."

"And if they'd caught you, they would kill you for it," Zayda said.

"That had occurred to me." He looked back again in the direction of the town. "It's a bit why I'm just a tad anxious to keep moving."

"You lied to me," she said. "I thought you were nobility."

"I am."

"You steal and pick pockets and know about loaded dice. You don't act like a noble."

"Then I would put it to you that you don't have a good working knowledge of the aristocracy."

"That . . . is perhaps actually a fair point."

"For starters, they can be just as underhanded as anyone else. Worse in many cases as a lot of them are spoiled and entitled." Peyne sighed. "I will confess I haven't always run in the best circles and may have picked up some bad habits as a result. My family was of the lowest rank possible to still be considered nobility, so I wasn't as finicky as I could have been about my acquaintances."

Zayda thought about that. "From now on we tell each other what we're doing. No more running off to taverns."

"By all means. Teamwork from here on." Peyne held up his right hand. "On my honor as a noble."

Zayda almost let a smile sneak back into her expression. Almost.

"Then climb back up here," she said. "We're wasting time."

When they made camp for the night, Zayda directed the dromadan to lie down between them and the direction from which any pursuit might come. "If the campfire is small enough, the animal will block it from sight in case they're chasing us."

"If they're chasing us on one of these enormous, plodding beasts, then I doubt they'll catch us," Peyne said. "I've seen glaciers move faster."

"I don't know what that is." Zayda began building a small campfire with a portion of their kindling.

"No, I don't suppose you have a lot of those around here," Peyne said. "Have you seen snow? Ice?"

"I've heard of them."

"Imagine an entire nation of snow," Peyne said. "An entire place that's just one huge block of ice. And the ice moves slowly. Maybe an inch a year. Something like that."

She gave him a sideways look, probably wondering if Peyne were pulling her leg.

Zayda finished the campfire, and they each ate a piece of fruit and a strip of the dried meat.

Chewing the tough meat made Peyne's jaw ache, but the blend of exotic spices was pleasant enough. "What kind of meat is this?"

"Chachu."

"Yeah, I don't know what that is any more than you know about glaciers, I guess."

"Like a rat. But much bigger."

Peyne froze in midchew. "I'm eating rat?"

"Chachu."

Peyne shrugged, began chewing again.

"How do you know about things like glaciers?" Zayda asked.

"Tutors," Peyne said. "The nobility prides itself on being educated, so as kids, our heads are filled with a lot of useless information from books. One of the reasons I was always sneaking away and learning things like how to throw dice."

Zayda stared into the firelight. "I don't believe in that."

"In dice games or glaciers?"

"In useless information," she said. "All knowledge is useful in some situation or other."

"Well, I was very unhappy for a year learning geometrical shapes and complex arithmetic," Peyne said. "I wasn't very good at it, and so far it hasn't come in handy."

"Do they have glaciers in Helva?"

"No. They have them very far north in the Glacial Wastes," Peyne explained. "I've not seen them myself. But Helva does have snow in winter."

"I would like to see snow," Zayda said. "I would like to see the whole world."

"I offered to take you to Helva, remember? You had other ideas."

"When I'm free," she said. "When I'm free, I will see the world."

Peyne believed her. The girl had an unwavering determination. But getting the collar off, well, that was another story. Sheer determination couldn't undo a wizard's machinations.

But Peyne didn't say any of this. No point in putting the girl in a bad mood. Let her have hope. She had little else. But he needed to get back to Helva as quickly as possible. If she'd only see sense and come with him, Gant's scholars could surely figure a way to get the collar off.

When the fire died down, they curled against the dromadan for warmth, the animal's slow, steady breathing hypnotic and comforting.

At last the sun rose from the horizon, like a mound of fire humping up from the desert, slowly casting its light over the world. Peyne stood and stretched, turning slowly to look in every direction. Lots and lots of desert.

His thoughts had turned to breakfast, and he almost didn't see them. He looked back, rubbed his eyes, squinted. Three small dots in the distance, only just noticeable against the even flat landscape. He couldn't make out what the dots might be, but the likely answers troubled him.

"Zayda."

"Yes?"

"Look at this."

She moved to stand next to him. "What?"

He pointed. "That."

She held a hand up to shade her eyes and squinted. Her face went blank in that way it always did when she was using her powers. "Three dromadan. Two riders on each."

"Anyone you recognize?"

She kept looking but shook her head slowly. "I'm sorry. It's too far. I can't make out details until they get closer."

"I doubt we want them to get closer."

"I think you're right," Zayda said. "We should load up and get moving."

She went to pack the dromadan, not wasting a moment.

Peyne stood watching the three dots a few seconds longer, then sighed. "Shit."

CHAPTER THIRTEEN

The feast was in Meddigar's honor. He sat at the center table of the dais, looking at the stage below.

He didn't feel honored. He felt nervous.

The wizard sat to Prince Kha'narahn's right. Other notables and those currently in the prince's favor spread out on either side. Meddigar spied Nila at one of the lower tables.

A dozen of Fyria's most buxom young ladies danced on the floor in front of the main table. Drummers hammered out a rapid beat, accompanied by a trio of twangy stringed instruments, the tempo increasing as the dancers rid themselves of veils until they were dressed in nothing but smooth skin. The crowd erupted in applause as the entertainers bowed, glowing with sweat.

Meddigar didn't quite see the point. He liked a pretty face as much as the next man, but such displays did little for him.

At least the food was good.

He dug into the razor-fish steak, grilled vegetables, and some sort of curried grain that was not quite rice. He kept his head down, attention on his cuisine, hoping not to be noticed.

The prince stood. "Ladies and gentlemen, your attention please!"

Meddigar shrank in his chair.

"Most magnificent and honored guests," Kha'narahn said. "We are here to celebrate our most distinguished magician, Meddigar the Bold."

The audience applauded dutifully.

The Bold? That's new. Meddigar didn't object. Supposedly he was the guest of honor, but he understood it was really the prince who craved the attention. Meddigar was merely an excuse for an extravagant party that highlighted Kha'narahn's rise in power and popularity. The prince relished the fact that every eye was on him.

Such a production. He can have it. I'd rather just be left alone.

"Nowhere in the world is there a wizard with more cunning or more courage," the prince said. "He has braved the deep desert where even native Fyrians do not come out alive. There he unearthed the ancient arcane arts of ink magic, invented in the cradle of Fyrian civilization and thought lost for untold generations."

He's laying it on a bit thick. Still, it does sound impressive. Maybe I do deserve a feast in my honor. He hid his grin with a napkin.

"And it is with Meddigar's humble assistance that the grand sultan has again made Fyria an empire for the ages!"

Applause was obviously required here, but to Meddigar the enthusiasm seemed genuine. As for Meddigar's humble assistance, well, that was simply a way to remind everyone that it was really to the prince that the grand sultan owed his gratitude. The prince lent his wizard to the cause the same way another prince might contribute troops or ships.

"But are we to let this brave man face the mysterious perils of the deep desert alone? Of course not," the prince assured the enthralled audience. "Naturally he will be accompanied by his trusty apprentice Nila L'inlei."

Nila came halfway out of her chair, bowing slightly to acknowledge the polite smattering of applause. The people wanted heroes, not sidekicks.

The sudden blare of trumpets almost shocked Meddigar out of his seat. The thunderous stomp of many boots in lockstep shook the banquet hall.

The prince raised his hands and shouted, "Behold the men of the Iron Guard, a company of men from my personal brigade. They will provide escort for our intrepid wizard into the deep desert."

Meddigar's heart sank. When the prince said *escort* what he really meant was *watchdogs*. It was unlikely the prince guessed Meddigar's contingency plan to flee Fyria, but the man wasn't a fool. Kha'narahn was aware of the possibility that his pet wizard might wander off in favor of a better offer or perhaps even be kidnapped. The prince was taking no chances, and Meddigar's scheme to dispose of Nila and slip away had just gotten exponentially more complicated.

He knew some fairly destructive spells, but Meddigar was no battle mage. A company of soldiers would be . . . difficult.

And the men of the Iron Guard were something more than mere rank and file troops. Each had been plucked from ordinary military units for displaying grit, strength, and tenacity beyond that usually expected of an ordinary soldier. They'd received special training and had to pass special tests.

Probably had to hunt down a dragon and wrestle it to the ground and then cut out its heart while still beating. Or some damn thing. Meddigar rolled his eyes, remembering too late he was at the head table and that his every move was probably being observed. He glanced around nervously but didn't think anyone had noticed.

The soldiers of the Iron Guard wore gleaming golden breast- and backplates, greaves and bracers. Gold mesh at the knees and armpits to allow free movement. Minimal skullcap helms of gold and without face guards. These men preferred a clear field of sight to facial protection. *Because who'd dare scar those pretty faces?* He stopped himself this time from rolling his eyes.

Never mind. Men are only men. They can be overcome.

"When it comes to protecting our invaluable magician, we do not send only mere men as his escort," the prince said proudly.

Oh, fuck you.

The prince raised his hands once again, eyes gleaming. "Behold the ink mages!"

The next three people to strut across the stage were probably the three scariest beings Meddigar had ever seen.

Ink mages. From what he'd heard, the trio had come a long way since he'd created them. Two women and one man. So few men were able to take the Prime that the wizard didn't even test them anymore. But this man, yes, Meddigar remembered him. This man relished the power too much. Nearly seven feet tall, barrel-chested, fat without being slow or awkward. A lot of skin under all that black leather, a lot of room for tattoos. Head completely shaved except for a flowing top-knot. Rumor had it the man had been scouring the world the past year, looking for more tattoos and had even found a few. Meddigar made a point to have a look. Any new ink would be of interest.

Hak, Meddigar remembered. That was the man's name. The women were only vaguely familiar.

With a company of the elite Iron Guard and three ink mages thrown into the bargain, the prince was obviously dead serious that the expedition not only succeed, but that his court magician come back in one piece.

Useless. I'll never find the lost city again, and now I can't even escape.

The audience's wild applause drew the wizard's attention back to the stage. The ink mages performed physical feats of strength and dexterity for the crowd. Hak tossed the two women into the air without effort. They twirled and flipped and landed perfectly. At one point, Hak again tossed one of the women into the air, and she came down on the feet of the other woman doing a handstand—a handstand on top of a hand-stand. The audience ate it up.

Such was the spectacle that nobody noticed the servant who set the silver goblet on the table in front of Meddigar. "The mead you wanted, sir."

Meddigar frowned. "I didn't order any—" He noticed the folded piece of parchment tucked beneath the goblet. "Oh, yes. Thank you."

The servant left, and Meddigar's eyes shifted back and forth quickly to take in the scene. The ink mages still held everyone's attention. He snatched the note, unfolded it in his lap where no one could see. He read.

And smiled.

The alley led to an enclosed square in one of Heberron's safer neighborhoods, but a dark alley was still a dark alley, and Meddigar kept his wits about him. He didn't need to glance over his shoulder to know the prince's man was following at a discreet distance. Meddigar pretended not to notice him.

The wizard had been obliged to wait for the end of the elaborate feast with all its entertainment, his impatience growing by the hour. At last, he'd been able to sneak away to follow up on the note.

He emerged from the alley and spotted the tavern across the small square, dirty orange light in the window. He slipped inside, pausing a moment to scan the room, patrons at the bar, a few scattered at tables. And then he saw his man at a table in the farthest corner, smoking a chuma stick and waiting.

The wizard crossed the room and took the chair opposite the man. Meddigar removed his floppy hat and set it in the empty chair next to him, then nodded. "Popo. Sorry to keep you waiting."

Popo shrugged. "I knew it would be awkward to slip away from the prince's feast. No worries. I'm a patient man."

Yes, patience would be a necessary trait in Popo's line of work. He was small and plain, almost hidden inside his robes, bland face, brown skin neither too dark nor too light. Everything about his appearance was unremarkable, another benefit, Meddigar supposed, considering the man's trade. There were often advantages to being forgettable. Popo's business was information. His spies could be found in every town and village in Fyria, a complex network of eyes and ears and tattletales. And as long as he was paid well, he didn't ask questions.

Popo looked past Meddigar toward the front door where a man entered and took a seat at the bar. "Your shadow."

"Never mind him," Meddigar said. "You've seen her?"

"Not personally. One of my people. But this is reliable information. I have a reputation to maintain."

"Tell me everything."

Popo spread his hands. "I don't mean to be a stickler, but we must observe certain etiquette, yes?"

"Of course. My apologies."

Meddigar took the leather satchel slung around his shoulder and shifted it into his lap, unhooked the brass latch, and rooted around inside among his spell components, spell book, and potion ingredients until he found the small coin purse. There were only five coins inside, but they were solid gold, worth many times more than silver or copper. A small fortune, but the prince had been generous. Meddigar could afford it.

He slid the purse across the table, and Popo made it vanish into his robes so fast that it might never have been there in the first place.

"Maurizan is in Tamtalla," Popo said.

"And you're sure it was the red-haired woman?" Meddigar asked. "The one who fights with two daggers gypsy fashion?"

A withering look from Popo.

Meddigar should have known better. Popo's information was every bit as good as Meddigar's gold. He held up a hand. "I withdraw the question."

"I assure you it was indeed Maurizan," Popo said. "One of my operatives got a little too careless and saw the two-dagger fighting style up close. He is expected to recover."

"I'm sorry to hear he was injured," Meddigar said, "but I hope that doesn't mean she's now aware she's being observed."

"Never fear," Popo said. "When he was caught tailing her, he made as if it were a robbery. Standard procedure. He'll get a bonus for taking a blade in the belly."

"Of course. You and your people are professionals. What else can you tell me?"

Popo opened his mouth to speak, then shut it abruptly as the barmaid approached. She set a pitcher of wine and two goblets on the table, nodded politely to each man, then withdrew.

"I took the liberty," Popo said.

"Obliged." Meddigar took the pitcher, filled each goblet.

Popo continued.

His report recounted all the woman's movements in excruciating detail, everywhere she'd been, to whom she'd spoken, what she ate at meals, if she drank and what and when, her room at which inn, if her room had a window or another exit, if she were traveling with a companion—she wasn't—and, well, if she'd sneezed. Popo's report contained meticulous details, all recited from memory. Popo might scrawl *meet me at the usual place* in a quick note, but he wasn't foolish enough to commit anything important or incriminating to writing.

One detail of the woman's activity caught Meddigar's attention. "You say she went to the mapmaker."

"Three times," Popo said. "Maybe more by now. My people continue to watch her."

Auvor Kre'Shama was by no means the only mapmaker in Fyria, but he was certainly the most famous and respected. For eleven generations, the men and women of Auvor's family had been cartographers. They had centuries of old maps to draw on, could tell if a river had changed course by three feet over the decades. Any river or stream, gully or canyon, any hill larger than a termite mound, if it were on a map, then it was almost a certainty that Auvor or one of his ancestors had put it there.

No one knew the deep desert. No one. But if anyone came close, it might be Auvor Kre'Shama.

"I wonder," Meddigar said. "Do you think he has a map? Perhaps she wishes to purchase it."

"Or"—Popo paused dramatically—"she's assembling one."

Meddigar frowned. "I don't follow."

"Auvor is the greatest cartographer of our time," Popo said. "If the woman brought him information . . . landmarks and so on . . ." A shrug.

"He might be able to piece together a particular location," Meddigar said.

"And the woman has been seen buying provisions, food and water for a long trek," Popo said. "She's purchased a dromadan and desert gear."

"Do you think she's headed for the deep desert?" Meddigar asked.

Popo took the pitcher, refilled his goblet. "When I sell information, I guarantee its accuracy. This opinion I offer for free since it is only a theory. Yes. The deep desert. She did make one more stop. I only just received this information an hour before your arrival."

"Oh?"

"A calligrapher," Popo said. "An old woman of some repute."

"I don't understand." Barons and counts needed calligraphers to make fancy party invitations. Why someone venturing into the deep desert might need one, Meddigar couldn't guess.

"There is a rumor the old woman also has some skill with alchemy," Popo said.

Meddigar scratched his beard, considering. "A glyph maker?"

"That was my guess also," Popo said. "As this information has come to me only very recently, I can't guarantee anything."

Perhaps Maurizan was guarding something. Meddigar himself used a glyph to guard his spell book. Anyone trying to read it without permission would be stunned into unconsciousness by a minor spell. Glyphs and wards were often better than an iron lock for keeping things safe. Food for thought.

They both drank in silence for a moment.

"I would like to ask a question," Popo said. "With the understanding you are not obligated to answer. I know it is not my place to pry."

"Please," Meddigar said. "I'll answer if I can."

"The woman intrigues. For obvious reasons," Popo said. "You've met her?"

Meddigar understood there was more to the question. For Popo to ask this question, as innocuous as it seemed, was to stretch the etiquette of their relationship almost to the breaking point. At least in Popo's mind, Meddigar thought. The wizard didn't really mind. He trusted Popo's discretion.

"She came to trade knowledge," Meddigar said. "We were both keenly interested in ink magic. Obviously. She told me about her tattoos and made an offer to trade. Information for information. She told me some useful things."

Popo may have suspected what came next, but he kept silent. He was polite enough to let Meddigar tell his own story in his own way.

"When it was my turn . . ." Meddigar sighed. "I'm sorry to say I did not quite keep my end of the bargain."

Popo's face remained blank. He was too much the professional to outwardly show his disapproval. Yet Meddigar could feel it radiating off the man, like heat from a glowing cook fire.

"The secrets of ink magic are precious. A mistake in judgment." Meddigar sighed again, more deeply this time, shaking his head. "I fear that crossing Maurizan may yet be a mistake that comes back to haunt me."

CHAPTER FOURTEEN

Night fell, and they built a fire, larger than the previous night's. Zayda didn't position the dromadan to hide the flames.

Instead, she and Peyne climbed back aboard the dromadan, and they moved off at a southwestward angle, not talking for fear voices might carry in the still night. They swayed in the saddle, and Zayda happened to glance up.

The stars spread themselves against the black velvet of the sky. A beautiful sight, although cold and distant. Yet also tranquil. Somehow it was a comfort, feeling small beneath the grandeur of eternity.

I'm here, she thought. *In the midst of all this, I'm here, and I'm trying. I won't meekly give up my life to servitude. No matter how big the world or vast the universe.*

It was pretty, the twinkle of starlight.

Peyne leaned in to whisper directly into her ear. "Sleep if you can. I'll keep first watch. If anyone follows, hopefully the fire will make them think we stopped for the night."

His warm breath on her ear raised gooseflesh on her skin.

She turned away from him abruptly, tried to find a position in the saddle that would allow her to sleep. She curled finally with her hands under one cheek, closed her eyes, knowing the effort was useless. The idea that she could get comfortable enough to sleep was ridiculous.

Zayda yawned.

She opened her eyes, seemingly only seconds later, to see the grungy pink of dawn lining the horizon.

Zayda thumbed the sleep from the corners of her eyes, turned to see Peyne's silhouette sitting tall in the saddle against dawn's light.

A warm feeling spread through her at the thought he'd stayed up all night so she could sleep. She immediately felt embarrassed. A gesture. Nothing more. He was being a gentleman. Was that really so surprising?

From Peyne? Maybe.

Still, she should at least thank him.

Zayda touched his forearm. "You shouldn't have done that. You should have let me take a turn."

Nothing.

"I'm thanking you," Zayda said. "I suppose strong and silent must seem a very manly way to—"

A light snoring sound and then Peyne twitched.

"Idiot!" She slapped him on the shoulder. Hard.

Peyne snorted, head coming up. "What?"

"You fell asleep!"

Peyne blinked. "Nonsense. I . . ." He glanced around. "Where are we?"

"Wouldn't that be nice to know?"

Peyne twisted in the saddle, squinted behind them. "I don't see anyone."

Zayda looked too. "Do you think it worked?"

"If they thought we'd camped, they'd camp too," Peyne said. "It was a good idea."

"It was just a thought," Zayda said. "I mean, if they saw our campfire . . ."

Peyne smiled. "It was a good idea."

Zayda felt herself blush and quietly cursed herself. Was she really some schoolgirl so easily swayed by such praise? "It seemed an obvious ploy. We got lucky."

"I'd rather be lucky than good, my father used to say." He looked ahead. "The dromadan is dependable even if I'm not. We kept the same course all night. I did fall asleep. I'm sorry."

Zayda sighed. The man made it impossible to stay cross with him. Was it something he did on purpose? She hated to think she could be so easily manipulated. It didn't hurt that he was devilishly good-looking, but there was something more. A bumbling sincerity about him that was almost irresistible.

No, she told herself sharply. *That's the trap. Don't fall for it.*

She lifted her chin, assuming a haughty air. "Just don't let it happen again." Zayda heard herself and cringed. *Ugh. I sound like a petulant child.*

Peyne must have thought something similar. He grinned and said, "A thousand pardons, your ladyship."

She rolled her eyes. "If we ride all day, we'll get there, or at least close."

"Get where?"

"Tamtalla."

"What's Tamtalla?"

"A city," Zayda said. "A proper city, not like that small town we just left."

"And why do you want to go there?"

"It's a river town," Zayda said. "People and freight move across Fyria to the port in Heberron."

"And that's why you want to go there?"

She hesitated.

"Zayda."

"I was born in Tamtalla," she said. "My parents still live there."

◆ ◆ ◆

The sun sank, the heat from the day ebbing.

At full dark, a glow rose in front of them, the fuzzy orange lights from the city shimmering in the distance, a beacon in the implacable desert night.

"Tamtalla," Zayda said.

"We're too close to stop now."

She smiled and nodded. "Okay."

They rode on, the dromadan slowly but doggedly eating the miles. The city lay ahead farther than they thought, but the idea of stopping in sight of it was off-putting. An inn with a proper bed called to Peyne, and damn if he'd spend another night on the ground.

They happened upon a road about three miles from Tamtalla and followed the path the rest of the way. Peyne guessed it was just after midnight when they reached the city walls.

The walls were built from desert stone, a pale rusty red, towers every hundred feet or so. The gatehouse was a big blocky affair with a high arched doorway large enough for two dromadan to pass each other coming and going. The gates were open, and clumps of coarse dry weeds in front of each made Peyne think it had been quite a while since they'd been closed. Flickering braziers on either side lit the entire entrance. A guard in cheap leather armor looked up as they approached and waved them through, not seeming very interested.

Zayda sat up very straight in the saddle, leaning forward, eager, eyes wide and alert.

This is her home. She probably never thought she'd see it again.

They passed beneath the gatehouse and into the city beyond.

It wasn't what Peyne had expected. What *had* he expected? Buildings crowding one another along narrow streets, he supposed, like so many other walled cities he'd visited. Instead, there was a wide open space, various corrals and hitching posts on either side. The dromadan, Peyne realized. They'd be too big for a cramped city. Now that he bothered to look, Peyne saw dromadan in various pens, men scurrying to tend them.

A ragged-looking man in dirty robes shouted up at them in Fyrian. He must have been at least eighty and had fewer teeth than he had fingers.

"He says ten copper to take care of the dromadan overnight," Zayda said.

"Is that good?"

"I don't know. My first time owning a dromadan." She shouted back to the man, and they went back and forth for a few seconds. She turned back to Peyne and said, "The price includes feeding and water. I think it's probably okay."

"Fine," Peyne said. "Tell him there's an extra copper in it for him if he shows Titan some special attention."

"Titan?" Zayda looked at him, deadpan. "You named it?"

"Of course I named it . . . *him*. I named *him*. He's our faithful traveling companion and mode of transportation."

Zayda shook her head. "That's . . . strange."

"Why?"

"It's like a fisherman hauling in a net full of fish and then giving them all names," she said. "Or naming a bush. It's not done."

"That's uncivilized. Titan is hardly a bush."

"I'm not telling him that," Zayda said.

"You tell him," Peyne said. "Go on."

Zayda shook her head again, sighing, and translated.

The old man threw his head back and cackled laughter.

"Uncivilized," Peyne said again. "The entire country."

"You're going to fit right in," Zayda said dryly.

They dismounted, and the old man gave them a numbered chit before leading Titan into one of the corrals. A flagstone path kept clear of dromadan dung led to the city proper. Peyne followed Zayda.

"We entered through the Trader's Gate. That's the one on the north side," Zayda said. "Most of the other gates are smaller. The Beggar's Gate and the Little Maid's Gate and so on, but the biggest one is River

Gate on the south side, which leads to all the riverfront docks and warehouses."

Peyne didn't give a tinker's damn what any of the gates were called, but he realized Zayda was excited to be home and didn't want to spoil her enthusiasm. "And what is this neighborhood ahead of us?" He wanted to seem interested. Let her talk.

"Ah, this is the . . ." She made a hand gesture, groping for the words. "There is no immediate translation. We have a word that means a combination of eating and relaxing but also travel comfort. Inns and taverns and so on. It is neighborhood for people passing through, which makes sense since it is near the Trader's Gate."

"Then that would seem to be perfect for us," Peyne said.

Zayda brightened. "Yes!" She laughed. "I didn't think of that since I'm from here, but I suppose we are passing through, aren't we?" She frowned suddenly. "I've come home as a stranger. I know it's late but . . ."

"Your parents would want to see you no matter the hour," Peyne said. "Let's find a good inn, and I'll get a room while you go home."

They entered the town proper, winding down a narrow cobble-stone street. There were lights in many windows, people out and about even at the late hour. They found an inviting establishment, and Zayda translated the sign out front. "The Indolent Imp." The sign displayed a fanciful image of a pointy-eared imp, passed out on a plush divan, an empty wine bottle in his grip.

"I happen to excel at indolence," Peyne said, leading Zayda in through the swinging double doors.

The common room was warm and inviting, conversation and laughter floating up to meet them. A man in a white robe and a red vest scurried across the wooden floor to greet the two, hands spread in welcome. A thin moustache twitched as a huge grin spread across his face. Obviously the proprietor and just as obviously eager to offer them his hospitality . . . for the right amount of coin.

With Zayda translating, Peyne soon negotiated a reasonable rate for a comfortable room.

"You must be tired," Zayda said. "You'll be fine here if I go?"

"See your parents," Peyne said. "I can manage." His eyes slid to the common room. "After such a long ride, I think a quick drink before bed will help me sleep. In the morning, I can see about catching a riverboat to Heberron. I rather like the thought of seeing Ambassador Korick's face when I walk in and announce I need another ship."

Zayda's face fell. "I hadn't thought of that. That you might book passage on a riverboat, I mean. Yes, obviously, you need to return to your people."

She smiled again, but Peyne thought it looked a bit forced.

Zayda wagged a finger at him, half playful. Half not. "No dice games."

Peyne held up a reassuring hand. "On my honor."

She smiled, shaking her head. "Wait for me. I'll see you off in the morning." Zayda turned to leave, looking back over her shoulder at him one last time. "Behave."

Peyne laughed and watched her go, feeling happy for her. She was off to see her family. He even envied her a little until he remembered the common room and the food and drink waiting there.

He entered, stuck his nose in the air, and inhaled deeply. Was there anything better than the smell of a tavern or an inn's common room? The smoke and the food, wine and ale, all of it mixing together with talk and bawdy jokes. A selection of humanity to be found here was the most interesting in any city, and Peyne loved it.

He found an empty table and sat, caught the eye of one of the serving women. Peyne generally preferred wine, but was in the mood for beer. The language barrier was making it difficult, and miming a drinking motion could mean water or wine or anything.

Peyne kept saying the same words in Helvan, and the serving girl kept saying the same words in Fyrian, nobody getting anywhere.

"The Fyrian word for beer is *cheleecha*." A woman's voice behind him, speaking perfect Helvan.

Peyne turned and saw her there, leaning back in a shadowed corner, boots propped on a stool in front her, a tankard in one hand. She wore a green cloak with the hood up even though it was warm. Peyne couldn't quite make out her face.

"And *cheleecha ka tita* is a spiced beer that's local," she said. "I recommend it."

"Join me," Peyne said. "I'm happy to trade a fresh drink for your translation services."

She hesitated, then stood, and he saw the long daggers, one hanging from either side of her belt. She wore travel clothes, worn but well kept, and a leather vest. She sat at his table, and they ordered two tankards of the spiced beer.

"I'm Peyne Erlich." He offered his hand. "One of King Gant's envoys to Fyria." He wasn't sure if this were technically still true, but maybe she'd be impressed.

She drew back her hood, revealing stunning red hair. She was perhaps ten or twelve years older than Peyne, skin pale and clear, eyes so penetrating he thought there hadn't been anything they hadn't seen. Her beauty alone would have been enough to turn heads, but the tattoos were what made people stop and look.

The mark of feathers at the corner of each eye, strange but striking in their own way.

She shook his hand. "I'm called Maurizan."

CHAPTER
FIFTEEN

Zayda crossed a sleepy district of craftsmen, much less active than the Traveler's Quarter, windows dark. She was the only one on the street, but it was a familiar area to her, and she strode through without concern. There were a few bad neighborhoods in Tamtalla of course, as with any city, but they were down near the riverfront.

She slowed her pace as she crossed onto a street of middle-class merchants. She turned her head slowly, side to side, taking everything in.

This was it. Her neighborhood. Her street. Her parents had raised her here. Her home.

Or it had been her home up until she was sold. She never thought she would see this place again as long as she lived.

Zayda wiped her eyes, vision suddenly going blurry.

No. She dabbed at her eyes with the scarf disguising her collar. *Control yourself. This is a homecoming. Go in smiling.*

It was late but not *so* late. It wasn't unheard of for her father to be up at this hour going over the week's numbers. Or her mother might be catching up on some sewing. And then she did smile, the thought of seeing her parents doing the simplest everyday things lent a spring to her step. Soon she was jogging toward her front door.

And then she was on her walkway, looking up at the house where she was born, a modest but handsome dwelling sandwiched between a rug merchant who lived over his shop and a tailor on the other side. A white facade over brick, a balcony on the second floor. She used to stand on that balcony in her adolescence and talk down to young boys who came to visit.

The boys were not allowed in, obviously. She laughed, remembering that her father had been just as adamant she not go down to meet them. They'd watched the High Season parade every year from that balcony, the string and drum band and the colorful veil dancers prancing past with the jugglers and bawdy puppeteers. She wondered if her parents had done anything to her room. How wonderful if she could sleep in her old bed tonight.

Zayda raised a fist to knock on the door, then hesitated, suddenly nervous. She took a deep breath, blew it out.

And knocked.

For a long time, nothing, or maybe it just seemed like a long time. Then she heard a stirring from within. Zayda held her breath.

"Who's there?"

Her mother's voice.

"Zay—" Her voice caught, and she put a hand over her mouth. Butterflies in her belly. She removed the hand slowly, took a deep breath. "Mother, it's me. Zayda."

A long silence from the other side of the door. Zayda began to suspect her mother hadn't heard her. Zayda was so nervous, her voice had barely come out above a whisper. She drew breath to speak louder, then froze when she heard her mother working the slide bolt on the other side.

Slowly the door creaked open a few inches, a wide-eyed woman peeking out, wary and unsure. She looked at Zayda as if seeing a ghost, and Zayda's heart broke.

"Mother?"

"Zayda?" A whisper so soft it might have been the breeze in the fronds of the fig trees.

A strange mix of emotions played across her mother's face, fear, surprise . . . and joy trying to fight its way past the first two.

"It *is* you!" She flung the door wide, gathered Zayda into her arms.

Any composure Zayda may have mustered before was shattered. She sobbed uncontrollably, clinging to her mother, fat tears rolling down her cheeks.

The older woman patted her back, rocking her back and forth. "My *tish*. Hush now, hush, my little *tish*."

Zayda laughed through the tears. How would she explain *little tish* to Peyne? A baked bite-size piece of bread with olive oil and goat cheese. *Little biscuit.*

Her mother stepped past her, suddenly looking up and down the deserted street. "Quick, come in. Before anyone sees."

Her mother ushered Zayda inside, hastily closing the door behind them. Halls branched off the foyer, one leading into a spacious living area. They turned the other way toward the kitchen.

"Have you traveled far? Are you hungry? I can fix you something."

"No, Mother. I'm not hungry. I'm just so happy to see you." Her mother had whispered, so she whispered too.

"Tea. I'll make a pot of tea." She scurried around the kitchen, stoking the cook fire, filling a pot with water.

Zayda almost told her mother not to bother, but she did want tea. She wanted her mother to wait on her, wanted to be a little girl, to be a family again here in her home, to have everything back the way it was.

They sat at the small table, sipping the tea, and whispering quietly to one another.

"I never thought I would see you again," her mother said. "Did you run away?"

"Not quite," Zayda said.

And then the story spilled out, all of it, from the *Pride of Klaar* sinking all the way to emerging from the jungle and traveling south through the desert. Zayda fatigued herself, telling the story, as if realizing for the first time all she'd been through. The miracle of her survival. And the battles. She didn't trouble her mother with the particulars of the tattoos, and she'd glossed over some of the bloodier parts of her story, but her mother still listened, rapt, not interrupting for nearly an hour.

The tea had gone cold.

Zayda sighed, rubbed her eyes. "It's so late. Is my old room . . . I mean, is my bed still . . ."

A cough from somewhere in the house, the sound of movement. Worry flashed in her mother's eyes.

"Are you up already?" came the voice from the hallway. "What hour is it?"

Zayda's heart leapt. *Father!*

And in the next second, he entered the kitchen.

She stood slowly. He looked thinner than before, pallid, hair tossed from sleep, bags under his deep brown eyes. A few days of stubble on his usually clean-shaven face.

He looked back at her in disbelief.

His expression quickly turned to anger.

"How dare you come here!" her father shouted. "How dare you dishonor this house!"

Zayda's mouth fell open, gut clenching.

"Please," her mother said. "She doesn't mean to—"

"Quiet, woman!" He spun back to Zayda. "I want you out of my house. You no longer belong here. I have given you to the ink wizard. Do you think I break my bargains? Would you have people say I go back on my word?"

Zayda trembled, nausea welling up in her. She felt dizzy.

"Father?"

Her voice weak.

"I said to get out!" He grabbed her under one arm, dragged her from the kitchen. "Go!"

Her mother gasped.

Zayda let herself be dragged down the hall toward the front door. Part of her understood that the grip on her arm wasn't so very strong. Her father was several years older than her mother. It would be simplicity itself to overpower him even without tapping into her spirit. She realized the truth for the first time. He was an old man. Given to the ways of an old man.

And yet this was her father, and part of her still saw him as larger than life.

He flung the front door open and shoved her outside. "Never come back! Never darken this door again!"

He slammed it shut.

Zayda stood a moment, stunned. Then she slowly sank to her knees and began to weep, shoulders bobbing, her whole body shaking as she cried and cried. She sat on the doorstep of her former home, head hanging, and cried until there was nothing left.

She looked around her at the quiet street. How long had she been there crying? It didn't matter. This was her street no longer, no longer her home. She'd cried, and now she was done crying, and there was only the future she would make for herself.

Still, she was so very tired. She stood, legs weak. Even when Zayda had swam ashore after the sinking of the longboat, dragging Peyne along with her, she hadn't felt so utterly spent.

Zayda turned slowly, began to walk away, feet leaden.

She'd almost turned the corner of the narrow lane when she heard the hurried steps behind. Zayda turned, saw her mother running, bare feet slapping on the cobblestones. Zayda waited and watched her come.

Zayda's mother reached her, threw her arms around her daughter, hugging her tightly, eyes glistening with tears. Zayda began crying again, softly this time.

Her mother pulled away, thrust a small coin purse into her hands.

Zayda shook her head, pushing the coins back at her mother. "I can't take—"

"You have to," her mother insisted. "It isn't much, but it might help. I love you."

"Oh, Mother."

"Forgive your father. He is ashamed to fail at business, to be put in a position where saving the family meant sacrificing you. Seeing you reminds him of this shame. He hates himself for it."

Zayda wiped the tears with the heel of her hand.

"He could save the business and save me," her mother said. "But not you. And every day it eats away at him."

"I'll come back one day," Zayda said. "I'll get this collar off and come back."

Her mother forced a smile, clearly not believing her, but said, "Of course. I have to get back before he realizes what I'm doing." She kissed her daughter on the forehead, turned, and ran back toward her home, not looking back.

Zayda stood in the middle of the street, the small purse still cradled in her hands. She tugged it open, counted the coins within. Eleven silver. She knew it must have taken her mother years to secret away such an amount, hiding a copper here and another there from her father. Perhaps not so much to show for twenty-five years of marriage.

But it was everything her mother had.

She cinched the purse closed again and stuck it into her belt. Zayda vowed to return in triumph, free. She'd pay her mother back. She'd make her father understand. Slinking away from her home in the middle of the night would not be the end.

Zayda headed back toward the Traveler's Quarter, wondering if Peyne were still awake. She brightened at the thought. She'd confess all her problems to Peyne, and he'd quip something witty, and she'd laugh and feel better.

She quickened her step, eager now and willing to forget the heartsick feeling brought on by her father. She raced ahead into the future.

CHAPTER
SIXTEEN

Zayda would have guessed the crowd within the inn's common room might have thinned out by now. She'd have been wrong.

If anything, the crowd had increased, men pushing their way up to the bar, shouting for the harried barkeep to hurry with drinks. Men constituted the bulk of the patrons, but there were women too, at tables here and there, even an obviously foreign woman with striking red hair. She leaned across the table, smiling, deep in an intimate conversation with—

Peyne?

Zayda frowned. *Well, it didn't take him long, did it?*

The red-haired woman and Peyne laughed together, both tilting back enormous tankards of beer. Zayda buzzed with irritation, stormed across the room toward their table. Men crossing in front of her spied her expression and scurried from her path.

She arrived at the table, stood glaring down at Peyne, clenched fists on hips. "And what do you think you're doing?"

He grinned up at her. "Having a drink!"

"Yes, well . . . well . . ." And why not? What claim did she have on him anyway? He was leaving in the morning. The time when they were shipwrecked, they'd had only each other, and she'd come to feel somewhat possessive of him, she realized. She was being silly, irrational. "Okay then . . . fine."

"Good news. I've been talking to my new friend Maurizan." Peyne gestured to the woman across the table. "She can tell us what waits in the deep desert."

Zayda offered the woman a tight smile. "Well, isn't that nice. Maybe she can—wait. What?"

"Do you two need to talk?" Maurizan asked.

"No, no," Peyne said. "She gets like this."

Zayda felt her face go red with fury.

Peyne turned back to Zayda, lowered his voice. "Look at her. Look at her face. She's like . . . you know . . ." He lowered his voice again to what he must have thought was a discreet whisper but was just as loud as his normal voice. He was clearly drunk. "She's like *you*."

Oh, she's like me, is she? Is that supposed to be flattering or something?

Zayda looked at the woman's face. The tattoos at her eyes looked like feathers. They gave the woman an exotic look, which only added to her beauty, annoying Zayda further. Is this the sort of thing Peyne found attractive? Because if so . . .

Tattoos!

This was what Peyne was trying to tell her. Another ink mage. If the woman knew something about the deep desert, then Zayda had to find out. Peyne had been trying to help.

Zayda felt like an idiot.

She looked at the red-haired woman again, this time without hostility. "You've been there?"

Maurizan met Zayda's eyes, nodded once.

"She can take us straight where you need to go," Peyne whispered drunkenly and loudly.

"That's not what I said," Maurizan said sharply. "I said we could *talk* about it. Perhaps we can make a mutually beneficial arrangement."

Peyne disregarded Maurizan's words with a sloppy wave. He looked at Zayda and winked. "Don't worry. I'll win her over."

Maurizan smiled. "He has a sort of juvenile charm, doesn't he?"

Zayda fought off another stab of irritation. There were more important things to consider now. If the woman could lead her through the deep desert, it might be the first step to removing this infernal collar from around her neck.

"Please." Zayda tugged her scarf away just enough to allow Maurizan a glimpse of her collar.

Maurizan recognized the collar and frowned. "I'm sorry. That's . . . barbaric."

"Can you help me?" Zayda asked.

Maurizan considered.

Peyne drained his tankard and set it back down on the table hard. "Of course she will! I've been talking to this woman, and I am a very good judge of character, so take . . . it . . . from me . . ." He trailed off, gaze shifting to something behind her.

Peyne's eyes went wide. "Oh shit."

Before Zayda could turn to see what had distracted him, an explosion of pain erupted at the base of her skull. A white flash of stars and a long dizzying fall into darkness.

Why couldn't these women understand that he had everything under control? Maurizan radiated danger, which had intrigued Peyne immediately. He'd had success with older women before, and they were both a long way from home, so . . .

And yet, when he'd found out she was an ink mage, Peyne's thoughts had turned to Zayda. Maybe this woman could be of some assistance. They talked. And drank.

Then Zayda arrived and seemed to be annoyed for some unknown reason but had come around quickly enough at the thought Maurizan could help her navigate the deep desert. Everything was going perfectly.

Zayda desperately wanted Maurizan's help. It was up to Peyne to assure her everything would be okay.

"Of course she will!" Peyne insisted. "I've been talking to this woman, and I'm a very good judge of character." One of his many talents. "So take . . . it . . . from me . . ."

The man coming into the common room looked very familiar. The gold teeth, the hawkish face. *Dumo help me, it's the men I cheated in dice back in Moizan,* he suddenly realized. There were others with him. *Maybe they won't notice I'm—*

The man's little rat eyes spotted Peyne immediately. He ran toward their table.

Peyne gulped. "Oh shit."

The man drew a dagger and smashed the hilt into the back of Zayda's head. Her eyes rolled white, and she went down.

"Zayda!"

Peyne reached for his rapier as he tried to stand.

This was when he fully realized the extent of his drunkenness.

He knocked his chair back with a loud clatter, tangled himself in the legs, and started to go down. The man with the golden teeth loomed over him, grinning vengeance, dagger coming in for a strike.

All heads in the common room turned to look, noticing the commotion now.

A blur of red hair, the gleam of steel, and blood sprayed from the man's throat as he staggered back, eyes surprised as he came to terms with his own demise.

The common room erupted in chaos, men climbing over one another to escape the fray. Peyne crawled around on all fours, glancing up to see Maurizan dancing among his attackers, twin daggers flashing.

She was there, and he'd blink, and she'd be somewhere else. Distantly he heard a bell ringing.

Ah, that will bring the watch. Best if I weren't here when they arrived.

He tried to stand, was jostled on all sides, slipped in blood, and went down again. Shouts and panic as men fled and fell. He heard a rush of steps enter the common room, saw the black tunics of the city guard. Peyne turned to crawl the other way but didn't get far.

His turn to get hit on the head.

CHAPTER
SEVENTEEN

The blow had dazed him. Peyne blinked the stars from his eyes in time to see a pair of city watchmen hauling him to his feet and snapping shackles on his wrists.

"There's been a terrible misunderstanding," Peyne said.

That earned him a scolding in Fyrian and a backhand across the face.

He looked around as they dragged him from the common room. The proprietor with the thin moustache was pointing and complaining loudly, a sleepy-eyed sergeant nodding sympathy. Another guard heaved an unconscious Zayda over his shoulder and followed after them into the street.

Dawn cast a dim glow over the city. The watchmen and their prisoners twisted through the quiet streets and arrived at a small, squat building. Some local outpost of the city watch, Peyne supposed. He noticed two jail cells. Peyne's shackles were removed, and he was shoved into one of the cells. He heard the creak and clank of the cell door next to him and assumed Zayda was being locked up in similar fashion.

He took stock of himself. He'd been relieved of his dagger and rapier but still had his purse. *An honest city watch. That's refreshing.*

He glanced around his cell. Small. A pallet of straw in the corner with a bucket next to it. A small window with iron bars. If Peyne stood on tiptoe, he could just see into the alley.

It wasn't Peyne's first time in a jail cell, but it was the first time his arrest had happened so far from home. No one would be coming from Gant's court to bribe the guards and set him free. The idea momentarily chilled him as he imagined himself growing old and dying in a dungeon, nobody ever knowing what had happened to him.

He dismissed the notion. Being dramatic wouldn't help.

He flopped onto the pallet and closed his eyes. He might as well sleep. There was nothing else to do.

◆ ◆ ◆

His eyes flickered open.

Something had happened, something to wake him.

Peyne sat up.

A rattling drew his attention, and he turned his head in time to see a small pebble bouncing in the corner. He frowned at it. Where could that have come from?

He turned toward the window.

Another pebble bounced off his forehead. "Ouch. Damn it."

He stood, went to the window, and looked out.

Maurizan stood in the alley looking up at him, hood up to hide her red hair. "Is it safe to talk?"

Peyne looked back through the bars of his cell, didn't see the guard. Perhaps they were out patrolling. "I think so," he whispered back.

"If you can figure a way out of there, you'd better do it fast," she said. "They usually let drunks out the next morning. But for more serious crimes, they'll round you up in a day or two and transfer you to the main dungeon. And escaping from there is next to impossible. You'll wait until the magistrate gets around to hearing your case."

"Can you help us?" Peyne asked.

She seemed to think about it and then spoke. "I don't think so. I'd have to fight my way in and out to do so. Killing some random thugs at the Indolent Imp is one thing. Dead city watchmen is another. I pass through this city a lot, and I'd never be able to show my face again."

"I can do it."

Peyne turned his head at the new voice. "Zayda?" She must have been at her window in the other cell, looking out just like Peyne was.

"I think I can get us out," Zayda said. "But not until tonight."

"Wait." Peyne opened his purse, took out the chit for the dromadan. He tossed it through the bars to Maurizan. "Get our animal, will you?"

"I'll meet you on the other side of the Beggar's Gate after midnight," Maurizan said. "You're less likely to be seen there or at least less likely to be reported. Beggars have no love for the city watch. I'll wait two hours, and if you're not there by then, I'll know it didn't work out."

"I have money," Peyne said. "Food and water for the desert."

"Pay me later," Maurizan said. "I know what to get. Good luck."

She glanced up and down the alley, then quickly and quietly jogged away.

"Can you really get us out?" Peyne asked.

"Maybe."

"Why not now?" Waiting to be transferred to the dungeons didn't sit well with him.

"Later," Zayda whispered. "After moonrise."

They waited, the day crawling along in no hurry to become night. Peyne alternated between snoozing on the pallet and pacing the tiny cell. Just before nightfall, a bored guard brought them each a wooden bowl of mush and a cup of water. The food was terrible, but he ate it greedily.

Night fell, and a couple of hours later, moonlight drifted in through the window.

He went to the window. "Zayda, is it time?" He whispered as loudly as he dared. "Zayda?"

◆ ◆ ◆

Zayda sat cross-legged on the cell floor, eyes closed, moonlight spilling through the window and washing over her.

She tapped into the spirit.

Zayda heard Peyne's voice like some distant echo from the bottom of a deep well but shut him out. She took a deep breath, released it slowly, opened herself to the moonlight, and let it fill her. In the past few days, the moon had filled in from the sliver of a crescent, and she felt the power come faster, her tattoo thrumming with energy.

The old woman had been awfully vague about the exact workings of the ink. Some instinct told Zayda that what she was about to try was possible, but there was no proof. Just a hope that she was right.

The moonlight seeped into her slowly but steadily, overflowing her storehouse of spirit, reaching the tip of each finger and toe and every strand of hair.

When she knew she couldn't hold anymore, she rose, feeling light on her feet, almost as if she might float into the air if she willed it.

Zayda considered the window bars. That would take her directly outside but would complicate Peyne's rescue. She turned to the bars of the cell door instead, gripping one in each hand.

And pulled.

She felt the power flow into her arms and shoulders, grit her teeth, every muscle tensing. Slowly the bars came apart. Zayda was slender and wouldn't need much. She bent, fit her head and shoulders through. She got stuck a moment at the hips, but twisted and wriggled until finally she stood outside her cell.

Zayda paused, listened. No jangle of armor or weapons, no rustle of clothing that might indicate the guards were coming. She moved in front of Peyne's cell.

"Peyne," she whispered.

The sight of Zayda startled him. He stepped back, eyes going wide, pointing at her and fumbling for words.

"It's me," she said.

"You're glowing."

She looked down at her hands. They shimmered with moonlight. The glow was all over her body. "So I am."

Peyne swallowed. "That's . . . interesting."

"It's a long story."

"You understand why I might be curious," Peyne said.

"Would you like to discuss it?" Zayda asked. "Or shall I spend these precious moments before the guards discover us effecting your escape?"

"Escape please."

She took the bars of his cell door in a tight grip. She grunted, straining to pull them apart. Slowly, they began to bend.

"You can do that?" Peyne gawked. "I didn't know you could do that."

And then the flow of power to her muscles faltered. She struggled, the bars bending much more slowly until the moonlight left her altogether. Her strength faded, bars refusing to budge any farther. Zayda pulled with everything she had, veins standing out on her neck and forehead, until she felt her face go hot, little stars flashing in front of her eyes.

Zayda let go, bent double, resting her hands on her knees and panting. She was covered in sweat.

"You're not glowing anymore," Peyne said.

She shook her head and searched within herself. There was still the spirit, waiting for her to tap into it, but the special energy provided by the moonlight had been exhausted. "Moonlight." She sucked in a ragged breath. Let it out. "Drained."

"Ah. Can you, uh, refill it?"

"It will take time," she told him.

"A doable amount of time, or a *ruin our whole plan* amount of time?"

The jangle of keys and the sound of the hall door creaking open turned their heads.

"I guess that's our answer," Peyne said.

The guard came around the corner and spotted them. All three froze for a split second.

They unfroze when he lifted the crossbow and fired. The bolt sped toward Zayda's face and—

—she tapped into the spirit—

The bolt floated so slowly, she stepped aside with ease, grabbed it out of midair, and tossed it to the ground.

The guard's eyes shot wide. He dropped the crossbow. It clattered on the ground, and he fumbled for the scimitar at his side.

Zayda was already moving, the heel of her hand breaking the man's nose. Blood gushed from both nostrils, and he staggered back. A punch in the gut bent him over, and a chop to the base of the skull put him down.

Two more guards must have heard the clamor. They crowded into the room, swords already drawn. She observed their every movement, every twitch and flex, knew what their bodies would do almost before they did.

The first swung at her throat, a sweeping horizontal slash hoping to take her head off.

Zayda ducked underneath, stepping forward and coming up fast, her tight fist connecting with the point of his chin. He grunted and staggered to the side.

The second came in fast, thrusting straight toward her belly.

She sidestepped, grabbed his wrist with both hands, and pulled down just as she brought her knee up. There was a sickening wet snap as the wrist broke, the sword dropping to clang on the floor.

His high-pitched scream was cut short by her chop across his throat. He gagged. She grabbed a fistful of his hair and drove his forehead into the wall, plaster cracking. He went cross-eyed and slumped to the floor unconscious.

The first one was just getting up again, but not to attack. He'd obviously had enough and ran for the door.

Zayda leapt on him from behind, driving him down. She banged his head against the floor three times until he didn't move anymore.

"You know, there are some fighting contests back home where we could make a lot of money." Peyne stood at the bars, looking impressed. "You look so small. We'd get amazing odds."

"Yes, well, we're a long way from your home." Zayda plucked the ring of keys from the first guard's belt and tossed them to Peyne. "Let yourself out, then help me drag these men into your cell. They'll awaken eventually, and we don't want them raising the alarm."

Peyne let himself out of the cell and helped Zayda drag the unconscious guards inside. He clanked the door shut and locked it.

"Toss the keys into that cabinet," Zayda said, pointing across the room to a rough-hewn cabinet. "They'll find them eventually."

"To blazes with that," Peyne said. "Let's toss them in the sewer."

She skewered him with a disapproving look. "These men are just doing their jobs. They don't know us."

"They tried to shoot you in the face with a crossbow and stab you with various swords."

"Like I said," Zayda insisted. "Doing their jobs."

Peyne held up a hand to forestall further debate. "Fine."

He opened the cabinet and brightened. "Hello!" His sword belt hung within, along with his rapier and dagger. He hurriedly strapped them on. There was another crossbow and a quiver of bolts. Peyne took them, slung them over his shoulder. Two cloaks the same black as the city watch tunics hung on pegs. He grabbed these also.

"Here." He tossed one of them to Zayda. "Disguises."

Zayda had already strapped on one of the guards' scimitars. She took the cloak, wrapped it around her shoulders, and pulled up the hood.

They looked like two sinister shadows. Zayda hoped they'd blend into the night as they made their way to the Beggar's Gate.

They cracked open the door and peered out. The street was empty.

"It's been a while, but I know the shortest way to the Beggar's Gate," Zayda whispered. "Follow me."

◆ ◆ ◆

Peyne followed her through the underbelly of Tamtalla.

Zayda paused occasionally at a crossroads to consider a left or a right but never for long. This was her city, and she knew it well enough. They soon entered a poorly lit neighborhood, most of the windows dark, many with shutters hanging loose. A good number of the buildings seemed abandoned altogether.

Zayda leaned toward him as they walked together, lowering her voice. "Be wary. The Beggars' Guild and the Thieves' Guild have an agreement, but you never know."

"An agreement?"

"The thieves don't rob anyone in the Beggar's Quarter," Zayda explained.

"Why would they want to?" Peyne asked. "Beggars rarely have anything worth stealing."

"The thieves don't rob the beggars," Zayda said. "They rob the people who come to give to the beggars."

Peyne cleared his throat. "I see. Let's come at this from another direction. *Why* would anyone go out of their way to *find* beggars? In

Merridan, beggars take it upon themselves to go where the money is. It's called initiative."

"The priests tell the people to give to the beggars, and then the beggars kick back a portion to the temple," Zayda said. "Everyone gets their coin, and the citizenry isn't tripping over beggars everywhere they go. And the watch doesn't have to bother with the place. They're always complaining they're spread too thin anyway."

"Efficient," Peyne admitted. "Yet strangely unsettling."

"Why should it be?"

"I'm not sure," Peyne said. "I guess it just seems there's no motivation for a beggar to better himself."

"Do you strive to better yourself?"

"I no longer wish to participate in this conversation."

The lane narrowed and curved. Zayda turned left, taking them through a stone arch and into a covered alley. Torches lit the way intermittently.

Beggars lined both sides of the alley, hunched inside ragged cloaks. The smell of unwashed bodies was overwhelming. Occasionally one would look up to see who passed, but none spoke. *They don't seem especially motivated to panhandle,* Peyne observed.

They emerged from the alley into a small square. Again, beggars lined the walls, the occasional cook fire the only illumination. A door stood across the square opposite the alley exit, two beggars sitting on either side. It was a thick wooden door, banded in iron, eight feet high and four wide. Large for a door. Small for a gate. But as Zayda had told him earlier, the Beggar's Gate was the smallest in the city. Certainly too small for a trade caravan of dromadan. The gate catered to a special variety of foot traffic.

"There it is," Peyne said needlessly, feeling nervous, eyes darting around the square. "Let's get out of here. Maurizan is probably already waiting on the other side."

She put a hand on his arm. "Wait. We need to ask the *onan* first."

"The what?"

"A general term," she said. "Like boss or chief."

They approached the gate, stopping short as one of the beggars lifted his head to appraise them. He smiled, teeth yellow and rotten. Skin wrinkled and scabby, beard white but dirty. His eyes were red-rimmed and watery.

"What brings you to the Beggar's Gate, children?"

Peyne noted the man addressed them in Helvan. They'd observed he wasn't a local, and Peyne wasn't sure if that were a bad sign or not.

Zayda took a half step forward. "We wish to pass, *onan*. If it pleases you for us to do so."

"I like you," said the old beggar. "So few young people have good manners these days."

"Thank you, *onan*."

The beggar shifted his gaze to Peyne. "Step forward. Show yourself."

Peyne stepped up next to Zayda and pulled back his hood. "At your service, *onan*." He offered a terse courtesy bow.

The *onan* frowned. "A foreign barbarian." He made a disgusted noise.

Barbarian? Have you smelled yourself? "I am humbled to be a guest in your exalted country." He cleared his throat. "Where a poor barbarian such as myself can learn of courtesy through your fine example."

The *onan* laughed. This seemed to be the signal to the other beggars, and a low chuckle rippled around the square.

"Very well," the old beggar said. "You both may pass."

Zayda ducked her head in a quick bow. "Thank you so much, *onan*. We are most grateful to—"

"For fifty silver pieces," the *onan* said.

Peyne made an abrupt choking sound. "I've paid many tolls in many places, and that's outrageous. You *know* it is."

"Toll?" An innocent look on the *onan*'s face. "I charge no toll. I am but a humble beggar. Fifty pieces of silver is simply the amount of charity I'm hoping from one so generous. There is no charge to pass through the gate."

Peyne blinked. "Passing through the gate is free?"

"Of course," the *onan* said. "We are more than happy to dump your body on the other side of the gate without charging you a single copper."

Ah.

Peyne lifted his chin. "Well, then, sir, we shall simply have to bid you good evening and take our business elsewhere. Yours is not the only gate in and out of this city." He turned to leave.

And stopped in midstep.

All of the beggars in the square had risen to bar his way. Those in the alley had moved forward to clog the entrance. These men were hardly crack troops, but there were enough of them, and doubtlessly some of those tattered cloaks concealed daggers and cudgels.

Peyne turned back to the *onan*. "Look, I don't *have* fifty silver pieces, okay? If I did, I'd give it to you." He took out his purse and shook it at the old beggar. "This is it. All I have."

"Then perhaps the woman should stay here and keep me company," the *onan* suggested. "While you go back and find the rest."

"*Onan*, wait." Zayda rushed forward, going to one knee. She tugged back her scarf, just enough for only the *onan* to see, revealing the collar.

For a moment, the old beggar narrowed his eyes as if not understanding what he was looking at, but then he caught a glint of metal in the firelight. His eyes slowly widened, and he nodded, understanding.

When the *onan* spoke next, it was in low tones, but Peyne was just close enough to hear.

"Beggars only eat by the generosity of others, but at least we're not slaves. Thank you for the reminder, child. There is always someone who has it worse." He raised his voice for everyone to hear. "I will let them pass."

Two of the beggars in the crowd came forward to slide the heavy bar to the side and swing the gate inward. A cool wind blew in off the desert, washing the beggar stink from the square. They were going to get out of here after all.

Zayda stood and bowed formally to the beggar. "Thank you, *onan*."

She passed through the gate, glancing back over her shoulder at Peyne.

Peyne offered the *onan* a more casual bow than Zayda's. "Obliged, sir. Truth to tell, I'm not sure where I would have come up with fifty silver on short notice."

"It's okay." The *onan* held out his hand. "Whatever's in the purse will do."

"You mean I still have to pay—" Peyne shook his head, sighed. "You know what? It's worth it." He dropped the purse into the beggar's open palm. "A pleasure doing business with you."

"Safe travels," said the *onan*.

Peyne followed Zayda through the gate, started when it slammed shut behind him with an ominous clang.

He looked at Zayda. She held her arms out, face turned toward the sky.

"What are you doing?"

"Absorbing moonlight," Zayda said.

"That's what the tattoo does? It turns moonlight into muscle?"

"It turns moonlight into power," she said. "Muscle is one way to use that power. I think. I'm still learning."

"Maybe you shouldn't absorb too much," Peyne said. "If you start glowing again, they'll see us for miles."

Zayda pulled up the hood on her cloak. "That's a thought actually."

A pause, then Peyne asked, "How did you know what he'd do?"

She looked at him. "What do you mean?"

"The boss beggar," Peyne said. "How did you know you'd have his sympathy?"

"That or he'd recognize it wasn't some random weak little girl who'd wandered into his territory. It was somebody who might cause him a big problem if he insisted on fifty silver."

Peyne smiled warmly. "So not just a pretty face, then."

She smiled and then tried to hide it but was too late. She *was* very attractive, Peyne thought.

He shuffled awkwardly, rubbed the back of his neck. "My plan had been to catch a riverboat back to Heberron. It goes without saying that I'm long overdue to report back to Merridan."

Zayda's smile wavered, but then she nodded quickly. "Oh. Yes, of course." She gestured to the left. "If you follow the wall that way, it will take you around to the riverfront. It's a busy place, boats coming and going at all hours, so it should be no problem to—"

Peyne cleared his throat. "Actually, I was thinking that I should probably come with you."

She blinked, face going blank.

"It's just . . . I mean, look, we've come this far . . . and I'd feel bad if . . ." He realized he was stammering like an idiot and felt himself go red. He hoped she couldn't see how flushed he was in the darkness.

"You would do this for me?"

Peyne remembered the panicked feeling in the jail cell, the dread thinking he'd be thrown in some dungeon never to see the light of day again. Zayda wore her prison around her neck, and everywhere she went, every day for the rest of her life, she'd take that prison with her.

"It's the right thing to do," he said.

She reached out, touched him lightly on the forearm, tentative. "I feel like I should talk you out of it. That it's too much to ask, and that I should tell you to go back to your own people, and assure you I can handle this on my own. But I don't want to."

And Peyne felt something pass between them, something he'd never felt before, and it was somewhat frightening and a little exciting and maybe he was just slightly dizzy. And he understood then that doing the right thing was only part of it, and that, really, if he left Zayda to take a riverboat and never saw her again, he would not be able to forgive himself.

He tried to think of something to say and failed.

"Come on," she said. "Maurizan must be near. Unless she sold us out and left with our dromadan."

He blew out a breath he hadn't known he'd been holding, and both of them scanned the landscape.

"There." Peyne pointed across the sand where a dune rose up a hundred yards away, the silhouettes atop the hill clearly two dromadan. "That must be her."

They hiked toward the dune, and when they were close, Maurizan waved. She didn't call out. Sound carried across the desert at night, and they weren't looking to call attention to themselves.

Peyne and Zayda climbed aboard their dromadan and settled into the saddle.

"Thanks for waiting," Peyne said.

"I'll want to know what she knows." Maurizan lifted her chin toward Zayda. "I want to know about whatever other tattoos she has besides the Prime. You seem like good people, but I'm not helping you for friendship. I'm hoping we can help each other."

"I'll tell you what little I know," Zayda said.

"Good." Maurizan jerked the reins, turning her dromadan west. "Follow me."

"The road is south."

"And if they bother to follow, they'll look for you on the road," Maurizan said. "I know a place."

Peyne and Zayda exchanged glances.

He gestured toward the gypsy. "Follow the lady."

Zayda clucked her tongue and flicked the reins. The dromadan lumbered into line behind the other, and they headed across the starlit dunes.

CHAPTER
EIGHTEEN

They came up the river on three huge barges like some invading army, labor gangs of prisoners rowing against the current. Meddigar stood near the blunt prow of the lead barge, watching the river city of Tamtalla grow bigger in the distance. Meddigar, the ink mages, and the military officers all traveled in the lead barge. It was the prince's personal barge and therefore the most comfortable. Meddigar had not suffered at all on the three-day cruise from the capital, servants and cooks and one of the prince's personal wine stewards all scurrying to make sure their honored passengers enjoyed every luxury. The trailing barges were of the more mundane variety and brought troops and supplies.

Meddigar's apprentice stood dutifully a few feet behind him, and he had been doing his best to ignore her.

She cleared her throat.

He kept ignoring her.

She cleared it more loudly.

Meddigar stifled a sigh. "What is it, Nila?"

"I'm still not sure why we're going to Tamtalla," she said. "Could we have not headed straight into the deep desert?"

"We've been over this," Meddigar said. "For one thing, we have a lot of men and supplies to move. Coming part of the way by river helps. Our backsides will be sore soon enough from endless days in a dromadan saddle. Are you really so eager to abandon the comfort the prince has generously provided?" He made a grand gesture, indicating the luxurious barge.

"No, of course not, master," Nila said. "But surely it would have been more expedient to disembark yesterday. It's my understanding that the road curves in such a way that—"

"Are you hoping to ascertain why I want to go to Tamtalla even though it is clearly out of the way?" Meddigar asked, voice dripping with exasperation.

A pause. "I am."

"Because I'm going to see Auvor Kre'Shama the cartographer."

"Oh." She was clearly taken aback by the straightforward answer. "For a map?"

"Why else would one see a cartographer?"

"Are we . . . I mean, do you *need* a map? Aren't we returning by the same route you took before?"

"Perhaps." The slightest of shrugs. "Perhaps not."

Nila regained her composure and said, "Visiting a cartographer will be instructive. I look forward to it."

"Sadly, you won't be able to accompany me."

Nila opened her mouth to protest, but Meddigar cut her off.

"Time is of the essence, and while I'm off to the cartographer, I'm afraid I'll need you to pack up my things," the wizard insisted. "Spell components, ingredients for elaborate potions, expensive and rare materials. I can't let just any servant ready them for travel. That's the job of a trusted apprentice, obviously. And I'm drying some kwikwi leaves for a medicinal elixir. They can't be packed until the last minute."

Nila started to object, then caught herself. Meddigar was quite right, of course. The care and handling of the spell components and other items couldn't be trusted to anyone else. The wizard smiled to himself. He'd spent the morning unpacking all these items specifically so she'd be occupied repacking them while he went into Tamtalla.

"I'll get started if you don't mind, master. We'll reach Tamtalla soon."

"Thank you, Nila."

She turned, walked toward the stairs that led belowdecks, shoulders straight, head held high, pride stiffening her spine. She'd sulk later, he knew, but never where the wizard could see her.

The three ink mages approached him, Hak in the lead, the two female ink mages behind him. When the ink mages first came aboard the barge, Meddigar had noticed something strange. The two women had handlers, as did all ink mages in Fyria, men who would use the control scepters to keep the mages obedient. The handlers had dutifully handed over their control scepters to Meddigar, who would take charge of them for the duration of the expedition.

Hak had no handler. A collar, yes, but nobody lording a scepter over him.

A fact that didn't sit well with the wizard.

Hak planted his impressive bulk in front of Meddigar, arms crossed. Power and arrogance radiated off him. "I was told you wished to speak to me."

"I want you to come with me when I go into Tamtalla," Meddigar said. "I'm seeking information from someone who might be reluctant to share it. Let's just say that your presence alone might be intimidating enough to make him talkative."

Hak's smile was half sneer. "Happy to oblige. The prince made it clear I am to be at your disposal."

"I notice you don't have a handler," Meddigar said.

Hak's sneer-smile wavered briefly. "I have been given the great honor of carrying my own scepter." He reached into the sash around his waist and produced the metallic scepter. "A gesture from the prince, showing his trust."

"A great honor indeed."

Not so much that he trusts you, Meddigar thought. *More that the prince doesn't trust me. I can't control you if you carry your own scepter, can I? Very shrewd. Hak both aids me and guards me. I'm going to feel his eyes on my back all the way to the deep desert.*

"May I ask how such an honor was earned?"

Hak's grin showed genuine pleasure. He liked this question and enjoyed giving the answer. "I saved the prince's life during an assassination attempt. A murder squad of insurgents broke into the palace, and I single-handedly killed them." His grin widened. "All thirty of them."

"Most impressive." *Look at the fool grinning. So proud of his body count. He thinks himself invincible.*

The wizard's hand casually dipped into a pocket of his robe, fingers closing around the cold metal device there. Meddigar thought of the item as his "skeleton key." *Perhaps we will need to put your invincibility to the test, eh?*

Ropes flew from the barges, and men along the docks caught them, hauling the vessels close. Activity erupted immediately. Supplies needed for the desert trek would be unloaded, additional food and water purchased.

None of these tasks concerned Meddigar. He was down the gangplank immediately after it was lowered, Hak following in his wake.

They wove their way through the city to a quiet street between the Scholar's Quarter and a neighborhood of craftsmen. A simple wooden sign hung from a bracket over the cartographer's door, a stylized image of the four points of a compass as if from a map.

Meddigar knocked.

A few seconds later, a young woman answered the door, pretty, dressed too well to be a servant, long black hair held back from a heart-shaped face with turquoise hairpins. "You wish to see the cartographer?"

"Yes, please."

"Do you have an appointment?"

"I'm afraid not. Tell him it's Meddigar. I'm sure he won't mind seeing me."

The woman's eyes lit with recognition. "Your name is known to me. Please come wait in the foyer. I'll see if he's available."

She ushered them inside and closed the door. "Sit if you like. I'll just be a moment." She took a wide, sweeping stairway up to the next level.

Meddigar considered the chairs but remained standing. A minute stretched to five and then to ten.

"Perhaps he's not as agreeable to seeing you as you think," Hak suggested.

Perhaps you can go fuck yourself. "Have patience."

A few seconds later, the woman came back down the stairs and signaled for them to follow. "This way if you please."

On the second floor, she took them down a long hall to the door at the end, opened it, and indicated they should enter. Hak had to duck his head going through the doorway.

This was clearly the cartographer's work area, tables and shelves filled with scrolls and papers. The space was well lit, tall windows in three of the four walls. Between two windows on the far wall hung a handsomely framed map of the known world . . . or at least the known world a few hundred years ago. To Meddigar's eyes, the map seemed very old.

"The work of my great-great-great-great grandfather," said the old man bent over the drafting table. He turned in his seat to face the wizard, bone thin, bald head speckled with brown spots, white sideburns

176

that dipped to his chin and curved back up again to join with his moustache. "It nearly ruined him."

Meddigar raised an eyebrow. "Oh?"

"A king from a long-forgotten kingdom," the cartographer said. "He commissioned the most accurate map of the known world and was willing to pay good gold for it. An arrogant and evil soul who fancied himself a conqueror. But difficult to conquer the world if you're not quite sure what all's in it."

"Thus the map," Meddigar said.

"Thus the map," echoed the cartographer. "My ancestor spent a small fortune sending ships in every direction to confirm certain landmarks. He traveled himself for a year to some of the farthest points on the map. A week after he finished—the greatest achievement of his life—word reached him that the king had been murdered by his own brother. It seemed not everyone shared his ambition for conquest. Alas, the map was never paid for, which is why you see it hanging here."

"I would imagine the episode was financially devastating," Meddigar said.

"Yes, but my ancestor recovered," the cartographer said. "And he learned a valuable lesson that he passed on to future generations. Always get half the money up front."

"A wise policy."

"Indeed. What can I do for you today, Meddigar?"

"The deep desert."

The cartographer sighed. "You too, eh?"

"Me too?" Meddigar realized immediately. "Maurizan."

Now Hak spoke up for the first time. "The red-haired foreigner?"

That caught Meddigar by surprise. "You know her?"

The cartographer turned to Hak, as if just now noticing the huge man standing there. "And you are?"

"Excuse my poor manners," Meddigar intervened. "This is Hak. He's assisting me in this enterprise. Hak, this is Auvor Kre'Shama, the world's greatest mapmaker."

Hak bowed. "World's greatest. That's quite a boast."

"There is a man in Sherrik more popular, I think, but that's probably just because he works cheaper."

"How do you know Maurizan?" the wizard asked Hak.

"As you know, the Prime is only the beginning," Hak said. "There are other tattoos of power if one has but the tenacity to pursue them. For many months, I crisscrossed the known continents chasing legend and rumor in pursuit of new tattoos. Wizards like to hoard their secrets, as I'm sure Meddigar will confirm."

"We go through a lot to unearth the secrets of the ages," Meddigar said. "We're not disposed to sharing them frivolously."

"Fair enough," Hak said. "Every wizard I visited, the red-haired woman had already been there. If they'd already shared the secret of the tattoo with her, then they were often not obliged to share with me also. It became . . . frustrating. I would very much like to meet this Maurizan in person."

"Be careful what you wish for," Meddigar said. "She's not one to be trifled with."

Hak grinned. "I look forward to it."

The mapmaker cleared his throat. "I'm not sure this has anything to do with me."

"My apologies, Auvor," Meddigar said. "But I take it she's been here."

"She has."

"I don't suppose you might tell me what she was after."

"I don't suppose I would."

Meddigar sighed. He looked around the room, saw a simple wooden chair against one wall. He gestured to it. "May I?"

Auvor nodded.

Meddigar pulled up the chair, sat, scooted a bit closer to Auvor's drafting table. "I completely understand that part of your service is . . . uh . . . discretion."

"Then you know I won't discuss another client's project," Auvor said. "It's simply not proper."

"Yes, of course." Meddigar scratched his beard. "You see, the thing is, this is maybe something of a special situation."

"I'm afraid I don't see how."

Meddigar looked back over his shoulder. "Hak, you said that often the wizards you found were reluctant to share their ink magic?"

"Yes."

"How would you come to terms?"

"I would offer them my services in exchange for the tattoo," Hak said. "They would set me to some impossible task. Not impossible for *me*."

"And most of these magicians would take you up on this offer?"

"Most," Hak said. "Not all."

"And those who didn't?"

"I was forced to become more persuasive." Hak cracked his knuckles. "I can be quite charming."

The cartographer sighed. "Really, Meddigar, this is beneath you."

Meddigar leaned forward, urgency in his voice. "I am on a mission for the prince. If it fails, he'll want to know why, and you know it's not in my nature to fall on my sword. I'll happily tell anyone who'll listen who failed to cooperate. Even if I spare you today, it puts your head on a pike tomorrow."

Auvor made an annoyed noise in his throat, rubbing his eyes as he considered the wizard's words. "Then I choose the task."

Meddigar blinked. "You choose the what?"

"Your ink mage said he would trade the wizards some task for the tattoo," the mapmaker said. "Only *persuading* them if they refused. If my only other choice is bodily harm, then I choose the task."

That wasn't exactly what Meddigar had in mind. Still . . .

"What is it you want?" the wizard asked.

Auvor sat back, took a deep breath. "I lost my son three years ago."

"I'm sorry," Meddigar said. "How?"

"He went to map the deep desert and didn't return."

"That is disturbing for multiple reasons," Meddigar admitted.

"He was a good mapmaker," Auvor said. "He would have taken over for me eventually. As someone whose work it is to document the physical features of our world, I think you can guess the allure of the deep desert. It is vast and unmapped. It would be my family's greatest achievement. My son died in the attempt. I wish for another chance."

"With respect," Meddigar said, "I think you may be a bit long in the tooth for such a perilous journey."

Auvor chuckled. "I cannot disagree. My bones ache. My fieldwork days are over. And I have no son."

A pause.

"But I have a daughter."

"The young woman who answered the door," Meddigar said.

"Yes."

"You realize the trek is dangerous. You've lost a son already."

"You are undertaking this trip for the prince, yes? My impression is that you are well equipped. Likely going under armed guard. Am I correct?"

"You are," Meddigar said.

"Then this is the safest chance she'll ever have."

"Are you so eager to send away your final child?" Meddigar asked. "She might not even want to go."

Auvor chuckled again, then raised his voice. "Venny, come in here please."

The door opened a second later. "Father?"

"I've been discussing the family business with these gentlemen," Auvor said. "Please inform them the subject on which you've been harassing me day and night without mercy."

She had the good grace to look embarrassed. "Mapping the deep desert, Father."

"As it happens, these nice people are taking an expedition into the deep desert," Auvor said.

Venny froze, her eyes going wide. She seemed to be holding her breath.

"This family has mapped most of the known world," Auvor said. "Some small bit remains. Do you think you might pop out with these gentlemen and map it for us?"

Her face blazed with sudden enthusiasm. "I can be packed and ready in twenty minutes."

She bolted from the room.

"Should you tell her we're not quite that much in a rush?" Meddigar asked.

"I don't want to dampen her enthusiasm," Auvor said. "In any case, twenty minutes is wildly optimistic. If she's packed all her gear in an hour, I'll eat my hat."

"And there's still the matter of what you told Maurizan," Meddigar reminded him.

"Don't fret. I plan to keep my part of the bargain." He pulled a large, rolled piece of parchment from the shelf above him and spread it out on the drafting table, fastening clips on either side to keep it flat.

Meddigar stood and stepped forward to get a better look at the document.

It was, of course, a map, but seemed to lack detail.

"It doesn't look like much," Meddigar said.

"It's not," Auvor admitted. "I consulted eleven different maps to cobble this together. The most recent one is nearly a hundred years old."

Meddigar squinted at the map. "This is in the deep desert?"

"The edge of it."

Meddigar looked more closely, still trying to understand why anyone would care about this. The center of the map was taken up with a vast blank area, ringed at the edges with low, rocky hills.

"It's just a wide open nothing," Meddigar said.

"It is now," Auvor agreed. "But before it was a large inland sea."

"And Maurizan was interested in going there."

"She was interested in going *back*," Auvor said.

They discussed the possible significance of that for another half hour, and then Auvor rolled up the map and handed it to Meddigar. "Take it. I don't know what good it might do you, but I wish you luck. It's possible that Maurizan has added something additional, is hoarding more information that makes the map more useful. I just don't know."

"Thank you."

"Meddigar?"

"Yes?"

"Please look after my daughter," the cartographer said.

She knows what she's getting into. "Of course."

"I'm obliged."

"If you don't mind, I need to confer with my associate," Meddigar said. "Please tell Venny to meet us down in the foyer."

"It shouldn't be long now," Auvor said. "I'll tell her."

Meddigar and Hak descended the stairs side by side in silence. When they reached the bottom, Meddigar glanced back one last time to confirm they were alone, then whispered to Hak, "Return to the barges as fast as you can. I'll need you to gather a squad of soldiers and the other two ink mages. Outfit a couple of dromadan. I want you ready to leave by the time I get back. The rest of our forces will have to catch up."

Hak frowned. "I probably should stay with you . . . for your safety."

Meddigar rolled his eyes. "I'm not going to run off. If we're going to pick up Maurizan's trail, we'll need every minute."

Hak brightened at the thought of confronting the red-haired foreigner.

"And anyway, you saw the young lady's face when her father told her she was coming with us," Meddigar said. "I couldn't possibly disappoint her. It would break the young girl's heart."

Hak laughed. "I'll need to tell the company captain where we're going."

Meddigar nodded. "Tell him we're going to the Last Village."

CHAPTER
NINETEEN

They traveled through most of the night, stopping only a few hours before dawn to steal a brief nap before pressing on again.

Several times, Peyne saw Maurizan closing her eyes, face lifted to the sky. He looked up, wondering what she was doing. Once, he saw a great bird with a huge wingspan circling high overhead.

He asked Zayda to urge their dromadan up next to Maurizan's, and when they'd pulled alongside, Peyne asked, "Any chance we're being followed?"

"No," Maurizan said.

Peyne glanced behind them at the empty desert, then back at the gypsy. "How can you be so sure?"

"I'm sure." Maurizan clucked her tongue, and her dromadan pulled ahead.

Not feeling conversational, eh?

The day dragged on. Peyne swayed in the saddle, drifting in and out of a doze. He spent his waking moments cursing his ugly hat but glad it kept the sun off. The miles were endless and dull and hot.

At last, the sun sank again, and they made camp in the low spot between two dunes to hide their meager campfire. They chewed tough pieces of overly spiced dried meat and drank their water rations.

"When do we turn south?" Zayda asked across the fire.

"Tomorrow," Maurizan said, "if we start early and ride all day."

"Why?"

Maurizan sprawled under a blanket, turning away from Zayda. "Food and water before we turn south. A good place to hide. Quiet now. I need my sleep."

Zayda turned to Peyne. "Did she just tell me to be quiet?"

Peyne paused in midchew. "Don't drag me into this."

"We are following her blindly into who knows where," Zayda reminded him. "I have every right to ask questions."

"She met us outside the Beggar's Gate just like she said she would," Peyne said. "I think we can trust her."

Zayda leaned toward him, pitched her voice low. "I wonder if it's her pretty red hair and white skin you find so trustworthy."

"Why, that's . . . how could you think—" sputtered Peyne.

"Not very quiet," Maurizan said from across the campfire.

Peyne pulled his own blanket up to his chin. "She's right. We all need rest. I'll expect your *apology* in the morning." He turned his back to her.

"Apology?"

"*Shush!*"

If Peyne listened carefully, he felt certain he could hear Zayda's teeth grind.

They were off again at the first light of dawn, following Maurizan due west. The day was an endless slog, the dromadan doggedly putting one gigantic foot in front of the other, dune after dune rising ahead of them and then dwindling behind.

If Peyne never saw another grain of sand as long as he lived, it would be fine by him.

And then, as the sun set, the desert aglow with the final burnt orange of fading daylight, Maurizan took a sudden left turn for no apparent reason. Their path curved around an enormous dune, lower and lower until they were all the way on the other side.

A rocky ravine opened up before them.

Peyne did a double take. The ravine had been unexpected and completely different from the surrounding geography. Maurizan led them inside, and they fell into shadow. Peyne looked up. The waning sunlight had diminished to what could fall between a twenty-foot-wide crack overhead. Peyne tried to imagine how the ravine must appear from above. Looking across the sand from a distance, it might be impossible to spot. Peyne suspected that travelers came to this place on purpose or not at all.

They traveled into the hidden ravine silently. Wind whistled past them. There was something eerie and claustrophobic about the place compared to the open desert. Every step of the dromadan, every stray pebble echoed strangely. For the first time, Peyne wondered if blindly placing their faith in Maurizan had been a good idea.

"I don't like it here," Peyne whispered to Zayda.

"Really?" Zayda whispered back. "Do you mean to say your white princess might not have our best interests at heart?"

"I feel that sarcasm is antiproductive at this time."

Zayda scowled at him. "You know I'm right. We've been near death and back again together, and yet this woman comes out of nowhere, and you swoon all over—"

"Now, that's not fair," Peyne insisted. "I've not shown any preference for—"

"Liar!" Zayda's whisper was like a sword blade leaving its scabbard.

"Hey! Now there's no reason to be rude, so just take your attitude and stick it up—"

"Stop." A deep voice, echoing along the ravine.

Zayda pulled back on the reins, and the dromadan lumbered to a halt.

Maurizan twisted in her saddle to look back at them. "Say nothing. I'll handle this."

"What's going on?" Peyne demanded.

"I said be quiet."

Peyne opened his mouth, shut it again. He glanced sideways at Zayda. Her expression said, *See? Your devious redhead has led us into a trap.*

Peyne shrugged back at her. *Get off my back. This isn't my fault.*

A man walked out from behind a boulder, stood in the center of the ravine's path, hands on hips. He was dressed head to toe in black, face covered, only dark eyes peering out at them.

"You know better than this, Maurizan." He spoke good Helvan with a heavy accent.

"This is important, Jaff," Maurizan said.

The man Maurizan called Jaff pulled aside the black scarf, revealing a handsome but scowling face. A full black moustache, no beard. Peyne thought he looked vaguely familiar.

"Get down from those animals," Jaff ordered.

Peyne cleared his throat, sat up straight in the saddle. "I think we may have gotten off on the wrong foot. I'm Peyne Erlich, and it might make a difference for you to know that I'm a duly appointed envoy of his majesty's—"

Jaff pointed at Peyne. "You. Foreigner. Shut your mouth or I'll carve your tongue from your head."

Peyne rolled his eyes. "You and what army, friend?"

Zayda gently laid a hand on his arm. "Uh . . ." She pointed upward.

Peyne looked up.

Dozens lined the cliffs overhead. Black-clad ghosts, many with bows, arrows trained on him. Others held torches. The sun had completely fled the world now, and the torchlight made their shadows long and distorted.

They're dressed just like the marauders who attacked the Pride of Klaar, Peyne thought. *I suddenly have a very bad feeling.*

"I'll tell you one last time," Jaff said. "Dismount. I'm using your ugly language, so I presume you understand me. Or are you just stupid?"

"Do what he says," Maurizan told them.

All three climbed down from their dromadan. Men in black oozed from the shadows to surround them.

"Told you," Zayda whispered from the side of her mouth.

"Not now," Peyne whispered back.

"Their weapons," Jaff said.

The men in black moved in fast, relieving Zayda and Peyne of all arms. Maurizan they left alone.

Jaff stepped up to Zayda. When he reached for her, Peyne tensed. Everyone must have sensed it, for suddenly there were a half-dozen sword points an inch from Peyne's body. He made himself relax, held up a hand to indicate *no worries here.*

The men in black didn't lower their swords.

Jaff pulled aside Zayda's scarf, eyes widening slightly at the sight of the collar. "She comes with us. Kill the foreigner."

"Excuse me?" Peyne said, voice a bit more high-pitched than he would have liked.

Maurizan's hand fell to the hilt of a dagger. "I come in good faith, Jaff."

"You know our rules," Jaff shot back. "This place is secret. You knew you were bringing this man to die. That's on you."

"Jaff." A warning tone in Maurizan's voice.

"If you're going to murder me," Peyne said, "may I at least ask a question?"

A predatory grin from Jaff. "By all means."

"How is it that Maurizan is allowed here, but I'm not?" Peyne asked. "She's a foreigner, too, isn't she?"

"My agreement with Maurizan is none of your concern," Jaff said.

"Tell him." Maurizan's gaze was hard, unwavering.

Jaff held the gaze for a moment before turning back to Peyne. "I said if she could beat me in single combat, I would spare her." He chuckled. "I didn't know about the tattoos when I made the offer."

"I accept your terms," Peyne said.

Jaff frowned. "What terms?"

"Single combat."

Jaff sighed, shaking his head. "Listen to me, soft man from Helva. You are already going to die. Don't add humiliation to your fate."

Peyne squared his shoulders. "Are we not men, sir? Is a man not permitted to die on his feet with a sword in his hand?"

Something not unlike respect crossed Jaff's face. "I'm glad to see you have some spine, foreigner."

"Thanks. I answer to Peyne actually, rather than foreigner."

"The duel will be to first blood only," Jaff explained. "If I bleed first, your life is spared. I draw your blood first, and it's the headman's axe."

"Why not just run me through during the duel?"

"Because we are not barbarians. The duel is to first blood," Jaff said. "You are in agreement?"

"Of course," Peyne said. "As soon as the wine comes, we can begin."

Jaff blinked. "As soon as the what comes?"

Zayda gave him a sideways glance and whispered, "Are you out of your mind?"

"We are going to toast, aren't we?" Peyne asked. "I thought you Fyrians were the civilized ones."

"With Maurizan there was no toast," Jaff said.

Peyne shrugged. "I can hardly be responsible for what gypsies do."

"You are stalling."

"Are you afraid it will make your hand unsteady?" Peyne's expression filled with concern. "If you don't hold your wine so well, I won't insist that—"

"I hold my wine well enough," Jaff snapped.

A low murmur ran through the crowd of black-clad men, and Peyne realized they were snickering.

"Check his back for the Prime." The hint of a mocking smile tugged at the corners of Maurizan's mouth. "If that will make you feel safer."

The snickering grew louder.

"Enough," Jaff shouted. "Bring the jug."

A few seconds later, another man appeared with an earthen jug and two cups. He handed one cup to Jaff and the other to Peyne, filled both.

"Go on and make your toast then," Jaff said impatiently.

Peyne lifted his cup. "To the good people of Helva and King Gant. I fight for their honor." He tossed back the cup of wine.

Jaff tossed his back too, winced.

Peyne held his cup out to the man with the jug. "Fill it for the next toast please."

"What next toast?" Jaff demanded.

"I've toasted to Helva," Peyne said. "Don't you want to toast to Fyria? I'd just assumed—"

"Yes, yes, fine." Jaff held out his cup. When it was refilled he held it up. "To Fyria."

Peyne took a very small sip from his cup.

"What are you doing?" Anger flashed in Jaff's eyes.

"What do you mean?"

"You guzzled your entire cup when saluting Helva, but only a sip when we drank to Fyria!" Jaff raged. "Do you think I will suffer such an insult?"

"I just didn't want to take unfair advantage," Peyne said. "If you can't handle your wine—"

"Insolent ass," Jaff shouted. "I will toast again, and you will drain your cup or so help me I will slit your throat on the spot."

"Very well."

Jaff raised his cup high. "To Fyria! The greatest nation in the entire world!"

They both drained their cups.

"This wine is actually quite nice," Peyne said. "I'm surprised."

"And why should that be?" Jaff asked. "Do you think Fyrian wine inferior?"

"I apologize," Peyne said. "Let us drink to my apology."

They drank.

Peyne motioned for the man to fill the cups again. "To the superior product of Fyrian vineyards."

They drank again.

This time Jaff motioned for the men to fill the cups. "To you, sir. You have good manners for a barbarian."

They emptied their cups.

Peyne contrived to come up with three more toasts. The men looking on had begun to stir and mutter to one another. Peyne doubted he could keep this up much longer, and anyway, the wine jug was empty.

"Bring the weapons!" Jaff announced loudly.

One of Jaff's lieutenants stepped forward, Peyne's rapier in one hand and Jaff's scimitar in the other. The lieutenant spoke in hushed urgent tones, but Jaff waved the man away with a growl, rebuffing his underling with harsh words.

Peyne didn't know a word of Fyrian but could guess the basics of the conversation. The lieutenant was suggesting that perhaps Jaff was not in the best condition to fight a duel. Jaff was almost certainly telling the man to mind his own business and that no soft foreigner was about to get the better of him.

Each man took his weapon, and they stepped back from each other several paces. Jaff looked more surefooted than Peyne had been hoping he would. The onlookers with torches formed a wide circle. Peyne spared a quick glance at Zayda and Maurizan.

Maurizan caught him looking and offered him an apologetic shrug.

Thanks a lot for bringing me here. If I get out of this alive, I expect a proper *apology.*

She was definitely a good-looking woman. Peyne admitted Zayda hadn't been completely off base about Peyne's overwillingness to trust her. *But, Dumo help me, she's not worth* dying *for.*

His eyes shifted to the Fyrian woman. Zayda's expression was a mix of alarm and anger. She was worried for his well-being, but if he got out of this alive, she would probably kill him.

"Begin!" Jaff lunged.

Peyne's attention was jerked back to the duel. The scimitar was usually more of a swiping weapon, but Jaff was fully extended, aiming a thrust at Peyne's midsection. Peyne sidestepped and tripped over his own feet.

Peyne had years of experience doing things while drunk. In fact, he considered himself a better swordsman with a few drinks in him, less tentative, not as anxious, the boost in confidence a slight compensation for his mediocre fencing skills. Most people tried to overcompensate for their sloppy moves when inebriated, attempting to bring an errant step or sword thrust back into line. That was wrong and almost never worked.

The key was to go with it.

Instead of trying to right himself, Peyne let himself fall.

Which saved him from Jaff's vicious backhanded swing with the scimitar. Jaff seemed to have momentarily forgotten the duel was to first blood. The blade whistled over Peyne's head. Jaff's judgment was off, and he swung too hard, stumbling after the swing. Peyne hit the ground and let his momentum take him into a roll, swinging randomly when he came out of it.

The wild swipe with the blade halted Jaff in midadvance. He had to jump back to prevent getting sliced across the shins, but he landed awkwardly and went down.

Both men were on hands and knees, trying to bring their swords to bear. A low muffled noise circled the crowd, and Peyne realized the men were laughing. *Good. Better than screaming for blood.*

Again, Peyne's instincts served him. He didn't bother trying to stand at all, but crawled forward as fast as he could, stabbing at Jaff's knees and shouting, "First blood! First blood!"

Jaff's men laughed openly now and loudly.

Jaff flushed red, infuriated.

"You mock me?" Spittle flew from Jaff's mouth as he shouted. He kept backing up to avoid Peyne's wild sword thrusts at his knees.

Peyne lunged forward, grabbed the man's left ankle as Jaff backpedaled. Peyne yanked hard.

Jaff's arms windmilled wildly, and he stumbled, hitting the ground hard. He spat a string of curses in Fyrian and struggled to rise. Peyne didn't let him, tossing his own sword aside and jumping on top of Jaff.

A war raged for control of Jaff's facial expression . . . anger, confusion, embarrassment. He tried to bring his scimitar to bear, but Peyne grabbed his wrists, leaned all his weight into holding the man down.

Peyne ducked his head toward Jaff's, and for a moment, Jaff looked horrified as if Peyne intended to kiss him.

But Peyne veered to the right.

And bit Jaff's earlobe.

Hard.

Jaff screamed, more rage than pain, thrashing and twisting and finally knocking Peyne back.

Peyne propped himself up on one elbow and spat on his hand. He held it up for all to see, blood and saliva dripping down his fingers. He grinned, teeth stained red.

"First blood."

Jaff staggered to his feet, face distorted with a sort of savage insanity. He raised his scimitar over his head, gripping it two-handed, and advanced on Peyne, murder in his eyes, an animal growl echoing off the walls of the ravine.

Jaff's men leapt on him, pulling him back, wrapping his arms to keep him from swinging his blade. Peyne hoped this meant he'd won the duel and Jaff's men were preventing him from committing some dishonorable breach of etiquette.

But Peyne worried he'd made a lifelong enemy. Humiliated and enraged, Jaff would clearly not be easily mollified.

It probably didn't help that Peyne couldn't stop laughing.

They hiked along the bottom of the ravine, Jaff's men both behind and ahead of them, lighting the way with torches. They'd taken the reins of Zayda's dromadan and had led the animal away . . . to be fed and watered, she hoped.

She glanced over her shoulder. Peyne's hands were tied in front of him, and one of Jaff's men led him by a rope. He wasn't laughing anymore.

Zayda hurried her pace to catch up with Jaff. The man was drinking water from a skin. One of his men had put some kind of powder in the water, concocting some brew to mitigate the effects of the wine. Jaff looked a bit haggard, but at least he was walking straight.

"Why did you tie him up?" Zayda asked. "He won the duel."

"I promised to spare his life," Jaff said. "Nothing else."

"You're being a sore loser," Zayda told him.

"He's impudent and crass," Jaff said. "He's lucky I don't drag him behind a dromadan. He made a mockery of an honorable duel."

"Peyne doesn't think like that," Zayda said. "He was just trying to find a way to save his own skin without anyone getting hurt. He's not your enemy."

"My ear *does* hurt, thank you very much. And I'll decide for myself who my enemies are."

"You're with the insurgents, aren't you?"

Jaff hesitated only a moment. "Yes."

"Then Peyne is on your side," Zayda said.

"No Helvan is on our side," Jaff told her. "We oppose the sultan and his blind ambition. But we are still Fyrian. We are patriots."

Maurizan moved up to walk on the other side of him. "If you don't need an ally, then at least think of your own reputation. Will you be gracious in loss, or do you prefer your men to think you petulant?"

He glowered, then ordered one of his men to bring Peyne forward. The man holding Peyne's rope dragged him up to walk next to Jaff and the two women.

Jaff abruptly drew his dagger. Peyne flinched.

Jaff cut through the bindings around Peyne's wrists, and the ropes fell away.

Peyne rubbed his wrists. "Thanks."

"Don't thank me. Thank your protectors." Jaff gestured to the women.

"Peyne, I've been trying to tell him we're on the same side." Zayda knew it wasn't quite true, but there was no need for them to be at odds either.

Peyne frowned. "Are we? Did you notice how these men are dressed? They're the same people who sank the *Pride of Klaar*. They killed your friend Kayman."

Something settled over Jaff, not the humiliated fury from before, but something deeper and more dangerous. "That's not true."

"Why should we believe you?" Peyne asked.

Jaff sighed and said, "Because Kayman was my brother."

CHAPTER
TWENTY

That explains why he looked familiar, Peyne thought.

Now that he knew the men were brothers, the resemblance was all too obvious. Light skinned, the same broad shoulders. Jaff had more hair, a thick black mass falling below his neck. Peyne had only momentarily known Kayman, but the younger brother Jaff seemed less brooding and sinister, proud and rash instead.

Peyne, Zayda, and Maurizan had been led deeper into the ravine until it opened into a canyon. They were taken up a zigzagging path on one side. The way up followed the natural contours of the ravine but had been worn smooth with much use.

They arrived at a series of caverns the insurgents used for their hideout, and Peyne and the two women were invited to sit around a cook fire where they were offered a bland stew and good black bread. They ate in silence for a while. Men moved in and out of the cave, attending to various tasks. There were bedrolls all along the walls. The place looked like it had been lived in for some time. Peyne spotted a few women, but they were wrapped in black like the men, scimitars hanging from wide leather belts.

Finally Peyne asked, "If the insurgents weren't who attacked our ship, then who was it?"

Jaff wiped his mouth with the back of his hand and set aside his empty bowl. "Prince Kha'narahn."

"That's hard to believe," Peyne said. "The prince's people were on board, traveling incognito."

"Believe it or don't. I won't lose any sleep over it."

"Please," Zayda said. "Help us understand."

When he spoke, he addressed the young ink mage. "My brother was a close advisor to the prince and deep in his counsel, but, like me, he opposed the war effort. The prince thought he was sending Kayman to flaunt a new weapon—you—under King Gant's nose. But my brother was really taking you to help the Helvans discover the secrets of ink magic. We thought if the sultan no longer had exclusive access to the magic, it might deflate his plans for conquest."

"Your brother never told me," Zayda said softly. "I wasn't fond of him, I must admit. I didn't know who he was. But I'm sorry for your loss."

Some of the hostility went out of him. "He couldn't risk telling anyone." Jaff cleared his throat, rubbed the back of his neck. "And, if I'm being honest, Kayman was never very pleasant. He always thought everyone else beneath him. Maybe that comes from being the eldest. I think my mother would want me to apologize for his behavior on behalf of the family." He smiled for the first time, straight white teeth making his face even more handsome.

Zayda blushed and turned away.

Peyne noticed. *Oh, I definitely do* not *like this fellow.*

Then Jaff's smile fell. "We suspected Kayman was lost when we'd heard about the *Pride of Klaar*. But to hear his death confirmed . . . well." He sighed again, shaking his head.

Zayda put a tentative hand on his shoulder. "I'm so sorry."

Peyne cleared his throat. "I still don't understand why the prince sent men to attack the ship. Nor why they were dressed as insurgents."

"One of our people was captured and questioned," Jaff said. "Not gently. The prince discovered that Kayman was a traitor, but he wasn't willing to attack a Helvan ship, not openly. Not yet anyway. There would be war, but on the sultan's schedule. So the prince's plan was to kill the traitor and blame it on the insurgents."

"You might not think of Helva as a possible ally, Jaff," Maurizan said.

"But obviously your brother thought differently if he was going to take Zayda to Merridan."

"My brother and I didn't agree on everything."

"You agreed you don't want war. Believe me, most people in Helva feel the same way." Maurizan stood, dusted off her backside. "I need some air. Zayda, walk with me?"

Zayda's head snapped up. "Oh, um, sure. Happy to." She rose and followed Maurizan out of the cave.

That left the two men sitting across from one another, staring into the fire.

Peyne cleared his throat again. "Sorry about your ear."

Jaff offered Peyne a withering look before his eyes shifted back to the fire.

Peyne wondered what the man might be thinking. *Probably dwelling on his lost brother. He'd held out hope Kayman might still be alive until we came along. Hardly our fault, but, still . . . the bearers of bad news and all that.*

The fire crackled and popped. The men sat quietly.

At last, Peyne said, "So what do you think of these ink mages?"

Jaff shot him an annoyed look. "I told you. If we can neutralize them as weapons, the sultan might rethink his war plans."

"No, I don't mean that," Peyne said. "I mean as people, putting them in collars and so on, making them slaves."

A noncommittal gesture from Jaff. "It is not uncommon when a family has debts. Accounts must be squared after all."

"It hardly seems fair," Peyne said. "That the daughters and sons should pay for the sins of the mothers and fathers."

"Perhaps. But that's not my concern for the moment. Averting a war is."

"It would be your concern if you had one of those collars around your neck," Peyne said.

Jaff frowned. "Do not insult my intelligence. Of course I would not find it agreeable."

"An understatement," Peyne said. "What is the likelihood ink slaves would fight for the sultan if they weren't wearing the collars?"

"Most wouldn't. Obviously."

"Then what would you say if I told you that just maybe"—Peyne paused for dramatic effect—"there was a way to get the collars *off.*"

A pause. Jaff's eyes slowly narrowed. "I'm listening."

The two mages stood at the mouth of the cavern, looking out into the darkness. Zayda hugged herself against a cold wind that washed through the canyon. The heat of the day had fled into the night, and not for the first time, Zayda lamented the loss of her cloak.

Maurizan smoked a chuma stick next to her. The smell of it was strange, bordering on sweet, off-putting at first but now oddly pleasant.

Zayda looked up. The moon had not yet shown itself.

"You know why I asked you out here," Maurizan said. Not a question.

"You want me to tell you."

"Yes."

So Zayda told her tale again, not hurrying, trying to be as detailed as possible, from Meddigar inking the Prime on her back all the way to the old woman in the jungle and the moon tattoo. Not quite a confession, but it felt good to tell the story, felt right to tell it to somebody who could understand completely, another ink mage.

Maurizan had been a good listener, interrupting only occasionally with a question to clarify some detail.

"I'm still learning what the tattoo does, how it works exactly," Zayda admitted.

"Let me know if something new happens," Maurizan told her. "Each tattoo is different, but in some ways they're all the same."

"I will." Zayda hated to admit it, but she was beginning to like the gypsy woman. Maybe it was some sort of ink mage camaraderie. *Sisters*, the old woman had said.

"My turn. I'll start with the obvious." Maurizan gestured to the feather tattoos near her eyes. "These tattoos have been handed down from mother to daughter for five generations. They bond me to my familiar, a great mountain eagle from the north. His name is Xarran."

Zayda nodded. "Peyne told me he thought he'd spotted a huge bird following us. That's how you knew we weren't being pursued through the desert."

"Xarran can see for miles and miles," Maurizan said. "He's been guarding us the whole time. I can see through his eyes, feel what he feels."

"That was your first tattoo? After the Prime, I mean."

"No." Maurizan tugged aside her shirt collar, and Zayda leaned in to look.

Three parallel lines slashing down the side of her neck.

"What do those look like?" Maurizan asked.

"I don't know." Zayda squinted at the tattoo. "Wait. Like a fish?"

Maurizan nodded. "Gills." She explained how the tattoo allowed her to swim fast and breathe underwater. "What I went through to get this tattoo, you wouldn't believe."

Incredible, Zayda thought. *Unbelievable.* But then she remembered what the moon tattoo allowed her to do. Not so unbelievable really.

"I found this other one in the same place." Maurizan looked around until she found a large flat rock and sat on it, turning toward the fire-light coming from the cavern. She bent, tugging off each of her high boots with a grunt.

She stretched her legs, feet out to show Zayda, toes pointed.

Zayda's first thoughts were unkind. Maurizan's feet were dry, heels calloused from constant travel. Zayda had always been vain about her feet, slender and unmarred with dainty toes. In her old life, her nightly routine had included rubbing them with various lotions and painting the nails to match the next day's outfit. She thought with embarrass-ment how dirty they must look now from her trek across the desert, sand gritty in her sandals.

Stop it. That's not what's important right now.

She focused on the tattoos on the top of Maurizan's feet. Zayda blinked, not sure if she were seeing correctly, but when she looked again it was the same. The tattoos moved, like smoke slowly swirling. When Maurizan shifted her feet, the tattoos caught the firelight differ-ently. The swirling smoke congealed into the shape of a hooded figure, crouched as if sneaking. Maurizan shifted her feet back, and the figure dissolved into smoke again.

"The tattoo is called the Phantom Walker," Maurizan said.

Zayda watched the swirling smoke, wide-eyed. "What does it do?"

"Are we interrupting something?"

The women turned to see Peyne and Jaff approaching.

"We'll finish this later," Maurizan said from the corner of her mouth as she pulled on her boots.

"I was perhaps hasty in dismissing Peyne as a possible ally," Jaff said.

Maurizan froze in the middle of pulling on her second boot, eyes narrowing with suspicion. "Oh?"

"A few of my men and I will escort you," Jaff said.

"Jaff pointed out that we were two foreigners and a runaway slave," Peyne said. "Not the best formula for navigating our way across Fyria, especially if we're trying *not* to draw attention to ourselves."

"And just where does he think he's escorting us to?" Zayda asked.

"To the Last Village," Jaff said. "Obviously."

CHAPTER
TWENTY-ONE

The name of the village—its *proper* name—had been lost to the centuries.

Everyone called it the Last Village for this simple reason: it was, in fact, the *last* village. The final outpost of civilization in Fyria before one reached the deep desert, a place to outfit, purchase food and water and gear, a chance to rest and perhaps even reflect and reconsider the folly of continuing south. The desert on the way to the Last Village was barren and treacherous and unforgiving.

The desert *beyond* the Last Village was death.

And yet the thought of continuing south had Venny positively giddy. She swayed in the saddle to the steady gate of the dromadan as the village sprung from the desert sand through the blur of heat in front of her.

Venny shared her saddle with the wizard's apprentice Nila. The woman was untalkative and unfriendly, and sharing the dromadan with her had made the nine-day trek across the dunes seem even longer.

Two more dromadan plodded ahead of her, one with the ink mage Hak in the saddle, the other carrying Meddigar. Of the six other dromadan trailing behind her, one carried the two female ink mages. Their names were Pinni and Priya, and they'd been introduced to Venny as sisters, chubby cheeked, cute rather than pretty, hair in tight braids. Venny knew very little about ink mages, but she was curious.

The rest of the dromadan carried a squad of soldiers led by a thick-necked, barrel-chested sergeant with a huge black beard. Venny was tempted to call their caravan a little army except she knew even *more* men and supplies would be following in a day or two.

But the wizard was eager to get to the Last Village in a hurry. Something about intercepting that red-haired woman Father had done some business with. It didn't interest Venny. She kept her eyes on the landscape, alert to any changes that might need to be updated on the current maps. Much of father's business consisted of selling maps of common caravan routes to traders who insisted on having the most up-to-date information possible.

But there was nothing new here. Venny's work would come later.

In the deep desert.

She adjusted her wide-brimmed hat against the late afternoon sun in her eyes and sighed, patiently waiting as the dromadan trudged toward the Last Village.

◆　◆　◆

"It's not what I expected."

"What *did* you expect?" Zayda slid down the back of the dromadan and dismounted using the little rope ladder.

"I don't know." Peyne hung his hat on the saddle horn, then followed her down. He stood in the middle of the hard-pack dirt street, hands on hips, surveying the village. "I'd assumed something called *the Last Village* would appear more . . . ominous."

It didn't look ominous at all. In fact, Peyne thought, the place looked boring. People seemed to be going about their business the same as in any other village. Frankly it didn't even seem like a village, more like something that was on the verge of becoming a small town.

The Last *Town* didn't have the same ring to it, Peyne supposed.

All of the buildings were made with the same brown stone and generally stood but a single story. As one neared the center of the village, a few of the buildings stretched to a second floor. It could have been any large village anywhere in Fyria.

The difference being that only sand and legend waited if one continued south.

Maurizan, Jaff, and three of his men joined Peyne and Zayda in the street. The insurgents had traded their black garb for ordinary clothing.

"My men will take the dromadan to be fed and watered," Jaff said. "I'm going to seek out someone here, a friend of the insurgency who acts as our eyes and ears. You'll understand if this person is a bit shy, so I'll need to go alone. If you need to supplement our supplies before we leave, now is a good time."

Jaff nodded to the group, then left. His men led away the dromadan.

"Any word from our spy in the sky?" Peyne asked Maurizan.

There had been plenty of time to talk during the journey to the last village, and with wonder, Zayda had related the tale of Maurizan's tattoos and all they could do. To Peyne, it just sounded like more unbelievable stories in a long line of unbelievable stories.

And yet he knew better than to disbelieve. He'd seen too much.

Maurizan closed her eyes for a moment, opened them again. "No doubt they're coming this way. A company of soldiers and a long supply column of dromadan."

"Still three days back?"

"Maybe more," she said. "Something bogged them down. Maybe a storm."

"Then we'll be long gone by the time they get here," Peyne said. "We should probably take Jaff's advice. Anyone need to do any shopping?"

"I'd like a cloak," Zayda said. "It gets cold when the sun goes down. There're a few other little things we need too. I can handle it. Unless either of you speaks fluent Fyrian."

"I do," Maurizan said. "But I don't look Fyrian. You'd have better luck."

Zayda looked at Peyne.

"Don't be ridiculous," he said.

Zayda grinned. "Where should I meet you?"

"We'll need a place to sleep," Peyne said. "I don't suppose there's a decent inn around here."

"Three actually," Maurizan said.

One of Peyne's eyebrows arched. "Oh? I wouldn't have thought there was enough traffic to support even one."

"As you might guess, the north-south traffic is notoriously one way," Maurizan said. "But there's a reasonably busy east-west trade route that passes through also. It crosses Fyria from one coast to the other."

"Suggestions?"

"The Dirty Djinn is the best place in spite of its name," Maurizan said. "If it's full, and it often is, I'd try the Sultan's Whore."

Peyne perked up at the name of the inn. Zayda frowned.

"Also not as bad as the name might suggest," Maurizan added.

"It's settled then," Peyne said and turned to Zayda. "Do your shopping, then meet us in one of those two places. We'll see about rooms for all of us and maybe a hot meal for later."

Zayda wagged a finger at him. "Behave yourself?"

"I'm not going to dignify that with a reply."

The local merchants marked her instantly as from some big city. As a result, prices went up.

I might as well be some foreigner like Peyne as far as these people are concerned, Zayda thought. She'd had to haggle extra hard, even walking out of one shop, but at last settled on a dark-green cloak with a twisting vine pattern along the hem and cuffs. The garment would be warm at night, but not too heavy. The price had seemed good to her, which probably meant by local standards, she'd been skinned.

She visited two other shops and perhaps spent a bit more than she'd intended, but the items she purchased were likely in short supply in this remote location.

Also, she was embarrassed.

The perfume and the nail polish and the scented soap were hardly the supplies she'd implied to Peyne and Maurizan she needed for the deep desert. The items were indulgent and under the circumstances, ridiculous. But with a new hope for freedom blooming within her, she'd found herself longing for the simple pleasures of her former life. She'd been long traveling, sleeping often on the ground, sand in every crevice.

Damn it, she wanted to feel good again, clean again, to smell nice.

And damn it, she was pretty.

It wasn't fair that Peyne should only see her dirty and bedraggled and travel worn.

The thought startled her.

Oh, who am I kidding? Of course I like him.

Which was beyond stupid. The man was a womanizer and a drunk and . . . and he just thought he was so witty. And father would *never* approve.

Isn't that half the attraction?

Ugh. Shut up, she told herself. *It's okay just to want to smell nice. I don't have to impress anyone.*

Zayda asked directions before leaving the shop. Peyne said he and Maurizan would try the Dirty Djinn first, so that's where she'd go. She thanked the merchant and headed out into the street and the glare of the late afternoon sun.

Meddigar sat on the veranda of the squalid café, sipping a mug of the strong local tea while he studied his spell book. He had sought the café specifically to escape the others. Hak was insufferably arrogant, and any day now he would murder his apprentice.

They'd been waiting and watching for Maurizan for two days, and everyone had become restless. Soon the rest of the troops would arrive—he *hoped* soon—and the wizard would be forced to make a decision. His attention returned to the spell book. Certain protective spells he renewed every day. One could never be too careful. The other spells he elected to memorize depended on his current circumstances.

This was one of the few times the wizard envied the ink mages. An ink mage's spells were inked directly into their skin, no tedious daily studying of complex spells from a book. Meddigar's magic had been hard earned from years of study. He'd been collecting spells for nearly three decades, and there were thirty-six now, each printed in Meddigar's precise lettering in one of the three ancient languages of magic.

But there were limits of course. An ink mage could empty her well of spirit. For more conventional wizards, there was a limit to how many spells the mind could hold. Meddigar could memorize nine. He'd once tried to hold ten in his mind, and it had nearly driven him mad. Spells were like living things, writhing and clamoring to get out. A mind had to be disciplined to hold them.

The great wizards of bygone days were allegedly able to hold twenty spells or more. Most of Meddigar's contemporaries could hold maybe five or six, so by comparison, Meddigar was above average.

Still, to choose nine from thirty-six. Meddigar selected his spells carefully, trying to anticipate his needs.

He looked up from the book, sipping tea, and saw her come out of the shop. Meddigar wasn't sure why she caught his attention, but she did.

He watched her. Trying to remember. He was *certain* he knew her.

Meddigar glanced at the sign above the shop door. His Fyrian was getting better but . . . *women's sundries*? Was he translating that right?

He wasn't sure what that meant . . . maybe didn't want to know.

Her head turned as she crossed the street, and something clicked in Meddigar's memory.

I've inked her. What was her name? Zeena? Zureen?

Zayda.

A scarf concealed the collar around her neck. Something was going on here, and Meddigar didn't believe in coincidences. He tossed a couple of coppers on the table and rose to follow her.

As they headed for the center of the village, Meddigar's hand slipped into one of the pockets of his robes, closing around something cold and metal. If Zayda had some secret to share, the wizard would know soon enough.

Maurizan and Peyne approached the Dirty Djinn, one of the two-story establishments in town, steps leading up to a wide double-doored entrance, fat columns on either side. Maurizan entered, Peyne right behind her. They paused just inside the doorway, letting their eyes adjust to the dim lighting as they slowly scanned the interior.

"Looks like a friendly place," Peyne said. "If they have any of that spiced beer—"

"Back out slowly," Maurizan whispered from the side of her mouth. "Don't make a scene."

"We've only just arrived," Peyne said. "I haven't had a chance to make a scene."

She hooked her arm into his as if they were a couple and smiled brightly.

Peyne smiled too.

She casually steered him back around toward the exit, still smiling, and softly said, "Did you happen to see the soldiers at the far table?"

In fact, Peyne had noticed the maid behind the bar with the alarmingly low-cut blouse but said, "I hadn't actually."

"I don't recognize the livery, but they're definitely not the village watch," she said. "Until I know why they're here, I think I'd feel comfortable someplace else."

"As much as I'd been looking forward to quenching my thirst with a tankard of the local brew, I'm forced to agree," Peyne said. "What was the other place called? The something something whore?"

Maurizan rolled her eyes. "Of course that's the part you remember."

Once outside, they turned left down the wide main avenue before Maurizan led him down a narrow alley toward the Sultan's Whore. Maurizan still held on to him, continuing the illusion of them as a couple, just a lord and his lady taking a stroll. Nothing to see here.

The common room of the Sultan's Whore was every bit as dim as the Djinn's. The place was also free of soldiers, and Peyne took note that the barmaid was every bit as attractive as the last one, so no damage done to his morale.

"Grab us a table," Maurizan said. "I'll see about rooms."

Plenty of tables were open, so Peyne took one near a window, thinking it might be handy to see trouble coming should there happen to be any.

He looked around.

There was something odd about the place. Not *bad*. Just . . . odd.

Most of the patrons were women, sitting in twos and threes at scattered tables. All of them were suspiciously attractive. Not that Peyne was surprised at the attractiveness of each individual lady, rather that so many beautiful women would be gathered in the same place. It had long been Peyne's opinion that truly attractive people represented a relatively small percentage of the population, and the odds seemed long that so many would randomly gather in one location.

A man entered, older, well dressed like some prominent merchant.

Three of the woman moved immediately to greet him, tickling him under his thin, white beard and leading him to his table. The way he bantered with the women made Peyne think the man was a regular.

Maurizan returned, took a seat across from him. "They remember me here, so I got a good rate on the rooms."

"This"—Peyne looked around the room again to confirm what he was seeing—"is a brothel."

"I was hoping you wouldn't notice."

"You frequent this place?"

"I did say it was second choice," Maurizan said.

"But . . . wait. Are you a . . . one of those . . . ?"

Maurizan's eyes narrowed. "I like men."

"Not that I would have a problem with that," Peyne said hurriedly. "Some of my best friends are—"

"You need to stop talking."

Peyne stopped.

"Because of the women, they have good security at this place in case a patron gets out of hand," Maurizan said. "And the rooms are clean and comfortable. You don't need to partake of the entertainment to rent a room."

"Are you sure?" Peyne asked. "If there's some requirement, I don't mind—"

"Talking again."

"Sorry."

"There's the third inn obviously," Maurizan explained, "but it's squalid. Maybe a good choice if you're trying to squeeze every copper, but frankly, if we're about to head into the deep desert, then this will be our last chance for a soft bed and a decent meal for the foreseeable future."

Peyne pointed to his own mouth.

"You may speak," Maurizan said.

"Your reasoning is unassailable," Peyne told her. "Perhaps when Jaff returns from consulting with his local contact, he can shed some light on who these soldiers are in the Djinn."

"Let's hope so. I'll feel better knowing if we need to worry about them or not."

"And since we seem to have accomplished our mission to secure rooms for the night, there's nothing left to do but relax and wait for our friends to return from their various tasks," Peyne said. "I suggest we order a pitcher of—"

One of the gorgeous women arrived at that exact moment, setting a tray on the table with a pitcher and two goblets. She winked at Peyne. "The good wine up from the cellar." She offered him a lingering look as she left.

"I'd already anticipated our needs," Maurizan said.

"If you're trying to win me over, it's working." Peyne took the pitcher and filled both goblets.

He lifted his, cleared his throat. "To a successful and hopefully death-free trek into the deep desert. May the divine gods bless us with shade, water, and—"

"Stuff the flowery talk." Maurizan grabbed her own goblet. "Let's get drunk."

Zayda was pleased to see that the Dirty Djinn was, in fact, a clean and well-kept inn and apparently popular since the common room hummed with activity, full of laughing, the clink of tankards, serving maids slapping away hands too eager to pinch and the ever-present aroma of something cooking in the back.

Peyne must love it here.

She felt a brief stab of anxiety as a table of soldiers paused to look at her. The big one with the huge black beard let his gaze linger an extra moment, but soon enough they turned their attentions back to their conversation and beer.

I hope they were just checking out my backside . . . and not my collar.

Her hand came up to touch the scarf hiding the collar around her neck. She hoped to eventually get rid of both. The collar for obvious reasons. The scarf because she usually never wore them. A boy had once told her she had a graceful neck.

She winced at her own vanity but didn't dwell on it.

Zayda glanced around the common room again, this time peering carefully into each dim corner, checking each face, but still not spotting Peyne. Maurizan had said the place was often full, which meant they might have moved on to the Sultan's Whore. Zayda frowned.

In spite of Maurizan's assurances, Zayda did *not* like that sound of the place, but she was feeling foolish standing in the middle of the Djinn's common room like a lost lamb.

She turned to go but was intercepted by a harried man in an apron.

"Please, madam." The man gestured to a closed door across the common room. "I was sent to fetch you. Your party awaits you inside."

A private room? Zayda thought Peyne would have preferred the rowdy clamor of the common room. Still, it was a relief. She wouldn't have to leave for the other inn after all.

She thanked the man, crossed the room to the door, and entered, smiling brightly, readying a greeting for Peyne.

When she saw the older man waiting for her, the smile fell. Recognition twisted her stomach with fear.

Zayda reached for the spirit and—

"Don't," Meddigar said sharply.

He held up one of the little scepters, and despair sank cold into her bones.

It was exactly like Zayda's control scepter but more ornate, jewels down the side. Slightly bigger maybe, although it was difficult to tell from where she was standing.

"Close the door," Meddigar told her.

She hesitated.

"You won't make it," Meddigar said. "And you won't be able to tap into the spirit fast enough either, not before I can activate the scepter, and you already know how unpleasant that can be."

Yes, she'd felt the sting of the control scepter before. But she still didn't close the door.

"I know what you're thinking," Meddigar said. "This isn't your scepter, and the scepters are specific to each collar . . . just as a key is specific to a certain lock." He wiggled the scepter in his hand for emphasis. "I like to think of this as my skeleton key."

Let him blather. Zayda only half listened, calculating her escape. If she darted through the open door, how fast could she get out of range? If she tapped into the spirit—

The soldiers who sized her up earlier were moving toward the open door. In a few short seconds, they'd block her path. Panic welled up and threatened to choke her.

"I'm not sure what brings you all the way to the Last Village without your handler," Meddigar said. "But I think it behooves me to ask a few pertinent questions while—"

Zayda ran for the door, reaching for the spirit.

Pain lanced through every inch of her like lightning, hair standing on end, eyes bulging, teeth rattling. The world spun for a split second before something hit her hard in the face. She realized it was the floor. Drool dribbled from her mouth. She tried to wipe it away, but her arm refused to move. Everything went cottony around her vision, darkness coming, and then . . .

"You men stand guard outside," Meddigar ordered. "Sergeant, close the door and help me with her."

The sergeant with the huge beard stepped in and closed the door behind him.

"I'd rather hoped she'd come quietly," Meddigar said. "I don't suppose we can carry a limp woman through the Djinn's common room without questions."

"I'll take her." The big sergeant grinned. "Let them ask *me* their questions."

Yes, he is a formidable fellow, Meddigar thought. *I certainly wouldn't presume to stick my nose in his business.*

"What's your name, sergeant?"

"Klamud." He thumped himself on the breastplate in case there was any doubt who he was talking about.

"Pick her up, Klamud, and bring her to my room. If anyone asks, we'll say she took ill. And send your men into the rest of the village," Meddigar said. "We need to know if anyone has seen the gypsy."

Klamud picked up the girl and tossed her over her shoulder as if she were a sack of feathers.

"And send somebody to find Hak and those two sisters," Meddigar told the sergeant. "I have a feeling things are about to heat up."

Jaff entered the Djinn's common room, trying not to show in his expression the nervousness he felt in his gut. His contact in the Last Village was an old woman, a widow, who had inherited her husband's tannery. Her two sons worked it. She managed the operation and kept the sons fed.

And she had no love for the sultan, which was why she fed information to the insurgents.

To Jaff she'd related the following. Soldiers were in town, men who belonged to Prince Kha'narahn. They'd come to the Last Village as a prelude to striking south into the deep desert. But they were also waiting for someone.

Someone named Maurizan.

Jaff scanned the common room but didn't see her or the other foreigner, Peyne.

Maurizan was not a stupid woman, Jaff assured himself. Even if she didn't recognize that the men belonged to the prince, she would likely want to get rooms elsewhere to avoid possible entanglements.

Jaff decided to leave. He'd try the Sultan's Whore and then . . .

He blinked.

One of the soldiers carried a woman over his shoulder as he passed through the common room, drawing stares from the other patrons. Everyone was obviously curious, but the big soldier's glare discouraged casual inquiries. Perhaps the woman had simply drank too much or—

Gods and fate be damned, that's Zayda. He realized he was gawking and stopped himself.

The big, bearded soldier carried Zayda upstairs. An older, dour-looking man in robes followed them. Jaff's contact had mentioned a wizard. Could there be any doubt whom he was looking at?

He turned and left. He needed to find the others. This was bad.

Very, very bad.

◆ ◆ ◆

They'd emptied the pitcher, and Maurizan waved to one of the girls to bring another.

The common room was beginning to fill, a mix of locals and travelers, a few coming just to drink but mostly men looking for attractive companionship. The place hummed with pleasant conversation, but nobody was rowdy or out of hand. Peyne thought it a very civilized brothel.

The new pitcher arrived, and Peyne filled both goblets. He sipped. He had that pleasant floating feeling, that *just right* feeling when he'd had just the exact right amount of wine. As he went along, the floating would gradually feel like falling, but that was something to worry about later.

"You know, I've had a bit of experience with older women lately," he said.

Maurizan leaned forward, resting her chin in her hand. "Oh, I can't *wait* to hear this."

"I'm just saying we have a free afternoon and comfortable rooms available upstairs."

Maurizan laughed, rolling her eyes. She sipped wine, then said, "I used to know a man just like you. Well, I still know him, but he's married now and more mature. He used to think he was *so* witty and charming. Back when he was your age."

"Are you implying I'm *not* witty and charming? That's hurtful."

A half shrug. "You are. Not as much as my friend used to be, but you have your moments."

"And who is this paragon of charm?" Peyne asked. "Tell me that I might seek him out and study his ways."

"The Duke of Klaar."

It was Peyne's turn to roll his eyes. "*You* know Brasley Hammish? Pull the other one. You gypsy women run in loftier circles than I'd been led to believe."

"He wasn't duke at the time," Maurizan said. "And the point I'm trying to make is that he was an indolent, womanizing drunk like some people I know—*ahem*—but now he's married to a good woman and much happier."

"I feel like I'm supposed to be taking some kind of hint."

She leaned forward more intimately, a mischievous grin tugging at the corners of her mouth. "You're telling me there's nothing between you and Zayda? I know what it means to be possessive, and I've seen it in her eyes."

Peyne opened his mouth to object but instead heard himself say, "We've been through a lot together."

"Without a doubt."

A long moment. Maurizan waited him out.

"She has that damn collar around her neck," Peyne said. "How can I ask anything of her or put anything on her? Would she even feel free? Could she even reciprocate?" He started to sip wine, but it turned into a gulp. "You need to be free in order to give yourself to someone. And I don't even know how she feels. Not really. I don't know anything. I don't know what I could promise her, and she doesn't need that right now." He emptied the goblet.

Maurizan sat back, looked him in the eyes for a moment before a slow, easy smile spread across her face. "There's more to you than meets the eye, Peyne Erlich. I think you have the makings of a decent grown-up."

"Sounds like a lot of bother."

"When I was a girl, I loved a boy," Maurizan said. "I'd fought hard for him, thought I'd earned him, and so he was mine. But we didn't have long together. Don't be so polite you miss your chance."

She pulled a chuma stick from a pocket, leaned toward the candle on the table, puffed it until the tip glowed. Peyne watched her. She inhaled, held it, then let out a long stream of blue-gray smoke.

"So I guess we're not going up to the room." Peyne smiled weakly, not meaning it anymore, never *really* meaning it if he were being honest with himself.

"We most certainly are not." She returned the smile. "But you are a *little* witty and charming. If that makes you feel better."

"You know, it does actually."

They held up their goblets, offering each other a friendly nod, then drank.

"It occurs to me," Peyne said, "that we've finished two pitchers of wine."

"You're suddenly concerned with moderation?"

"I mean we've been here *long enough* to drink two pitchers," Peyne said. "Where's everyone else?"

"That's not a bad question." She turned her head, glancing about the place. "Damn."

"What is it?"

"Look at the front door," she said. "Don't be obvious."

Peyne brought his goblet up to his mouth, let his eyes slide to the front door.

"What do you see?"

"Two soldiers," Peyne said.

"What are they doing?"

"Looking this way."

"Shit."

Meddigar pulled the simple wooden chair up close to the bed where he'd tied Zayda. The girl had hovered in and out of consciousness. His ministrations with the control scepter had kept her subdued. He adjusted the dial just below the scepter's sphere, and Zayda arched her back, a loud moan escaping her lips.

Damn, too much. He dialed it back, and she relaxed.

There hadn't been many opportunities for Meddigar to practice, but through trial and error, he'd managed to put Zayda into a sort of daze, not conscious enough to resist, yet just awake enough to answer simple questions. Some instinct had motivated him to ask her about Maurizan, and, indeed, the women were traveling together and might be found at the Sultan's Whore. He'd tried to ask more, but the girl had swooned.

Behind him, Klamud cracked his knuckles. "Let me question her the old-fashioned way."

Meddigar sighed. "Don't be foolish. She'd tap into the spirit and simply tell herself not to feel whatever you were doing to her."

A snort. "When Klamud hurts somebody, they feel it."

Idiot.

A knock at the door.

"Check it," the wizard told him.

Klamud opened the door a crack and stuck his head out. Meddigar heard a low back-and-forth muttering, and then Klamud came back inside and shut the door again.

"It's just as she told you," the big sergeant said. "The red-haired woman is at the Sultan's Whore."

"Alone?"

"With some man."

"Just one?"

"That's all they saw," Klamud said.

"Good." Meddigar tugged at his beard, thinking.

"You want me to round up the men, go get them?" Klamud asked.

"She'd kill you."

The look on Klamud's face indicated he seriously doubted that.

"She's an ink mage," the wizard said.

A flicker of uncertainty across Klamud's face, but he said, "Still just a woman."

Meddigar smiled tolerantly. *They are building them big and dumb these days, aren't they?*

Meddigar stood, bent over Zayda, examining her. No tattoos on the arms, nothing for strength. She'd been tied with strong rope and tight knots. Even if she woke up, she wasn't going anywhere.

Meddigar went to the window, threw open the shutters, and looked out across the village and into the desert beyond. He was in one of the two-story buildings, and the view was good, facing south toward the vast and perilous expanse of the deep desert. Night had fallen, and it was beginning to cool.

Klamud shuffled impatiently behind him. "Orders, my lord?"

"Go to Maurizan," Meddigar said. "Tell her I'd like to propose a trade."

◆ ◆ ◆

"Have they come back?" Maurizan asked.

Peyne glanced at the doorway again. "No."

The soldiers had looked straight at Maurizan and Peyne, looked at each other, and then left. Twenty minutes had crept by, but the soldiers hadn't returned. Maybe they wouldn't.

Peyne tried to feel optimistic about that and failed.

"It's possible they were just checking the place out," Peyne said. "They're soldiers after all. And this is a brothel."

"You don't believe that for a minute," Maurizan said.

"I do not."

"Want to get the fuck out of here?"

"I'm right behind you."

Maurizan stood, took one step away from the table, and nearly fell over. Peyne hurried to catch her, preventing an awkward crash to the floor. One of his arms went around her waist. He took one of her arms and draped it around his shoulders.

"I'll guide you," he said.

"How in blazes can you hold so much wine?" Maurizan slurred.

"Years of practice."

"Out the back."

Peyne guided her at first, but she gently pushed him away.

"I can walk," she said. "Just standing up went a little funny. Jump in and catch me if I head for the floor."

The back door led into the kitchen. A harried cook started to tell them they couldn't be in there, but Maurizan calmly assured him it was all fine. He shrugged and went back to his cook stove.

She grabbed an earthen pitcher from a counter as she passed through, sniffed it. "Water. Hold this." She passed the jug to Peyne.

The next door took them to a narrow alley. It was dark, but light from windows across the alley lit the scene well enough. Maurizan leaned over, braced herself with a hand against the wall.

"Uh . . . are you okay?" Peyne asked.

"I will be in a minute."

Peyne watched her, concerned. She'd assumed classic vomit posture, but he hadn't thought her that far gone.

Maurizan's face went calm and blank, the same way Zayda's did when she was about to use one of her powers. Peyne continued to watch, fascinated. The gypsy took in a deep breath, held it a moment, then let it out slowly. One at a time, each of her limbs went stiff then loose again.

Then her back humped up, shoulders hunching, a series of little grunts coming out of her. Peyne took a step back. Maurizan's mouth opened wide, and she vomited acrid liquid against the wall.

The smell hit him, and he winced.

Maurizan stayed like that a moment, spitting a few times. Then she stood, held out her hand. "Give me the water."

Peyne gave her the jug.

She rinsed her mouth and spit. She drank again and swallowed.

"Well, that was appalling," Peyne said.

"You'll get over it."

"You did that on purpose?"

"I drew the wine from everywhere in my body. Then I got rid of it," she explained. "Instant sobriety."

"I didn't know you could do that."

"Spend twenty years with the Prime down your back, and you learn a few tricks," Maurizan said. "Not pleasant, but it works."

"You." A new voice, gruff. "You're the one called Maurizan?"

They turned to see a trio of soldiers at the mouth of the alley, big men outlined in silhouette against the light from the street behind them.

"Who wants to know?" Maurizan asked.

Perfect, Peyne thought. *Antagonize the big men with swords.*

The spokesman for the trio ignored her question, instead saying, "You have a map from Auvor the cartographer, yes?"

Maurizan frowned. "I still don't know who I'm talking to. Give me a name or piss off."

"How about Zayda?" the soldier said. "That a name you recognize?"

Peyne felt his stomach clench.

A pause.

Then Maurizan said. "What about her?"

"She's safe. For now."

"Do you know what I am?" Maurizan asked.

"A woman with a map," the soldier said.

"Zayda stays safe or you don't," Maurizan said. "You understand me?"

"I'm terrified," he said flatly. "But frightening me won't do you any good. I'm just delivering a message. Bring the map to the Dirty Djinn common room in an hour. We'll trade your friend for it."

They turned to leave without waiting for an answer.

"We've got to get her back," Peyne said hurriedly.

"Calm down. I know. We will."

Peyne took a deep breath, forced the panic he felt down to some acceptable level. "Those were lap dogs obviously. I wish we knew who they worked for."

"Meddigar."

They turned to see Jaff standing there in the doorway.

"You were listening?" Peyne asked.

223

"I thought it best not to show myself," Jaff said.

"Good." Peyne nodded, thinking. "If they haven't seen you, then that might help us. Maybe they don't know how many of us there are."

"We don't know how many *they* are," Maurizan pointed out.

"A dozen give or take," Jaff said. "According to my contact. And there's more bad news. This Meddigar is—"

"A wizard. I know," Maurizan said.

Jaff frowned. "That's disappointing. I wanted to say it."

"Wait," Peyne said. "You know him?"

"He's double-crossed me before," Maurizan told them. "I don't trust him."

"Then we need a plan," Peyne said. "And we have an hour."

"Right." Maurizan fished a chuma stick from the pocket of her cloak. "Step one. Find me a light."

CHAPTER
TWENTY-TWO

Maurizan stood in the street, looking at the front door of the Dirty Djinn. The hour was almost up, but she intended to wait until the last second to make sure everyone had time to get into position. Jaff had told them he'd seen an unconscious Zayda being carried to the second floor of the inn. If she'd been moved, this might all be for nothing.

She tucked the rolled up parchment under her arm. It was tied with a bit of twine. If Meddigar wanted a map, then he'd get a map. He'd want to examine it, of course, before giving up Zayda. Maurizan was counting on it.

She took a deep breath, felt foolish to be nervous. She was an ink mage and had survived perils many wouldn't believe.

But there was a wizard inside the inn, and she'd never known a wizard that didn't have some trick up his sleeve. *He can die on the end of a dagger like anyone else. If I can get close enough.*

Big *if.*

She let out the breath and tapped into the spirit. Maurizan entered the inn and . . .

. . . the world slowed.

Her eyes took in everything. Tapped into the spirit, no detail escaped her. Five men at a table in the corner. Four of the soldiers and another man she'd never seen, chubby red cheeks, a patchy dishwater beard and greasy hair to match. His eyes landed on Maurizan as if he'd been expecting her.

Other patrons sat at tables here and there. Not many, but not few enough. She hoped they wouldn't get in the way.

Her eyes darted to a group of men three tables from the fellow with the patchy beard. Three of Jaff's men sat there, making a point not to look as Maurizan entered, chatting and drinking beer as if they were ordinary patrons. They'd been instructed to stay out of her way unless things went bad. One never knew when a few extra sword blades might come in handy. Jaff was elsewhere, making ready for a fast departure.

A trio sat a table away in the other direction, a man and two women in cloaks, hoods up. There was something in their postures Maurizan didn't like.

No more stalling. Get on with it.

Maurizan stuck a chuma stick in her mouth and approached the nearest table. She gestured to the candle there. "May I?"

A glassy-eyed man looked up from his tankard of beer. "Have it." He handed her the candle.

She lit the chuma stick, puffed smoke, and set the candle back on the table. "Thanks."

Maurizan narrowed her eyes, shifted the chuma stick from one corner of her mouth to the other, puffing.

Let's do this.

◆ ◆ ◆

Peyne wished he could puke himself sober as Maurizan had.

Fortunately, the wine hadn't affected him as severely as it had the gypsy woman.

Still, he would have preferred to be completely sober while scaling the back wall of the Dirty Djinn.

A slanted roof overhung the outdoor kitchen, and an empty barrel had provided a boost. He pulled himself up on a dusty ledge, grunting and panting, slinging his leg up, his foot almost losing purchase and sending him flailing back to the ground again. But he reached the window ledge and heaved himself up and through.

And landed on the other side in an awkward heap, stifling another grunt.

Peyne gathered himself, stood, took a look around. He was at the end of a long hall, doors on either side. The inn's guest rooms. His job was to locate where they'd stashed Zayda, but it was only just occurring to him that he had absolutely no plan. Running up and down the hallway, knocking on random doors, seemed like the perfect way to call unwanted attention to himself while simultaneously failing to locate Zayda.

He cocked his head, held his breath, and listened.

The low murmur of conversation.

He snuck down the hall toward the conversation but tried not to *look* like he was sneaking.

Fool. Just go. You're not doing anything wrong. At least not yet.

Peyne walked down the hall, acting like he belonged there, until he found himself at a railing that circled the interior of the second floor. From here, he could look down into the first-floor common room. Maurizan approached a table where some of the soldiers he'd seen earlier were sitting.

Damn. It's about to happen, and I haven't found Zayda. I should have climbed faster.

A heavy hand grabbed his shoulder and spun him around.

Peyne gulped, looked up at an enormous soldier with a huge black beard. The man scowled and muttered something in Fyrian that had a definite hostile tone.

Peyne smiled weakly. "Sorry, friend, I don't speak the local lingo."

The way the big man squeezed his shoulder made it all too clear that pain was a language in which all were fluent.

♦ ♦ ♦

The chill brought her around.

Zayda walked some narrow path between dreaming and wakefulness. Meddigar? She pictured him opening the shutters, looking out into the night. Was that a memory? She thought so. Then all was darkness, and when she came around again, the room was empty. The window was still open, letting in the cool night air, but the wizard had gone.

She tried to sit up, but something tugged at her wrists. She tapped into the spirit, took stock of her situation. Flat on her back in a narrow bed. Tied with thin rope around her wrists and ankles. She tugged as hard as she could but realized she was only making the knots tighter. She tried to contort her hands, reach the knots with her fingers.

Impossible.

Frustration rose up in her, and she thrashed on the bed.

Then she stopped herself, mastered her emotions. The spirit gave her perfect calm. There was a way out of this. There had to be.

Zayda glanced at the open window again. Night. How long had she been here? If she could only free herself from the ropes, she could climb out the window and away.

Think, girl. You're not stupid.

A faint glow in the corner of her eye caught her attention. She turned her head again to face the window.

Slowly, the moon began to rise.

Maurizan approached, stopped at the edge of the table. She puffed her chuma stick and scowled at the man with the patchy beard. She waited. Let him talk first.

His eyes shifted to the rolled up parchment under her arm. "That's the map?"

Maurizan eyes narrowed as she examined the man. "Nice try, Meddigar."

Patchy Beard froze, then he slowly grinned. "I should have known I couldn't fool you. It was the voice, wasn't it?"

"Yes."

"This glamour spell is cheap," Meddigar said. "It only changes my appearance. Tried to disguise the voice myself." He muttered a quick, unintelligible syllable, and the air around his head shimmered, features contorting, the patchy beard face blurring and reshaping into Meddigar.

"Not much of an improvement," Maurizan said.

"Can't blame me for trying," Meddigar said. "We didn't part on good terms last time, and I thought posing as a stranger might facilitate things."

"If you want to stay on good terms with people, then don't double-cross them," Maurizan said.

"I'll store that bit of advice away for another time," Meddigar told her. "In the meantime, I believe we have some business to transact."

"Then let's get on with it. Where's Zayda?"

"Safely tucked away."

"I want to see her."

"Give me the map and you will," Meddigar said.

"I don't think so."

"This doesn't need to be difficult," Meddigar said. "But it can be if you insist."

She glanced at the men at the table with him. The soldiers seemed formidable enough, but they were still only men. Meddigar couldn't really think they'd be any trouble for her, although she shouldn't forget that Meddigar himself was a wizard. Maurizan could only guess what spells he might unleash.

"I need to know she's in the building at least."

"She is," Meddigar said. "Upstairs."

This confirmed what Jaff had told her. Peyne should already be up there. She hoped.

"But if I see you make any move toward the stairs, I'll make a signal, and she'll be dead in an instant," Meddigar told her. "Even tapped into the spirit you won't be quick enough to prevent it."

Maurizan looked him in the eye. He might have been bluffing.

She couldn't risk it.

She took the rolled up parchment from under her arm, reached across the table, and put it into the wizard's hand.

"You'll understand I need to look at this first," he said.

"Of course."

Meddigar set the parchment on the table in front of him, took the ends of the twine between thumbs and forefingers.

Maurizan tensed.

"Before I examine the map," Meddigar said. "A question."

Peyne could hear the voices rising behind him from the common room below, Maurizan and the man at the table.

But most of his focus was on the enormous brute who had hold of him. The language barrier remained a hindrance, but Peyne inferred the soldier was saying something along the lines of, *What are you doing sneaking around here where you don't belong, small fragile man with the easily breakable bones?*

The brute gestured emphatically to a closed door behind him, tone growing more threatening.

"Stay away from that door," Peyne said, nodding and smiling. "Understood. No problem."

So that's where Zayda is. Good. All I need to do is overpower this mountain, break in, and rescue her.

What could be easier?

"Listen, friend, I think there's been a misunderstanding." He kept smiling, tone genial. "Also, I bruise easily, so if you could just let go of that shoulder before—"

An explosion.

A blast of hot air lifted him, the world spinning. Ears ringing. Peyne landed hard.

The brute with the black beard landed on top of him.

That. Hurt.

◆ ◆ ◆

"Ask your question," Maurizan said.

"How did you happen to find yourself in the company of a runaway slave?" asked the wizard.

"She's not a slave. She's a person."

A wan smile from the wizard. "I understand. Truly. But you'll have to take *that* up with the sultan. I just do what I'm told."

"Yes," Maurizan said. "You're so innocent."

"Does she have a tattoo other than the Prime?" Meddigar asked. "It didn't occur to me to check her. Slaves seldom have the same freedom you do to travel the world, searching for ink magic."

"You're not going to check her because I've given you the map, and you're going to bring her to me," Maurizan said. "You're going to keep your bargain this time, Meddigar."

She watched him, knew he was thinking it over.

"Very well," he said. "Today's not the day to press my luck, I suppose."

He pulled the twine loose and unrolled the parchment, spreading it out on the table in front of him.

As soon as she saw the wizard frown, Maurizan leapt to one side, going to the floor, arms covering her head.

◆ ◆ ◆

Maurizan's interest in Zayda was almost certainly connected to a new tattoo. The ink might be something valuable.

It's a bad time to bite off more than I can chew, Meddigar thought. *Stick to the business at hand.* He sighed.

"Very well. Today's not the day to press my luck, I suppose."

He pulled the twine loose around the rolled parchment, spread the map out in front of him.

It wasn't a map.

Meddigar frowned. There was nothing on the parchment but a single word in the center of—

He twisted around, pushing away, just as the explosion shredded the table to splinters, a ball of fire bathing him in searing heat even through the shield of magic that crackled with bright purple light around him. It was a spell he always kept in place for just such surprises and the only thing that had saved him from the glyph.

Popo said she'd been to see the glyph maker. I should have guessed.

He shook his head, trying to clear the sound of bells, discovered he was on the floor amid dust and the debris of shattered furniture. He lifted his head, blinked. Smoke hung in the air. A five-foot square scorch mark blackened the floor where his table had been. The four soldiers who'd been with him lay charred and dead, bodies sprawling from the blast zone like wagon wheel spokes.

An arm lay smoldering, disconnected from its owner.

Get up. It's not over. Get up before she does.

Where were the others? He called out. Meddigar's voice sounded cottony and muffled in his own head. If anyone answered his call, he couldn't hear it. He pushed himself up to his knees, dusted off his robe.

A clatter and rustling drew his attention.

Maurizan crawled from beneath a layer of rubble, plaster and chair legs and broken crockery. She stood, drawing her daggers, face so calm that Meddigar knew she'd tapped into the spirit.

She came for him.

His head swam with spells. The wizard was still dazed from the explosion. Casting required perfect concentration, and Meddigar could barely keep his eyes from crossing. Maurizan lunged, and even with the dagger coming straight for his face, he couldn't help but notice how lithe and graceful she was, precise balance and control, the perfect marriage of a seasoned warrior and virtuoso dancer.

Even though he'd seen ink mages in action countless times, the movements were still a sight to behold.

A shame it will be the last thing I ever see, Meddigar thought.

Peyne pushed the brute off him, coughing and sore. He blinked dust and smoke from his eyes.

Where . . . am I?

He remembered. Effecting Zayda's rescue. He shook his head, staggered to his feet, legs like noodles. He paused to look at the wreckage of the common room below. Bodies and debris covered the floor haphazardly as if dropped there by some indifferent god.

No time for this. Get Zayda.

Peyne stepped over the brute, rushed to the door behind him, and flung it open.

Dark within, but Peyne heard Zayda gasp from her place in the narrow bed to the left. The room itself was small, two beds and an open window in between to let in the night air.

Some racket reached him from below, the telltale clamor of fighting and the clang of swordplay. He needed to hurry.

Peyne sat on the edge of Zayda's bed, took her by the shoulders. "Zayda, it's okay. It's me, Peyne. I've got you."

Zayda sat up abruptly, her face coming into the light that spilled in from the hall.

It wasn't Zayda.

"What you do? Who are you?" Pretty and young, passable Helvan with a heavy accent. "What you want in here?"

Peyne stood up immediately, backed away. "Ohhhhh, shit."

The young woman exhausted her Helvan, and a flood of angry Fyrian poured from her mouth.

"A mistake! Sorry!" Peyne said. "Uh, could you maybe quiet down a bit?"

Somebody was hitting him from behind. Peyne turned to look.

Another young Fyrian woman had risen from the other bed to beat him mercilessly with a straw hat, very similar to the one Peyne used to keep the sun off. Unlike the first woman who was clearly alarmed at the sight of a stranger in her room, this one seemed more angry, a bitter expression twisting her otherwise attractive features.

She spat words in Fyrian like daggers.

"Ladies, I assure you this is all a dreadful misunderstanding."

An earsplitting roar from the hall froze all three of them, the one woman pausing her assault, the hat held high ready for another strike.

Then the floorboards rattled. Thundering footfalls like the end of the world.

The brute filled the doorway, blood dripping from one ear down the side of his face, an expression of such mad animal rage that both women screamed, shrinking against opposite walls.

Their shrieks were drowned by another furious roar.

Peyne stood transfixed, eyes wide, stunned that this would be the way he'd die.

The brute leapt, slammed into Peyne, encircling him with arms like iron. Both men flew back.

And out the window.

♦ ♦ ♦

Zayda lay back and relaxed, took a deep breath, letting the moonlight slowly fill her. The moon wasn't quite full, but it had grown bigger than the thin crescent it had been when the old woman had first given her the tattoo in the jungle.

The moon tattoo pulsed beneath her skin, veins humming with the power that flowed through every inch of her body. She knew she could break the bonds now. The idea she could be held captive, that anyone could stop her seemed a feeble joke, but she forced herself to be patient.

Not yet. Soak it all in until you can't hold any more.

The room blazed with her glow, brighter almost than daylight. She felt invincible.

But there was more. She felt . . . giddy. A wild euphoria roiled within her, a feeling she never wanted to end.

Zayda tugged lightly with one arm, and the rope around her wrist snapped like a single strand of sewing thread. She untied the other one, sat up, and untied the ropes around her ankles. When she stood, she felt like she'd float away. She went to the window, feet barely touching the floor, and stood there, spreading her arms, letting the moonlight lift her above mere mortality.

Finish the wizard first, Maurizan thought.

And then the rest would be easy.

She drew her daggers, tapped into the spirit, and lunged, driving the tip of the dagger toward a spot between Meddigar's stunned eyes. The wizard blinked once, obviously still dazed from the explosion, not even trying to dodge.

A blur at the corner of her eye, a flash of steel, and the ring of metal on metal as Maurizan's thrust was parried. A girl, her cloak fanning behind her as she spun, bringing the scimitar around to strike.

Another ink mage!

Maurizan swept the scimitar aside with a dagger, already spinning to face the second woman she'd sensed coming up behind her, swinging her dagger, striking nothing but air.

She's an ink mage too. Where the blazes did they *come from?*

They came at her from two sides. Thrust. Block. Spin. Duck. Parry. The clang of blades, grunts of exertion. It all happened in a second, but it was enough. Maurizan could tell she still had a slight advantage. It was often the case with these new ink mages. Their perfect reflexes and situational awareness made them deadly with a blade, but they'd had no training.

Maurizan had.

Since she'd been old enough to hold a weapon, she'd been trained in the gypsy two-dagger fighting style. She and these other two ink mages might be on even footing physically, but Maurizan had been educated in the ways of combat.

All the edge she needed.

Maurizan thrust, avoided a block as her blade sliced a shallow gash in the girl's side, drawing a surprised gasp. Maurizan went low as she turned, made a lightning backhanded move, and the other ink mage staggered, blood spraying from behind her knee.

When Maurizan spun again, she saw him.

The third ink mage.

She saw his hand coming toward her in slow motion and knew he saw events unfolding in the same way. In the eternity of the split second before his blow landed, she looked him over with an expert eye. A huge man, tall and fat, but in no way clumsy or sluggish. His cloak was thrown back, revealing tattoos along his enormous arms. *He's got more than just the Prime, more dangerous than the other two put together.* She was too late to counter him, and knew that he knew it too and that there was nothing to do but watch it happen.

In the instant the heel of his hand struck her breastbone, she saw the tattoo of the oxen on his upper arm. *One of the strength tattoos. This is going to be rough.*

Twenty men slamming her with a battering ram could not have hit harder. She flew back, the turtle tattoo a few inches below her belly button humming to life. Her skin turned to the hard, deep green plates of the turtle shell. The wizard who'd tattooed the symbol on her body had been an old tribal shaman from the Glacial Wastes and had told her it needed to be inked near her center of balance. Unlike other wizards she'd dealt with, he wanted nothing in return. He was old and lived a hermit's life and simply thought the tattoo might fade from history if there weren't somebody walking around with it on her skin.

Maurizan thought all this in less time than it took to blink an eye.

She slammed through the wall of the inn and into the street, only the turtle armor preventing multiple bones from shattering.

Maurizan lurched to her feet amid the rubble, coughing from the dust.

The gigantic ink mage stood in the hole in the wall she'd just created, not in a hurry, grinning. Maurizan glimpsed the two female ink mages behind him.

"You're Maurizan," he said. "I've been looking forward to meeting you. I'm called Hak."

Introducing himself in the middle of a fight struck Maurizan as a bit theatrical. Was he really so arrogant? *He either thinks a lot of himself or little of me. What other tattoos does he have?*

"We're rare creatures you and I," Hak said. "Ink mages are rare enough, but those who have tattoos beyond the Prime are rarer still. How many do you have? Three? Four?"

Maurizan said nothing, took up a fighter's stance, and raised her daggers.

"And how do beings as powerful as we test ourselves?" Hak asked. "How do we push ourselves to know what we can truly be, what we truly are?" His grin widened. "I think you will make a fine test for me, Maurizan."

Kiss my ass.

He paused, and when she had no reply, his grin fell.

"A shame," Hak said. "I'd hoped to find a like-minded being. Adversaries, yes, but birds of a feather still. I suppose we might as well get on with it."

He stepped through the ruined wall and into the street.

And was immediately flattened by two men falling out a window.

They landed hard, and the brute let go of him.

Peyne rolled off the pile of bodies—only two, but huge enough to constitute a pile. He groaned, felt along his ribs. There would be bad bruising at the very least. There was no part of him that didn't hurt. He looked up, knowing that no matter what he saw, he wasn't going to like it.

He observed two young women erupting from the hole in the inn's wall, throwing themselves on Maurizan, blades flashing in a whirlwind of death. Maurizan danced between them, her daggers coming up to block, then thrust as she spun and dodged, taking on two . . .

Ink mages? They had to be. Nobody else could move like that.

Peyne shifted his gaze to the two big men sprawled a few feet away. The unconscious brute with the black beard was huge, yet he seemed like a child compared to the giant on which they'd landed.

"Oaf!" shouted the giant. "Idiot!" The giant tossed the brute off him and rose to his feet, his enraged glare falling on Peyne.

Shit.

Peyne looked at the giant, the tattoos on his arms.

Another ink mage? Where the blazes are they all coming from?

The huge mage started toward him, and Peyne felt his bowels quiver.

A scream. Both Peyne and the big ink mage paused to look. One of the female ink mages slid off Maurizan's dagger, leaving it red and dripping. The girl backed away, eyes wide, clutching her stomach, blood thick as syrup oozing between fingers. She opened her mouth as if to object, as if to declare it impossible that there could be an end to her.

Then her legs gave and she went down.

Maurizan and the remaining female ink mage circled each other, blades up and ready, faces calm, all business. Grief or pain or relief would come later.

Peyne took this moment to start crawling.

He'd been hoping to slink away unnoticed. No such luck.

He felt an iron grip on his ankle. Peyne clawed at the ground to keep from being dragged back. When Peyne heard the sinister laughter, he glanced over his shoulder into the grinning face of murder.

"You've stumbled into the wrong fight, little man," the big ink mage said. "But you're lucky. I'm going to kill you quickly, so I can give all my attention to the gypsy."

Peyne felt the grip tighten on his ankle. He thrashed and twisted. No escape.

And then the world exploded with light.

Everyone froze, half blinded.

Peyne looked, one hand up against the blinding glare. It was as if the sun itself fell to earth.

No, not the sun. This light was colder, impossibly white and a pale blue at the edges. The glow streaked toward the ground like a falling star, but instead of a cataclysmic impact, there was a graceful landing.

Peyne's mouth fell open in awe. "Zayda."

She stood in the street, legs slightly apart, fists at her side, moonlight rolling off her in waves and washing the street white with its brilliance. Maurizan and the other ink mage had stopped fighting, gawking instead. Even the brute was awake now, stumbling away, eyes squinting, face half turned away from her blazing glory.

The female ink mage who'd been fighting Maurizan took two tentative steps toward the male ink mage. "Hak?"

"Let me handle it," said the one called Hak. He let go of Peyne's ankle, stood to face Zayda.

This time, Peyne thought the grin on Hak's face looked forced.

Don't gawk. Move!

Peyne started crawling away again, slowly so as not to draw attention to himself. Terrible things were about to happen, and Peyne didn't want to be in the middle of the cataclysm. As he crawled, his ribs protested loudly. *More than just bruised. Cracked? Dumo, help me, not now.*

"You might just be the test of my skills I'm looking for," Hak said. "I think Meddigar underestimated you. Zayda, is it?"

"Call me whatever name you give to death." Zayda's voice filled the world, echoed off the buildings of the Last Village. Her words made Peyne's skull vibrate, and he winced.

Hak abandoned all pretense at bravado, a scowl replacing the cocky grin. "You have tattoos beyond the Prime. Obviously. How many?"

A hint of a smile so slight from Zayda it might not have been there at all.

"One." The single syllable rolled across them like thunder.

"You lie," Hak said.

"You only have to believe one thing," Zayda said. "Just this. If you don't walk away right now, you'll die. It won't even be difficult. I might not even remember it later. There are so many important things to remember, and this is just a moment, a chance crossroads where you live or die, but I go on. The choice is yours."

"I have *seven*," Hak boasted. "Seven beyond the Prime."

"Then you'll be buried with them," Zayda said.

She means it, Peyne thought. *Dumo save us all, she's not fooling.* He crawled faster.

Hak's face went tight, and his whole body quivered from a mix of rage and indecision. Peyne knew the man was about to try something . . . run or fight or . . . ? He didn't know. He desperately hoped Hak wasn't the sort of prideful asshole who could never back down for fear of losing face.

Hope in one hand and crap in the other. See which one fills up first had been a favorite saying of Peyne's father.

And for a split second, it all stood on a razor's edge. Maurizan and the other female ink mage watched, mouths hanging open. The black-bearded brute cringed against the wall of the inn near the new opening. Peyne held his breath.

Hak's eyes were wild and unreadable. Any second he could—

And then Hak was moving.

It happened so fast, Peyne wasn't sure he saw all of it. He hadn't even seen Hak draw the sword, but the ink mage flew toward Zayda faster than the wind, bringing his scimitar down straight at Zayda's face.

Zayda brought both of her hands together in a clapping motion. It was the fastest Peyne had ever seen a human move, and yet, at the same time, the gesture seemed as casual as someone shooing a fly. He blinked and saw she'd captured Hak's blade between her hands.

Hak's ink mage composure collapsed, and he gasped. He tried to tug his sword free but couldn't.

Slowly, Zayda twisted her hands, bending the scimitar to a ninety-degree angle. Then Zayda released the blade, taking a step back.

Hak tossed aside the mangled scimitar.

"Bitch!" he shouted. "I am the greatest of ink mages. You seek to mock me? You think I'm intimidated by your tricks? Let this be the end of it."

He leapt for her, hands going for her throat. Again, to Peyne, Hak's motions were almost too fast to follow.

Zayda's strike he didn't see at all.

Suddenly Hak was flying backward. He flew through the air, smashing into the building across the street. The roof caved in, dust and rubble kicking up, and Hak came out the other side, smashing into the next building beyond.

Howls of terror filled the night. Villagers streamed from the surrounding buildings, many in nightclothes, all fleeing the scene of the melee, some clutching small children to their breasts.

Peyne staggered to his feet, holding his side. He turned back to Zayda, saw her standing there, face utterly calm, her arm still outstretched, hand in a tight fist from the move she'd put on Hak. Slowly she opened her hand, lowered her arm to her side.

Maurizan stepped up behind the remaining female ink mage and slammed the hilt of her dagger into the back of the woman's head. The girl's eyes rolled back, and she wilted into the dust.

"We shouldn't linger," Maurizan said. "I guarantee you Hak is clawing himself out of the rubble right now with revenge on his mind."

A wan smile from Zayda. She turned to Peyne. "Hello, Peyne. Are you all right?"

He almost couldn't look at her. Her voice filled the world like a song from some goddess. The light radiating from her was too much to look at directly for more than a few seconds.

"I'm fine, I guess." He swallowed hard. "How are *you*?"

She tossed her head back and laughed, seeming human again. "Is it so strange to see me like this, so filled with power?"

Peyne cleared his throat. "No, not at all. It's . . . it's fine."

"Don't be afraid," Zayda said. "It's still me."

Zayda smiled warmly at him, looked about to say something more. Then her face twisted in pain, and she screamed.

"Zayda!" Peyne rushed to catch her, and they went to the ground together. He gathered her in his arms, and she twitched, eyes rolling back white as she bleated agony. "What is it? What's happening?"

"M-Meddigar."

Peyne looked, saw the wizard standing in the hole in the inn's wall, a scepter held tightly in his fist. Not Zayda's scepter, but it didn't seem to matter. Meddigar was obviously controlling her. He held the scepter aloft.

He's going to kill her.

Peyne held on to her tightly, a useless protective instinct. His mind raced. *Do something!*

A crossbow bolt flew past the wizard's face, coming within an inch of his ear. It had come from inside the inn. The wizard turned.

Where the blazes did that come from?

Meddigar turned, scanning the interior of the inn. A trio of men stood near the bar, one reloading a crossbow, the other two with scimitars in their hands. He remembered them from earlier but hadn't paid them any attention, thinking them random bar patrons.

I should have known Maurizan wouldn't meet me without a plan.

The one with the crossbow had reloaded, lifted the weapon, and aimed.

I don't think so.

And then there was fire.

It poured from the palm of the wizard's hand like dragon's breath, completely engulfing the man with the crossbow. Screams high-pitched and terrifying as he fell to the ground, body writhing in agony.

The other two leapt to the side, one frantically slapping at his burning sleeve. Stray flames ignited the bar behind them.

The burning crossbowman lay still, his shrieks finally ceasing.

The third one drew a dagger as his comrade struggled to douse his flaming arm. He tossed the dagger, and it tumbled end over end toward Meddigar.

The wizard waved his hands, rapidly babbling the words to another spell.

Everything froze.

The dagger hung in the air, the tip six inches from Meddigar's face. The Time Halt spell was one of his most powerful, but it would barely give him three seconds to act. He sidestepped the dagger and approached the man who'd thrown it. He stood frozen, arm still extended from the follow-through. His face was a mask of grit and determination. These men had attacked a wizard. They were brave and doomed and must have known their fate.

Meddigar reached out and grabbed the man's wrist just as the flow of time resumed. His expression turned to surprised. To him it seemed as if Meddigar had blipped from one side of the room to the other in the blink of an eye.

Meddigar uttered the quick words to another spell, and the man's surprised expression shifted to one of pain, his body quivering from head to toe.

Shocking Touch was the junior version of the much more powerful Lightning Bolt spell but it worked well enough in close quarters. He released the man, who fell in a heap, dead eyes open and staring at nothing.

The last man had recovered from the surprise of the Time Halt and rushed the wizard, scimitar thrusting. Meddigar's hand flashed into his robe and came out with a short sword, straight flat blade clanging as he parried the attack.

Meddigar was far from a sword master but had trained in the basics enough to defend himself. *Nobody expects the old gray-bearded wizard to whip out a sword. Fry them with a spell, yes. That they expect.*

He blocked two more lunges, backing away as his opponent pressed his attack. It was clear Meddigar would not win a sword duel. He didn't need to. He just needed to keep the man off him until he completed his next spell.

Meddigar stepped back as the last syllable of the spell escaped his lips. A ball of eldritch green light blazed from his hand, spanned the distance between him and the other man in a split second, and hit the man in the chest. He was lifted two feet into the air, then came down hard, landing flat on his back. Smoke rose from the black hole in the dead man's chest.

Meddigar spun, sword up and ready, scanning the common room for more opponents. Nobody came at him.

The flames crackling along the bar spread to the far wall. Black smoke filled the room. There was no one left in the inn to fight the fire. The whole place would go up soon.

Meddigar headed for the hole in the wall. Time to go.

"Now!" Maurizan said. "While the wizard's distracted!"

Peyne gathered Zayda's limp form in his arms. He tried to stand, and pain lanced through his side. He grunted and went to one knee.

"What is it?" Maurizan asked.

"My ribs," Peyne told her. "At least one cracked, maybe two."

She knelt next to him, slipped a hand up under his tunic, her cold skin on his startling him. She prodded the tender area. "Here?"

He winced. "Yes."

"Hold still." She pressed her palm firmly to the ribs, his flesh growing warm then hot.

Peyne stood, lifted Zayda. Only a vague ache remained in his side.

He looked at Maurizan. "Are you okay?"

She'd turned ashen, swaying on her feet like she might topple over any second.

"Healing nearly drains me." She held up her hand to show him the tattoo on her palm.

The tattoo wasn't obvious. It had been done with some kind of glossy, clear ink, invisible at first but obvious when she turned her hand and it caught the street light just right. The tattoo depicted a stylized heart on her palm, flowering vines radiating out from the heart to creep along each finger and thumb.

"I can barely walk after I use it, so don't come to me every time you stub your toe," Maurizan said. "Now let's get the blazes out of here."

Maurizan somehow summoned the energy to leave at a jog, Peyne right behind her with Zayda in his arms. She led them through a zigzag path of side streets and narrow alleys. Peyne alternated between looking where he was going and looking down into Zayda's face, eyes closed, mouth slack.

Please be okay. Please be okay. Please be okay . . .

They emerged from an alley into a wide expanse of sand, and Peyne realized Maurizan had led them to the southern edge of town.

Jaff waited with their dromadan. "My men?"

Maurizan shook her head.

Jaff's face looked tight for a moment; then he said, "I opened the stable gates and ran off the other dromadan. They'll eventually return for feeding time, but it will give us a head start."

"Then let's make the most of it," Maurizan said, climbing onto her dromadan and taking her place in the saddle.

Peyne situated himself in his own saddle, a sleeping Zayda's head in his lap. She seemed to be breathing well, face calm. Peyne sighed relief. She would be okay. She had to be. He lightly stroked her hair.

He twisted in the saddle, looking behind him. A flickering orange glow hovered over the village. It seemed to Peyne the fire might be spreading. He remembered Hak smashing through buildings.

"They're going to need a new Last Village," Peyne said idly.

The dromadan plodded on, the deep desert stretching ominously before them.

CHAPTER
TWENTY-THREE

Meddigar stood in the street and watched the inn burn.

The two women on their hands and knees coughed behind him, splashing water from a skin into their eyes. He felt bad for Venny. This probably wasn't what she'd been expecting. She'd said a man had burst into their room. Alarming but probably fortunate. If she'd slept while the inn burned, she might not have gotten out alive.

As for his apprentice, it would have been a favor for Meddigar if she'd perished in the fire. He had no affection for Nila, had in fact come to despise her.

He heard someone approach and turned to see Hak. The man was bruised and scraped head to foot, minor rips in his clothing, but Meddigar wondered if Zayda hadn't damaged his pride more. The woman had literally been glowing with power. Meddigar was unaware a tattoo could do that. He'd been studying and collecting ink magic for years, but still so much was lost to the ages.

"The stable master has boys out looking for the dromadan," Hak said. "It will take time."

"Damn." Meddigar scratched his beard, thinking. How far would Maurizan get ahead? What did she know? He'd hoped to see her map on the chance she'd added to it significantly and might shed some light on his destination. Failing that, he thought he could make her talk. With Hak and the other two ink mages standing with him, it hadn't seemed an unreasonable thought.

Meddigar hadn't considered Maurizan might have another ink mage backing her up. He certainly could not have predicted Zayda would have some powerful tattoo he'd never heard of.

"Find the best tracker in the village," Meddigar told Hak.

"Finding him is one thing," Hak said. "Convincing him to go into the deep desert is another."

"If the prince's gold won't convince him, I'm sure you'll persuade him somehow."

Meddigar had expected one of Hak's arrogant grins, but instead, the ink mage returned only a curt nod, his expression tight and grim.

Zayda took the piss out of him even more than I thought, Meddigar mused. *I hope he's up for a rematch. I don't need him hesitating at the wrong time.*

They would follow Maurizan and her companions into the deep desert. Meddigar *would* know the woman's secrets. He had no choice. He couldn't find his way back to the lost city without some hint, some clue. Wandering aimlessly until something looked familiar would only be feeding more corpses to the deep desert. Running would mean silencing Hak and all the others, and he wasn't sure he could do that.

Oh, he had the will for it. But perhaps not the ability. He'd weighed the odds carefully and still thought catching up to the gypsy was his best bet.

"As soon as we find the tracker and retrieve the dromadan we're going," Meddigar said.

"You don't want to wait for the supply column and the rest of the troops?" Hak asked.

"Every minute we delay, Maurizan gets farther ahead of us."

"As you wish." Hak left to make ready.

Meddigar felt eyes on him and turned to see Nila watching.

The deep desert.

Even in the most inhospitable regions of northern Fyria, life could find a way. Big animals hunted the smaller ones. This was often a matter of extreme patience, but the circle of life endured. Even water could be found by those who knew where to look. Life, brutal as it might be, went on.

Not so in the forbidding desert land south of the Last Village. Nothing lived there. Nothing had for centuries, perhaps for even longer than that.

History gave way to legend, the stories growing threadbare with the telling and the retelling, many of the details lost or reinvented, often replaced by colorful lies until nothing was known about what used to be in the deep desert or what had turned the region into a wasteland in which no living thing venturing into it ever came out again.

And really even *that* was untrue. On the rarest of occasions, some explorer, like Meddigar, through skill or luck or the will of the gods, would enter the deep desert and somehow stumble out again.

These were the exceptions to the rule.

One other thread of truth steadfastly endured even in the most obscure of legends. While it was self-evident that the deep desert was lifeless and deadly, all agreed that it hadn't always been that way.

Once upon a time, if the legends were to be believed (and they generally were) the region of the deep desert had been lush and fertile, indeed, the garden spot of Fyria. Rivers cut through green fields, crisscrossing the landscape, and amid this verdant land sprung a magnificent city unlike any other in the world, a place of magic and technology and innovation and learning unsurpassed.

So it was that in one breath the deep desert was cursed as a desolate wasteland, while in the next it was held in awe as the cradle of Fyrian greatness.

One might not have sensed the appropriate respect for this sentiment if they'd heard Peyne shouting from the saddle of his dromadan, "I hate this fucking place!"

Maurizan twisted in her saddle to look back at him. "Give it a rest."

"I'm hot."

"We're all hot," Maurizan said. "It's Fyria. It's the *deep desert* in Fyria. It's always fucking hot. Shut up already."

Peyne wiped sweat from his brow and adjusted his hat. "It's been a week. Excuse me if I'm not having the time of my life."

"It's not a holiday!" Maurizan snapped.

Zayda stirred in the saddle next to Peyne, opening her eyes long enough to say, "Everyone, shut up," and then she turned away, curling into a tight ball and closing her eyes again.

"How can you sleep?" Peyne complained. "Every part of me is sweaty and gross. I feel like some hot greasy pork chop."

Jaff brought his dromadan alongside Peyne's. "Enough. We're all miserable. There's no point in sniping at one another."

"You're Fyrian," Peyne said. "You're used to this heat."

"This?" Jaff made an irritated gesture toward the sun. "Nobody is used to *this*, but complaining won't help."

"I'd feel better at least if we could take a day to rest," Peyne said. "Maurizan, are you sure they're still following us?"

The gypsy closed her eyes, her face going calm and blank. "Xarran's coming back. Hold on."

Peyne craned his neck, one hand up to shade his eyes from the sun as he scanned the sky, but he failed to catch a glimpse of the great eagle.

Seconds stretched to minutes.

Then suddenly a gigantic feathered mass fell from the sky, seemingly out of nowhere, startling Peyne. Three feet from the ground, its wings spread and it swooped upward again, rich brown feathers glossy in the sun. Its wingspan was at least a dozen feet, beak yellow and hooked, talons that could grip and carry away a pig with ease.

Peyne looked on with wonder as the eagle made slow, majestic circles around Maurizan. The gypsy's eyes closed as she presumably communicated with the creature.

Finally, Maurizan's eyes popped open, and she frowned. "They have a tracker."

"How do you know that?" Peyne asked.

"I can see whatever Xarran sees," Maurizan said. "And his eyes are sharper than any human's. All the same, I told him to go low so I could get a good look. There's a man out front of the column. He keeps stopping, climbing down from his dromadan, and checking the ground. I can only assume he's a tracker."

"How can anyone track us in this?" Peyne waved his hand at the endless sand in every direction. "The wind covers our path."

"The best trackers can tell the difference," Jaff said. "They know if it's wind that's shifted the sand or a dromadan's step. Rest stops will have to be brief. We can't risk their catching up. I lost three good men. I don't intend to tangle with a wizard again if I can help it."

"They'll have to stop and rest too," Peyne said. "The bird can tell us when. They stop. We stop."

"No," Maurizan said. "I'm sending Xarran away."

The look on Peyne's face would have been comical under other circumstances. "Why in Dumo's bloody name would you do *that*?"

"Because he's starving," Maurizan said. "There's nothing here for him to hunt."

"Then feed him."

"Do you know what a giant mountain eagle eats?" Maurizan asked. "Do you have a goat in your pocket? And anyway there's barely enough water for us. Xarran is loyal and will stay with me until he starves and drops from the sky if I ask him, but I won't ask that. I'm sending the eagle away. He'll pass the column of soldiers on the way, so we can see if they've picked up their pace."

"Excellent," Peyne said dryly. "Just really fantastic. Let me see if I completely understand our situation. We're fleeing *into* an uninhabitable wasteland. We're being pursued by a wizard and his pet ink mages from whom we barely escaped the first time. A few days behind them is an army of soldiers. And we're sending away our only chance at an early warning. Oh, and by the way, it's still fucking unbelievably, mind-bogglingly *hot*."

Maurizan rolled her eyes. "Maybe I'll feed *you* to the eagle."

Zayda snorted a quick laugh, then went back to sleep.

Peyne watched the eagle a long time as it faded into the distance. He was sorry. Truly sorry to see the bird go.

The days blurred into one another.

By unspoken agreement, they deferred to Jaff to decide when to stop and for how long. To Peyne, the rests were all too brief. It seemed he'd barely had a chance to stretch and rub his saddle-sore ass when Jaff would order them to mount up again. Peyne's back and legs hurt. All of them lingered on the edge of total exhaustion. Peyne no longer had the energy to complain, and they'd ride for hours in silence, the muffled plod of the dromadan and the hot wind the only sounds.

Food had turned out not to be a problem, not because they had it in such abundance but because the heat had sapped their appetites. Peyne could barely bring himself to choke down a few small bites of jerky tough as boot leather.

Water *had* become a problem, and Jaff had cut their ration to a mere mouthful each day. At least once a day, Zayda would tap into the spirit, closing her eyes and hoping to smell a nearby oasis. She'd come up empty every time.

Peyne anticipated his mouthful of water each day with a sort of desperate insanity. The relief provided by the lukewarm drink vanished almost immediately. His mouth was constantly dry, lips cracked, throat parched.

Five hours after sunset, Jaff called for a longer than usual rest stop. They all needed sleep and would have to risk it. And in any case, surely their pursuers would have to stop also. They circled the dromadan and slept among them. No one talked. As soon as they stretched out on the ground, all fell asleep immediately.

Peyne dreamed.

The air was cool, and the world was blue. He stood under a waterfall, water splashing down on him, his skin breaking out in gooseflesh. He realized it was the waterfall he and Zayda had found after the *Pride of Klaar* sank and they'd finally found their way ashore.

The acute realization he was in a dream disappointed him bitterly. Still, he lingered under the waterfall, willing himself not to wake, loath to be returned to the waking nightmare of the desert.

But slowly the dream world faded to be replaced by harsh reality. Peyne propped himself up on one elbow and squinted at the faded orange light of dawn. The feel of the cool, wet waterfall had vanished, the grit in his eyes and mouth begging for water. Only the smell remained, moist and verdant.

He lurched to his feet and stumbled between two of the shaggy dromadan across the sand toward the sunrise.

The simmering orange sun humped up from the horizon, looking huge and impossibly close. Its light shimmered and danced strangely on the desert floor like shimmering fire. Peyne wondered if it were some sort of illusion, a trick of the light, the desert sand seeming to swell and fall as if waves lapping at the—

Peyne blinked.

Water. He rubbed his eyes, looked again. Water. A huge lake. That was why he could still smell it. It was so close. The lake must have invaded his dreams. They'd almost come upon it in the night but hadn't seen it in the total darkness, the moon having set before they'd stopped.

He ran.

"Water!" He'd tried to shout, but it came out as a dry croak. "Water!" Louder this time.

He sprinted up a dune and down the other side, almost tripping, until he reached the water's edge. He splashed into it knee-deep and then dove, going completely under into a world that was cool and dark.

Peyne kicked, going deep, thrilling to the feel of the water on his skin.

And suddenly he was lost.

Everywhere Peyne looked he saw the same endless depths. Up and down became meaningless. He paddled and kicked, going nowhere, seeming to hover in the same spot. His lungs burned for air. The cool, refreshing water now turned ice cold, numbing his bones. He panicked and thrashed but couldn't seem to move. His lungs threatened to burst, darkness pulling him down and down and . . .

Stinging pain across his cheek. The feel of his face going red and hot.

Peyne's eyes popped open. He was screaming.

Zayda sat on top of him, hand raised to slap him again.

Peyne flinched. "Don't."

She lowered her hand. "You'd gone mad."

"What?" Peyne sat up, looking around. "Where is it?"

"Where's what?"

"The water," Peyne said. "There was a huge lake."

"The fool is seeing things," Jaff said, coming up behind them.

Peyne gawked at the empty desert. "What?"

"It happens," Zayda said gently. "The heat of the desert can affect a person after so long. People imagine things, see mirages."

Peyne stood, knees weak, brushing the sand from his clothes. "Embarrassing."

"Never mind." Jaff wiped the sweat from his brow. Barely after dawn and already the heat was rising. "We'll all probably go mad sooner rather than later. The water is becoming an issue."

"I rather thought it was already," Peyne said.

"We left the Last Village in a hurry," Jaff said. "I packed the dromadan with as much water as possible on short notice, but when traveling into the deep desert, how can one know what is enough? I think we need to cut our rations."

"How about if I just lie down and die right here?" Peyne asked.

"That would leave more water for the rest of us," Zayda said.

"You're quite a humorous little thing, aren't you?"

"The problem is the dromadan," Jaff said. "They can go an astonishingly long time without water. But not forever."

"Don't tell me we have to share our remaining water with the animals," Peyne said.

"It wouldn't do any good," Jaff explained. "The beasts are big, and the water we have left wouldn't matter a thing to them. They need the lake you were imagining."

"I'm starting to regret ever coming on this ridiculous expedition," Peyne said.

Zayda frowned, took a step away from him, crossing her arms.

"Maurizan is already packing," Jaff said. "I suggest we get moving. We have an army behind us, and we slept too long." He turned and left, not waiting to see if Peyne and Zayda followed.

She looked at him, clearly hurt.

"You know I didn't mean it," he said. "I know you want that collar off, and something in the deep desert holds the secret. Of course I don't regret coming. Look, I just thought I was swimming in a lake. Obviously I'm not in my right mind."

The hint of a smile.

She hooked her arm with his, and they walked back toward their small camp.

"You have a sort of natural charm, you know," she said. "It's quite annoying."

"My charm is what's kept me alive this long."

"It's certainly not your swordsmanship."

"Hey!"

Two days later, the first dromadan dropped dead.

It came to an abrupt halt in its trek across the dunes, made a low grunt from deep in its belly, then toppled over. Maurizan had to leap from her saddle to avoid being crushed under its weight.

The great shaggy beast huffed and puffed for a few minutes, belly expanding and contracting, until it let out a final plaintive sigh and expired.

They transferred the meager provisions to Jaff's dromadan, and Maurizan shared his saddle. They set off again, gloomy and silent, the dromadan's corpse an inert lump dwindling behind them.

The next morning the dunes gave way to hard, baked ground, cracked and gradually dotted with more and larger rocks as they proceeded. By midafternoon, they reached the edge of a minor cliff that stretched east and west as far as the eye could see. The slope down the cliff was gentle enough, and the ground flattened out again thirty feet below.

"This used to be a great inland sea," Maurizan said.

Peyne sat up in his saddle, tried to see to the other side but failed. "What happened to it?"

"Good question." Maurizan turned her dromadan east. "This way."

"Why *that* way?" Peyne asked.

"Because I've been here before."

Two hours later, she spotted it, pointing about a half mile along the floor of the dried seabed. Something stuck up from the ground. Peyne couldn't quite make out what it was and didn't have the energy to ask. What did it matter at this point which direction they went? Unless someone happened to spy water, he was beyond caring. When Maurizan guided her dromadan over the edge, Peyne dutifully followed.

The bank was steeper than it had first appeared, and Peyne had to grab onto the saddle horn to keep his seat. Zayda latched onto Peyne.

A few moments later, the two beasts were on flat ground again, walking side by side to whatever the thing was Maurizan had seen.

A half hour later, Peyne recognized it. A ship.

Or, more accurately, half a ship.

The front half rose up from the ground at an awkward angle, prow sticking in the air twenty feet off the ground. No sign of masts. Peyne wondered how long the vessel had been there. It seemed to be made of some dark-red wood. Hewn from forests long gone? He couldn't guess, but when they drew closer, he realized it wasn't wood at all.

The ship was made of metal. The dark-red color was rust.

It had once been a large vessel, twice as long as the *Pride of Klaar* had been and several feet wider, a sleeker design, possibly meant for speed rather than shipping tons of cargo. The prow had been fashioned into the likeness of a winged woman, long flowing hair, wings folded back to suggest speed in flight. The metalworker must have been a master artist, for her features seemed almost soft, only the rust giving away she'd been made of harder stuff.

They reined in their dromadan where the ship sprung from the ground like some old, rotting stump, and dismounted.

"I didn't know they made ships of metal," Peyne said.

"The ancients were advanced in more than just ink magic," Maurizan said. "Twenty years ago, I found one of their cities on a remote island and was almost killed by men of metal."

"They had advanced armor?" Peyne asked.

"Not men *in* metal," Maurizan said. "Men *of* metal. They were powered by steam."

Peyne and Zayda exchanged disbelieving looks.

"No, it's true," Jaff said. "I've heard of this."

"You've heard of steam-powered men?" Peyne asked.

"No, of course not. But the scholars and engineers at the university in Heberron are always inventing new wonders. They somehow harnessed the pressure of steam and were able to turn a mill wheel with it." Jaff shrugged. "Or at least that's what I heard. I can't claim to have seen it with my own eyes."

"This is where I found the healing tattoo. It was in a small chest, the stencil and a small vial of ink. The chest must have been magically preserved over the centuries." Maurizan turned her head, squinted across the dry seabed. "I wanted to explore further, but I estimated I had only just enough water to get back."

Nobody said what they were all thinking. Their remaining water was a mere fraction of what they'd brought with them from the last village. There was no going back. The only choice was to press on and hope that somewhere in the unknown land ahead they would stumble upon a well or oasis.

Peyne was intimately familiar with gambling, enjoyed it a bit too much. And he knew a bad bet when he saw one.

Zayda went toward the ship, stepped over the gunwale.

"There's nothing more in there," Maurizan said. "The tattoo was the only thing of value."

"I didn't come this far not to look," Zayda said.

Peyne fell into step behind her. "I'll come with you."

Maurizan sighed and followed. "I suppose I could have missed something."

"I'll watch over the dromadan," Jaff said. "I'll leave the ghosts of the ancients to you."

The deck slanted upward, but not steeply enough to prevent them from climbing. They entered an open doorway. Dim light drifted in from portholes. Peyne grabbed the handle of a heavy iron door and pulled, the door creaking open slowly on rusted hinges.

Sand filled the passage beyond floor to ceiling, spilling out over Peyne's boots.

"Is it all like this?" he asked.

"Everything aft as far as I can tell," Maurizan said. "My theory is the ship sank and mud poured in through the portholes, filling all those compartments. Only the cabins forward are accessible."

They explored the cabins forward, finding nothing but broken bits of furniture and dust. The last cabin was best preserved. Scattered bones lay about, including a skull, the lower jaw missing, eyes hollow and haunting.

"I found the tattoo in here," Maurizan said.

Zayda knelt, staring into the eyes of the skull. "This was a wizard's cabin?"

"The whole ship could have been the wizard's for all I know," Maurizan said. "Or maybe he was the sultan's royal wizard sent on some errand. We'll never know. But the ship is pointing north. I'm thinking it came from the south, so that's where we need to go."

"That's a stretch," Peyne said. "It could have tossed and turned in some storm before sinking. It could have come from anywhere."

"Yes," Maurizan agreed. "But with no other information available, I'll go with my gut instinct."

"You're talking about crossing this dry sea. Who knows how far that is?"

"That's exactly what I'm talking about. And however far it is, then that's how far we go. There's no other choice anyway. If you have a better idea, I'm all ears."

Peyne didn't have a better idea.

"There's a little daylight left. We might as well make use of it."
Maurizan turned to go. "Take a last look if you want but don't linger."

Peyne sighed. "She's right. There's nothing here. Zayda?"

Zayda stared at the skull, her face blank.

Peyne knelt next to her, put a hand on her shoulder. "Zayda."

She touched the collar around her neck. "I don't know what I
thought I'd find. I mean, I didn't think the key to removing this collar would be hidden in this old wreck of all places, but I thought I'd
find . . . something. Or see something to give me hope. That we were
doing the right thing."

Peyne reached for the collar, hesitated. "May I?"

"Go ahead."

He examined the thin metal circle. It was perfectly smooth all the
way round, not a sign of any latch or mechanism of any kind. "How
the blazes was the damn thing put on?"

"The ring was a single long strand, limp like *strillini* . . . ugh, what's
the word? Noodle! That's it. Like a metal noodle, a little brassy, not like
any other metals I've seen. It was solid but almost moving like liquid,
like it might drip out of Meddigar's hands," Zayda said. "Then he put
it around my neck and joined the ends while muttering some spell. The
ends merged together, the metal hardening."

"Want to know what I think?" Peyne said.

"Tell me."

"I think all the ink magic came from the same place, the control
scepter, the noodle metal for the collars, the ink for the tattoos, the spell
to put the collar on your neck. All ancient magic," Peyne said. "And
that's the place we're going to right now. And if there's a spell to put a
collar around your neck, then there's one to take it off again, and we're
going to find it."

Hope bloomed in Zayda's face. Or maybe it was simply gratitude,
Peyne thought. Gratitude that somebody would believe in her futile
errand to free herself.

She leaned forward suddenly and kissed him, lips mashing hard against his, one slender arm going around his neck to pull him close.

Peyne returned the kiss without reservation, gathering her in his arms. His thirst and hunger and fatigue, the entire desert vanished. Zayda became the whole world, and nothing else mattered.

When she pulled away, there were tears in her eyes.

"I've killed you," she said. "I've dragged you along on this fool's errand and killed you."

"Now, listen. You know me," Peyne said. "I'll eventually find some way to get killed anyway."

And they kissed again.

They emerged from the ship to find Maurizan looking grim.

"We lost another dromadan," she said.

CHAPTER
TWENTY-FOUR

The tracker's name was Krokett, a wiry little man, three teeth missing from the left half of his smile, and mahogany brown skin so leathery it might have been a saddle. Meddigar had trouble guessing the man's age. Krokett could have been forty or sixty. The promise of gold and glory had seduced him enough to take the job of leading them into the deep desert.

Also, Meddigar thought the man a bit cracked in the head.

Krokett squatted in the shade of the ancient hulk, a ship from a bygone epoch, sticking halfway out of the dry seabed, and examined the hard-packed ground.

Meddigar and Hak stood off to the side, watching and waiting, the rest of their party a dozen yards back with the dromadan.

The trip thus far had been miserable, a pall descending upon the group after they'd lost a man, one of the soldiers. He'd been sickly before and had dehydrated and died. They'd buried him in the desert and moved on. Meddigar again wondered about the water supply. They still had plenty, but it wouldn't last forever. He guessed they might be better off than the gypsy and her people. Maurizan had left in a hurry. They were likely short of supplies.

That would be just fine with the wizard. He wasn't a hero, had no desire for a glorious rematch. If he found them dead from thirst, that would do fine.

Except for Maurizan. He needed her to talk.

In fact, Meddigar wondered if catching up to Maurizan *too soon* might be a mistake. If the woman knew where she was going, it might be better to simply let her get there and keep following.

A babbling in Fyrian drew his attention back to Krokett.

"He says he's figured it out," Hak translated.

"Let's hear it, then."

Krokett spoke rapidly, gesticulating, indicating the ship first and then the desert, finally gesturing at the carcass of the dead dromadan baking in the sun several feet away.

"Four of them," Hak said. "Three went into the ship. One stayed outside. Then all four left on a single dromadan."

"How long?" Meddigar asked.

Hak asked, and Krokett answered.

"Late yesterday," Hak said.

Meddigar nodded, considering. They were catching up. Slowly yes, but catching up. He adjusted his hat, squinting at the sun still high in the sky. Four or five hours of daylight left at least. "Are we still placing the markers? I don't want Captain Bevelakwa and his company getting lost behind us."

"We've left them a clear trail," Hak assured the wizard.

"Okay then. Let's get moving."

They marched on until nightfall, then made camp. They'd brought a supply of firewood, but it had dwindled fast, and so the cook fire was meager and provided little warmth. Venny sat near the fire across from Meddigar, squinting at a notebook in her lap, the campfire offering insufficient light. She dipped a quill into a small inkwell and scribbled notes. Around them, others made ready, fixing the evening meal, preparing bedding, and seeing to the animals.

"What are you writing?" Meddigar asked.

"Guesses."

The wizard grinned. Venny had an energetic charm Meddigar admired. The hardships of the deep desert seemed to bother her not at all. "Enlighten me."

"A good deal of southern Fyria is on a downward slope."

Meddigar thought that was insane. His expression must have given him away.

"I know. I know," Venny said. "It looks flat as a board, and for all practical purposes, it is. It's too subtle to sense it or for it to even matter, but cartographers must often look at the big picture, the *really* big picture, and that means considering the flow of rivers and so on."

"Fair enough," Meddigar said. "Continue."

"On the coast, at roughly the same latitude where we are now, there is a feature of the landscape we think was once a river delta," Venny said. "I'm extrapolating—quite liberally, I might add—but considering the various features around an unknown area often allows us an educated guess at what that area might be like."

"And?"

"And if I had to guess," Venny said, "I'd guess this sea used to be quite wide east and west but not so far north and south. Like a crease across the bottom half of Fyria in which water gathered and drained out the delta and into the sea."

"So we're rather fortunate," Meddigar said. "To be crossing the short part instead of the long part."

"Fortunate if my guesses are right," Venny said. "The ship gives us more hope than any of my guesses."

"Oh?"

"A ship that size suggests ports," she said. "Any number of rivers might feed into and out of the sea. Or used to. Rivers and seaports mean commerce and civilization. It's not a bad guess that a lost city would be found near a lost coastline or riverfront. It narrows our search."

"Search?"

Something subtle changed in Venny's expression. "Maybe *search* is the wrong word. You know where you're going. Obviously. I just meant in terms of mapping. I'm looking for landmarks, trying to fill in the blanks."

Meddigar's eyes shifted to the figure a few yards away. Nila lay in her bedroll, eyes glittering in the shadows, watching.

Always watching and listening.

The next day brought a tedious march across a baked land. They plodded from sunup to sundown, the landscape never changing, only Krokett's word they were still on the trail of their prey.

The next two days were identical.

On the third day, they found the edge of the world.

The group stood on the cliff's edge looking down. Krokett spit out a warning in Fyrian, and Hak translated. "He says the sands can shift suddenly, so be wary."

They all took a half step back from the edge.

The brute Klamud took five steps back. The man might have been strong enough to wrestle a bear, but heights gave him trouble.

It had been Venny who'd called it the edge of the world and had known even as she was saying it that she was being colorful. She explained cartographers were always looking for exciting ways to list new landmarks on a map.

Her mark in history, Meddigar thought. *The woman who mapped the edge of the world.*

But standing there, trying to take it all in, Meddigar could see how this might seem like the end of the world.

The cliff went down almost straight for half a mile before sloping more gradually to the floor below. A few miles beyond that—scale was difficult from Meddigar's vantage—an enormous round hole gaped darkly, depths unknown. The cliff stretched out of sight both east and west.

"It's a crater," Venny said.

Everyone looked at her.

"I mean it *looks* like one," Venny said. "See how the cliff bends in the distance?" She gestured in the other direction. "And it bends that way too. I wonder if it meets on the other side and makes a circle. Then it really would look like a crater."

"No, you're right," Meddigar said with wonder. "It's a crater."

Venny was already shaking her head. "I was being figurative again. It's far too big to be—"

"I've read the histories," Meddigar said. "Even the ancient accounts from the Great Library in Tul-Agnon. A war among the master wizards of old. It was said they pulled rocks from the sky to hurl at one another. Their wrath almost broke the world."

Nobody had the nerve to say *bullshit* to a wizard, but the looks on their faces were unmistakable.

"Maybe that's where all the water went," Klamud said.

Could it be that simple? Had the muscle-bound idiot stumbled upon the answer? Maybe the sea had simply swirled into the gigantic hole, bathwater down a drain.

A high-pitched voice came to them on the wind, and all heads turned to look. While they'd been standing and debating the crater, Krokett had skirted the rim of the cliff. He'd hiked partway to some mass humping up from the ground in the distance.

They hurried after him.

As they approached, the hump coalesced into the shape of a dead dromadan.

"They're on foot now," Hak said.

Krokett jabbered at them again. He knelt next to the cliff's edge, pointing down. They joined him, all looking.

"He says they climbed down here," Hak told Meddigar. "It's a difficult climb, but a slightly better spot than where we were standing before."

"Well, they didn't have to decide," Meddigar said. "We do."

Nila raised an eyebrow. "Decide what?"

"If we follow them down or look for a path the dromadan can take," Meddigar said.

"They'll get too far ahead if we don't follow immediately," Hak said.

"The deep desert on foot?" Venny's expression made it clear what she thought of that idea.

"Whatever we decide, it'll be too late to try it until morning. The sun sets soon," Meddigar said. "Make camp. We'll debate it over a hot meal."

The others drifted away, leaving Meddigar to stare across the vast crater, contemplating the implacable hole there. Did the old wizards really have such power?

He sensed somebody and saw Nila in his peripheral vision, moving to stand next to him. *Of course. Who else would ruin a quiet moment with my thoughts?*

"You're lost, aren't you?" his apprentice said.

He went stiff, hesitated, and then said, "Don't be ridiculous. We're following the tracker. Krokett hasn't led us astray."

"That's not what I mean," Nila said. "You don't know the way, or otherwise you could have gone straight there. That's why you're following the gypsy. She's your only hope. I heard you and Venny talking last night, and I know I'm right. Venny knows it too. She's just too polite to call you on it."

"You're jumping to conclusions."

"Do you know how much gold the prince spent on this expedition?" Nila said. "He will be furious."

Meddigar sighed. He'd need to handle this just right.

He put a hand on her shoulder. She tensed.

"I need you to listen, Nila. This is important. Maybe the most important thing you'll ever hear. I respect you and your intelligence, so I know you'll recognize the gravity of what I'm about to tell you. Will you listen?"

A pause. Then she nodded, the tension leaking out of her.

And then Meddigar shoved her as hard as he could.

He caught the briefest glimpse of her astonished face right before she went over, too bewildered to even scream. He watched her go down, bouncing once and then again off a particularly jagged outcropping and then rolling and rolling until she came finally to a stop at the bottom.

He glanced over his shoulder. No one had seen.

He looked back, watched her a moment. She didn't move. Really, there could be no doubt of the outcome.

Meddigar turned, clearing his throat. "Help!" he shouted. "There's been a terrible accident."

CHAPTER
TWENTY-FIVE

Climbing down the cliff hadn't been as difficult as it had looked, plenty of handholds and footholds. They descended slowly and methodically, avoiding mishap.

"How far across?" Peyne asked.

"No idea," Maurizan said. "I told you. I've been as far as the shipwreck. This is all new."

Peyne sighed. "Great."

They distributed the waterskins and backpacks of supplies among the four of them. Peyne carried five skins and a canvas bag slung over his shoulder with jerky and dried apricots. The supplies were simultaneously too heavy and too light.

How long to trudge across? Will there be water on the other side? Will there be anything?

Maurizan led them east of the great yawning black hole in the ground. They traded theories on what it was and what might have caused it. At last, curiosity got the better of them, and they veered toward it to have a look.

The hard, cracked ground gave way to loose sand again, and within a hundred yards of the edge, the ground began to slant steeply toward the hole. The sand shifted suddenly beneath Maurizan's feet, and she went down. The sand slide would have carried her all the way to the hole and over the edge if Jaff and Peyne hadn't each grabbed an arm and hauled her back.

They decided they weren't that curious after all and gave the hole a wide berth as they continued on.

They marched silently, single file, putting one foot in front of the other, the hours endless. After nightfall, they camped without a fire, dropping where they stood and falling immediately to sleep, none appreciating the stars brilliant and close overhead. They rose with the dawn to repeat the process.

By midafternoon, they reached the cliff on the far side, similar to the one they'd climbed down before. They rested for an hour, no one eager for the climb but knowing it was inevitable.

Going up was harder than coming down had been. It took hours to reach the top, and even though there was still daylight enough to march, they collapsed and slept within a dozen yards of the cliff's edge.

Halfway through the next day, Jaff stopped suddenly, squinting into the sky. "Maurizan, your eagle. Look!" He pointed.

Maurizan shook her head. "No, Jaff. I sent him away."

Peyne and Zayda looked as well, but the sky was clear.

"Are you blind?" Jaff said. "He's right there. Can't you see—"

He lowered his arm. "Never mind."

Normally, Peyne would take some satisfaction knowing he wasn't the only one susceptible to hallucinations. Instead, it was a reminder of what could happen. Dying of thirst or starvation wasn't the only peril in the deep desert. They could all literally lose their minds.

They came to the end of the dead sea the next day and found themselves again traversing dunes. Just when Peyne thought the trip could not possibly be more miserable, a hot wind kicked up, not quite a storm but enough to sting their eyes with sand. They trudged on, heads down.

The land took on a gradual upward slope. The desert seemed to be actively working against them, pushing back the impertinent intruders.

The next day, the water ran out.

A pall descended over the group. Nobody said it aloud, but they knew. They were going to die. Still, they plodded on. There was nothing else to do.

Peyne remember how thirsty he'd been lost at sea after the *Pride of Klaar* had gone down. That thirst was nothing compared to this. The wind continued to lash him with sand. His skin was raw.

They headed up a steep dune and stopped halfway. As if by unspoken agreement, they all collapsed into the sand, exhausted. They lay there, not speaking, not caring, hopeless.

An hour crept by.

Peyne's eyes popped open. He had to pee.

He almost had the energy to laugh. How could there possibly be enough moisture in his body to make urine? He tried to remember the last time he'd had to relieve himself but couldn't. Well, it had to happen eventually.

He ignored it and closed his eyes.

Peyne opened his eyes. He couldn't ignore it.

If I'm going to die, I'm not going to die pissing my pants.

With great effort, he stood and began trudging upward, looking for a private spot. He crested the dune, unlaced his breeches, and did his business. A sad dribble. He laced himself up again.

He looked up and saw them. People standing in the distance, barely visible in the swirling sand. The sight startled him momentarily, and then he laughed and went back down the dune.

The others roused as he approached. He plopped down in a sitting position, rubbing his eyes and chuckling to himself.

"What's with you?" Zayda asked.

"Nothing. Seeing things again."

"What things?"

"People. It's nothing. A mirage."

"What did he say?" Maurizan asked. "People?"

"I told you it's nothing," Peyne said.

"I want to look." Zayda rose, began climbing the dune.

"Me too." Jaff followed her.

A second later, Maurizan lurched to her feet and followed also.

Peyne sighed. "Fine." He climbed back up the dune, much more slowly than the others.

He joined them at the top. All three looked through the blowing sand, eyes squinting.

"Not people," Maurizan said. "Statues."

It had been a trick of the desert and the poor visibility in the blowing sand that had made Peyne think people were standing relatively close by.

The statues were actually forty feet tall and an hour's hike from where Peyne had originally spotted them from atop the dune. They grew larger as the group marched closer, the statues and their environs taking shape gradually but clearly.

There were seven statues in all, three on each side, lining a wide, shallow valley, and then one in the middle at the far end. The statues were of winged women, reminiscent of the wrecked ship's prow. Some held swords aloft, eyes looking skyward. Others held shields in front of them, heads down as if in prayer.

The seventh statue stood tall with her head thrown back, arms spread wide in triumph or welcome or both.

"Made of copper, I think," Peyne said. "The metal turns that sort of pale green."

"Big statues," Jaff said. "That's a lot of copper."

"Probably not solid," Peyne said. "The statues in the Hall of Kings in Merridan are made with copper over an iron frame."

Jaff considered, still looking at the statues. "Still expensive."

"The Valley of the Seven Guardians," Zayda said.

Peyne looked at her. "What?"

"Something the old woman told me." A wan smile from Zayda. "It seems like so long ago. Like a lifetime."

"It's not a valley," Maurizan said.

They looked at her, waited for her to explain.

"I mean, it's a valley *now*, I guess, but look at that line of stone columns between the statues." Maurizan pointed along one side and then the other. "And over there. With a little imagination, you can see piers. This was a harbor."

"Can we assume a harbor means a harbor *town*?" Jaff asked.

"If so, it'll be up there." Maurizan pointed where the rock wall of the valley rose up another thirty feet behind the final statue. "Since we've no other pressing engagements, I suggest we have a look."

They set out again, hiking along the floor of the valley. Peyne paused, looked back, and saw that Zayda wasn't coming with them. He went to her. She stood still, eyes closed.

"Zayda?"

Her eyes popped open. "I smell water."

The statues stood on bases at least twenty-five feet high, contributing to the looming effect as they walked among them. They found a landing behind the base of the seventh statue. They climbed up to it. Once on top, Peyne looked back out into the valley, tried to imagine a harbor filled with water, boats tied up along the piers. Had this been the gateway to some thriving civilization millennia ago? Or some powerful wizard's private domain?

A zigzagging staircase had been carved into the natural rock and went up to the top of the wall. The stairs were smooth and wide enough to accommodate groups passing one another going up and down. Again, Peyne tried to imagine it. People disembarking from ships after a long journey, climbing the stairs home. Or those coming down the stairs, eyes on the sea that stretched out before them, excited for the journey, new people in new ports.

What sort of cataclysm could erase an entire people?

They started up the stairs with a renewed energy, the news of possible water nearby temporarily lifting their fatigue.

As they neared the top, they saw rusty chains hanging from multiple pulleys.

"For lowering cargo?" Jaff guessed.

Maurizan shrugged. "I would imagine so. Zayda, is this still the right way?"

"I think," Zayda said. "Yes."

They made it to the top to discover they were on a large plateau.

The ruined city lay before them. Peyne simultaneously marveled at its magnificence while gasping at the destruction that had obviously befallen it once upon a time. Their spot above the harbor stood at a slight elevation, offering a good overall view of the city. The plateau stretched perhaps a mile east to west and half again as far north to south. In terms of area, it would have fit ten times into his home city of Merridan. The ancient dwellers here had compensated by erecting their buildings very close together, narrow avenues crisscrossing the cityscape. They'd also built high. Peyne saw no single-story buildings.

Many of the structures, especially those nearest the harbor, had been wrecked to the point that only iron frames remained, ghostly skeletons of the edifices they'd once been. Sand piled high against the walls of the intact buildings, spilled from the windows of the lower floors.

Amid the destruction, two landmarks, basically intact, drew the eye, both domes.

The first dome stood more or less in the center of the city, a wide area of open space around it, odd perhaps in a place where square footage was at a premium. Three wide boulevards led away from the dome, stretching in straight lines east, west, and south. They were far wider than the other lanes and divided the city into sections.

The second dome was much larger and sat atop a once magnificent palace directly across from the harbor on the other side of the plateau, at the same elevation. The palace appeared to be the least damaged structure in the city but had clearly seen better days.

"How does a nation lose an entire city?" Peyne wondered aloud. "There must have been thousands of people here at one time. Tens of thousands."

"You don't look for something you don't believe in," Jaff said. "Why risk your neck in the deep desert for a fairy story?"

And yet that's exactly what they'd done. They stood another moment, gawking at legend.

Zayda pointed. "The water's down there."

And just like that, legends would have to wait, awe vanishing in a puff of thirst. They found another wide stone stairway and descended into the lost city.

They tried to find a direct route to the city's center, but it was difficult going. They sank ankle deep into the sand as they went, buildings rising high enough on either side to block the sunlight. At one point, they turned a corner to find a ship blocking the way, lodged between two buildings. It was made of the same metal as the ship they'd passed days earlier, now rusted, and almost as big.

"How did this happen, do you think?" Jaff asked.

"A tidal wave," Maurizan said.

"I don't know what that is," Jaff said.

"But you know what a wave is, right?"

"Of course."

"Now imagine one two hundred feet high," Maurizan said.

Jaff shook his head. "Impossible."

"Sherrik," Peyne said.

Maurizan nodded. "Exactly."

"You mean the port?" Zayda asked. "There was a storm or something, yes? This was many years ago."

"Not a storm," Maurizan said. "An ink mage. She created a wall of water and smashed the city. She destroyed the outer wall. Flooded every street. Ships smashed against the stone wharves like nothing."

Jaff snorted. "You *believe* those stories?"

"Not stories," Maurizan told them. "I was there."

◆ ◆ ◆

"And you think the same thing happened to the lost city?" Venny asked from across the fire. "An ink mage attacked it like Sherrik?"

It had become customary the last few nights for Meddigar and Venny to converse around the fire at day's end. Frankly, he didn't enjoy anyone else's company. Venny had not shown any particular affection for him, but she was well mannered and educated. She'd been the first to offer sympathies upon hearing of his apprentice's accidental death.

It had only occurred to Meddigar just in time he should pretend to be sad. His skills as a thespian had proven adequate.

"I thought it might be something like that until I saw the crater," Meddigar said. "I didn't see the crater my first journey. I originally approached the lost city from . . . a circuitous route. I believe the crater was created by one of the cosmic rocks pulled from the sky by one of the great wizards of old."

Venny's eyes narrowed. "How does that result in an enormous, destructive wave?"

"Isn't it obvious?" Meddigar asked. "The rock striking land might actually have done less harm. A water strike has far worse consequences. What happens if you drop a pebble in a puddle?"

"Ripples?"

"Yes."

She thought about it. "The bigger the rock, the bigger the ripples."

"Ripples taller than the prayer tower in Zinevah," Meddigar said. "Traveling faster than an avalanche in the Glacial Wastes."

Venny's face had gone blank. She was trying to imagine such a spectacle. "When the ripples reached land . . . that would be catastrophic."

"The city sits atop a rocky plateau, so some of the wave's destructive power might have been absorbed by the harbor wall," Meddigar explained. "But not the bulk of it. I've spent some time considering the aftermath. The initial wave would have killed most of the populace, and when the water eventually receded, the bodies would remain, stacked like cord wood and left to bake in the merciless sun. The dead would have outnumbered the living. Disease would rise, taking more of the survivors, if any, and vermin would feed upon the corpses and spread more disease. Rebuilding would have been an impossible task. Fleeing the city would have been the only sane option, but flee where? The sea had gone and all the boats wrecked in any case. And so the dead took management of the city, and it faded into legend."

"Suddenly I'm less eager to see this place," Venny said.

Meddigar chuckled. "Don't worry. The bones have long turned to dust. Most of my previous visit was quite dull actually. The majority of the buildings are empty husks."

"There had to be something of interest," Venny said. "Or why bother coming back?"

"Of course," the wizard said. "The great wizards knew how to keep their secrets safe, how to seal themselves away from the elements, away from time itself. The ink magic had been preserved, the means to create ink mages and control them. I am considered by some to be an accomplished wizard." Meddigar sighed, shaking his head. "Compared to the magicians of old, I am nothing. I'm looking forward to exploring the lost workshops of the ancient wizards again. There is much to learn."

"Hopefully these workshops are well hidden," Venny said.

"Not especially," Meddigar said. "I remember the location well enough, so that might give me some advantage over a newcomer.

We lost some time finding a path down the cliff that would allow the dromadan to descend safely, but Krokett assures us we're only two days behind, three at most."

"I'm not as eager to catch up to them as you are," Venny said. "They almost brought the Last Village down around our ears. I just want to make maps. Sorcery and swordplay are out of my league."

"We'll do our best to keep you out of harm's way," Meddigar said. "As far as Maurizan and her people are concerned, I wouldn't be surprised if we stumbled over their corpses any day now. The desert is merciless to the unprepared. Thirst and hunger may have taken them."

"Can I ask you a question?"

"Of course." Meddigar felt suddenly wary. The girl was naturally curious, and she'd never before felt the need to ask permission before a question.

She pitched her voice lower and asked, "Why do you want Maurizan's map so badly?"

He could almost hear the question she was really asking. *You're lost, aren't you?* Did Venny suspect what had really happened to Nila?

Meddigar's first impulse was to lie. And then suddenly there was an overwhelming desire to tell her the truth, to unburden himself. He realized that he was deeply lonely, realized further that this was something he'd known on some level for a long time. The prince could provide him with any number of females to satisfy his carnal needs, but none of these women were companions or confidants.

The wizard ultimately settled on a less damning version of the truth.

"As I mentioned before, I came via a different route the first time," he said. "If she knows another path, a faster or safer path, then I want to know also. And consider this. Your father is unsurpassed in mapmaking, is he not? What information could Maurizan have possibly unearthed to fill in the blank space on a map if your father could not?"

He could see Venny giving his words serious thought.

At last, she said, "But these are guesses, surely. For all you know, she has no map at all."

Meddigar had worried himself over that very notion. If that were the case, then the lost were following the lost, and likely the desert would take them all.

CHAPTER
TWENTY-SIX

"What in the bloody blue blazes do you mean there's no map?" Shouting hurt Peyne's dry throat, but under the circumstances, he felt a little shouting to be justified. "We've been following you as if you know where you're going."

"I do," Maurizan said. "And there *is* a map, so keep your voice down."

"But you just said—"

"You said you wanted to *see* the map, and I said I didn't have one to *show* you," Maurizan snapped. "It's not on paper. It's up here." She tapped the side of her head with a stiff index finger. "Ink mage recall, remember? If I tap into the spirit, I can see every crease and ink blot on the map. I destroyed it so it couldn't be stolen. Then I rolled up some parchment as a decoy. An exploding glyph on the inside so any thief would get a nasty surprise."

Peyne sulked. There had seemed no point in looking at the map before, but now that it seemed they might actually find water and live another day, his curiosity had resurfaced. Where were they? How had they gotten here?

What does it matter now? We're here, aren't we?

Except maybe it would be nice to get back home again. Alive.

Maurizan's theory that the city had been destroyed by a tidal wave had given rise to a myriad of other questions, but Maurizan had told them she was dead on her feet and might murder all of them if forced to answer questions.

In light of such a pronouncement, they agreed to table further conversation until they'd located the source of the water.

They picked their way through the narrow lanes, debris or a collapsed building often turning them aside. There seemed to be no straight path to where they were trying to go. They were following Zayda's nose, an inexact process at best.

Maurizan tapped into the spirit and tried to catch the scent of water also. Although successful, her sense of smell was not as keen as Zayda's.

"The chuma sticks," Maurizan speculated. "I smoke too much."

It seemed to hit the gypsy hard that after twenty years as an ink mage, she was just discovering this limitation.

After three hours of slowly plodding through the ruined city, they happened upon one of the wide boulevards they'd spied from atop the harbor wall.

Except it wasn't a boulevard.

It was a canal.

Or at least some of them thought it was a canal. They couldn't guess what else it might be.

The way was smooth, tiled in white with an intricate blue pattern of lilies. Peyne marveled. The fountains on the royal grounds in Merridan were tiled in such a way, but this canal stretched a mile. It must have been fabulously expensive, boasting a city that had riches to squander. Many of the tiles along the canal were chipped and weathered with age but still a testament to artisans long dead. The canal was a dozen feet deep and forty feet wide.

And it was, of course, as dry as a bone. The sand seemed to barely collect here.

"I don't believe it's a canal," Jaff said. "Such an extravagant use of water is unheard of. What's the purpose? There are no crops here to irrigate."

"Maybe it was some kind of transportation system," Zayda said.

Jaff shook his head. "Absurd. How many millions of gallons of water would that take when one could just walk?"

"There are places where water isn't so scarce," Peyne said. "Canals like this wouldn't be uncommon."

"This isn't other places," Jaff said. "This is Fyria."

"Who knows what it was a thousand years ago," Peyne shot back. "People might have been farting water, for all you know."

"Insolent ass!"

"Enough!" Maurizan shouted. "First we find water. Then we can debate whatever idiocy you like."

"Yes, shut up your stupid bickering," Zayda said. "What difference does it make right now when we're dying of thirst? Shut up! Shut up, both of you!"

They all stood silent a moment.

Then Peyne slowly raised his arm, pointing along the path of the canal. "Just tell me plainly. Is there, or is there not, water in *that* direction?"

"Yes," she said. "I think."

"You *think?*"

She lifted her chin, expression hardening. "Yes. I *know.*"

Peyne shrugged and started walking. The other three followed.

Walking along the dry canal turned out to be a good choice. It provided a straight, uncluttered path, and Peyne sent up a silent prayer of thanks to any gods who might happen to be listening. He wasn't particularly devout, but he'd take help from anywhere he could get it.

Ten minutes later, they came upon the boat.

It lay on its side in the center of the canal. They circled the craft, examining it with interest. It was made of some light, durable metal

Peyne had never seen before, not rusty like the previous vessels. It was twenty feet long with bench seating around the interior, a rudder in back, and something like a miniature windmill sticking out of the aft end. An odd piece of machinery like a sealed metal barrel sat in the middle of the boat, and a tube the diameter of a cup sprouted from the top of the barrel. Coiled tubes went in and out of the barrel, gears on the side for no purpose Peyne could guess.

Still, the boat was obviously a boat. He turned to Jaff, gesturing at the vessel, face smug.

"That proves nothing," Jaff said. "We've seen ships out of place already. The tidal wave could have dropped them anywhere."

"To me it looks exactly like the size and type of boat perfect for canal travel," Peyne said.

Jaff made a dismissive gesture. "Now he's a boat expert."

Zayda started walking, didn't wait to see if anyone followed. "We're close. Stay and argue about the boat if you like."

Jaff and Peyne exchanged brief looks.

Then hurried after Zayda.

The dome was made of a dark brassy sort of metal that had somehow retained its color, unlike the copper harbor statues. The canal led directly into the dome. More specifically, the canal led into the gaping maw of a gigantic fish, a stylized sculpture affixed to the side of the dome and cast from the same metal. Huge fins and scales gleamed in the sunlight.

The fish's open mouth arched ten feet above the canal. They craned their necks gawking up at it as they passed underneath and into the enormous dome.

Peyne heard a slight splash and looked down. He stood in an inch of water.

The four of them dropped to their bellies immediately and began to drink. At first, Peyne simply stuck his lips directly into the water, sucking from the floor of the canal. The water had a strong metallic taste, but Peyne didn't care. To him it was the sweetest, most refreshing thing he'd ever put into his mouth. He started scooping in water with his hands, looked up briefly to see the others doing likewise. He splashed a handful onto his face.

Nobody talked for the next few minutes. Only the sounds of slurping and lips smacking and contented sighs.

When Peyne's belly was tight and full, he forced himself to stop drinking. He didn't want to make himself sick. He paused now to take in his surroundings.

The pool of water was only an inch deep, but it covered the floor of the canal, leading into the dome. This part of the canal must have been subtly lower, just enough to keep the water from flowing onward.

Peyne stood, moving farther into the dome as the others continued to drink.

It was cooler beneath the dome. Twenty feet ahead of him, the canal terminated at a gigantic door, apparently made of the same metal as everything else. As he approached, the water became slightly deeper. When he was close enough to place his palm against the door's cool metal, the water was three inches over his ankle.

It seemed an extravagant amount of water after all the time spent in the desert.

The door looked formidable. Again, made from the same metal as the dome itself, it looked like it joined in the middle, two heavy bars with interlocking mechanisms keeping it sealed.

But perhaps not completely sealed after all.

A slight trickling sound drew his attention. Peyne ran his hand down the crack where the two halves of the door met. Water was coming through, leaking through the crack, but not much. He wouldn't have noticed at all if the trickling sound hadn't tipped him off. How long would it have to drip like that to form a pool like this? Months? Years? A long time but certainly not as long as the city had been deserted. So the leak had begun relatively recently, he supposed. The builders of this city had been far more advanced than today's, but nothing lasted forever.

He bent and scooped in another mouthful of water, wondering if the metallic taste came from the door. Maybe it was some kind of storage tank.

Peyne heard the others splashing up behind him and turned.

"Is there water behind this door?" Peyne asked Maurizan.

Peyne wasn't sure why he thought she would know. She'd never been here before, was seeing the place for the first time just as he was.

And yet some instinct told him she did know. Maybe not everything. But something. "You knew we'd find this."

Maurizan shook her head but with hesitation. "Not this exactly."

"But something."

The hesitation again, but then she nodded. Her eyes flicked to Zayda and Jaff.

Everyone waited.

Maurizan sighed. "I need to tell you a story."

She led them up a narrow metal staircase that wound around the outside of the dome, taking them gradually upward.

"Is this strictly necessary?" If not for the water, Peyne wouldn't have been able to climb so many stairs. As it was, his legs still ached. He preferred the cool shade underneath the dome.

"I want to show you something," Maurizan said. "It'll help my story make sense."

"What a view this must have been at one time," Zayda said with wonder. "A shame what happened."

They arrived at the top of the dome where there was a ten-by-ten landing encircled by a metal railing. A large curved brazier sat in the middle of the landing. This evidently was why the stairs existed, Peyne thought. Was the brazier a signal, lit for specific ceremonies?

Maurizan called them to the south side of the landing. She leaned against the rail and asked, "What does a city need to live?"

"My father would say a good economy," Zayda said. "Trade."

"Not to thrive," Maurizan said. "Just to live. The basics."

"Water," Jaff said. "Obviously."

"Food," Zayda said.

"Which can't be grown without water," Jaff said. "Nor can you keep livestock without water."

"Water. And food too," Maurizan said. "What else?"

"Wine," Peyne guessed.

Maurizan frowned at him.

Peyne shrugged.

"What else?" prompted Maurizan. "What does a body need in a climate like this?"

A long, thoughtful silence.

And then Zayda said, "Salt."

Maurizan smiled. "This is a story of water and salt. Peyne, you wanted to know what was on the map in my head, yes?"

"Yes."

"Rivers," Maurizan told him. "Or what had been rivers once upon a time."

Peyne nodded, crossed his arms. "Okay. Let's hear the story."

CHAPTER
TWENTY-SEVEN

The story.

When Maurizan was young, she'd been given the Prime. Other tattoos came later. She understood firsthand the power of an ink mage. She'd seen an ink mage destroy a city simply by calling the wind and creating an enormous wave of seawater. The variety of tattoos and the powers they granted fascinated her.

So for the next twenty years she traveled the world in search of ink magic.

She quickly discovered that the study of ink magic was also the study of history. The origins of the arcane were thought by the learned to be in Fyria, but not the Fyria of today. An ancient Fyria now lost to the ages.

And so Maurizan searched. She chased rumors, cobbled together scraps of information from here and there, piecing together legend and lore, leaving no stone unturned. She haunted civilization's great libraries and listened to stories told by the elders of any tiny village she happened upon. Slowly a picture began to form, and over the years, Maurizan began to feel she intimately knew a city she wasn't sure existed.

The key, of course, was the aquifer.

Find any village or town in Fyria, and it would soon be obvious it had been built around a well or along a river. Jaff had been correct. Farming, the raising of livestock, life itself depended upon water. And so when the greatest store of clean water in Fyria was discovered, naturally a city was built on top of it. Who had done this? A sultan or king of old? Perhaps. The information Maurizan had unearthed suggested one of the original wizards himself.

There were no salt mines in Fyria. Not one. But the sea provided ample salt. It was extracted on the coast and carried inland and traded for other goods and services.

The lost city perched atop a plateau next to what once had been an inland sea. A salt sea. By whatever luck or blessing of the gods that made it possible, a plentiful source of salt and a limitless supply of freshwater had existed side by side in this place without contaminating one another.

And so a great city rose and prospered. Not only were the wizards more advanced then, but so too were the architects, engineers, physicians, and so on.

From the city sprang three rivers. One flowed more or less to the east. The second west and the third south. Swaths of green flourished along these rivers. Villages were built. Farms raised crops. Foodstuffs flowed into the city. Salt and manufactured goods flowed back out. A thriving, unparalleled paradise.

These were guesses, but good guesses, Maurizan thought, based on puzzle pieces she'd been trying to fit together for two decades.

How long had this magnificent civilization stood? A hundred years? Five hundred?

But all things end.

The calamity was so sudden and utterly complete that it had nearly wiped the city from all memory.

Maurizan had long pondered what had caused the great wave. She'd talked to the southern islanders on one of her visits there, and an old woman had told her offshore earthquakes could generate such waves. Or perhaps it had been the work of some mage.

In the end, what caused it didn't matter. The wave hit. A destructive force several times larger than the wave she'd witnessed so long ago in Sherrik.

The city took the brunt of the hit, but by no means was the catastrophe an isolated incident. The momentum of the wave carried along all three rivers, a massive surge of water, smashing riverside villages as it went, sweeping away huts like handfuls of twigs. The paths of the rivers funneled the destruction hundreds of miles and into the oceans on both coasts.

Since the water was salt, it ruined all farmland. Nothing would ever grow there again, even if anyone had been alive to plant.

And then the rivers themselves vanished.

Slowly, inevitably, the desert took over. The region became so inhospitable that travelers shunned it. And several generations later, nobody could think of a good reason to risk journeying there. Stories? Oh, yes. A lost city filled with untold wonders. The foolish could risk their lives on such nonsense. Not the wise.

A lesser empire grew up along the coast and the rivers in the north. Sultans had vowed to return Fyria to its former glory with only the barest inkling of what that glory had looked like.

Few found their way to the city now. Fewer still returned.

And Maurizan had spent half her life getting here.

"What do you mean the rivers vanished?" Jaff asked.

"It's not unheard of," Peyne said. "The courses of rivers can change over the centuries or dry up altogether as the climate of a region shifts."

In spite of his best efforts to avoid his tutors as a child, some of the learning had evidently stuck.

Jaff hit Peyne with the side eye. "Always the expert."

"Peyne's right," Maurizan said. "It can happen that way. But I don't think that's the case here."

Jaff crossed his arms. "And?"

"I think the rivers were turned off," Maurizan said.

They stared blankly at her.

Maurizan shifted nervously. She must have known how her theory sounded. "I'm actually not being figurative."

The blanks stares did not abate.

"Look." Maurizan turned and pointed at the canal they'd used to approach the dome. "One river leading east." She shifted her pointer finger to the next canal. "A river going south." She pointed at the final canal. "And one going all the way to the western ocean."

Very slowly, the blank stares became incredulous.

Finally Jaff said, "You're telling me they created their own rivers? I don't believe it."

"I'm forced to agree with Jaff," Peyne said. "Aquifers are replenished by rain, and it doesn't rain in Fyria. The biggest aquifer in the world would eventually run dry."

"I'm thirty-four years old," Jaff said. "I've seen it rain four times."

"You didn't even think they were canals," Maurizan said heatedly.

"Fine. I'll concede the canals," Jaff said. "I do not concede rivers."

"Peyne said climates can shift." It was Zayda finally speaking up. "For all we know, it rained every week back then."

"I'm not saying I have all the answers," Maurizan said. "I don't know everything about rivers or aquifers or wizards. I wasn't even sure I believed this city would be here until I saw it. But now that I have seen it, I have to think almost anything's possible."

Peyne waved his hand in front of him, as if trying to banish the clutter of guesses the conversation had become. "Look, we're going about this all wrong. Let's say the rivers were made by the ancients. And let's suppose they did turn them off. So what?"

Maurizan sighed. "Because King Gant wants me to turn them back on again."

CHAPTER
TWENTY-EIGHT

"You know Gant?" Peyne asked. "Wait, he wants the rivers back on? No, forget that. You know Gant? He *sent* you here?"

"It's not as simple as that," Maurizan said. "Gant was more interested in the ink magic. He knew I'd been investigating it for years and that the key lay in Fyria."

Peyne nodded as he listened. Ambassador Korick had told him something similar. If Fyria was raising an army of ink mages, then Gant needed to know. That had been Peyne's mission until he'd postponed it to help win Zayda's freedom.

"But when I told Gant my three-river theory, it intrigued him," Maurizan said. "It's why I sought you out, Jaff. If people had another place to go, out from under the sultan's thumb—"

"And I told you then we're not separatists," Jaff said. "We want to remake Fyria into something we can be proud of again. Not run away and start over somewhere."

"But there *are* separatists," Maurizan said. "Anyway, Gant didn't specifically tell me to turn on the rivers. How could he have guessed that? It's impossible. He simply told me to show them. Show the people of Fyria such a place exists. Then whatever happens will happen."

"And why would anyone in Helva care about such a thing?" Jaff asked. "For what purpose?"

"To stir the pot," Peyne said. "To make the sultan look inward instead of north toward Helva."

"We don't need foreigners stirring anything," Jaff said.

"It's what you and the rest of the insurgents are doing."

"We're not *foreigners!*"

"We should turn them on." Zayda's voice was so quiet and calm that it somehow demanded their attention more than if she'd shouted. "The rivers. All three. Let them flow again."

"You agree with *them?*" Jaff didn't use the word *foreigners* again, but it was clear what he meant.

"I agree to turn them on," Zayda said. "But not to distract the sultan or win a war or do anything like that. We should do it because it's an amazing thing. An impossible thing. How can we come this far and look something impossible in the face and not try? Because if ever this place had been green and living, how could we not know that? Not know how it happened? We must know. I *demand* to know."

They all looked at each other.

"Works for me," Maurizan said.

It had been only the promise of an opportunity to prove them all wrong that finally got Jaff to agree.

But Peyne could see it plain enough on the man's face. Curiosity. Zayda had been right. To come all this way and *not* investigate such ancient wonders? Folly.

The four circled the dome a few times, attempting to divine the workings of the three great doors. The other two didn't leak. Knocking on the doors produced a sound like knocking on a great tank of water.

"If we open the doors, we can release the rivers," Maurizan said. "I'm sure of it."

"I don't see levers or crank wheels anywhere," Peyne said. "And those interlocking mechanisms . . . well, we're not going to *force* them open. That's for sure."

"We're missing something obvious, I'm sure. Keep looking."

They fanned out, each methodically searching some section of the dome's interior. The structure actually consisted of two domes. The large outer dome was merely a hollow covering for the structure beneath, the huge ornate fish affixed to the outside, their gaping mouths set to vomit the rivers in three directions. The inner dome was somewhat smaller but seemed to be made of a thicker metal. Was that because it was holding back tons of water? Peyne could only guess. The enormous doors occupied three sides of the dome. He casually circled the structure to the fourth side.

Before he could begin his examination, Peyne heard someone coming up behind him, turned to see Zayda approaching. They'd had the presence of mind not to toss aside the empty skins when they'd run out of water in the desert. Zayda had three of the skins, refilled, slung over her shoulder.

"I have to go," she said. "I've already told the others."

He blinked. "Go *where*?"

Zayda flicked the collar around her neck, and it rang dully. A wan smile. "This is why I came, remember? There are answers somewhere in this city, and that domed palace is my guess. I need to get this thing off."

"But . . . but . . ." He gestured vaguely at the dome and its environs. "We're turning on rivers and whatnot. It was *your* idea."

"It was Maurizan's idea. I just agreed," Zayda said. "And anyway, three can do this as well as four. Three of you for the three rivers. That's good symmetry, don't you think?"

Peyne frowned. "I don't like the idea of you mucking around an ancient lost city all by yourself."

"I'm an ink mage. Is there really anything extra you could do to protect me?"

"I still don't like it."

She stepped closer to him, touched his cheek. She tilted her head up and leaned in, lips softly touching his. They stood like that a moment, and then she stepped back, smiling, and he could see she was trying to be cheerful.

"You're not allowed to get yourself killed while I'm away," she said.

"You be careful too."

She gave him a final peck on the cheek, then turned to go, leaving at a jog as if she wanted to be away before changing her mind.

Peyne watched her round the dome and vanish from sight. The possibility of not seeing her again struck him harder than he'd anticipated.

He immediately turned back to the task at hand, trying to put her out of his mind. Zayda had been right. That he might go with her as some sort of guardian was laughable. She was an ink mage.

Whereas Peyne was just some fool who'd somehow stumbled into this mess.

He ran his hand across the cool, smooth metal of the doorless side of the dome. This was going to take longer that Maurizan thought. They could be here for weeks trying to figure out the doors' mechanisms, and Peyne was acutely aware there was a wizard two days behind them.

But we can't be sure of that. We don't have Maurizan's bird spying for us anymore. They could have caught up. They could be here any minute. Or maybe they ran out of water and perished in the desert.

One could hope.

In any case, it wasn't in his best interest to dawdle. The sooner they achieved—well, whatever the blazes Maurizan thought she was trying to achieve—then the sooner Peyne could go after Zayda. And Gant was his friend. If this was something the king wanted, then . . .

He paused. *What was that?*

He ran his hand back over the spot, his fingertips barely feeling it. In the waning light beneath the shadow of the dome, he'd had no chance to see it. He went to one knee, squinted. A crack? A seam? He traced the seam from the floor to a spot at least a foot over his head. He quickly examined the area to either side of the seam, cursing the ancient builders for their seeming disdain for obvious doorknobs and latches. He gave up using his eyes and began feeling along the metal again.

He'd almost given up hope when his fingertips ran across another crack four feet to the right of the first. This one didn't run straight up and down. Instead, it made a small circle about the size of a soup bowl. Peyne casually gave it a push and gasped, startled, when it flipped open.

He bent, peeked inside. A valve wheel the size of his palm.

This is when you should call the others and consult about what to do next.

Instead, he reached in, took hold of the wheel, and twisted.

It turned easily.

A sudden hiss of escaping air made him jump back. "Shit!"

The crack in the metal wall opened half an inch as the hissing faded and then died all together.

Peyne pointed at the crack. "Hey!" He looked around. Where was everybody? "Hey, I found . . . I found . . ." What in blazes had he found? "I found *something!*"

Jaff and Maurizan appeared from opposite directions, converging on the spot where he stood. A second later, he was explaining what he'd found and how.

Maurizan tried to cram her fingers into the crack. "We need it just a little wider. Jaff, your dagger."

Jaff drew the dagger, jammed it into the crack, and very slowly pried it open enough for Peyne and Maurizan to insert their fingers. He pulled one way, she the other. Slowly, grudgingly, the two halves of the door began to slide in opposite directions.

"It's coming," Maurizan said. "I think it's on wheels or a track or something. Keep pulling."

They grunted and pulled, stopping when the two halves stood open three feet apart. They stepped back, panting and looking into the darkened interior with wonder.

Maurizan slipped her backpack off her shoulder. "I've got a lamp."

A small oil lamp. She lit it with flint and steel, then held the light aloft, the three huddled together as they entered the chamber.

They stood inside, trying to see everything at once, trying to understand, hulking machinery all around them glinting in the lamp's flickering light.

"What . . . the blazes . . . is this?" Peyne asked.

"Just don't touch anything yet," Maurizan said. "Just . . . wait. Let's figure this out."

So they stood and looked and took it all in.

Immediately to their left sat a huge metal thing that looked like a fat oven with a heavy metal door. A smaller door stood to the left of it, only five feet high. Directly over the "oven," hanging down from the ceiling, was the bottom half of a big metallic sphere. Pipes crisscrossed the ceiling. Some as thin as Peyne's wrist, others as big around as his thigh. A huge gear wheel hung on the far wall. It missed meshing with the bottom half of a second gear wheel by six inches, the top half disappearing into the ceiling.

"Like a giant clock," Peyne said.

"I've never seen one," Jaff admitted.

"I have," Maurizan said. "But even the gears in the great clock tower of Merridan aren't *that* big."

Ten feet in front of them, a row of levers sprouted from a mount in the floor. Six levers, three sets of two. Each set consisted of a lever that came up to Peyne's waist and another lever right next to it about six inches shorter.

Maurizan moved toward the levers for a closer examination. Peyne followed. "Look." She pointed.

A marking had been carefully etched into the floor in front of each set of levers. The first was a circle with a slash through it. The next a circle with two slashes through it, and the last a circle with three slashes.

"Doors number one, two, and three," Peyne said. "Simple."

"Don't knock simple," Maurizan said.

She grabbed the first lever.

"Uh, maybe we should pause here a moment," Peyne suggested. "You don't know what might—"

Maurizan pulled.

The lever didn't budge.

Maurizan grunted, muscles tense, face turning red. Finally she let go.

"Yeah, that's not going anywhere."

Peyne glanced over his shoulder at Jaff who was still looking at the big oven with the iron door. "You remember the boat we passed on the way here? The smaller one in the canal, I mean."

"So you admit it was a canal?"

Jaff frowned. "Close your mouth and listen for a change."

Peyne drifted back to stand next to Jaff. "Yes. I remember."

Jaff pointed at the oven. "There was a smaller one of these on the boat. I remember because it reminds me of a still I saw once. Old men making grak."

"What, pray tell, is grak?" Peyne asked.

"A rather foul-smelling homemade booze," Maurizan said. "It's terrible. Even *you* wouldn't drink it."

"Don't be so sure," Peyne said. "It's been a long time since my last goblet of wine. Beggars can't be choosers."

"I was actually trying to make a point," Jaff said.

Peyne held up a placating hand. "Apologies. Please continue."

"The old men lit a fire under the still, the big round part they called a boiler," Jaff explained. "The pressure inside would build. Sometimes if they were not careful, the pressure would build and the boiler would explode."

Peyne looked at Jaff.

Jaff looked back.

Peyne cleared his throat. "I fail to see how explosions help us at this particular moment. One might even argue they'd be counterproductive."

"The explosions were not on purpose. That's not the point," Jaff said. "It's because the pressure would build up."

Peyne looked at Maurizan. She shrugged. He looked back at Jaff. "And?"

"Don't you remember Maurizan's steam-powered men? The pressure builds up and then is released in such a way that"—Jaff waved vaguely at the machinery around them—"that . . . makes it do *something.*"

Maurizan's eyes played over everything in the room. "He might be right."

Jaff pointed at a huge pipe leading into the sphere-shaped container over the boiler. "This could fill that big bowl-looking thing with water." He indicated a smaller pipe leading away. "And then the steam goes into there perhaps. The built-up energy is released in a way that turns the gear wheels."

"How do you know this?" Peyne asked.

"I don't *know* anything."

Maurizan nudged Peyne out of the way and spoke directly to Jaff. "So what would you do next?"

"I have no idea."

"You've seen a still," Maurizan said. "Of the three of us, you're our official expert."

"I have no confidence in this enterprise," Peyne muttered.

They ignored him.

Jaff went to one knee, opened the heavy metal door, and peered inside. "I think we need to start a fire."

"With what?" Peyne asked. "Everything's gone to dust that isn't metal."

"They wouldn't send out for firewood every time they wanted to get the thing going," Jaff said. "There'd be a store of it close at hand surely."

He reached for the latch of the little door on the side, yanked it open. A miniature avalanche of lumpy black rocks spilled out and around his ankles.

Maurizan squinted at them. "Charcoal?"

Peyne picked up one of the rocks. "No, but some kind of coal, I think. In the Glacial Wastes, the tribesmen mine this and use it for heating. Not a lot of trees up there. I mean, if it's the same stuff. I've never seen any. No idea how to light it."

"Some of the lamp oil," Jaff suggested.

A determined look on Maurizan's face. "Do it."

"Wait," Peyne said. "How big was this still you saw?"

"Much smaller than this."

"But you said they exploded sometimes," Peyne insisted. "Could this thing explode the same way?"

"The same way? No." Jaff shook his head. "This explosion would be much bigger."

The going was much slower than Zayda had anticipated.

The domed palace didn't seem so far as the crow flies. Crows, however, didn't have to bother with narrow streets clogged with debris. She'd often have to backtrack and circle around, hunting for a clearer path. By the time the sun set, plunging her into darkness, the palace had drawn only a little closer.

Zayda found a quiet place to sit on a broken column. She supposed it had once been part of the magnificent entrance of some magnificent abode. Now it was a marble stool. She didn't want to stumble and break her neck in the dark, so she sipped water from a skin, ate a piece of jerky, and waited.

The silence was stunning and complete. Even in the deep desert, she'd been with the others, and when she'd slept at night, there'd been the rustle of clothing, Jaff's light snoring, or the occasional snort of one of the dromadan when they'd still been alive.

It was with some relief an hour later when the moon rose, and she opened herself to its cold light. She let the power of it fill her. There had been so many times as they'd traipsed through the desert she'd been tempted to fill herself with moonglow and tap into the spirit to fend off the agonizing thirst and crippling fatigue. But she'd been warned. One could not simply stay tapped into the spirit indefinitely. Ink mages had burned themselves out that way. At least, that's what she'd been told. She believed it. She'd felt the seductive power. There had been times she hadn't wanted to let go.

Ten minutes later, she rose from her perch on the broken column, the path lit by her own glow.

Eventually, the debris and rubble lessened, allowing Zayda to pick her way along more easily. Soon she stood before the wide steps leading up to the palace. She climbed them slowly, head up as she took in the structure's enormity and grandeur. A line of columns guarded the front of the palace, each at least ten feet around and forty feet high. The dome that topped the palace was of the same brassy-looking metal she'd seen elsewhere in the city.

She passed between the center columns onto a wide terrace. Life-size statues stood on marble bases about thirty feet apart all along the length of the terrace. She paused to look up at the one nearest her. It was the same pale green as statues in the harbor. A man, tall and broad chested, a warrior by the look of his armor. It wasn't the armor of connected metal squares she'd seen most Fyrian soldiers wear. This was full plate, spread wings across the top of the breastplate. One hand rested on the hilt of a sheathed sword, not a scimitar, but a short, very wide blade. The man's helm had a topknot of hair that flowed over one shoulder. His face was clean-shaven, calm gaze staring into the distance. He looked noble and strong.

And he's been dead for centuries. All of them have.

But she couldn't stop herself wondering who they'd been. Were they a just, intelligent people? Were they conquerors? Some historian might know. It had never come up during any of Zayda's family dinner conversations. Her mother had always been full of gossip, her father obsessed with business. She felt a sudden stab of longing to hear that mindless chatter again, to be with her family.

The large front doors were metal also and stood open, a wing etched onto each. When the doors were closed, they'd form the same spread-winged image that was on the statue's armor.

She held her breath and passed through the doorway, half expecting to be accosted by ancient ghosts.

She wasn't.

The layer of sand on the floor failed to detract from the entrance hall's majesty. The ceiling soared above her, arching and richly detailed with the carvings of winged figures, her glow not even filling all the space. Grand staircases on either side led to the level above.

Zayda realized she wasn't exactly sure how to begin. The palace was vast, and even if she found what she was looking for, would she recognize it when she saw it? Her task suddenly seemed daunting and impossible.

Stop it. You crossed the deep desert and lived. Look what you've done, how far you've come. Just handle it already.

Zayda eyed the closest staircase. The steps made a slow, elegant curve upward. *The most important people are always higher up, right?*

She climbed the stairs. Slowly. Footfalls echoing. She'd never felt more like an intruder in all her life.

She paused on the second-floor landing. Halls branched off in three directions, and the stairs continued upward. No sand here. Explore this floor or keep going?

Up.

Her glow began to fade. Zayda no longer had direct contact with moonlight. She circled the third level until she found a room with a balcony. She went out and opened herself to the moonlight again. Slowly, the power refilled her. She would need time to completely learn how all this worked. In the Last Village, Zayda had felt so full of power that she felt she might burst. Was it possible to go too far? What were the limits?

Once the collar was off, she'd need to spend some serious time discovering the exact parameters of the tattoo.

When she felt bright enough again, she went back inside.

Zayda methodically explored every hallway. Most rooms were empty except for a layer of dust. Anything made of cloth or wood had disintegrated over the centuries. Some of the rooms were obviously bedrooms, evidenced by the metal bed frames that had survived the years. She found a kitchen, metal stove, and pots and pans. Silverware. Goblets made from the strange metal omnipresent in the city.

Room after room of nothing.

I'm wasting my time. This is hopeless.

She persisted.

Be smart about this. Okay, I'm an ink mage. How can I make that work?

As she walked, she looked down, examining the floor. She was tapped into the spirit, and no detail escaped her. It took her only a minute to find what she was looking for, disturbances in the dust, footprints. The city's citizens might be long dead, but Meddigar had been here a relatively short time ago. He'd discovered the exact secrets

Zayda was looking for. Wherever he'd gone, that was exactly where she intended to follow.

The tracks led down a long, back hallway that seemed to stretch the entire width of the palace. She followed it. No doorways. No branching hallways. She picked up speed after noticing her moonglow was fading again. Push on or go back and look for a window so she could recharge herself?

The hall took a sharp right turn and ended at a door.

Her glow faded further.

Looking at the door, Zayda knew immediately that the room behind it wasn't just any other room. The metal of this door was darker and heavier than anything she'd seen before, and the winged image was etched across the top half, similar to other occurrences of the image but with a significant difference. A fanciful image of a heart sat in the center of the wingspread, the heart encircled by an iron chain. What the image might symbolize, she couldn't guess.

Of more immediate interest were the scorch marks near the doorknob and along the wall. Somebody had been serious about getting inside.

Meddigar's work, Zayda supposed. *I guess you don't need a key if you can blast the lock open with a spell.*

She took the knob tentatively and pulled. The slightest resistance, then a sucking sound when it came open, air wafting across her feet.

And then her moonglow faded completely, returning her to darkness.

Damn it.

She dithered a moment. Should she go back, find access to the outdoors, and absorb more moonlight? It would take time, and she might go all the way and come back only to find out she'd discovered some overblown closet. Better to step inside and try to determine at least if it were worth the time. And anyway, if Meddigar came here, then she needed to investigate.

Zayda tapped into the spirit again as she stepped inside, opening all her senses so she might form some sense of the space.

A light flickered overhead.

She gasped, stepping back, hand falling to the hilt of her scimitar. A glass globe, perfectly round, hung from the ceiling. It was the size of a caba melon and emitted a soft glow, gradually brightening until the entire room was well lit.

Zayda stood perfectly still, holding her breath as her eyes made a slow survey of her surroundings.

The first thing she noticed was that, unlike what she'd seen throughout the rest of the city, everything here was intact, as if this chamber had been sealed against any possible disturbance.

She didn't know what a wizard's workshop would look like but supposed it would have been close to this. She remained tapped into the spirit, so she could make an exact inventory, recall every precise detail should it be necessary.

The room was thirty feet wide and more than double that from the door she'd entered to the other side. The space was split down the center by a series of five workshop tables, the surfaces covered here and there by odd instruments or various mixing bowls and other items like some kitchen for cooking up magic instead of food. The walls along both sides were lined with shelves, bottles and vials of various sizes, shapes, and colors. Some were filled with liquids, others with powders, and at least one was filled with what Zayda suspected were human eyeballs.

For mixing ink? Zayda had been given to understand that the ink mixtures varied from tattoo to tattoo. The wizard's workshop was filled with curiosities and wonders.

But it was the chair that intrigued her most.

She'd been holding her breath. She let it out nervously, lips flapping.

The chair sat all the way against the far wall. Zayda walked toward it, resisting the urge to stop and examine the other oddities along the way. A curtain to one side hid some alcove. Her curiosity again tugged at her, but she refused to be distracted.

The chair wasn't so much up against the wall as it was built directly into the metalwork. It was blocky with sharp angles and cast in the same metal as everything else, wide seat and arms but padded in dark leather. Other than the chair's bulk, two things stood out.

An enormous glass container, spherical like the ceiling light but completely transparent, hung over the chair. It was two-thirds filled with a thick metallic liquid the same color as her collar. Glass tubes curved down to connect to metal rods on either side of the chair, affixed to the wall about neck level. Copper wiring had been looped in tight coils around the rods. To the right of the chair, a row of levers sprouted from the wall, various symbols under each.

The realization struck her suddenly. *This chair makes the collars.* She'd seen the metal in "noodle" form. Now before her there was a huge tank of it but fully liquid. If there was a way to make the metal solid, then there must be a way to reverse the process.

Zayda sighed, lowered herself to sit cross-legged in front of the chair. Being tapped into the spirit didn't afford her any additional knowledge but did give her control of her mind, allowing her perfect concentration. She would examine every inch of this contraption.

Until she figured it out, Zayda didn't plan to budge.

CHAPTER
TWENTY-NINE

Sweat poured off their skin. All three were slick and greasy with it.

Peyne and Jaff went shirtless. They'd also kicked off their boots. Maurizan stripped down to a thin shift. She'd taken a dagger to her own breeches, cutting them off several inches above the knee, revealing a *lot* of smooth white leg.

Peyne had gone to great lengths *not* to notice.

Coal dust mixed with the sweat, streaking them black. Their hands were covered completely. They'd been working all night to figure out the workings of the great steam machine. Outside the dome, the sun was rising.

"You'd think there would have been a shovel," Peyne said.

Jaff rolled his eyes. "Yes. We know. You've said that at least ten times."

They scooped the coal by hand, tossing it into the oven that now washed the chamber in a sinister orange glow. The heat was so intense they almost couldn't approach the boiler.

"That's got to be enough," Maurizan said.

"Agreed." Jaff pushed the door shut with his sword. It was too hot to touch. He gestured to a large valve wheel. "Turn it, foreigner."

Peyne took the wheel in both hands, grunted. It turned slowly at first, and then they all heard the sound of the boiler filling.

"It will make steam now," Jaff said.

"Then what?" Peyne asked.

"The steam will build pressure."

The word *explosion* rattled in Peyne's head. "Are you sure you know what you're doing?"

Jaff grinned. "Not in the least."

Maurizan's eyes widened. "What's that noise?"

They all heard it, a low rolling rumble.

"Like a teakettle coming to a boil," Peyne said. "If the teakettle were the size of a barn."

They felt the rumbling in their feet now. The boiler began to rattle.

Peyne took a step back. *Don't explode. Don't explode. Don't explode.*

"Do something!" Maurizan shouted.

Jaff grabbed another valve wheel, this one connected to a thinner pipe leading away from the boiler. He twisted, and the pipe vibrated, the rumble easing as a clanking mechanical racket rose all around them. The vibration of *thunk tunk clank* rattled in their feet.

A high-pitched screech of metal on metal. Slowly the enormous gearwheel on the far wall began to turn.

A whoop from Maurizan as she fist-pumped the air.

I don't believe it, Peyne thought. *This is actually working.*

Maurizan rushed to the first set of levers, grabbing the longer one in both hands.

She pulled.

The lever came forty-five degrees back, locking into place with a loud *clunk*. The entire chamber now shook with the workings of hidden machinery.

The large gear moved upward to mesh with the smaller gear over it, both turning now.

For a fleeting second, Peyne considered turning and running. The rattling, rumbling chamber, the whir of machinery, the oppressive heat, the rotation of the meshing gears—it was all overwhelming. And yet, it was exciting too. He stood transfixed, watched the gears turn.

And then a sound, muffled and distant, echoed throughout the dome. *Clank . . . clank . . . clank . . . clank . . .*

"The door!" Maurizan left the chamber at a run.

The two men followed.

They heard it as they approached, the roaring rush of water. When they rounded the corner, they saw it. Fresh water foamed and spewed from the opening as the two halves of the door separated, the torrent rushing down the canal.

They'd done it. They'd unleashed the river.

They shouted in triumph, Maurizan pulling the two men into a three-way hug as they cheered.

The flow of water eased, the door continuing to open, until the flow died to a trickle and then nothing.

"What happened?" Confusion on Maurizan's face.

The door still clanked open. Maurizan jumped down into the canal, the water waist-deep as she waded toward the doorway. Already the water level was going down. "What . . . where is it?"

"Maurizan, be careful!" Peyne went to the canal's edge where it met the doorway, leaning in to watch the gypsy's progress.

She climbed out of the water and into the area beyond the doorway. It arched dozens of feet over her head. She made a quick circle, looking at everything. "I don't understand."

"I told you," Jaff said behind Peyne, but he obviously took no pleasure in proving the others wrong. He'd been as excited as anyone else when they'd thought they'd set the river free. "Perhaps it was just a place to store water. Nothing more."

"But the canals," Peyne said.

Maurizan went to one knee, running her hand across the wet floor. "There's a crack here down the middle. This opens!"

Peyne and Jaff looked at each other.

Jaff's eyes shot wide. "The other lever!" He turned and ran back toward the boiler room.

"Wait!" Peyne called after him, but Jaff was already around the bend of the dome.

To Maurizan he shouted, "Move back! Jaff's going to pull the other lever."

The ink mage looked at Peyne, then down to the floor, then back at Peyne, understanding blooming in her eyes. She leapt back into the water. It was still draining, the level now down below her backside. Maurizan backed away from the open door, watching and expectant.

Peyne guessed her thoughts. If the aquifer was below them, then the hatch in the floor must be what was really holding it back. The levers were in sets, a longer and a shorter. If the longer one opened the outside door, then it was a good guess the shorter lever might open the panel in the floor.

"Maurizan!"

Her head snapped around. "What?"

He pointed. "Where you're standing."

She looked down, back up at the open door and the closed hatch beyond. If the hatch opened and released the aquifer . . .

"Shit!"

Maurizan splashed to the wall of the canal and reached up. "Help me out of here. Hurry!"

Peyne went to his belly, extending a hand. She jumped and caught it, bracing bare feet against the canal's smooth tile, walking herself up slowly as he pulled.

They heard the *clunk . . . clunk . . . clunk* of the hatch sliding open and froze, heads turning to look, expecting water to spew violently from the opening.

That didn't happen.

She let go of Peyne's hand, slid back down the wall into the water, only knee-deep now. "Hold on."

"Maurizan, don't."

"It's okay," she said. "I'm just taking a quick look."

He watched her climb back up to the doorway and peer over the edge of the open hatch. "It's empty."

"Can you see the bottom?" Peyne asked.

She shook her head. "It goes a long way down." She took a deep breath and yelled, "Hello!"

Her voice echoed back to her.

"Don't fall in."

She frowned at him. "Really? Don't fall in. I would never have thought of that."

"Back away from the edge," Peyne suggested. "You're making me nervous."

"I don't understand," she said in a small voice. "I guess Jaff was right."

"Do you think it's gone dry?"

"I don't know. Maybe . . . an earthquake?" She groped for answers, disappointment raw on her face. "It could be blocked or . . ." She shook her head slowly. "I don't know."

Peyne tried to think of something comforting and failed. Zayda had come to learn more about ink magic, to discover its ancient secrets, to see if it was possible to free herself from the collar. And Peyne had come for Zayda. Jaff had come because if one ink mage could be freed, then maybe all of them could, and that would put a kink in the sultan's ambitions of conquest. Only Maurizan had known about the great aquifer. Only she had suspected this forgotten place had once been green and thriving.

And yet they'd gotten caught up in her dream, the idea that they might together work some miracle.

Peyne stood and turned when he heard the shouting.

"What's that?" Maurizan asked.

"Jaff, I think."

And a second later, Jaff came storming around the corner, running full speed. "Run!" he shouted. "Run for your lives!"

Peyne frowned. "What in blazes is he talking—"

A sharp crack like thunder and the ground tilted.

Peyne fell back, arms windmilling, ears ringing. He had only a moment to glimpse a cloud of steam rolling past Jaff, who'd been thrown to the ground. Peyne was floating. No . . . falling, until—

A sting as his bare back hit water. Followed by a bruising smack as he hit the bottom of the canal.

They all heard it and looked up to see.

Although at this distance there was nothing they *could* see. Still, like a crack of thunder but sharper, the noise rolled across the dunes.

"Any sign of Krokett?" Meddigar asked.

Hak sat up in his saddle on the adjacent dromadan, squinting into the distance. "No."

Meddigar grunted. Typical. The man came and went as he pleased, skulking about, always looking at the ground and muttering something or another. In the wee hours before sunrise, he'd taken one of the dromadan and headed south. The wizard had assumed he'd see the man again before now.

"Do you see . . . *anything*?"

Hak scanned the dunes. Meddigar knew that tapped into the spirit, Hak could see farther than anyone else, except for perhaps Priya, the other ink mage.

"Yes," Hak said. "Statues. Big ones."

Meddigar didn't remember seeing any big statues last time. Then again, he'd approached the city from a different direction then. "How far?"

"Far."

"So helpful."

Hak smirked. "By sundown. Maybe."

They pressed on and made good time, arriving with the last remains of daylight by which to gawk at the harbor statues. They dismounted, a welcome rest from the dromadan saddles, and stood in a small group.

"Winged warriors," Hak said.

"You'll find the winged motif throughout the city," Meddigar said. "Although what cultural or religious significance it might have I don't know. I was otherwise occupied."

A frenetic scratching sound drew the wizard's attention, and he turned to see Venny madly sketching. He moved to look over her shoulder. His proximity didn't seem to bother her. He'd thought she might be mapping, but she was rendering an admirable likeness of one of the statues. "You're quite the artist."

"I wanted to get as much as possible before we lose the light," she said. "Amazing, isn't it? These things have been here . . . what? Centuries? Millennia?"

"A long time," Meddigar said. "Are all cartographers such gifted artists?"

"No. But my father likes that I can do little flourishes to adorn the maps. Fanciful sea serpents and so on. Gives his work a little something extra."

"You're quite good."

"Thank you." She said it casually. "I suppose I should be mapping the details of this valley . . . used to be a harbor, yes?"

"Yes."

"Interesting. Just think. A city lost to history, and my map will be the one that brings people back again."

Meddigar stiffened, frowning. He quickly made his face go blank to hide his reaction. He hadn't quite connected the fact of her mapmaking with the idea that others would return to follow in their footsteps. There were untold treasures yet to be discovered, the wizard was sure.

Venny stopped sketching abruptly, eyes coming around slowly to regard him in her peripheral vision.

Meddigar cleared his throat. "Yes. A triumph of mapmaking to be sure."

She smiled weakly in return.

A high-pitched call rescued them from the awkward moment.

"It's Krokett," Hak said. "Here he comes."

The tracker stood before them a few minutes later, his dromadan in tow. He began talking, punctuating his report with gestures back toward the city.

"There's no way to get the dromadan up from here," Hak translated.

"What else?"

"They've found a water source," Hak said.

Oh? That would have been helpful during my last visit. Meddigar scratched his beard, considering. "Are they still there?"

"Except one," Hak reported. "Hak says one of them broke off, the trail heading toward a big palace on the other side of the city. From the size of the tracks, Krokett thinks it's a woman."

Meddigar frowned. *Maurizan. She's always been greedy for ink magic. Well, I'm not going to let her take what I worked so hard to discover.*

Except she has a head start.

"I'm going immediately," Meddigar announced. "I'll want a few of the waterskins and some other provisions."

"Now?" Hak asked. "It will be dark soon."

Meddigar muttered the words to a minor spell, and a glowing ball the size of a walnut bloomed to life a foot from his ear. It made a slow orbit around his head, casting pale light over the area. "I don't intend to stumble around blind."

"Well, you shouldn't go alone," Hak insisted.

"I'll take Priya," Meddigar said. "Satisfied?"

Hak shrugged. "You're in command."

That left Sergeant Klamud and one of his men to accompany Hak to the water source. Krokett would show them the way. "Leave the dromadan. Pack up as much equipment as you can carry and follow when you can. And take all the empty skins. Fill them at the water source."

"And what about those we find there?" Hak asked.

"Kill them."

Hak grinned. "My pleasure."

"I'll come with you," Venny told the wizard. She was already gathering her pack and slinging a waterskin over her shoulder. "A palace sounds worth sketching to me."

Meddigar opened his mouth to object, then stopped himself. He did enjoy her company, but that could no longer be a consideration. He was still uneasy about her map and the flood of ambitious adventurers it might bring to the city. Meddigar wasn't ready for that to happen, could not foresee ever being ready. At one point, the wizard had contemplated fleeing Fyria and going into hiding, but now that he'd found the city and could successfully navigate his way back at any time, he was loath to share the place with anyone else. To Prince Kha'narahn, Meddigar was the secret holder of the ink magic. The wizard meant to keep it that way, and Venny's map threatened that. Better to keep her close.

After all, if an accident could happen to Nila, then it could happen to anyone, yes?

"Your company would be most appreciated," Meddigar told her, voice light as if murdering her were the furthest thing from his mind.

CHAPTER
THIRTY

"Well, you did warn us the explosion would be bigger," Peyne said.

The three stood in the smoking remains of the boiler chamber. The blast had shredded metal *like thin parchment and blackened most* of the floor and walls. The doorway was now twice its normal size, the edges jagged with ripped metal. The great gear hung askew, as if a good sneeze would send it tumbling across the floor.

"I suppose I should have considered some way to vent the steam," Jaff mused.

"The next time we're fooling around with ancient machinery in a lost city, we'll remember that." Peyne rolled his shoulder and rubbed his neck. He was sore and bruised all over. His backward spill into the canal could have been much worse if there hadn't been three feet of water to break his fall.

Maurizan stood with shoulders slumped, abject failure on her face as she sullenly shook her head at the wreckage. "This was not what I had in mind. We'll never get the other two doors open now."

"Not that it would matter, if the aquifer has gone dry," Jaff said.

Maurizan shot him a look that said I'm not in the mood for I told you so.

"For the record, I wish it had worked," Jaff said. "I wish I was wrong."

Daylight had fled hours ago. The oil lamp's tiny flame felt like some futile rebellion against the darkness.

Maurizan let out a long, exhausted sigh and said, *"There's nothing left to do here.* We should get some sleep and set out after Zayda in the morning."

"Not here," Peyne said. "There's no air."

They slept along the canal near the dome's opening. There wasn't what anyone might recognize as a cool breeze, but at least there was a minimal flow of air, unlike inside the claustrophobic boiler chamber.

Peyne lay down, his pack making an uncomfortable pillow, but nevertheless he was asleep instantly, the deep, dreamless slumber of one utterly spent.

But sometime later . . . an hour? Three? It all melted together in this place. Something stirred him. Splashing and voices. His eyes came open. He lifted his head very slightly, not wanting to draw attention to himself.

Torchlight. Somebody was coming up the canal toward the dome.

Peyne turned over to wake Maurizan. She wasn't there. He turned the other way. Jaff wasn't there either. Peyne was alone.

Well, that's just fucking typical.

He squinted down the length of the canal. Two men tromped through the shallow water. Peyne swallowed a lump of fear as he realized one of them was the huge bearded bruiser from the Last Village.

Peyne stood slowly, looking around for his sword and boots. Damn it, they were back in a pile with his shirt near the boiler chamber. He'd stripped it all off to shovel coal and then—

An iron grip around his throat yanked him upward until Peyne was standing on tiptoe gasping for breath. He looked up into the grinning face of the huge ink mage they called Hak, his hard eyes glinting in the torchlight coming up behind Peyne.

Peyne tried to pry the fingers from around his throat. He might as well have been trying to bend iron.

"The others?" Hak asked the men behind Peyne.

"No sign of them." Peyne recognized the brute's voice.

Hak's eyes slid to Peyne. The ink mage's predatory grin wid*ened.* "Never mind, Klamud. This one will tell us. How about it, little man? Where are your friends?"

Peyne opened his mouth to say something but could utter only a strangled squawk.

Hak released his grip on Peyne's throat.

Peyne flopped to the ground, coughing and gasping for breath. He glanced up at the ink mage looming over him. Peyne had seen the power of the tattoos, had seen Zayda outmatch men twice her size. There was no chance *he co*uld take on this giant. A scimitar hung from Hak's belt. His tunic was sleeveless to show off tattoos Peyne didn't recognize. One of the little control scepters sprouted from his sash.

He doesn't have a handler. Probably ate him.

Hak went to one knee to get eye level with Peyne. "Now, I believe you wanted to say something."

"They're dead," Peyne said. "No water. I barely made it here myself."

Hak grabbed Peyne's hand, took his pointer finger. And bent it.

Snap.

Peyne's eyes shot wide, mouth falling open as he took in a ragged breath, pain shooting through him. A cold sweat broke out across his face, mouth falling open, a disbelieving groan.

"You've got nine more," Hak said.

Peyne shook his head. "I don't know."

Hak moved to the next finger. Snap.

This time, Peyne screamed.

"Please," Peyne said. "They were here but gone when I woke up. Maybe they heard you coming. I don't know where—"

Snap.

Another scream. The world spun, and a second later, his head hit the ground. He convulsed once, twice, then vomited.

"Maybe he really doesn't know," Klamud said.

"That's fine too," Hak replied.

Snap.

Meddigar was forced to pause every time Venny stopped to gawk at something. Her delicate hands flew over the sketchbook, trying to draw everything at once. She'd said she wanted to wait for daylight to draw the great domed palace. But the statue of the armored man caught her attention on the way inside, and she stood looking up at it with the same wide-eyed awe she had with everything else in the city.

"I'm sorry, my dear," Meddigar said. "Normally, I'd indulge you, but we're in a bit of a hurry."

"Someone's been here," Priya said. The ink mage pointed at a trail from the statue to the palace's main entrance where the sand had been disturbed.

Once the tracks were pointed out, the trail was obvious. In this particular case, one didn't need Krokett's tracking skills to see someone had passed through here recently.

It has to be Maurizan, Meddigar thought. He regretted suddenly not bringing Hak along. Maurizan was formidable. She'd demonstrated that already. Surely Meddigar and Priya together could handle her.

He hoped.

Meddigar noticed the two women were staring at him.

"Come," he said, trying to sound confident and decisive. "I remember the way."

He was pleasantly surprised to discover it was true. He led the two women directly to the workshop of the ancient wizards. The door stood open, but the interior was dark.

"Someone's been here," Meddigar said.

He readied a spell and entered, Priya and Venny following closely.

The globe of light flickered and brightened overhead, startling the two women.

"It's normal. Don't worry," the wizard told them. "One of the many miracles to be found here. I think it's a spell triggered by movement." The wizard scanned the room quickly. No sign of Maurizan.

"Amazing." Venny's voice was barely above a whisper.

Priya lingered near the doorway, examining the floor and the tracks in the dust. "Lots of coming and going."

"Which set of tracks are the freshest?" Meddigar asked.

Priya shook her head. "That's a question for Krokett. Not for me."

Meddigar scratched his beard, pondering. He didn't like the idea of Maurizan lurking around out there, ready to pounce at any time. "I need you to find her."

Priya nodded.

"Do not engage her," the wizard said. "Just find her and report back. I don't want her sneaking up on us."

"She killed Pinni. My *sister*," Priya said. "If I find her, I'm going to—"

"She'll destroy you," Meddigar said flatly. "Find her. Stay hidden. If you find nothing in an hour, come back."

Priya held the wizard's gaze for a long moment, eyes intense. Reluctantly, she nodded.

"You have a torch?"

"If I'm trying to stay hidden, then a torch is a bad idea," she said. "Don't worry. I'll find my way."

She turned abruptly and left.

"She's hot tempered," Venny said a moment later.

"You're good at reading people," Meddigar said.

"I am. But you don't need to be for her. She's liable to go for blood, in spite of what you told her."

"Then she'll die."

Venny looked around. "And this place?"

"The workshops of one of the city's wizards."

"*One* of the wizards?"

"I don't know anything for certain," Meddigar admitted. "A bit of history. A bit of legend. A lot of guessing. But scholars believe there was a great Fyrian wizard with many apprentices. Each of these apprentices was a master wizard in his own right. On my last trip, I made a careful examination of everything in this workshop. They're almost exclusively items connected with ink magic. I believe this was the workshop of an apprentice assigned specifically to the task."

"Then the workshop of this great master wizard is still out there somewhere," Venny said.

A wan smile from Meddigar. "If it is, I didn't find it."

Venny walked past the shelves, eyeing the various jars and vials. "These are ingredients?"

"Yes. For ink mostly. I must confess I've only barely started figuring it all out. With food and water in short supply, I was forced to head back to civilization."

Venny paused to squint at a jar filled with what looked like small, dried bat wings, leathery and black. "These are . . . interesting."

"Come this way." Meddigar gestured she should follow him. "The really interesting things were kept under lock and key. Here, I'll show you."

He approached the little alcove and swept the curtain aside. "The needles and specialized—shit!"

He stepped back as Zayda emerged from the alcove, his hand going toward his pocket.

The tip of Zayda's scimitar was underneath Meddigar's chin in an instant. "Don't."

The wizard froze.

Zayda's eyes flicked to Venny. "I've no quarrel with you. Just stay back."

Venny took two large steps back.

"Thank you."

Very slowly, Zayda leaned in, reaching into Meddigar's pocket, the other hand keeping her sword tip against Meddigar's throat. She came out with the jeweled scepter and took a step back, the scimitar never wavering.

"Say one word I don't understand, and I'll assume it's a spell and run you through," Zayda said.

"You don't want to kill me. You could have done that straightaway."

"And I still can whenever the whim strikes me," Zayda said. "But if you can be helpful, you might live."

They stood that way a moment while he considered. If he began a spell, she'd skewer him. And he no longer had the scepter. His options appeared limited.

"How may I be of assistance?" Meddigar asked.

"The chair makes the collars, yes?"

Meddigar's eye went to the chair, then came back to Zayda. "Yes."

"Tell me."

"It's rather complicated. I'm not sure—"

"Use small words."

The wizard cleared his throat. "When you pull the first lever, the rods with the coils move in around the subject's throat. They create . . . uh . . . a field. A disturbance in the air."

Confusion on Zayda's face.

"You know how the air feels different during a lightning storm?"

A pause. Then Zayda nodded.

"Similar," he said. "The liquid metal flows down the tubes. The rods create an energy that alters the structure of the metal, changing it from liquid to solid. The person in the chair gets a new collar."

"There was no chair for me," Zayda pointed out.

Meddigar grinned. "I had to cheat a bit. The chair isn't exactly portable. I managed to create a spell that duplicated the effect."

Zayda took a deep breath, then asked, "Is it reversible?"

A long pause. "Yes."

"Show me."

Meddigar hesitated.

The pressure of the sword tip on his throat increased just enough for Zayda to make her point.

"Very well," he said. "The final lever makes the rods spin the other way. I deduce it somehow reverses—"

A flash of metal tumbled through the air toward them. No one in the world but an ink mage could have reacted quickly enough.

Zayda wheeled, her scimitar striking the flying dagger out of midair with a sharp clang.

Priya was already running along the tops of the tables, rattling beakers and vials as she went and drawing her own scimitar as she aimed a flying kick at Zayda, a look of intense focus on her face. Zayda ducked beneath the kick and popped back up just in time to block Priya's sword thrust.

Meddigar stumbled back, hand automatically going to his throat, relief flooding him. He readied a spell, intending to spray Zayda with fire, but stopped himself. He couldn't strike one ink mage without hitting the other.

The workshop rang with the flurried swing, block, thrust, parry of their blades. The movements were almost too fast for Meddigar to follow. Venny pressed her back flat against the wall, trying to make herself small, watching the duel wide-eyed, mouth agape.

Priya thrust, and instead of blocking it, Zayda sidestepped and brought her other hand around, smashing the jeweled scepter against the side of Priya's head.

Priya grunted, her other hand coming up to grab Zayda's wrist. She twisted.

Zayda grimaced and let go of the scepter.

Meddigar followed it with his eyes as the scepter bounced on the nearest worktable, rolled, and fell off the other side.

The wizard went for it.

In the corner of his vision, he saw Zayda thrust her scimitar into Priya's belly, angling the blade upward. Disarming Zayda of the scepter must have left her open. Likely it had been Zayda's ploy all along. Priya shuddered, mouth falling open. Then a cough, blood flecking over her bottom lip. Priya slid off Zayda's blade and crumpled to the floor with a lifeless thud.

Zayda was already leaping across the table at the wizard.

Too late.

Meddigar activated the scepter.

Zayda fell out of the air in midleap, screaming. She crashed against the table, rolled off, and hit the floor hard, air whuffing out of her. Meddigar activated the scepter again. More screams as she writhed on the ground, agony shooting through her.

Meddigar moved around the table, putting himself between Venny and Zayda, scepter still held aloft, ready to unleash punishment again in an instant. "No need to worry now, my dear. Everything is under control."

Venny nodded dumbly, mouth still hanging open.

"You had me worried there for a moment," he said to Zayda.

Zayda tried to lift her head, tried to focus her eyes.

"I believe you've illustrated beautifully the need for these collars," Meddigar told her. "I thought it cruel at first, but ink mages are dangerous. Useful tools, yes, but dangerous, and precautions are necessary. Thank you for helping reinforce this point. However, you, young Zayda, I have deemed more trouble than you're worth. Time to say goodbye to the world."

The wizard activated the scepter again. If possible, Zayda's screams were even more agonized, back arching off the floor, tears leaking from the corners of her eyes.

◆ ◆ ◆

Peyne cradled his right hand against his chest, four fingers and a thumb broken. He curled in a fetal position, feeling dizzy and sick, the ink mage, bruiser, and other soldier standing in a little circle looking down at him.

"He doesn't know," Klamud said.

"They're around here someplace," Hak insisted.

"Or maybe they don't like him. Left him behind."

Peyne wanted to object to that but worried if he moved, he would vomit again.

Splashing and the clank of metal in the distance. All three men froze.

"Somebody's out there," Hak said.

"Trying to sneak away maybe."

Hak thought about it. "Go out there and take a look. Both of you."

The other two men looked at each other, and then Klamud said, "Us?"

Hak scowled at them. "Just take a look."

The two men left the dome, skulking along the canal.

Hak made a slow turn, attempting to peer into every shadowed corner. It was quiet except for Peyne's low groaning.

"Something's odd," Hak said.

Go fuck yourself. Peyne wished he'd had the balls to say it out loud. *No, I don't.*

Hak examined the group's belongings. "The waterskins are still here. They might leave you if they were running away, but they wouldn't leave those. Where are your little friends hiding, eh?"

Peyne closed his eyes, pretending he'd passed out.

A moment later, he opened his eyes again. He couldn't help it. He had to know what the big ink mage was doing.

Think. There's a way out of this. There's always a way.

Except that wasn't really true, was it? The first rule of luck was that it eventually ran out.

He watched as Hak moved toward the open doorway to the aquifer. "What's this then? This where the water comes from?"

It used to.

Hak climbed up through the doorway, then stood at the edge of the gaping hole leading down into deep darkness.

And then suddenly Maurizan was there.

She must have been hiding around the corner within the aquifer chamber the whole time, standing totally still, waiting for her chance.

Peyne would have cheered, if he'd had the energy. He lifted his head, and seeing her in action sparked hope in his chest.

She'd launched herself at Hak, a flying kick that landed in the small of his back.

Peyne struggled to one knee. He had to see this. His hand throbbed, but he grinned.

Hak flew forward, hands flailing, over the side into the dark drop below.

To the center of the world with you, you son of a bitch!

Hak turned in midair as he fell, face utterly calm. One of his hands shot out and grabbed the edge, supernaturally strong fingers sinking into the metal for purchase.

Peyne's triumphant grin fell. *No!*

Hak pulled himself up, but Maurizan was already on him, stabbing a dagger straight toward his face. His free hand shot up with impossible speed, catching her blade three inches from his nose. Hak's arm had turned to gray stone up to the elbow. He twisted his hand, and the dagger blade snapped with a *ting*.

Hak swept the stone hand in a wicked backhand toward Maurizan's knee. She backflipped out of the way, landing in a fighter's crouch, shifting her remaining dagger from her left hand to her right. Hak was already climbing out to face her.

He stood with legs apart, drew his scimitar, and grinned.

Maurizan bent slowly, never taking her eyes off Hak, and drew a short knife from her boot. A poor substitute for the broken dagger but better than nothing.

"I'd hoped we would meet again, Maurizan," Hak said. "Your glowing friend is not here to save you this time."

◆ ◆ ◆

The world was a blur of pain.

The wizard was saying something again, but it was all a muffled chatter beyond the haze of agony. Zayda tried to lift her head and failed. All she could do was writhe on the ground and wait to die.

And then suddenly the pain stopped,

Zayda's eyes creaked open. A line of drool had spilled down the side of her face to drip on the floor where she lay. The blur looming above her gelled into the figure of Meddigar. He'd come forward to gloat one last time maybe, the jeweled scepter held tightly in his fist.

"You're made of stern stuff. I'll give you that, girl." Meddigar thumbed a dial beneath the scepter's little globe. "But I think one more good jolt on the highest setting should finish things, don't you agree? A shame it had to come to this, but—"

Meddigar's eyes shot wide. Face twitched. He sucked in a sharp breath. Then turned to look behind him.

Venny stepped back, pulled the thin stiletto from the wizard's side. Blood stained two thirds of the blade.

Meddigar's face twisted in pure astonishment. "Why?" His voice a weak whisper.

Her answer was another sharp thrust into his gut. Blood washed over her hand. She pulled the blade out and stabbed again.

And again.

He collapsed to his knees, blinked once, then fell over, hand coming open, the scepter skittering across the floor.

Venny stood over him, panting, stunned at what she'd done. She looked at the bloody stiletto in her hand for a moment, then tossed it away in disgust.

Zayda lifted her head. "What . . . just happened?"

"He was going to kill me, I think. Because of the map I was making. I think he killed his apprentice too." She knelt next to Zayda. "I'm Venny. Can we be on the same side please?"

Zayda tried to tap into the spirit but couldn't. She reached for it, stretched within herself, but it hovered just out of range. She was exhausted, she realized, body trembling. She needed to flop into a soft bed and sleep for a month.

But there was something to be done first.

She grabbed her collar, took a deep breath, and said, "I want . . . this damn thing . . . *off*."

Venny helped her to her feet, and they staggered toward the chair. Zayda moved to sit in it, but Venny stopped her.

"Let's see if it actually does what he claimed," Venny said.

Zayda braced herself against one of the worktables, nodded. "Okay."

Venny reached up with two hands, grabbed the first lever, and pulled down. It *thunked* into place. For a tense moment, nothing happened. They held their breaths.

Then the muted *clunk clank* of machinery awakening behind the walls. The floor vibrated beneath their feet. The rods hummed and began to spin, picking up speed, the copper wires now a glowing blur.

And then they saw it. A disturbance in the air between the two rods.

"Like heat waves coming off a hot road," Venny said.

"Try the next lever," Zayda told her.

A hesitation, but then Venny nodded, stepped forward, and pulled the second lever.

The big glass tank of liquid metal began to bubble. It flowed down the tubes, and a second later, the rods shifted toward each other, spitting the metal out, two halves forming a ring that hovered within the disturbance in midair.

Once the collar was formed, the rods shifted back, the second lever rising back to its upward position again. The fully formed collar fell, bouncing off the seat's leather padding.

Zayda edged forward, tentatively plucked the collar from the chair as if half expecting it to burn her. It was cool. And solid.

"He said the final lever would reverse it."

"You're not really going to sit there," Venny said. "Who knows what it'll do to you?"

"Dead ink mages aren't worth anything," Zayda said. "It must be safe."

She sat in the chair, leaned back against the headrest.

"Do it."

Venny balked. "I don't really want to be responsible for—"

"Please. Do it."

Venny blew out a nervous sigh, took the final lever in both hands, and pulled.

The rods slowed their rotation gradually and then finally stopped altogether. Slowly, they began to spin the other way, picking up speed until they were again a copper blur. Zayda's hair stood on end.

The rods shifted, moving toward her.

Zayda's skin crawled. Her teeth vibrated, every bone in her body seeming to hum with the energy of the rods, not painful but strange and frightening.

Maybe this is a bad idea after all.

Bright light began to crowd her vision, becoming brighter and brighter as her sight narrowed, a noise in her mind growing to a roar until finally—

Somebody was helping her up. A voice coming from far away as if at the bottom of a deep well. Zayda blinked, looked up into Venny's face.

"I said, are you okay?"

Zayda shook her head. "I . . . don't know." Had she fallen out of the chair? She looked back. The rods were still now, all the levers in their normal upright positions.

Something was on her hand, gooey and thick. She wiped it on her halter top. Like jelly but glinting metallic.

Zayda gasped.

"It just melted off," Venny said.

Zayda's hand went to her throat. When she didn't feel the collar, her other hand came up reflexively, feeling all around her as if she couldn't believe what had happened.

"It's off," Venny confirmed. "You're free."

Zayda stared at the other woman for a moment.

Then she broke down into tears, sobbing uncontrollably.

She fell into Venny's arms, and the other woman patted her on the back. Zayda's whole body shook, tears streaming down her face. At last, she pulled away, dragging her arm underneath her nose to wipe away snot, rubbing her eyes with the heels of her hands.

Zayda sniffed. "Venny, is it?"

"Yes."

"Sorry, Venny. I got carried away."

Free. They said the damn thing would never come off, but I did it. I'm free.

"I've never been a slave," Venny said. "But I imagine I might react the same way."

Zayda looked around the room. Was the world any different? She wasn't completely sure how to feel. Her eyes landed on the corpses of the wizard and the other ink mage.

"Are there others with you?" Zayda asked.

"Don't worry. They didn't come here," Venny said. "They're going to some water source."

Zayda's head snapped around. "What?"

"Somewhere else in the city," Venny said. "The tracker said there was water, and the others—"

Zayda had already tapped into the spirit. It was easy now with the burden of the collar lifted. She was out the door at a dead run. Venny called after her. Zayda ignored the mapmaker.

Peyne!

Tapped into the spirit, Zayda remembered her path perfectly, running at full speed through the darkness, never putting a foot wrong.

She burst through the palace's front door, flying past the statues, across the wide terrace, and down the steps, eyes turned toward the sky.

The moon was still there, barely. It would set soon, and then dawn would come.

But it's enough, she thought. *It has to be enough.*

The moonlight filled her, the glow from her body gradually banishing the night.

She needed to get back to the aquifer dome, back to Peyne. And fast. She remembered how slow the going was crossing the city to get here in the first place, the narrow lanes too often blocked with wreckage. She had to think of something else. Zayda would never get back in time to make a difference if she returned by the same route.

Zayda craned her neck, looked up.

The roofs. They wouldn't be blocked, would they?

She ran to the nearest building and climbed, the moonlight feeding her speed and strength. Where there were no foot- or handholds, she made her own, gouging into the stonework. Seconds later, she heaved herself up and over and onto the rooftop.

It was clear.

She became a perfect running machine, flashing across the roof, launching herself into the air and landing on the next roof, running and jumping again, a beacon of cold light blazing across the top of the city, the wind a roar in her ears.

The moon set. Her stored power began to fade. *It's enough,* she kept telling herself. She was almost to the dome.

The pink-orange of dawn crept over the horizon.

It's enough.

Maurizan didn't like the feel of the little knife in her off hand. The balance was all wrong. Tapped into the spirit, she could easily compensate, but that wasn't the point. She didn't like it. Didn't like the limitations, that it would force her to make alternate decisions when countering attacks or initiating her own.

She also didn't like Hak's smug face. At all.

They hadn't fully had the chance to test each other when they'd last met. Zayda had intervened . . . which had been just fine with Maurizan. Hak was all too eager for the rematch.

Maurizan wasn't.

Yet here we all are. Wonderful.

She spared Peyne a glance. The man watched but seemed to be making no move to help her. Which was for the best. He'd only get in the way, and he was obviously in pain. If she survived her encounter with Hak, she'd need to apologize. She hadn't enjoyed keeping perfectly still and hiding while listening as Hak had broken Peyne's fingers one at a time, but it had been necessary. Jaff had needed time to draw the other soldiers away, giving Maurizan a one-on-one chance with the other ink mage.

She hoped Jaff was still alive out there. Not that she could worry about it now.

"Let us make it a duel for the ages." Hak's smug grin never wavered. "Something the bards will sing about."

"I don't see any bards around," Maurizan said.

"Don't worry. I'll fill them in on every detail," he assured her.

"What if we just took a pass on the whole thing?" Maurizan suggested. "You go your way, and I'll go mine."

Hak's grin slowly dissolved. "That's disappointing. Truly."

"What is it you want, Hak?" Maurizan asked. "To be the best. What would that prove? Who would be impressed? Do you have so little in your life that you feel the need to—"

Hak lunged, would have instantly killed any normal opponent.

His blade sliced through the center of Maurizan's face.

Except it wasn't her face.

Her image dissolved into smoke, swirling away as she appeared behind Hak, thrusting her dagger. Hak spun, parried the dagger, and sliced through smoke again on the back swing.

The Phantom Walker tattoo was one of the first she'd gotten after the Prime. She was always just a little ahead of her own image, the enemy constantly striking in the wrong place. In this manner, she danced around Hak, trying to hurt him from the back or sides.

But he was *fast*. His scimitar would slice through smoke but always return in time to block or parry her own blade.

And then he anticipated her.

He missed with the scimitar again, but when Maurizan reappeared, the Stone Fist was waiting for her. In the tiny fraction of a second between seeing the fist and the fist landing, she switched from Phantom Walker to the Turtle Shell tattoo, the skin all over her body hardening.

The ink was the only thing that saved her.

Instead of her head flying off her body and across the dome, the blow was merely brutally painful, sending her staggering back. She righted herself, blades up, and blinked the stars from her eyes. She felt along the inside of her mouth with her tongue. At least three teeth were loose. She spit blood.

Hak laughed. "Come now. Are you telling me this is not the best sport? That you do not feel *alive?*"

Maurizan tried to grin back at him and winced. The side of her face was already swelling badly. Her tongue felt thick. She composed herself and said, "There's a place called the Purple Pirate near the docks in the Red City. The spices in the fish stew will make you feel so alive, you'll wish you were dead."

Hak laughed. "Noted. I'll think of you when I have a bowl."

Movement at the edge of her vision. Jaff, staggering back into the dome.

And he didn't look good.

Not for an instant did it occur to Peyne to join the fray. If Maurizan couldn't handle the big ink mage herself, then they were all screwed. She was apparently holding her own until she suddenly took a savage blow. Peyne had flinched at the sound.

There was a time when he'd have run. Let these two fight it out while he fled. The thought simultaneously appealed and appalled.

A groan and the sound of shuffling pulled him out of his thoughts.

Jaff stumbled into the dome. His right eye was swollen shut, tunic torn, blood down one arm and dripping from his left ear. He held his scimitar loosely, the blade dripping red.

"Jaff," Peyne whispered.

Jaff looked at him, smiled weakly. "I . . . I got them. I got . . . both. Both of them."

Peyne frowned. "Are you okay?"

"No."

A huge shadow loomed behind Jaff, and Peyne shouted, "Jaff, look out!"

Klamud lurched into the dome, swinging his axe. Jaff turned just in time, stumbling backward, the axe passing within two inches of him. One side of the brute was smeared with blood, left arm hanging limp. Jaff brought his scimitar up, his hand shaking, barely able to lift the blade. He backed into Peyne, knocking him over, and kept going.

Klamud ignored Peyne, stepping over him, pressing his attack, lifting the axe one-handed over his head for a kill strike. Jaff was still stumbling back, the tip of his scimitar dragging along the ground. He didn't have the strength to lift it.

The brute growled. "And now you die. Now Klamud makes an end of you."

Peyne reached out with his good hand, grabbed one of Klamud's ankles.

The brute went down, landing hard on Peyne, knocking the wind out of him.

Peyne grunted with the impact. *Fucking . . . again.*

Jaff threw himself at Klamud, grabbing the arm holding the axe, refused to let go, refused to let the man use the weapon.

Klamud head butted Jaff in the face, and Jaff's nose flattened, both nostrils shooting blood. Jaff fell back, eyes rolling up.

Peyne reached up, grabbed a fistful of Klamud's beard. *Hang on. Don't let him do anything. Just hang on.*

The grunting brute covered Peyne's ruined hand with an enormous paw. And squeezed. Already broken bones crunched like dry twigs. Peyne wailed.

"Now you die," Klamud said. "Both you fuckers die."

A flash of metal, and Klamud sat up stiff. A knife stuck out of his right eye. He twitched, tried to speak, making only awkward gagging sounds, twitched again, and fell dead across Peyne.

Peyne pushed the big man off him. *That's the last time you fall on me, you beefy son of a bitch.*

Peyne looked down at his mangled hand, the broken fingers aiming in multiple directions, and fainted.

◆ ◆ ◆

Even with all her skills, and tapped into the spirit, Maurizan had to admit it.

That was a damn good throw.

And yet at the same time, Maurizan fully realized that pausing to throw the knife and save Peyne's life had left her open. She turned back to Hak.

Too late.

The Stone Fist caught her on the same side of the face, sent her staggering back. She pushed the pain aside, righted herself, brought her dagger around for—

Hak punched her again, and this time Maurizan went down. Her eyes crossed. She almost faded, but commanded herself to focus, then realized she was being lifted. Hak had her by the throat. He drew his Stone Fist back for a final blow.

"In the end, disappointing after all," Hak said. "All too easy."

Maurizan forced herself to remain conscious, clinging to the spirit. Maintaining the Turtle Shell was her only chance.

The Stone Fist connected with Maurizan's forehead like a charging bull. The sound of the world breaking. Maurizan lifted, flew through the air and across the canal. She landed hard, rolling, and then briefly, lost consciousness.

When her eyes popped open again moments later, she'd lost the Turtle Shell. She looked around, barely able to move, wondering if there was anything that could save her. Peyne lay two feet away, looking too damaged to help himself.

This is it. This is how I die.

Orange light spilled into the dome. Dawn. *Good,* thought Maurizan absently. *Somehow it's better to die in daylight.*

Hak chuckled. "Good all of you are together. We can make an end of it finally."

"I wouldn't do that if I were you."

Hak squinted into the blooming dawn, at the silhouette of the girl standing there.

Zayda.

Hak frowned. The last time he'd faced Zayda, he hadn't had the better end of it.

Zayda slipped into the canal, strode toward him through the water. Hak watched her come and stepped back when she climbed up into the aquifer chamber. He seemed unsure of himself, and after their battle in the Last Village, Maurizan couldn't blame him.

They faced each other.

"Whatever you've planned for my friends, you can forget it," Zayda said. "Because I'm here to stop you."

Well, thank Dumo for that, Maurizan thought and passed out.

Zayda lifted both her scimitar and her chin, defiance in her eyes. "You can call off this nonsense. Or you can die."

Hak was wary, but his eyes narrowed, and he said, "Something's different."

Light from the rising sun filled the dome. Zayda was lit with it from behind. She stood tall, legs apart, ready for anything.

"Walk away," Zayda said. "Or I'll be forced to destroy you."

A pause. He considered.

Then a smile lit his eyes. "Where did your glow go, little girl?"

She said nothing, returned his gaze.

"You filled the night with your radiance in the Last Village," Hak said. "Tell me your secret. Some tattoo of course, but where did you get it? Tell me, and I might let *you* walk away."

Her smile was colder than his. What would Peyne say in this situation? "Fuck yourself sideways with a crooked stick."

Hak charged.

His blade came down hard. She parried, thrust, stepped to the side as he took a backhanded swing at her. The interior of the dome rang with clashing steel. They circled each other, feigning, striking, blocking.

They both stepped back, panting and gleaming with sweat.

"I've been waiting to see your other tricks," Hak said. "I'm guessing you don't have any."

Zayda refused to let her fear show. She took the fear and squashed it down into some inaccessible corner of herself. "I don't need tricks."

Hak nodded slowly, figuring it out. "Every tattoo has a power," he said. "And every tattoo has a limitation."

She said nothing.

"Last time, you made me . . . afraid," Hak admitted. "It has been a very long time since anything made me afraid. So what's different?"

His eyes shifted to the fresh daylight creeping across the floor of the dome.

"It was *night* in the Last Village when we first met, wasn't it?"

"You're grasping at straws," Zayda said.

Hak shook his head. "No, I'm not. And by the time I'm finished with you, you'll tell me all your secrets, I promise. For you see, I haven't used a single one of my tattoos beyond the Prime. I've been testing you, matching you move for move. And guess what I've discovered. You've got nothing."

Zayda swallowed hard. "I beat you before. It was easy."

"Yes," Hak agreed. "So why not now? What's holding you back?" He chuckled. "No, this will be finished very soon, and then you'll tell me everything. You'll *beg* to tell me everything."

"I'll never beg you!"

She leapt at him, sword aimed for his heart.

Hak didn't bother to counter this time. He sidestepped her thrust, ducked beneath her back swing, rolling out of the way. When he sprang to his feet again, he sheathed his sword, that infernal grin of his spread across his arrogant face.

Zayda pressed her attack with renewed fury.

She swung the sword every way possible, thrusting and slashing, but whenever her blade arrived, Hak simply wasn't there.

Too fast. Without the moonlight, I simply can't match him. Can't even come close.

She leapt at him again, screaming frustration, sword thrust straight at his gut.

He reached in and plucked the sword from her grasp like he was picking a flower. He laughed as he tossed it over his shoulder, the scimitar clanging down the bottomless aquifer shaft.

She blinked, gasped.

Then Hak had her wrist. She tried to pull away, but he was far too strong. He turned her around, twisted her arm behind her back. She winced.

"Now we talk, eh?" Hak said.

Zayda said nothing.

Hak applied pressure to her arm, and she squealed, high-pitched and sudden.

He leaned down, pressing against her from behind, his cheek against hers, hot, fetid breath assaulting her as he spoke. "I can hurt you, yes, but let's be clear. I can do many things to you, anything I want. Humiliations beyond imagination. And then you'll tell me everything you know anyway. Get your mind around it, girl. Trust me. It will go easier for you if you do."

◆　◆　◆

The clamor of swordplay pulled Peyne out of his swoon.

The bearded brute still lay dead to one side of him, Jaff and Maurizan unconscious a few feet away on the other side. He twisted his head around and saw Zayda battling the gargantuan ink mage. It was clear after watching only a few seconds what the outcome would be. Zayda was overmatched.

He blew out a ragged sigh, head sinking back to the floor. What could he do? He was spent, sword hand mangled. Even if he'd been in peak condition, he was no match for Hak.

Peyne felt cool fingers on his broken hand and winced.

Maurizan had crawled toward him. Her eyes looked unfocused, barely conscious. She covered his broken hand with one of hers. A moment later, his hand tingled with sudden warmth, hummed with the healing energy of Maurizan's tattoo.

Maurizan's head fell, eyes closing.

Peyne flexed his hand. Healed.

It could hold a sword.

Jaff's scimitar lay nearby. Peyne picked it up.

He realized he was still barefoot and shirtless. He wished he had some armor and his own sword.

Fool, if you're going to wish, then wish big. Wish for a company of Gant's personal guard to come do the fighting for you.

But there was only Peyne.

And if Zayda was going to die, then the least he could do was die with her.

As quietly as possible, he slipped over the side of the canal and into the water. Slowly, he moved toward the doorway of the aquifer shaft.

No splashing. The urgent need to hurry was almost overwhelming, but it would all be for nothing if Hak heard him coming. Slowly but steadily he moved forward in the knee-deep water.

Zayda swiped frantically at Hak now, but the other ink mage dodged her thrusts easily.

He's toying with her.

Peyne kept moving, slowly, methodically. No splashing. Almost there.

He reached the edge of the doorway, pulled himself up so very carefully, holding his breath. Now he was glad he had no armor to clank and give him away. Even being barefoot might help him approach with stealth.

Hak now twisted Zayda's arm. He was saying something to her. It didn't matter what.

All that mattered was that Hak's broad back was to Peyne. A wide-open target.

Peyne put one foot in front of the other, scimitar ready to thrust. He hadn't made a sound, still held his breath. Hak was still talking to Zayda, mockery and threats.

That's fine. Keep talking. Pay no attention to the man behind you with the sword.

With five feet to go, Peyne charged full speed, sword blade aimed for the center of the big man's back.

Hak spun to meet him, the Stone Fist coming around in a blinding backhand, shattering Peyne's blade into a dozen pieces.

"The little man again." Hak grinned.

He hit Zayda at the base of the skull, and she wilted to the ground, eyes rolling back.

"Zayda!" Peyne rushed Hak, fists swinging.

Hak laughed, caught Peyne by the throat, and lifted him. Peyne's feet dangled three inches off the floor.

"And here we are again," Hak said. "Did you really not learn your lesson the first time?"

Peyne couldn't breathe, felt his face going hot, spots floating in front of his eyes. He pawed at Hak's tunic, groped at the man's sword belt, hoping to find a dagger or something to use as a weapon. Hak was so close. Peyne could hurt the man if he only had a weapon.

Peyne's hand closed around cold metal.

Hak screamed pain, looked down.

Zayda had bitten the fleshy part of Hak's calf just below the back of his knee. Blood spilled red from her mouth.

"Bitch!" Hak kicked and sent her flying across the chamber to land hard on the other side.

"I'll attend to you in a moment, little man." Hak tossed Peyne aside. "The bitch dies first."

Peyne rolled, stopping himself inches away from tumbling over the side and into the aquifer shaft. He gulped breath, blinked the spots from his eyes.

Hak stalked toward Zayda. "Enough. I know longer care for your secrets. I will content myself with feeling your neck snap in my bare hands."

"Hey!" Peyne called.

Hak ignored him.

"Hey, you dumb tub of shit!" Peyne yelled.

Hak stopped, turned slowly. "Are you really so eager to die first?"

"I was just thinking you might need this." Peyne held up Hak's scepter. "You know, so your ugly fat head doesn't explode off your body."

Hak's face erupted with panic, eyes wide as he frantically patted his sash, searching for his scepter as if there'd been some mistake, as if the cosmos were playing a cruel, impossible joke.

Peyne waved the scepter. "Right here, friend." He held the scepter over the yawning darkness of the aquifer shaft.

Hak was already moving, closing the distance like a charging bull.

Peyne threw the scepter down the shaft as hard as he could.

And then Hak was there, and Peyne knew he was going to die.

But Hak ignored him, flew through the air, reaching after the scepter, raw fear on his face. The big ink mage went over the side.

And down.

Peyne elbow crawled to the edge and peered down into the darkness, waiting, listening.

"Come on. Let's hear it. Come on."

Nothing. Hak didn't even scream. It was almost as if the mage hadn't simply fallen down a hole but had fallen out of existence.

The silence stretched.

And then.

Boom.

"Yes!"

Three seconds later, a blast of hot air erupted from the shaft, washed over Peyne, blowing his hair back.

Peyne wished he could have seen it, Hak's surprised face as the collar exploded, Hak's head popping off his body. Peyne began to laugh. Relief and dismay flooded him. He laughed and laughed, unable to stop himself.

And then the ground began to rumble.

CHAPTER
THIRTY-ONE

Peyne pushed away from the shaft's edge and tried to stand, failed, tried again, and stumbled toward Zayda. The floor shook, a deep rumble coming up the shaft. The entire dome rattled, and Peyne feared the whole place might come down around their ears.

He grabbed Zayda under one arm, lifted her. "Come on! We've got to get out of here."

She latched onto him. "What's happening?"

"An excellent question," Peyne said. "Let's discuss it later."

They slid out the door and into the water, splashing knee-deep, her arm around his shoulders.

"Up here!"

Jaff leaned over the edge of the canal, reached out a hand.

Peyne boosted Zayda up. She took Jaff's hand, and he pulled her out of the canal.

Behind them water erupted from the aquifer shaft, shooting up violently with a metallic ring against the chamber's roof.

Jaff reached down to Peyne. "Take my hand."

Peyne tried to grab for it, slid back down the slippery tile.

"Reach, you stupid foreigner!"

Peyne reached.

A wall of water slammed into him.

He was driven under, rolling along the bottom of the canal, bouncing off tile. He kicked, surfaced in daylight, and had just enough time to gulp a lungful of air before going down again. His shoulder hit the bottom hard. He righted himself and kicked for the surface again.

He treaded water. The swift current carried him along, but it was no longer the foaming, violent torrent that had tried to drown him. If he could swim to the side, he could probably climb out and—

He slammed into something and almost went under again but turned and grabbed onto whatever it was.

The boat. The one they'd passed coming up the dry canal. It bobbed in the current, a chain leading away to a mooring stone on the edge of the canal. Peyne grabbed the gunwale, heaved himself over and inside. He lay in the bottom of the boat. Panting, bruised, and sore.

Somewhere in this damn city there must be a cask of wine.

And then he passed out.

Two days later, they stood, looking down into the little boat, considering last-minute preparations. It had been stocked with food and water, and cloaks had been roughly sewn together to spread over the vessel's metal canopy frame aft for shade. They'd filled a bin with coal. Jaff had gotten the small steam engine working, basically a smaller version of the huge machine used to open the door to the aquifer shaft.

"Which exploded," Peyne reminded Jaff.

He frowned. "I told you. This valve releases excess pressure." He pointed at something sticking out from the side of the contraption. "Just make sure it's open."

"And the steam power makes the little windmill thing in the back spin."

"Yes," Jaff said. "It should propel the craft. Then you steer with the rudder like any other boat."

Like any other boat, Peyne thought. *Other boats don't explode.*

Peyne looked at the rest of them. "And nobody else wants to come with us? You're sure?"

Maurizan shook her head. One side of her face was still badly bruised from Hak's treatment, but she seemed in good spirits. "There's still all the ink magic here. I need to investigate. And now I can without Meddigar breathing down my neck."

Jaff's injured arm hung in a sling, but he seemed otherwise in good shape. "I'm staying too. Zayda is evidence the collars can come off. That's important to my cause."

"I'll stay with them," Venny said. "I plan to map the entire city. It's too good an opportunity to miss." She turned to Zayda. "You'll tell my father what I'm doing? That I'm safe?"

Zayda smiled back at her. "I'll remember."

"And Krokett?" Peyne asked.

Venny had told them about the odd tracker. There'd been no sign of the man. Jaff and Maurizan had gone to fetch Meddigar's dromadan and the much-needed supplies and had discovered one of the animals missing. Perhaps Krokett had taken it and returned home. Or maybe he was still lurking around somewhere. They'd had to circle the plateau for miles but eventually found a path the dromadan could use to enter the city. Those who remained behind would be well provisioned for a while.

"Don't worry," Maurizan said. "We'll keep an eye out for Krokett."

"Well then," Peyne said. "I guess we're off." He looked at Zayda.

She beamed at him. Since the collar had come off, she'd been relentlessly cheerful.

Zayda jumped down into the boat, steadying herself as it bobbed with her weight. Peyne climbed in more carefully. He turned some valves on the steam engine and looked back at Jaff, who nodded approval.

Please don't explode.

Maurizan cast off the chain, and the current took the boat. Peyne took his place at the tiller, keeping the vessel in the center of the canal. Maurizan, Jaff, and Venny jogged alongside the canal for a while, calling out good wishes and waving.

Zayda waved back. "We'll see you again!"

Peyne didn't wave. He held on to the tiller with a white-knuckled grip.

At last, they left the others behind, the canal taking them to the edge of the city.

They'd scouted ahead, of course, and knew that the canal turned north as it took them down a gentle incline, delivering them from the plateau. But from inside the boat, the incline seemed much less gentle as they shot through white water, bobbing violently. Peyne worked the tiller. Zayda clung to the gunwale. Water splashed into the boat.

But then it was over. They leveled out, and Peyne realized they were no longer in the canal. They followed the natural course of the river now, a river that had not existed for centuries.

Zayda and Peyne looked at each other. She still held the gunwale in a tight grip. Then she started laughing. Her laughter sounded sweeter than music and was contagious, and he laughed too.

She moved aft to sit with him under the makeshift canopy.

"Now we just sail to the ocean," she said. "Easy."

"Let's not be hasty," Peyne cautioned. "That aquifer could go dry tomorrow. Then we'd be stuck. And there's no guarantee Maurizan even knew what she was talking about. The river might not go where she thinks, might not be a river at all."

Zayda sighed. "You worry too much."

"Whatever happens, one thing's for sure," Peyne told her. "We've got a long trip ahead of us."

She turned to him, one of her slender hands sliding up under his tunic to caress his chest. "Then we'll need to come up with some way to pass the time, I suppose."

He raised an eyebrow. "Oh?"

She kissed him softly. Then her hands slid to his breeches, unlaced them. She reached inside, grabbed him.

Peyne hung on to the tiller, kept the boat in the center of the river. "Uh . . . um . . ."

"You just steer the boat," Zayda said. "I'll steer you."

EPILOGUE

I.

Captain Bevelakwa was pretty sure he was going to be in trouble.

Meddigar had ordered him to follow as quickly as possible with the bulk of the expeditionary force. Doing this had been problematic. They'd been late leaving the Last Village because the merchants there were unaccustomed to provisioning a force of their size. The fact there had recently been some sort of conflict, destroying a good bit of the village, further complicated matters.

When they'd at last set out to follow the wizard, the captain had ordered the troops to march double time in order to get back on schedule. He slowed them down again after the third soldier had dropped dead from dehydration.

And then the sandstorm had hit out of nowhere.

They'd circled the dromadan and hunkered down. The storm blew for a day and a half.

Bevelakwa sat high in the saddle atop his dromadan and surveyed the damage. He was tall and thin, braided beard clasped with brass at the end, and no moustache. A single thick braid down the center of his head, shaved clean on the sides. He was young for a captain but had fought in many battles, and the men knew it.

An older, world-weary sergeant tromped across the dune, stood before his dromadan, looked up, and saluted.

"Report, sergeant."

"The men have picked up most of the supplies," he said. "Storm blew 'em around pretty good. Lost some. Not enough to worry about. It took us a good while to find the marker the wizard left, but we're back on the trail now. Worst thing is we lost two more men."

"How?"

The sergeant shrugged. "Get turned around during the storm. Walked off in the wrong direction and couldn't get back. It happens."

Bevelakwa sighed. Losing men in battle was one thing. But this . . .

"Orders, Captain?"

"We have our orders already, sergeant."

The sergeant looked disappointed to hear it. "Yes, sir."

"How far behind are we now?"

"At least five days," the sergeant said. "Maybe more if they're moving fast. Or they could be dead."

"Until we find corpses, we'll assume they're not."

"Yes, sir. Uh . . . sir?"

"Speak freely, sergeant."

"Seems like the odds are against us. We've lost men. Been some bad luck. Maybe we should consider . . . alternative orders?"

Bevelakwa smiled. "Alternative orders. I like that. A diplomatic turn of phrase. No, sergeant, we will follow the orders we have. Whatever lies ahead, we'll find it. And we'll deal with it."

II.

Mardis Kain had taken a hundred men with him into the jungle.

He'd come out with eight.

His failure in part was the result of underestimating the Katoki. He hadn't thought so many of the savages would unify to mount such an attack. His early success had made him complacent. He would go north and confess his incompetence to his superiors. He would accept whatever punishment was handed down. Perhaps they'd allow him to attempt some impossible task in order to redeem himself.

He wasn't holding his breath.

Mardis and his eight men made for a ragged sight as they marched out of the jungle and north along the grasslands' road. They were all bloodied and bruised in some way. A grimy rag was tied around Mardis's head, covering the left eye. He'd need to practice with the sword until he felt comfortable again. The loss of the eye had ruined his depth perception.

It was near dusk when they saw the column coming down the road toward them. Mardis stood atop a slight rise, and the vantage allowed him to see the column stretched farther than he'd originally thought.

A group of horsemen broke off from the column and galloped toward them.

Mardis waited.

The squad of horsemen reined in their mounts ten paces from Mardis and his men. Officers in gleaming helms and breastplates flanked by bannermen. They looked exactly the opposite of Mardis and his muddied, blood-spattered troops.

One of the riders spurred his mount forward a few steps, gray moustache, gold trim on his armor. "Mardis Kain?"

"Yes."

"I'm General Parnov."

Mardis had never heard of the man but saluted.

"It looks like you've had a rough time of it," Parnov said.

"Yes, sir," Mardis replied. "The details do me little credit, I'm afraid."

"We'll hear all about it later. Looks like some of your men could use medical attention. I'll have my people see to them."

"My gratitude, sir," Mardis said. "General, I can't help but notice the force with you seems much larger than what I was expecting for the garrison. You must have at least three thousand men with you."

"Five thousand," the general corrected. "There's been a slight change of plan."

III.

Shouting roused Ambassador Korick from a sound sleep.

He sat up in bed, rubbing his eyes.

Then somebody kicked in the door of his bedroom. Korick had a sword around somewhere but didn't bother looking for it. The blade was an ornate ceremonial weapon, not that he really knew how to use it, and anyway it was too late.

Three Fyrian soldiers rushed into the room, oil lamps in one hand, naked steel in the other. A moment later, a Fyrian with a gold officer's sash entered, a rolled piece of parchment in one fist.

Korick sighed. "Okay then. Let's hear it."

"You and your retinue are being expelled from the city of Heberron and the nation of Fyria," the officer said in good Helvan but with a thick accent. "I have the order here if you'd like to read it."

"Never mind," Korick said. "I believe you. I presume I can at least get dressed first."

"Yes, but hurry," the officer told him. "A ship is waiting, and you must catch the tide."

Korick dressed in sturdy, practical travel clothes. "What about all our things?"

"They will be sent on later."

Of course they will. After you've searched everything carefully.

The ambassador was taken downstairs, where the rest of the Helvans, a dozen of them, waited in the foyer, looking worried and harried, surrounded by Fyrian soldiers. They were escorted outside as a group and marched through the street toward the docks, grim-faced Fyrian soldiers marching along on either side.

Fyrian citizens appeared on their balconies along the path, jeering, calling insults. Then they started throwing trash and rotten fruit. An oily, half-eaten fish slapped Korick in the neck. He flinched but held his head up, ignoring the assault.

Mullen pushed his way past the rest of the Helvans until he walked next to Korick. "This is *outrageous*."

"Yes," Korick said. "Isn't it?"

"But what's the purpose?" Mullen said, voice high-pitched with anxiety. "What does it mean?"

"It means the war has started."

ABOUT THE AUTHOR

Victor Gischler is a world traveler who earned his PhD in English from the University of Southern Mississippi. The recipient of Italy's Black Corsair Award for adventure literature, Victor was nominated for both an Anthony Award and an Edgar Award for his mystery writing. He is also the author of the fantasy trilogy A Fire Beneath the Skin, which includes *Ink Mage*, *The Tattooed Duchess*, and *A Painted Goddess*. Born in Sanford, Florida, he currently lives in Baton Rouge, Louisiana, and would grill every meal if his wife would let him. For more information, please visit www.victorgischlerauthor.com.